FIRE AND FORTITUDE

Erin P.T. Canning

H.C. Brown LLC

To all the readers who have wished they could step into their favorite fantasy story and take the lead role.

Lameiría
The Wastelands
Aerytol
Alderton
Ama-doras
Druin
Caraloria
Glennock
Menor

CONTENTS

Chapter One

THE SEED

"I don't understand how she knew." Morgán's words drift in and out of his tent, his voice hoarse, his words abrupt.

He's been alone in his tent for the last three days, not once emerging—not for food or water, not to speak with his soldiers, and not to ease the tension that's been building between Āranol's shoulder blades, making his back stiff and his neck sore. The muscles in his neck twinge as Āranol turns his head and his eyes drift to his father's tent, again.

The camp's vibrant sea-green, turquoise, and teal canvas tents and silk coverings brighten their dull surroundings and conceal the mountains looming in the distance, barring Āranol from sneaking into Aerytol. Granted, sneaking is no longer an option. At this point, he'd much rather head home and plan contingencies, should that wretched girl invade his home and threaten his people. Well, his father's people. Not that Morgán's lived in Feídra né Morna in the last century.

Why couldn't she stay in the Immortal Realms?

The image of that little girl curled around his horse's hoof, her long brown curls wilting into the grass before she faded out of existence, haunts him behind his eyelids. He did the right thing. He did what his father asked. He secured this world's future. Her kind doesn't belong here.

Then how did she manage to come back?

"You look gloomy," Ameira says, sitting down beside Āranol in front of his own tent. Her long auburn hair spills over her shoulders. "I'm certain our lord will have news for us soon."

Āranol throws a rock across the empty terrain, away from camp. He ought to join his soldiers during this morning's drills, considering they have little else to do while they wait for Morgán to emerge. "Do you need something?"

"Well, if you're looking to kill time—"

"Not now, Ameira. Maybe when we return home."

She's been an agreeable companion for the last fifty years, but they both know their relationship's ebbing. At least, he does.

"You haven't found someone else yet?" he asks.

"If you keep up this attitude, I will."

Pulling her hair around her neck, she nudges his shoulder with her own, providing him with a direct view of her cleavage pressed together. She waggles her eyebrows, and they both exhale a soft laugh, reminding Āranol why he's considered more than once choosing her to become his life partner.

Getting up, she rests her hand on his shoulder. "Everything will work out. Have faith."

He takes her hand and kisses the backside. "Thank you, my friend."

When she walks away, swaying her hips from side to side in those tight tan trousers, he smirks for half a moment. Then his eyes drift back to his father's tent.

Behind him, designated soldiers finish packing up their gear and food and redistribute supplies while the horses finish snacking on the hay. Āranol's troops ought to have released the horses three days ago—when they were to climb the mountains and cross the river into Aerytol. But Morgán's unannounced arrival has left them stranded and Āranol uneasy as they wander aimlessly and squander resources.

Why hasn't he given new orders, and who has he been speaking to all night?

Brushing his brown locks away from his eyes, Āranol stands, exhales a large breath that puffs out his cheeks, and walks toward Morgán.

I'm just a son approaching my father. Nothing wrong with that.

Stepping closer to the tent's entrance, Ãranol slows his breathing and lightens his steps so he doesn't make a sound. One by one, the hair on the back of his neck rises. With his muscles locked, he stills himself so that he doesn't accidentally sway into his father's line of sight.

With a low growl that sounds more like a mad dog, Morgán paces back and forth, his shadow appearing every so often close to Ãranol's side of the tent. "Yes, yes," he hisses. "I'm aware I have no other choice now. I'll begin tonight."

Begin what?

Espestus, one of Ãranol's lieutenants, steps around Ãranol's abandoned backpack and hurries over. He opens his mouth to speak, but Ãranol shakes his head profusely and waves the lieutenant away while cringing that he caught Ãranol spying on his own father, on the savior of elf kind.

His father stops pacing. A chair scrapes across the ground. "Come in, Ãranol."

This is why humans curse.

With a sigh, Ãranol walks around the wooden stakes and string holding up the tent, pushing aside the flaps, and enters. The bedding lies undisturbed. His father's armor rests on the ground, the breastplate upside down in a pile of mud and his sword plunged into the earth. Ãranol bows his head. Then he lifts his eyes and waits patiently, waits for that moment when their eyes meet and Ãranol knows he's talking to his father, not his lord and savior.

Sitting at a small table, Morgán stares into a bowl of water, its dark interior reflecting his face. The skin beneath his eyes sags like half-moons, and more sliver streaks have claimed portions of his light-brown hair, which he's pulled back and tied neatly at the base of his neck. His left hand, resting on the table, draws Ãranol's focus, specifically Morgán's gnarled pinky that looks as if he first crushed that finger between the lid and lock of his storage chest and then set the small appendage on fire. The burns, deep and thick, wind around his bent finger like vines squeezing an animal to death.

When did that happen?

Not wishing to continue staring at that broken finger, Ãranol clears his throat.

Morgán's eyes snap to him, and he pushes away the bowl, still full. "Have the soldiers finished packing?"

"Yes, sir. We're almost ready to move on again. If you're prepared for us to ascend the mountain, I estimate we'll need three days to make up for—"

"Forget the mountain."

"Sir?"

"Turn back. Keep the horses and return to Camp Three. Get more hay there."

"Camp Three? But why?"

"Because that abominable girl discovered our plans, and now Alderton and Lameiría have agreed to defend her. Yes, you heard correctly. The mule has won both sides to her cause, and she's ascended the throne."

"And Lameiría accepts that, given what happened to Queen Arraya? Don't they know the mule was born and raised in Alderton? How did she convince them to—"

"She married Élara's son."

His father's words lodge in Ãranol's throat, making him gag. *He wants to take a human into his bed? It's an act of bestiality.* "How revolting."

"Indeed."

No wonder father's been irate since hearing from his spies. "How did she discover us?"

"You mean how did she escape you?"

Ãranol lowers his head and grinds his jaw. "I saw her return to the Immortal Realms. She vanished in front of me. I did as you asked." Those bright-green, innocent eyes flash into his mind, how they peered up at him as he got her to trust him, to take his hand. He flexes his fingers, then curls them into a fist.

"Yes, well, it would seem she's a traveler. She can travel great distances in the blink of an eye."

Those loathsome Aerytolians. Why must they be so difficult to eliminate? "How does returning to Camp Three aid our cause?"

Morgán doesn't respond. Rising from his chair, he worries his hands and mumbles to himself while his eyes dart around the tent. The closer he approaches his nine-hundredth birthday, the more he slips away from the father Ãranol knew. Granted, he remembers little before those stupid human boys killed his brother. He remembers most his mother wasting away from grief and his father succumbing to his rage at Arraya's leniency. From that day on, Ãranol's life revolved around hunting the humans who escaped Aerytol and helping his father create a new order that exemplifies to the world what life could be like, if only elves taught humans how to be their best selves. They're too unpredictable and prone to emotional outbursts for elves to leave humans on their own.

"What would you have me do, father?"

Morgán's head pops up, leaving behind his thinking. For a moment, he sees only the child he didn't lose. "Do? Nothing, my son." He walks forward and places his hand on Ãranol's shoulders, his warm brown eyes taking in how much taller Ãranol is than himself. His thin lips rise into a smile. "Lead the troops there. That's all. I've left some extra supplies with Espestus. All you need to do is wait for my next orders. I'll send word soon enough."

"What else are you planning?"

Morgán shakes his head slowly. "I'm sorry, but trust your father. I cannot risk my only son." His expression shifts into stone as his eyes darken and his thoughts recede, taking the light with them. "Go now. Lead the way. I'll see you soon."

Before Ãranol can figure out how to challenge his father's wishes, five of Ãranol's friends step into the tent and bow deeply.

"Ah, good. Thank you for coming." Morgán claps his hands together and steps around Ãranol, leaving him behind. "Thank you for volunteering to stay behind with me. You're going to help me on an elite mission, one ordained by the fae themselves, to correct the course of this world. What fine soldiers we have here, some of our best, indeed."

Ãranol's friends bow low. He's known each of them since they first arrived in the Wastelands, when they crossed the barren plains, and when they built Feídra né Morna brick by brick. These lieutenants have always been loyal. So too has Ãranol. But Morgán has changed all his plans without consulting or including Ãranol once.

After he exits the tent, Ãranol glances back at Morgán, his face shrouded in shadow. He whispers to his followers and leans closer to them as they fall onto their knees. The fact that Ãranol can't hear his father, who's standing only ten feet away, makes him furrow his brows. The soldiers bob their heads thrice, and their shoulders round forward in unison, as if something has fallen upon them simultaneously.

As Ãranol turns back into the tent, Morgán whips his head up, and his irises flash dark red. Ãranol halts. A moment later, his father's eyes are their usual brown again. Perhaps he imagined that. But his father's cold, emotionless expression belongs to a stranger, to someone who's willing to do whatever's necessary to fulfill his mission before his time runs out. Ãranol backs out of the tent, but the cold follows him, creeping up his spine and numbing his limbs, even when he's thirty feet away and in direct sunlight.

He's never questioned Morgán before.

When did I become afraid of my father?

Each step that leads Ãranol farther away from his father makes the bile in his stomach more volatile. He should have eaten breakfast. With a thousand soldiers behind him, he places one foot in front of the other, his hand on his hilt and the other stuffed in his pocket. Miles of flat, light-green grass stretches before him. At least this portion of the Wastelands has one color other than gray. He's been gone from home nearly a month. How he wishes he could hear the sea breaking against the cliffs, the fishers laughing as they haul up baskets of salmon, cod, and mornel, and the ease of conversations in the streets below his home.

But no, now we need to visit Camp Three. When Father sent word for us to destroy the Neutral Territory, he was adamant about our timing. Why now send us to Camp Three with no orders beyond that?

Espestus slaps Ãranol on the back. "Cheer up, will you? We're heading toward home this time."

"Not quite."

"Fine. One detour."

"Why?" Ãranol asks, not concealing the agitation in his voice.

Espestus raises both hands and shakes his long, wavy black hair. "Whoa. Come on now. I've never been one to question Lord Morgán."

Ãranol chews his tongue. How can he explain the changes he's been seeing in his father? "You don't think my father's been acting not like himself?"

"Don't take it personally." Espestus throws his head back and watches the one cloud lazily drift past them. "Ever since Queen Arraya prophesized the mule's birth, he's spent most of his life trying to save this world from her, and she not only keeps escaping him but has also grown stronger. He's scared to leave you with his burden."

Ãranol recalls the moment he left his father's tent. *That wasn't fear in his eyes.* And if Morgán has run out of options, what might he do next? Whatever his plan, he refused to share a single detail, aside from the fact that he retained five of Ãranol's soldiers.

I cannot risk my only son. Morgán's words reverberate inside Ãranol's head, along with knowing that desperation leads to poor choices.

Ãranol glances back at his soldiers. Half a day separates him from his father.

Gripping Espestus's shoulder, Ãranol says, "I leave you in charge while I'm gone."

"What? Gone?"

"I'm worried about my father. Something's not right. I'll be only a day or two behind, not much more."

"But, but Lord Morgán gave explicit orders."

"Not really. He said wait at Camp Three. So do that. I need to know that he's alright." *And what he's planning.*

Espestus raises his hands and strangles the air in front of Ãranol. With a loud grunt, he drops his arms and turns away. "Fine. I'll do as you say. But I'm not covering for you."

"I wouldn't expect you to." Ãranol smacks Espestus's arm with the back of his hand. "Keep them going until nightfall."

Without another word, Ãranol disappears down the ranks, praising his soldiers, his people, his friends, as they march past him. He slips out the backside of their formation and continues to backtrack for half a day until he finds his father's turquoise tent along the horizon, at the base of a hill that rises gently toward the mountains. Debating whether to approach his father directly or wait for signs of movement, Āranol sits down, slips his backpack off, and rests his hands in his lap.

With nightfall descending, the soldiers should pitch their shared tent and light a fire. But the campsite looks as barren as when Āranol and his soldiers marched away. His father's large commander tent remains the only object visible on the horizon. No volunteers emerge either, not even as the moon rises higher in the sky, and candlelight makes the interior of the tent glow.

What are they doing in that tent?

Considering he's neither seen nor heard anyone, Āranol creeps closer, pausing every so often to listen for signs of life, only to observe nothing. He crouches next to the tent's side, holding his sheath to prevent the leather from tearing the grass. Lowering his head to the ground, he peeks under the canvas and spies his friends lined up, side by side and on their knees. The tent limits Āranol's view to their torsos. Beyond them, his father's hands set down on his table a pewter chalice decorated with foliage and intertwined stems. A drop of thick, dark liquid slips down the side and pools between two leaves. Morgán stands in front of the first soldier, the one furthest from Āranol.

Remaining as quiet as possible, Āranol cannot leave until he learns his father's plan, to verify its validity. The last few decades, Morgán has become despondent, mostly absent, and impulsive. The fact that he had Āranol's soldiers roam the Wastelands for three days, without purpose, proves that Morgán's calculations have stalled, that his mind has slowed down—that fulfilling his destiny, his purpose, to rid the world of Aerytolíans has consumed him.

Whatever the reason, Morgán's become less of a father and more of a liability. Sooner than Āranol would like, he'll need to make a choice: whether to help his father yet again complete this mission, or whether it's time for Āranol to take matters into his own hands.

CHAPTER TWO

THE PLAN

THREE DAYS EARLIER

Adaline kicks her legs and twists her torso to free herself from the sheets that have wrapped around her body like vines trying to bury her alive. Yanking herself free, she sits up in bed, brushes her curls out of her face, and pulls her hair out from beneath her bottom. She kept tossing and turning all night, her dreams replaying various scenarios of Seira's prophecy that Morgán might soon break the world.

Adaline reaches out beside her, her fingers subconsciously seeking her husband's arm, but her hand falls onto an empty bed. She pulls her hand back from the cold sheets and rubs her eyes that burn from lack of sleep.

As her vision clears, Ëólas's chambers in New Leira come into focus. Given the absence of digital clocks, she cannot guess the time of day. Darkness shrouds the room, muting the rich, sage-green- and navy-themed upholstery into drab grays. In the grandiose marble hearth, last night's fire has dwindled into a pitiful pile of dust. The drawn curtains, at least, reveal a streak of bright sunlight beneath their hem.

Adaline slides out of bed and tugs one of the four curtains open, revealing the arched windows that look toward Lameiría's forest and the backside of the castle. The sun warms the meadows covered in Purple Stardust, those periwinkle flowers that at night make the fields look like the sky turned upside down.

It's nearly midday. Why the hell didn't anyone wake me sooner?

She spins around, hoping to discover that Ëólas snuck in the moment he heard her stir, that he's lounging on the sofa, cheek in hand, his dirty-blond hair framing that handsome face, while he watches her in amusement. But she finds nothing, not even a note on his pillow. She can't say for certain if he ever came to bed.

Since yesterday, he's been treating her like a wounded puppy, refusing to touch her, all because one lousy citizen stabbed her. Correction—nicked her.

I've survived three assaults since I first came here. He should be used to this by now.

Granted, Adaline hasn't had the energy to tease Ëólas into giving up his self-restraint, not after hours upon hours of meetings during which the council drafted announcements to the neighboring kingdoms about the return of Aerytol's heir and calculated the economic implications of Aerytol becoming its own sovereign again. Today would be no different, not when they had yet to discuss the city's defenses and plan for the thousands of soldiers arriving from Lameiría and Alderton over the next three days—not to mention the whole matter of Ãranol's army disappearing last night. Yet Ëólas didn't bother to wake her up on her first official day as queen.

How many meetings has he run this morning, without me?

She slams her fist into the mattress. Hurrying to her armoire, Adaline swings the doors open, only to discover bare shelves. From the pole, her two remaining dresses hang, the periwinkle ballgown that's far too fancy for a workday and the green one she wore when No-Nose and Shorty attacked her at the ruins.

Adaline throws back her head and groans. At this rate, Seira had better not gift Adaline anymore clothes, given that she lost one dress and her only cloak to a river and the other to the fake guard who shredded her skirts—and her legs.

At least my legs healed. And my shoulder.

Her duffle bag slumps against her armoire. She could toss on jeans and a flannel, but what message would that send to her people? That she doesn't take her role as queen seriously? Or she could wear her grandmother's dress. Slip into her shoes. Become the new Queen Arraya.

Adaline thumps her forehead against the armoire door. *Oh my god, Adaline. Get your shit together and stop stalling.*

She yanks the ballgown off the hanger and walks over to the gilded full-length mirror. When she holds the dress in front of herself, the periwinkle color makes her green eyes more vibrant. Her hands fall to her sides, the dress slipping down to her waist.

She stares at her irises, at the green specks the color of moss and meadows, and walks closer to the mirror, her dress pushing against the glass. She touches the eyes reflecting back at her, and a tear slips down her cheek.

Those aren't my eyes.

Not the eyes she was born with. Her father changed them to hide her in Alderton and then Maryland because humans don't have periwinkle irises. Only elves do. Like Seira. Like most of their family does.

He didn't give Adaline any old pair of green eyes either. No, he changed hers to match her mother's. For the last twenty years, even without her memories, Adaline has been staring into her mother's eyes.

She drops the dress, letting the layers fall to the floor, and returns to the one open window. Leaning forward, she waits until a cool breeze caresses her cheek and then whispers, "Please, find my mother. Tell her I'm back, that I'm stronger, that I'm looking for her. That I love her."

She claps her hand over her mouth to stop herself from crying; she doesn't want her mother to hear that too. Pulling her head back inside, she sits down on Ëólas's side of the bed. His warmth must have dissipated hours ago.

He said we'd do this together.

A knock on the door gets Adaline to stand up and wipe her cheek dry. "Come in," she says once she's certain her voice won't betray her.

Kayla pushes the door open and steps into the room. Per usual, she's neatly secured her light-brown hair in a gold-threaded snood, and she pinches the folds of her dark-burgundy dress as she curtsies, keeping her head low. The sight of her lady's maid, who never called Adaline out for her lack of knowledge about all things proper, encourages her to leave behind the window.

When Kayla rises, she scurries to the armoire and picks up Adaline's ballgown. "May I assist you with dressing?"

"Thank you." *On so many levels. Including insisting you want to keep working with me even though that means frequenting the elven side of the castle.*

As Kayla helps Adaline step into the gown, Nuríel enters the room, her long raven hair fluttering at her sides. She makes the bed as quickly as possible, touching only the corners of the sheets, never the center, while her eyes focus on the floor or headboard, as if looking at a marital bed embarrasses her—or thinking about the occupants and their different backgrounds offends her.

I don't know her well enough to assume the worst.

Even though Nuríel has spoken little since Adaline met her last night, Ëólas said she's been tending to his chambers since they built the castle. He trusts her, and that's enough for Adaline to do the same. Besides, everyone will need time to adjust to having a human-looking queen and an elven king.

Standing near the door, Nuríel gathers her hands together and bows her head. "My lady, the seamstress awaits in the sitting room. Lord Ëólas insisted that you meet with her first, after you break fast. I have readied your meal."

As soon as Adaline finishes expressing her gratitude, Nuríel flees the room. Adaline stares after her but keeps her mouth clamped shut.

Once again wearing her ballgown, Adaline secures her belt around her waist and ties her sword to the leather strap. What peculiar accessories for a festive dress.

Adaline pushes open the doors to her chambers and hurries down the hallway toward the study where she's certain Ëólas has been since daybreak. Maybe earlier. Without her.

Before taking four steps, her entourage of guards falls in line behind her, along with the seamstress who showed Adaline fifty designs while she shoveled her breakfast into her mouth.

"What about this design, my lady?" The elven seamstress scurries beside Adaline, holding up another piece of parchment that displays a dusty rose dress, matching shoes, jewelry for every exposed body part, and an ornate hair comb with dark-pink rhinestones.

I'll need an entire armoire just for shoes and accessories. Adaline shudders.

She halts and faces the seamstress whose eager eyes make Adaline soften her tone. "It's lovely, thank you. Every design you've shown me is equally beautiful."

"I'm so glad you think so, my lady."

"Can you start with this dress and three more?"

"That's all?" Her face falls.

Maybe being seamstress to the Queen of Aerytol is her current passion? "Um, just to start. What I could use right now are trousers and tops. I'll need them more in the coming days."

"Of course, my queen. I'll start on those immediately."

"Thank you! And if you have questions, Seira knows my preferences." *Somehow.*

As if having foreseen this precise moment, Seira opens the doors to her chambers at the opposite end of the hallway and calls the seamstress into her own quarters.

With a wave and thank you smile, Adaline picks up her pace and rushes along, her periwinkle skirts and the sheer, ruffled, elbow-length bell-shaped sleeves swishing in tune with her long strides. Fortunately, the distance to the study from the elven side of the castle matches that from her old chambers. The only difference is that everyone pauses their activities to curtsy or bow, which makes Adaline walk faster.

Reaching the study, the guys' muffled voices rumble behind the thick wooden doors. A guard pushes one open, and when she steps inside, all six guys immediately stop talking and turn to her. Most of them surround Ëólas's desk, the closer of the two, in the center of the spacious room.

To her left, standing in front of the grand fireplace, Merith bows his head, his silver hair falling forward. Fólas, sitting on the far back table, hops off and jumps to attention, slapping his hands at his sides. Behind Ëólas's desk, Magnus takes his hands off the map, letting the parchment curl shut, while Thoren, next to his king, grunts as if Adaline purposely left him waiting hours. Hamon shakes his long blond Westley-esque bangs out of his face and straightens his spine, his thigh bumping the desk chair. When Ëólas lifts his golden eyes from the maps, his dour expression shifts into sheer joy, as if he has her to thank for filling the room with light.

"Adaline." He rushes over, places one hand on her cheek, and kisses the other.

Her anger evaporates under his warm gaze, her lips tilting upward, drawing nearer to his. *How can I stay mad at him when he looks at me like that?* Her lips curl into a smile, drawing his eyes to her mouth, which makes her heart beat faster.

Finding her hands, he clasps them against his chest. "Good morning, my love."

"Morning?" She leans back, the corners of her mouth dipping downward. "You should have woken me."

"There was no need."

"No need?" She turns to the guys, who suddenly find their fingernails or the ceiling endlessly fascinating. Tugging her hands free from Ëólas, she takes a step back. "Have we found Āranol, or Morgán, for that matter?" When no one replies, Adaline clicks her tongue and strolls toward Ëólas's desk. "How long have you been at this?"

"Not very," Magnus says, hooking his thumbs on his belt and leaning backward. He's wearing the same gold velvet long coat from yesterday.

Adaline purses her lips. "Define *not very*. Since before sunrise?"

Ëólas, having moved past her and resuming his spot beside his desk, crosses his arms over his chest. "Yes."

"Is it really that bad?" she asks.

"No." Ëólas dismisses the idea with a wave of his hand. "We're just being extra cautious. Because we don't know where, when, or how Āranol and Morgán will strike, we must consider every possible scenario, along with response procedures, and ensure we have enough guards in each location to respond effectively. It's a lot of coordination and logistics, especially with Alderton's reinforcements arriving tomorrow and Lameiría's a day or two after that. I'd rather we work through the logistics first, then report back to you."

Adaline presses her fingertips together and taps her chin. "Thanks. Still, someone should have woken me up at a normal hour."

"Yes, but…"

"But what?"

"Well." Resting his fists on his desk, Ëólas grinds his knuckles into the oak. "Given all you've endured this past week, you deserve a decent night's rest." His tired tone makes Adaline hesitant to argue.

But I did rest, back in Maryland, before I retrieved my memories and shit hit the fan.

Not wanting to argue, she moves next to him and points at the top map, one of many. "So where are we at?"

Magnus unfurls the parchment, and Thoren places a bronze tree-of-life trinket box on one end as a paper weight. Merith, positioning himself between Ëólas and Magnus, holds down the opposite end of the parchment, and Fólas and Hamon gather closer too. The map of Aerytol shows at least a hundred small villages throughout the land, but all of them have a large X drawn on top, which Adaline assumes to mean that those villages were abandoned or destroyed long ago.

Magnus points to a few different locations near New Leira, each progressively further away. "We've heard from scouts in these five quadrants, and they've not seen anything amiss."

"That doesn't give us much to go on," Adaline says. "What about those in the Wastelands?"

"They haven't seen Āranol and the Morgai either. But my spies did find tracks that suddenly stopped."

Adaline looks to the others, waiting for someone to explain how that's possible.

Thoren translates, his fingers tugging at his curly red beard. "They turned around."

"Wait, what?" Adaline almost smiles, until she realizes no one else is too. "I don't get it. Isn't that a good thing?"

"Āranol's not done. He must have something else planned." Ëólas stares intensely at the map as if he's willing it to reveal the Morgai's current location.

"Ãranol could try something stealthier, or cover his tracks to confuse us, or—It doesn't matter. We're considering the options. All of them."

Ëólas stands up, takes Adaline's hand, and leads her a few feet away from the maps. "Trust me, my love. In addition to the scouts I sent ahead, Magnus and I also have spies dedicated to weeding out Morgán. I have this. We all do."

In the corner of her eye, the guys shift uncomfortably from side to side. *Do they want me to leave?*

Maybe she's just a distraction. They do, after all, have decades of experience studying warfare and strategy. All Adaline knows is history, what's already happened, what decisions *other* people made. She'll strive not to repeat past mistakes. But in terms of the present, she has only her moral compass to guide her, and even that's limited to what she perceives as right and wrong.

"Besides," Ëólas kisses the back of her hand, "you have other things to focus on today."

"I do?" she asks.

"Yes," Merith says. "We need you to choose Aerytol's new council members."

"Oh." *I thought I might get to do that, but changing what Magnus and Ëólas have established doesn't feel right, especially when I don't know what I'm doing.* "Um, sure. No problem. Anything else on my schedule for today?"

"Lord Otto would like a word with you," says Magnus. "He's worried about his investments in the city."

Adaline rolls her eyes. *Of course he's worried about money. Oh, wait. Is that a problem?* "Do we owe him money or something? How do we pay him back or—"

"We'll handle that later." Ëólas shakes his head with disgust. "But I know at least two people who are anxious to know if they might have a place on your council."

He juts his chin in Fólas and Hamon's direction, both of whom jump forward. Fólas, his hair pulled back in a half bun, bends his knee to kneel but stops and bows like Hamon.

Crossing his arm over his chest, Hamon bends at the waist, his bangs swinging beside his eyes. "I'd be honored if you'd consider me for captain of the city guard, my queen. I will devote every moment of the day and night to safeguarding this city and her people."

Adaline looks to Magnus, who for some reason doesn't interject even as he drills holes into Hamon's backside. "But Hamon, isn't Alderton your home?"

"I made New Leira my home when His Majesty first established this city." Hamon waits without breath.

Holy shit. Is Hamon defecting in front of Magnus?

Fólas, however, takes this chance to speak. "I also would be honored for you to consider me for the position, my queen. I too have made New Leira my home, and I—"

"Okay, both of you need to relax." Adaline gestures for them to stand up. "Let me know, privately, if you have any concerns about collaborating. Otherwise, you two can keep doing your thing. If Magnus is okay with that."

Picking up a paperweight, Magnus rolls a brown and white stone from one hand to the other. "I certainly don't plan to order anyone living here to return home with me. But," he emphasizes loudly, "I do expect that those who owe any of my citizens—what did Adaline call it, ah, yes—child support, continue meeting those requirements."

Hamon's face turns beet red. "Of course, Your Majesty."

Oh, Hamon. How many kids do you have? "Then it's settled." Adaline pats both of their shoulders. "If you think anything can improve what you're doing, let me know. I'd love to hear your ideas."

Fólas and Hamon retreat to the back of the room, elbowing each other as they snicker and talk among themselves.

They'll be celebrating at the pub tonight.

She turns to Merith, who hasn't moved once, his feet firmly planted in front of the hearth. "I assume you'll be sticking around?"

His silver eyes lock on hers. "As long as I draw breath, my queen."

"Whomever you deem captain of the queen's guard will take Thoren's role on our council," Ëólas says.

Merith raises a finger. "I have sugges—"

"Sora," Adaline blurts out. *I need more ladies to balance out this room.*

Merith perks up, lifting a whole eyebrow to change up his typical, stoic expression—when he's not singing and dancing at the tavern, that is. "Sora?"

They must be good friends too. "Yeah. She helped me in Lameiría. Do you think she'd want the job?"

"She'll be thrilled, truly." Ëólas runs his hand up Adaline's spine, his fingers rediscovering the gown's open back. He grazes her bare skin, making her body tingle and cheeks flush. Dropping his hand, he steps away, adding space between them even though none of their friends cringe or turn green. "You're off to a good start. Mercia's offered to explain the positions on the current council so you can choose replacements."

Thank God. "Wonderful."

"You also have a speech to plan," Magnus says.

"Huh?" *Didn't I give a damn good one yesterday?*

Grumbling at her inexperience, Thoren sits his meaty thigh on the edge of Ëólas's desk. "The people yearn for news and stability."

"They should find that through you from now on," Magnus says, his tone empathetic.

Picking up a pile of papers from his desk, Ëólas scowls as he sifts through them. "Given our need to focus on strategizing, we've instructed the people to come here."

"Sure, no problem." *What the hell am I going to tell them?* "So, while I prep for a speech and choose a council, you'll be in here?"

She waits for someone to share that she has other affairs to attend to today as well, that she should come back in an hour or two, that they'll soon adjourn the boys' club. But, aside from nodding, the guys don't move to resume their conversation, not while she's still in the study.

"Okay, then." *I guess a lunch date is out of the question.* She meanders toward the door. "We'll reconvene later."

Ëólas peeks up from his papers. "You sound disappointed?"

Adaline waves him off. "Oh, I just wish we had some clue as to what's going on with Āranol."

"So do we," Thoren growls. "As Seira said, they're getting desperate, and desperation leads to unpredictability." He smashes his fist onto his palm. "Give me another round with the prisoners, and I'll get them to give up more—"

Ëólas gives Thoren the death stare to shut up, not that Thoren cares.

"What do you mean?" Adaline's stomach flips upside down as she tries to push out of her mind what her kind, loyal husband might be capable of. "You've been torturing the prisoners? Ëólas, I'm not okay with that."

"I know," he squeaks, as he searches the room for a way to gloss over this topic, "which is why you needn't worry about this business. I handled it."

"Meaning what?" Adaline aims a cold, hard stare at him. *I don't want him tainting himself in my name.* "Are they alive?"

He nods, his dark golden eyes reflecting his discomfort.

"But?" she asks.

"You know the penalty for attacking members of the royal family."

"Ëólas!"

He drops the papers on his desk, tightens his jaw, and faces her. "I will not let anyone think they can get away with attacking you. And yet, knowing your feelings on the matter, I've already been more lenient that I should. Magnus and I have given them an option: Cooperate with us now, and we'll ease their sentences."

"Or?"

"If they give us nothing, *then* they'll be executed."

"Ëólas, no. Absolutely not." She stares them all down. "I'll speak with them. If they despise me, then maybe I can provoke them into revealing something."

"No!" the guys protest together. Even Fólas and Hamon cut off their conversation, shaking their heads and looking at her as if she has no sense.

Taking a deep breath, Ëólas speaks calmly, but each word sounds strained, tempered, ready to burst. "I won't have you visit the dungeons and face the very people who seek to destroy Aerytol yet again. They don't deserve the air they breathe."

"Oh my god." Adaline throws her hands in the air, knowing no one in this room will side with her on this matter. Dropping her voice, she makes sure her tone confirms that this isn't up for debate. "No executions. Ever. I mean it."

Ëólas's nostrils flare. But he lowers his head, they all do, the way Magnus's subordinates submit to his commands or the way Ëólas does when Queen Élara issues orders. And the fact that Adaline can force Ëólas to do as she says, simply because of her title, opens a weird emotional fissure between them. Her views have left her stranded on the other side. Alone, once again.

Peeking up through his thick lashes, he pleads quietly, "Please, try my methods first. I'm still the commander general, unless you revoke my title."

Unless I take everything away from you.

Adaline closes her eyes. This is political, not personal. She knows that, but it doesn't feel that way. Is he going to refer to her as his queen, like he did his own mother, to separate those two dynamics? What if Adaline doesn't want that between them, doesn't want him to see her as his queen first and wife second? But she also can't condone the death penalty.

"We'll try it your way." Her shoulders drop, and her voice reduces to a whisper. "But I don't want people executed. If you can promise you won't start killing people without my consent, then we can try your method first."

Oh god. Did I just give him permission to keep torturing prisoners? Apparently I don't know the difference between right and wrong—or that's not enough.

Approaching her, Ëólas takes both her hands. "Thank you, my qu—"

"No." Adaline yanks her hands free.

He furrows his brows but doesn't touch her again.

She walks away from him, remembering the others in the room who look equally agitated that she's messing with their methods, or fighting with Ëólas in front of them, probably both. "Send someone when it's time for me to address the people." She avoids Ëólas's eyes when she adds, "and let me know what other duties you think are more appropriate for me to handle."

She leaves the study, wishing more than anything they could redo that conversation. But he'd need to meet her halfway, and he's still operating without her. Because he doesn't need her. Or because she's not ready.

Yeah, she's definitely not ready for this.

CHAPTER THREE

A SPEECH

"Now this is a nice room!" Adaline descends five steps into the open lounge.

In the center of the room, ample seating forms an airy circle. The plush, deep-purple velvet sofas, with their button-tufted backrests and rolled arms, and the wide armchairs, painted white and decorated with silver-leaf accents, invite everyone to recline lazily and chat about current affairs or weekend plans. The embroidered tapestries hanging from the ceiling add more color to the room and warm the white stone interior. Opposite the doorway, ornate marble pillars divide four open archways that lead to the balcony and a cloudless blue sky. Overall, the furnishings and ambiance are fit for a queen.

With Seira and Mercia behind her, Adaline skirts around one of six sofas and the massive central coffee table, topped with white marble, and hurries onto the balcony. The sun casts a soft glow over New Leira's terracotta buildings and vine-covered facades, which at this distance look like dollhouses. The balcony's height perfectly accommodates giving speeches, so the citizens will see her clearly, and she won't have to scream at the top of her lungs.

Why don't Magnus and Ëólas give speeches from here more often?

As far as Adaline's witnessed, they intentionally went into the city and addressed the people from the Rialto bridge. Then they'd continue to another location, repeat themselves, and answer questions. They prided themselves on that personal touch, that they traveled to their people, rather than making the people come to them.

So why change plans today? Why limit her to the castle?

Because Ëólas still thinks I'm recovering from yesterday's incident?

Resting her elbows on the balustrade, Adaline drops her head in her hands. During her trek through the Wastelands, she dreamt about returning to New Leira, about roaming the market and chatting with friends and strolling across the bridges and smelling the freshly baked bread from the corner bakery. But she can't see the Rialto from here. Or Sallie's shop. And Kian and Jósep's deaths feel like a lifetime ago.

After this speech, I need to check on Sallie. God, I hope she doesn't think I intentionally deceived her.

Seira, prancing onto the balcony, joins her cousin and leans on the balustrade. She tilts her head toward Lameiría's forest and closes her periwinkle eyes, her platinum blonde hair cascading around her shoulders, a few strands dancing in the wind. Whatever she's thinking, she doesn't share. Thankfully, she doesn't look pensive or troubled, as though she's forgotten Morgán altogether, as though the mere mention of his name hadn't caused her to collapse last night, scream in terror, and warn them that he's on the cusp of making the world come undone.

Damn, I can't get that image of her out of my mind. I hope Seira can stay like she is now, like her usual carefree self.

To fight back the darker memories, Adaline inhales a deep breath of fresh air, which carries scents of freshly harvested squash and the salty sea air beyond the old palace. "What a lovely view."

With her head tilted downward, Mercia stands eight feet back, her snood sagging around her shoulders from the weight of those compressed red curls. "I'm glad you find this lounge agreeable, my lady."

"Mercia, we talked about this. I need my friends to be my friends. If you anger me, I won't toss you in a dungeon" *where my husband might torture people for information. With the same hands he uses on me—but for far different reasons. Well, he did, before we returned to New Leira.*

Focus, Adaline. "If you have questions, ask me. It's that simple."

Mercia's buoyant cheeks turn rosy, matching her hair. "I'm honored, Your Maj—er, um, Adaline."

"See, I'm still the same girl you met weeks ago." As the first cluster of citizens crosses the bridge and begins the climb uphill to the castle, Adaline scurries into the lounge. Fanning her face, she paces around the marble coffee table. "Mercia, can I see the list you put together?"

From under her arm, Mercia retrieves the parchment and passes it to Adaline, who unfurls the list and scowls at the blank spaces for her own council.

"You don't have to address this right now," Mercia says, selecting an ink bottle and quill from the writer's desk against the back wall. She sets both on the coffee table. "You could simply transition a member from Alderton's or Lameiría's council to the equivalent position on yours."

But I don't know the current council members well. I don't know their qualifications or motivations or what it's like working with them. I can't stick someone in a position if I don't know these things. And do I choose elves or humans?

Laying the list on the table, Adaline hugs her stomach and regrets the ten mince pies she ate for lunch. Which Ëólas missed. Because he still hasn't emerged from the study.

She rubs her thumb along the underside of her wedding ring, spinning the floral gemstones from side to side, and resumes pacing to walk off her stomachache. "I don't suppose you have any suggestions, Mercia? Any tips or information that will help me?"

Smushing her lips to the side, Mercia teeters her head back and forth. "I just know that most of the elven council members are nervous you'll send them back to Lameiría because they were rude to you."

"Ha!" Seira laughs, sashaying off the balcony. "As she should. The humans too, the ones who are vicious little vipers." Seira hisses like an angry kitten and sinks onto a sofa, draping her head backward.

"But that means I need to fill four positions with new people." Making her next lap past the balcony, Adaline peers over the balustrade to watch a steady stream of people make their way to the castle.

"Five, actually," Mercia whispers.

"Huh?" Adaline spins around, crinkles her brow, and checks the list again. She needs to fill the master of logistics, the treasurer, the city planner, and the head of restoration. Oh, and a commander of the army. "Why is Ëólas's job on here? He wants to keep that position for now, at least until we've dealt with Āranol." *And Morgán.*

Mercia clasps her elbows in front of her garnet-red dress. "Yes, but then Lord Ëólas will need to pass that title onto someone else until you have an heir. From what I've learned through my studies, an elven prince consort can't hold the title of commander general because that position is for the firstborn."

An image of a preschooler with gold eyes and long curly brown hair fills Adaline's mind, making her pause her pacing and worrying so she can hold on to that dream, until she replays Mercia's words a second time, and another thought pops that vision. "Wait, prince consort? I don't understand. I married him, and—Ooooh. Because I'm a higher rank, as Aerytol's heir."

Seira chimes in. "Exactly. He married you, not the other way around."

That's bullshit. We married each other. In our vows, we chose to share everything equally. I know I felt that. "I don't care what anyone says, Ëólas and I are a team."

At least, we were in the Wastelands. Adaline repeatedly slides her ring off and on her finger.

"Regardless of what title you give Lord Ëólas," Mercia says, "everyone expects you to name someone as the temporary commander general, at least until you have a little one running through the halls."

"Okay, so that's five positions." Adaline strides over to the table, sits on the edge of an armchair, and dips the quill into the inkwell. "Lady Síena can continue handling the city's restoration efforts." If only Adaline could work beside her, digging up discoveries and rebuilding the palace. Maybe she can once this war is behind them. "And I'd like to meet with Lady Áwen tomorrow to discuss her conservation plans, if she doesn't intend on returning to Lameiría."

Adaline scribbles the two ladies' names on the list. *That's progress.* Granted, now the list comprises mostly elves. She should probably choose humans for the three remaining positions. But whom? *Maybe I can ask Ëólas tonight, before bed.*

Pushing the parchment aside, Mercia gently touches Adaline's arm. "Just focus on your speech, on letting the people know you'll do what's best for them. Be your sweet, kind self, and you'll win them over."

"Thank you, Mercia. And thank you for agreeing to be my envoy while you're still here."

"Oh, well, I'm glad to help." This Mercia, the one who readily shares her thoughts, has so much potential, beyond managing some future husband's estate. Yet, when Adaline first asked for help during lunch, Mercia's hand wouldn't stop shaking, causing her teacup to rattle every time she held it. Now, she seems taller and livelier. Even her voice sounds stronger.

"My lady," Tumin announces from the doorway, "Lord Ëólas and King Magnus are on their way."

When she hears Ëólas's voice, Adaline's body sways toward the hallway. Going to him would be easy, natural. But she grips a sofa's backrest to anchor herself. After rolling up the parchment to hide the blank entries, she sits on a chair facing the balcony, rests an elbow on the armrest, and crosses her legs as if she's been that way for the last hour.

When the guys' heavy boots stomp into the lounge, a set of warm hands slides under Adaline's curls and massages her shoulders. Leaning over, Ëólas kisses her cheek. The instant connection makes time slow down enough for Adaline to inhale that lavender scent, to treasure his fingertips grazing her skin, to reset her nerves. She reaches for his hand, to kiss his palm, but a few seconds later, he's gone, taking his reassurance with him. Adopting his all-business persona, Ëólas steps onto the balcony with Magnus, Thoren, and Merith.

Adaline slumps in her chair, prompting Seira to slide off the sofa and fall onto her knees at Adaline's side. She lays her head on Adaline's lap and steals her cousin's attention with those bright periwinkle eyes.

"No hiding," Seira hums.

Nodding, Adaline stands and pretends to adjust the neckline of her gown. Even though she's overdressed, it's almost showtime, and she can't flee the room to consider a costume change while Ëólas and Magnus address the crowd.

"What are they saying?" Adaline asks.

Mercia creeps toward the balcony, positioning herself so she's not within her father's line of sight. "Lord Ëólas is explaining the plans for defending the city against Ãranol."

Wait, he has plans now? And he's telling our people before telling me?

A few minutes later, Mercia waves for Adaline to come near. "King Magnus has announced his intention to help restore Aerytol's legacy. That's your cue, Adaline."

As Magnus and Ëólas wait for Adaline to take center stage, she adjusts the layers of her skirts one last time and steps forward, only to stop and extend her hand to Seira. "Tíer Nía, come with me."

Seira flutters to Adaline's side and curtseys. "My queen." When Adaline rolls her eyes, Seira's whimsical laughter stirs the wind and ruffles the tapestries. "I'm here. And your love is waiting."

Gathering her skirts with one hand, Adaline elongates her neck and emerges from the shadows with Seira. While Adaline walks to Ëólas and Magnus, taking her place between them, Seira prances next to Merith and hugs his arm.

Most of New Leira's people fill the meadow inside the castle wall, creating a crowd larger than Adaline imagined. Fólas and Hamon must have their hands full, overseeing the city guards and ensuring order. She scans the crowd quickly, praying she'll find Sallie or Delós in a sea of thousands, but she has no such luck. Aside from the council members up front, most of the faces staring at her belong to strangers.

With a commanding voice, Ëólas says, "The coronation will take place after we've eliminated Āranol's threat."

"In the meantime," Magnus booms, "Alderton acknowledges Queen Adaline's authority over her homeland."

At the word *authority*, a cool breeze brushes Adaline's curls across her exposed back, making her shiver. Ëólas and Magnus take a step back, leaving her front and center and alone. She keeps her hands interlocked in front of her lower abdomen the way Nan did when addressing participants at PTA meetings. Feeling queasy, Adaline chooses a single spot to focus on, to keep her balanced—a child with disheveled hair and a smudge of dirt on his cheek. The corners of her lips perk up into a natural smile.

Showtime.

"Thank you, King Magnus, Commander General Ëólas, and all of Alderton and Lameiría for everything you've done to ensure Aerytol's future. I'm grateful our kingdoms have rebuilt a firm foundation of trust and kinship that will aid in our prosperity and friendship for centuries to come." She projects her voice loudly, and the wind assists, carrying her words across the meadow, while she keeps at the forefront of her mind why this moment in history matters.

"I want every citizen here to know that I value the work you've invested in creating a new and stronger Aerytol, and I hope you will stay and consider this land your home. I promise to serve you as faithfully as King Magnus and Lord Ëólas have done so, and I will always act in the best interest of our people, human and elf alike."

The crowd murmurs, but only slightly. Pushing aside their minimal reactions, she mentally lists the next talking points she and Mercia mapped out. She's given enough lectures to faculty and students to make this a breeze. But her words feel like a boring monologue from a new dean who vows not to make changes, even though everyone knows that's bullshit.

Adaline click-clacks her thumbnails against each other. "I will continue to listen to Alderton and Lameiría's council as we work together to address the challenges..."

Adaline stops.

The child yawns and drops his chin to his chest. A spectator coughs. A few sighs float above the crowd shifting on their tired feet. One man sticks his finger in his ear and examines the wax. A woman closes her eyes, dreaming of going home or thinking about the chores awaiting her.

Even now, the crowd has mostly divided itself into a human and elven side. The middle's a bit mixed, but overall, the people chose separate sides. Adaline can't blame them. It's only natural they'd default to what they're most familiar with, comfortable with, especially when Ãranol has placed their homes and lives at risk. If only Adaline knew how to help ease their fear.

Shit. Where was I?

As Adaline runs through her talking points again, Mercia's and Seira's words echo in her mind. *Just be yourself, and you'll win them over. No hiding.*

Adaline drops her hands. "I can only imagine how unnerving yesterday must have been for you, whether you witnessed the events firsthand or heard about it later. I'm sorry you had to learn about what we're facing, and who I am, under those circumstances."

Now the people pay attention, their eyes wide open.

"I never meant to deceive you. Any of you." *I hope you're down there, Sallie.* "I didn't know myself until a few days ago."

Murmurs weave through the crowd as neighbors turn to neighbors, as parents attempt to silence their children, as people angle one ear to hear better.

Lifting her chin, Adaline projects her voice louder. "When I was seven years old, the Morgai found my family in Alderton. They took my mother and tried to execute me and my father. Like yesterday, my magic saved us, just like it saved Queen Arraya, and I found myself in a new home where the Morgai could never find us."

Resting her hands on the balustrade, Adaline leans forward, and the crowd does too. "I grew up in another world. A world so different from this one you can't even imagine. And even though my grandmother sealed away my memories to spare me from the trauma, I found my way home. To you. To fulfill my destiny of reuniting our peoples and being your queen."

The pressure in her chest eases up, enabling Adaline to continue, her thoughts and words flowing smoothly. "That other world did more than just hide me from the Morgai. There, I became a scholar. I studied ancient histories and vastly different cultures, but I always found the ways in which we're similar. The common threads that link us. I see that here too. Our diversity is our strength. When we lean on and learn from each other, we create new opportunities and possibilities. Look at what you've achieved thus far."

"So, in the spirit of collaboration," Adaline pauses, her mouth spreading into a wide smile as she lifts her arms and turns her palms to the sky, "I'm opening the council member positions to everyone in Aerytol."

The crowd gasps. Excited and confused whispers grow louder.

She doesn't dare to look at Ëólas or Magnus. They left this to her, so she's doing her own thing. "I invite anyone who wishes to remain in New Leira to submit their name for consideration on my council. For each position, I will require an elf and a human to work together as a team, just like how Lord Fólas and Lord Hamon co-manage the city guard. I will review all applicants equally, regardless of whether you have a title in the court. And regardless of gender."

As conversation erupts among the crowd, Adaline strains to listen for hints of agitation. Surely some won't like the changes ahead. But mostly Adaline hears Seira clapping, her giggles skipping over to Adaline.

Lowering her arms, Adaline infuses her words with warmth and encouragement. "We have a chance to set an example for the world, to show other kingdoms what's possible when elves and humans work together. I believe in Aerytol. I believe in you."

Her father flashes in her mind, him sitting in front of the fireplace, his wife on his lap, their foreheads pressed together. Blinking away her tears, Adaline can't conceal the lilt in her voice as she says, "Your safety is my primary concern. Because we will always have to stand up to those who don't support our efforts, we must come together as *one* people."

Squeezing the railing, Adaline deepens her voice and narrows her eyes. "To anyone who follows Ãranol, I hope you will choose to think for yourself. Judge our results with your own eyes. If you do not wish to be a part of Aerytol's future, then you are free to leave. But," she gives the crowd a moment to process the severity of her tone, "if you try to harm my people or thwart our efforts, I will punish you accordingly."

The crowd pauses, their faces a mix of pride for their city and fear of what may lie ahead. No one gives away if they support Ãranol—at least, no one Adaline can spy as she sweeps her eyes over the thousands of individuals. A few people throughout the crowd begin clapping, their cheers picking up momentum until the people applaud and shout their praises with enthusiasm.

Thanks for the indirect lessons, Nan.

Magnus and Ëólas rejoin Adaline. Standing united, the three of them wave to the crowd while Seira dances around Merith, still standing at attention. Magnus, his blue eyes shining brightly, congratulates Adaline and heads into the lounge.

Before following his king, Thoren nods at her like a father who just watched his daughter graduate.

When they're alone on the balcony, Ëólas steps closer to her. The sunlight highlights the gold in his dirty-blond hair, and the gleam in his eye displays his contentment. Maybe, now that he has a plan, they can spend the rest of the day together, work together.

He kisses the back of her hand. "You're a natural, and your idea for the council is brilliant."

"I can't take credit for it. You and Magnus set that up first."

"Yes, but that was with the city divided. Aerytol itself never had humans on the council, and you've just made that mandatory. Well done, my love." He rubs his thumb over her hand, over the ring he gifted her.

She closes the remaining distance between them, her chest brushing against his, and lifts her lips toward his. "Are you done for today?"

"Ah, um." His expression darkens. Sliding his hand to the small of her back, Ëólas turns her toward their friends and guides her into the lounge. "Almost. Magnus and I still have aspects to complete. I'll fill you in tomorrow, I promise." With another peck to her cheek, he dashes out of the lounge, forcing Merith to follow.

As Adaline watches Ëólas's back disappear, Magnus walks over to her. "I'll make certain he joins you for dinner."

She forces herself to sound peppy. "No, it's fine. He likes to be thorough, and I don't want to rush him."

Magnus pats her arm and leaves with Thoren. Seira and Mercia don't utter a peep while Adaline stares at the scroll Ëólas never asked about.

He must be stressed. He'll, he'll be more himself tomorrow.

"Hey, Moren? Tumin?" Adaline calls. Both of her guards emerge from the hallway and enter the lounge. "When the crowd dissipates, I'd like to go into the city and visit with Sallie."

"Oh, no my queen," Moren blurts out, then smacks his lips shut. As Adaline waits for him to elaborate, the seconds drag into eons. Not once does he unlock his mouth.

Adaline clears her throat. "Why, Moren? What happened?"

"Nothing, Your Majesty. Nothing at all. I'll send word immediately for the city guards to find and escort Sallie here."

"But I want to get out of the castle for a bit."

Moren side-eyes Tumin, who refuses to budge from standing at attention. "Perhaps you'd enjoy the private gardens, Your Majesty? I'll have Sallie brought there."

Crossing her arms over her chest, Adaline addresses Mercia. "Want to join me in the city?"

Seira covers her grin with both hands and sinks onto the sofa and out of sight, leaving Mercia to whisper, "They don't want you leaving the castle."

"They?" Adaline asks.

Mercia stares at her toes. "Father. His majesty. Lord Ëólas. All of them."

"Apologies, my lady," Moren says. "But you've survived three assassination attempts thus far. No one wants to give the enemy a fourth opportunity, especially not my lord."

Adaline's chest flutters and then tightens, like a bird hitting the sides of its cage. *He didn't discuss any of this with me.* "And if I walk out the front door?"

"I must follow my commander's orders, my lady." Moren lowers his head. "He told us to keep you in the castle."

Fire burns through her veins, making her cheeks flush and throat burn, as Adaline growls, "He said what!"

Moren and Tumin walk into the lounge and stand at attention on either side of the doorway. An elven butler steps between them, his sage waistcoat and its silk-embroidered floral stems and leaves peeking out from beneath his navy overcoat.

Clearing his throat, the butler announces, "Sallie, Your Majesty."

Then he steps aside, revealing Sallie, clutching the hands of her two girls, who bob next to their mother and crane their necks to see into the luxuriously furnished room, a true gilded cage. The boys and baby Lori must be at home with Abuela, not that Adaline can ask yet, given that Sallie appears not to be breathing. When her eyes land on Adaline, Sallie pulls her head back, her face stiff, lifeless.

Swallowing her anger at Ëólas, at least for the time being, Adaline rises from her seat and hurries to the doorway. "Sallie, I'm so happy to see you. Are you in a rush to return home? Do you have a moment?"

Sallie, remembering to let her lungs work, exhales and shakes her head. She bows low, her gray-streaked dark hair once again piled high in a tight bun. "How might I be of service to you, Your Majesty?"

Her formality bruises Adaline's chest. "I just wanted to check in on you. Please," she says, gesturing for Sallie and the girls to enter the room. "I don't know the etiquette here, so please forgive me, but Sallie, this is my cousin, Seira."

Right on cue, Seira skips next to Adaline and hunches over, resting her hands on her knees, and flashes her pixie-like smile at the girls. "Would you like to see the view from the balcony?"

The girls glance at their mother. After Sallie's hesitant nod, they each take one of Seira's hands and scamper to the balcony, filling the room with giggles and oohs and ahs.

Seeing the girls at ease, Adaline massages the kink out of her chest and turns back to Sallie. "And this is my good friend, and now envoy, Mercia." *Lady Mercia. Oops.*

Pinching the sides of her tan frock, which matches her beige skin too well, Sallie curtsies. Her muddy hem brushes the floor. "An honor, my lady."

"I'm pleased to meet you, Sallie. Lady Adaline speaks highly of you." Mercia, ignoring the horror her mother would display if she found out, curtsies in return, making Sallie blush and her lips curl upward.

With her arm looped around Sallie's, Adaline guides her friend into the heart of the lounge and offers a seat on the same sofa. Adaline angles herself sideways, her muslin skirts rustling against Sallie's linen frock, and looks into her friend's careworn eyes. "How are you? Really?"

Sallie lowers her gaze to her lap. "I'm managing. One day at a time."

"I'm so sorry I haven't been around."

"You were on quite the adventure, Your Majesty."

"Please call me Adaline."

"I cannot presume to be so informal."

"It's okay. We'll work on that." Adaline pats Sallie's hand, then returns her own to her lap, giving her friend space to breathe. "How are things with the shop?"

"Oh, business is good. Everyone's been very supportive, and his majesty approved my request that my brother-in-law should inherit the shop. It'll take him months to sort his affairs, and I might yet convince him to let me keep running the business for him. He's not keen to come—to own a candle shop—so I expect us to be fine. He might even relinquish the shop to Adem once he's of age."

"Wait, wait, wait." Adaline holds up her hand like a stop sign. "Do you not want the shop yourself?"

Sallie's eyes dart about the room, but Mercia, taking a seat across from them, offers an explanation. "Women can't own property in Alderton, my lady."

Adaline springs off the sofa. "What? Well, this isn't Alderton. And Alderton's laws no longer apply here, not to my people. That's ridiculous. I want that law amended, immediately. All women over the age of eighteen can own and inherit property. We'll iron out the specifics later, but I want it in writing, today, that Sallie owns her shop. That is," Adaline sits down quickly and searches Sallie's eyes, "if you want it. I mean, the law's changing no matter what, but at least you have the option now."

Sallie doesn't move.

If she keeps forgetting to breathe, she's going to pass out.

"My, my lady. I d-don't know what to say," Sallie starts. "I, yes, thank you. Yes."

"It's done then," Adaline says, turning to Mercia, who's already writing down Adaline's new law.

Oh, Mercia. Can I keep you too?

The girls clamor into the room, dragging Seira with them, her long blonde hair flowing behind her like a fairy in the wind. The joy on her face has erased all traces of yesterday's panic attack.

The girls should come by more often. They all should. "Sallie, please know the castle is always open to you." *Consider me your kiddos' godmother. Oh, right. We don't have that here. Um, they're fairy godmother? Whatever.* "If you need anything, just let me know."

Sallie stares in disbelief. Finally, she leans forward and touches Adaline's elbow. "My lady, you must be careful. There are those who would seek to take advantage of your kindness."

"I know. And I'll keep my eye out for those." Adaline winks and sits back on the sofa more casually, hoping to encourage Sallie to loosen up. "But don't feel like that's what's happening here. You brought a social injustice to my attention, and I'm—Oh! Sallie, would you consider being on my council?"

Sallie falls backward into the sofa cushions, partially because the girls leapt onto their mother and partially because of Adaline's words. "I, I, I know nothing about being a, a—"

"I know little about being a queen, but here we are. And you do know the people. That's what matters to me. You heard my speech. I need people like you on my council. Will you at least consider it?"

After a long pause and her girls hugging her around her waist, warmth returns to Sallie's eyes. "Yes, Your Majesty. I, I'll consider it. May I have some time to think it over?"

Adaline beams. "How about a week?"

Sallie bows her head, and her entire posture relaxes as she hugs her girls. Her voice and mannerisms become less rigid, less formal, over the next hour. Mercia speaks to Sallie as a peer, not a commoner far below her, while Seira plays a game of cards with the girls on an area rug off to the side. Overall, the conversation and laughter ease the ache in Adaline's chest. But knowing the person she loves most of all has practically trapped her in this castle contaminates the joy she should feel from coming home.

Chapter Four

A Mule

As the sky dims into deeper shades of burnt orange and plum, Adaline meanders through the private garden. Thank goodness Seira knows when Adaline needs alone time, and the royal guards agreed to block anyone else from entering the enclosed garden. Sitting down on a stone bench, Adaline stares at a patch of dirt and moves her hand back and forth. The earth doesn't respond. It lies dormant at her feet. Unmoved. Unphased. Uninterested.

How did I tear open the road when that elf attacked me? What's different?

If negative emotions weaken Aerytolían magic, then maybe her abilities have shut down because Ëólas missed dinner. Three nights in a row. And all other meals, for that matter. Granted, he has gifted her the occasional peck on the cheek and a sentence or two to make sure she's doing well or what tasks she could focus on, like welcoming Alderton's troops outside New Leira. And he changes his clothes daily, so he must enter their room at some point—just not when Adaline's present or conscious. Overall, his duties as commander general come first, leaving no time for them as newlyweds.

But that can't turn off her magic. She can't depend on her spouse to make her abilities function. Hell, she spent weeks denying her feelings for Ëólas. Yet she still subconsciously performed feats of magic.

Or did she?

She didn't *make* the tree root trip her abductor. The tree chose to help her. Same with the cave collapsing and the wave pushing her out of the river. They've been friendly toward her, just like when she was a child. Well, mostly. Water has always been unpredictable, and the wind comes and goes as it pleases. Even so, in her youth, the elements felt like friends who came over and played until they needed to go home.

But that day in New Leira, when she tore open the road, her magic felt different. The earth moved in sync with her, as if they were connected, as if they understood each other.

I have no idea how to replicate that.

Sitting up, Adaline rubs her bare arms that throb from today's sword practice. A cool breeze drifts past her, its scent infused with rust. Or blood. The hair on the back of her neck rises.

All day she's felt uneasy. Yes, she's still pissed at Ëólas's disappearance. He did after all promise her they'd do this together. But the insecurity that's been nagging at her started when Seira said Morgán's becoming desperate. Her internal compass has been going haywire ever since. Maybe Ëólas's has been too. Maybe, like her relationship with the earth, she and Ëólas are out of sync.

If she wants to escape this castle and protect her people, she doesn't have the luxury of waiting for him to make time for her. She needs to figure out how her magic works and quickly. Who knows what Āranol and Morgán have planned? Surely one of the prisoners must know something. The elf, at the very least, considering No-Nose and Shorty didn't know who she was when they attacked.

An image flashes in Adaline's mind, her face pushed into the grass, the ribbons of her bodice coming loose, No-Nose holding down her wrists.

"Can't you get her to hold still?" No-Nose bellowed.

"You try undoing these damn laces," growled Shorty.

"This is taking too long."

Adaline jumps up from the bench and clutches her stomach. Neither of them sounded sadistic. They sounded angry, worried even, that someone would catch them. Why would two men sneak into the palace ruins, risking the wrath of Lameiría's border patrol, only to make a ruckus to assault her? In fact, Shorty didn't take an interest in Adaline until he heard her accent.

It never made sense how those men got past border patrol. An elf had to let them in.

But why would two men want to help Ãranol?

Maybe they're his brainwashed pets from Feídra né Morna.

"Oh my god. They weren't trying to rape me," Adaline says to herself.

If they were, they would have focused on pulling up her skirts, not getting her bodice off. They even spun her around, trying to tug the fabric off.

Adaline places her hand on her ribs, over her birthmark. The day she met Ãranol, the day he tried to kill her, he'd told her that their families were old friends. "I know a lot about you too," he said, leaning against the doorframe to her parents' bedroom, his hands clasped innocently in front of him. "I bet you even have Aeríoléna's kiss, right?"

When he mentioned the birthmark she shared with Nan and her father, Adaline had touched the left side of her ribs. His eyes had snapped to that spot below her heart, and that asshole smiled as if he'd already won. She'd given herself away.

Damn it. After Ãranol stabbed her, he saw her disappear too. He could have been keeping an eye out for her, especially when he sent his spies to sabotage the Neutral Territory. And then Adaline showed up at the ruins with an otherworldly accent. "Those bastards knew."

Adaline hurries out of the garden, past the trees and rows of pink dahlias and purple asters, and steps through the archway that Moren and Tumin and four more guards have been watching. "I need to go to the dungeons."

"Um, but," Moren's eyes widen. "My queen, I have orders to—"

Adaline glares at him. "In Lameiría, if Queen Élara gave you an order that contradicted Ëólas's, who's orders would you follow?"

Moren gulps. "Queen Élara's."

"Ha! I'm the queen here, so I'm going to the dungeons. Right now. And you can either stay with me, or you can go tell Ëólas, but I'm not waiting for you." Adaline pushes past them and makes her way to the courtyard, where she asks a squire to bring her Ëólas's horse immediately. When the tall steed stands in front of her, she rubs the bridge of his nose and looks into his big brown eyes. "I had a horse once. His name was Benley, and I loved him dearly. I haven't ridden by myself since that day, so will you please help me get to the training grounds?"

The horse neighs and swishes his tail, telling Adaline that he understands even though she's not speaking Elvish. It's the connection that matters.

Adaline pulls up her skirts, steps into the stirrup, and pulls herself up and over the saddle, her new dusty-rose dress falling in layers down the sides. As her six guards scurry onto their own steeds, Adaline nudges her horse's sides, and they race to the training grounds.

Once she reaches the arena and dismounts, a pair of city guards tends to Ëólas's horse while Adaline hurries to the left side of the surrounding buildings. Another guard opens a door to a building that resembles where Fólas has been training her. Only, instead of having different weapons and dummies, this room has stairs that descend into the ground. Torches light the damp corridor, and two more guards jump to attention at her arrival.

Following the guards' directions, she turns right and keeps her body close to the back wall as they pass nine cells, each containing full bedding, desks, carpets, and a musical instrument. When she reaches Shorty, he's lying on a plush mattress and staring at a painting of a waterfall. He's crossed his feet at the ankles and folded his arms behind his head. Seeing her, he tilts his head up, grumbles, and lays back down.

Moren barks, "Stand up for your queen."

"I don't have a queen," Shorty says.

Tumin steps forward, ready to stab Shorty's foot through the bars, but Adaline raises her hand to stop him. She walks up to the bars so that the light of the torches clearly illuminates Shorty's face. She studies him for a moment, and her instincts feel nothing, telling her to move on.

Five more cells down, she finds No-Nose, sitting on the ground and sketching a face into the dirt floor. The moment he sees Adaline, he wipes the image away with his foot and sits on his bed perfectly still, facing the wall so that Adaline can see only his profile, which accentuates the jagged stump that should be his nose.

She hears his voice in her head, how he defended his actions the last time she saw him, how he insisted that any woman traveling alone must be in want of company. Then she kneed him in the groin and sentenced him and Shorty to working in the quarry. The memories make her cringe.

"How's work going?" Adaline asks, her tone detached.

He looks at his hands, torn and dry as leather, but doesn't speak.

She had hoped to never see him again. But she came here for a reason. So instead of seeing the monster at the ruins, she thinks about the man in the pillory in Hell City and all the other brainwashed humans with no choice but to earn their mentors' favor. "I traveled a great distance recently, all the way to Feídra né Morna. What I saw in that city was quite alarming."

No-Nose's thumb twitches. Adaline moves to the far right of the bars so she can see more of his face. He doesn't glance at her but also doesn't turn away. With his shoulders slumped, he looks beaten down, exhausted.

She softens her voice. "I saw what happens when humans break Āranol's rules. I can't stop thinking about those people, how terrified they must be, having to do what their mentors say to keep their freedom, to avoid punishment."

No-Nose still doesn't move.

She leans closer to the bars, making Moren move his hand to his hilt, and points to her nose. "Is that the price you paid for disobeying your mentor?"

The man flinches. His eyes blink rapidly, and he tightens his jaw to control himself. Watching him struggle to hold back those memories reminds Adaline of Seira, screaming on the ground when she remembered Morgán.

Adaline swallows hard. "You knew about my birthmark."

His eyes dart to her ribs, giving her all the evidence she needs. She turns to Tumin. "Let him go."

"What?" Tumin squeals. "But, my queen—"

"He's a victim in all of this. And now that I know the truth, I won't continue to torture this man, who—"

"No!" No-Nose leaps to his feet, making Adaline jump back as he grips the bars and crushes his face between them. "You can't let me go. I'll stay here. I'll continue working in the quarry."

"Why?" Adaline shakes her head. "If you're afraid of Āranol, you can earn a place here. Help us, and we'll make sure you never have to see him—"

"I'm not afraid for myself." No-Nose clamps his mouth shut and turns away. "I won't help you. If you let me go, I'll only try to kill you. I promise you that."

Tumin places himself between Adaline and the cell. Despite him urging her to leave, Adaline can't stop staring at No-Nose's hunched back. He doesn't look determined. He looks defeated. And even though his words are cold, he doesn't sound like a psychotic murderer. He sounds like Adaline did, when she stood up to Calvden, when she would have done anything to save Ëólas.

"You have family in the Wastelands?" she asks.

No-Nose sits down on his mattress, drops his head, and dangles his hands between his knees.

He is one of them, one of Ãranol's pets. "My husband and I will leave with our army in a few days. We're going to overtake Feídra né Morna and free all the humans in the Wastelands. I have two armies at my disposal. Queen Élara and King Magnus have lent me their forces. I will not lose this war."

No-Nose shakes his head. He probably thinks Adaline's lying. What promises did Ãranol make that convinced this man to travel to Aerytol, to the Forbidden Lands, and search for Aerytolíans?

Adaline looks at the patch of dirt that No-Nose had been drawing on with his finger. She takes a deep breath and imagines herself touching the ground. "Please, show me what he erased," she whispers.

This time, the earth listens, wriggling like snakes. No-Nose gasps and pulls his feet onto his bed as the floor turns into an Etch-A-Sketch, outlining the face of a young girl with a button nose and big, sad eyes. But the dirt doesn't stop with today's etching. It keeps going until the entire floor of his cell displays portraits of the same three youthful faces.

No-Nose's expression shifts from awe to agony as he stares at the girls' vacant eyes.

"Who are they?" Adaline whispers.

"My daughters. Aster, Iris, and Norin."

Adaline nods. "My mother used to plant norin beneath my bedroom window. When the sun shined directly on them, their sweet perfume filled my room. What's your name?"

"Marcus." He can't tear his eyes away from the floor.

"Nice to meet you, Marcus."

"If Āranol suspects me to be disloyal, my girls will pay the price. I'd rather die here than betray him."

"I understand. But I need to know how many people came with you."

Marcus's body shakes with frustration, prompting Adaline to tell Moren, Tumin, and the other royal guards to back up until they cannot see Marcus. With the guards gone, he glares at her with the same intensity as when he hunted her through the ruins. "Fuck you," he shouts, his cuss echoing off the walls. But he lifts his hand in front of his chest and holds up five fingers. Then he traces the round curve of his ear and changes the number of his fingers to three.

If their group started with six, then Adaline's abductor, Shorty, and Marcus account for the three humans. The elf she caught four days ago means that two remain, if Āranol didn't send more. But that's not the point. Adaline didn't ask that question to get names. She wanted to know if Marcus would help, and he did.

There's hope for Marcus after all. And there's hope for Feídra né Morna.

Taking one last look at Marcus staring at his daughters' faces, Adaline leaves him be. When she reaches the stairs that lead to the surface, she pauses and looks left, toward the elven side of the dungeon. Even though she came to see Shorty and No-Nose, she can't leave without seeing the elf she nearly buried alive—and knowing with absolute certainty his condition.

Instead of stopping at one of the many cells she passes, the dungeon guards halt in front of a wooden door. They slide a rectangular piece of metal to the side, revealing a gap large enough for mail delivery but at eye level. Peering inside, Adaline discovers the elf bound to a chair in the middle of the room, his head hung low, his shirt missing, and blood dripping from his wrists and torso.

Hearing the metal side open, the elf lifts his head and glares at Adaline, his lip busted open and his eyes swollen in shades of black and blue.

"Open the door," Adaline says.

When a guard hesitantly does so, Adaline steps inside and approaches the elf. His eyes follow her the entire time, waiting for an opportunity to finish what he started.

"Where's my mother?" she asks.

His lip curls into a snarl and begins bleeding again. "Your husband didn't tell you?"

Adaline clenches her jaw. "I want to hear from you."

He blinks slowly and rolls his head backward, letting his hair, caked with dirt and blood, fall to the side of his face. One of his top teeth is missing. "We killed that wench years ago."

Adaline locks every muscle in her body to stop herself from strangling him. She could grab a torch off the wall and ram it into his chest. But he's defenseless now, and rage won't do her any good.

"You never returned," he continues. "And she caused more trouble than she was worth."

Is that what happened, Poppa? You were driving home from work when you felt half of your soul die? Is that what caused your car to swerve and crash into the river? Adaline's lip quivers, which makes the elf grin.

Looking him dead in the eyes, Adaline whispers so that the human guards can't hear her. "Do you know what happens to elves kept underground?"

His grin falters.

"You have one day left, maybe less," Adaline says. "You might want to consider telling me the truth because your savior isn't coming. He won't risk attacking when we have the advantage. And that must burn him, knowing I've slipped through his fingers yet again. Your lord wouldn't have been so stupid as to kill my mother, to destroy the only leverage he has. So you're on your own. Tell me where she is, and I'll find you better accommodations."

The elf chuckles. "Do you know what we call you? The mule." He spits in her direction, but Moren jumps in front of her. The prisoner's spittle drips down Moren's breastplate.

Knowing she won't get anything more from him, Adaline leaves him behind. But she can't forget the sight of him. Did Ëólas inflict those wounds himself, or did he instruct someone else to do that? Did he bother to try reaching the prisoner another way, a better way, than through torture and threats?

Nan and her mother always said to choose kindness. But where does she draw the line? And she can't entirely be angry with Ëólas when she too felt the urge to burn her enemy to the ground. She even threatened him.

Is this how rulers become tyrants?

As a guard opens a door to the study, Adaline overhears Fólas say, "I've set up the elven campsites behind the—"

"Adaline." Ëólas doesn't approach her this time. Instead, he releases a deep breath, nods with relief that she's in front of him, and crosses his arms over his chest. "Did you find what you wanted in the dungeon?"

Of course he knows I went.

The guys have moved the long table from the back of the room into the center, between Ëólas's and Magnus's desks, and they've added tons of figurines to represent troop deployments. In fact, the navy and burgundy toys occupy nearly every square inch of Aerytol.

Dang, he is over planning.

Adaline leans her back against the closed door, keeping her distance from everyone, especially Ëólas. She cocks her head to the side and mirrors his posture. "Yes, actually, I did. When were you going to tell me they killed my mother?"

Ëólas leans his hands on the table, using it to hold himself up. "I didn't say anything because he was lying."

"I know that."

Ëólas glances at her. "You do?"

"Ãranol and Morgán have been hunting my family for centuries. He wouldn't give up his only leverage."

Magnus arches a brow. "Good reasoning."

"I've said before that I'm a scholar. History includes thousands of wars too, you know." Pushing off the door, she walks toward the table. "Marcus is from Feídra né Morna."

"Who?" Thoren asks.

"Marcus. No-Nose. One of the humans who attacked me at the ruins." Adaline bites her lip to stop herself from gloating that she learned something they hadn't. Her thorough-yet-absent husband missed a piece of the puzzle. "Like I said earlier today, we'll accomplish a lot more if we work together. What aren't you telling me? What has kept you held up in here for days?"

Because Ëólas won't speak up, his knuckles turning white as he grinds his fists into the desk, Adaline looks to Magnus. "What do you think Āranol's planning?"

Magnus hems and haws, but Thoren says matter-of-factly, "If I were him, I'd send more spies to assassinate you. Everyone knows you're too curious, wanting to explore the city and make friends. He'd be wise to take advantage of that."

Yes, he would. "Which is why Ëólas ordered my guards to trap me in the castle?"

"That wasn't an order, not that you would listen," Ëólas says through clenched teeth.

"Not that you explained your reasoning to me." Pinching her lips into a stiff smile, Adaline turns to Magnus and the others. "Would you all please excuse us? Ëólas and I need a moment."

"Of course." Magnus quickly ushers everyone out of the study.

When the door bangs shut, Ëólas stands perfectly still with his rigid jaw, flaring nostrils, and eyes burning holes into the map.

Adaline tiptoes up to the table. "Say what's on your mind."

"I would rather not. I need time to think and continue strategizing."

"You've been strategizing for three days. I know you like to be thorough, but, Ëólas, you can't plan for everything."

"Yes, I can. I've done so before. And it'd be much easier if you'd trust me."

Wait, who needs to trust whom? She bites the tip of her tongue. "You're mad I went into the dungeons."

"Yes!"

"Why?"

"Because you don't need to see all of that, to expose yourself to—"

"Being called a mule? I can handle more than you think."

"But you shouldn't have to. You have your hands full as it is. You're learning so much every day, and the people need you front and center, not getting your hands dirty." Pulling his hair at the roots, he walks away from the war table.

Adaline stares at the back of his dark-green long coat, the brown leather belt cinching his waist that she would normally desire to hug. "But you can get your hands dirty? You think I'm okay with what you did to that elf?"

"I know you're not. But your sincerity will jeopardize my planning and your life." He scoops up one of the navy figurines from the table. "I have fewer guards stationed in the dungeons right now with the hope of luring his accomplices out. But you had to go down there and place yourself in the middle of my scheme. You're just handing yourself over to them, Adaline. Is this how it'll be going forward? I'll carefully plan our moves, and then you'll do whatever you want? Please, let me know so I can adjust my expectations going forward."

"You can't blame me for not knowing your plan when you didn't share it with me!"

The fire in the hearth roars, sputtering ash onto the stone floor. Adaline's cheeks burn as well. She clenches and unclenches her fists as she walks back and forth between the table and Ëólas's desk.

He tosses the figurine on the table, knocking two more over. "I said I'd fill you in soon. You couldn't wait one day?"

"I've been waiting. Day after day. And I've needed you. You said we'd do this together, and you left me alone since day one."

"To handle a speech and choose your council and welcome Alderton's forces. I knew you could handle that."

"It's more than that, and you know it." Oh, how she'd like to shove him. "You're shutting me out. You have been since Seira's end-of-the-world prediction. What do you think is going to happen?"

"I'm uncertain," he mutters. "I'm still figuring out humans and how unpredictable they can be."

Adaline stumbles backward. There it is—the separation between them. The elf and the mostly human. The precise and the messy. Harmony and chaos. They both look away, taking a moment to breathe.

"If you're going to keep shutting me out, then don't blame me for foiling your plans. I'm not a mind reader, Ëólas."

"I'm not asking you to be. I'm asking you to be patient."

Adaline scoffs. "Oh my god. You still don't get it. You know what? It's fine. Take as much time as you need to figure out whatever is really going on with you. Because whatever's happening between us, it's not normal. It's not *our* normal. Until then, you can sleep in here. Not that you would have come to bed tonight anyway."

Adaline storms out of the study, past all the guys waiting in the hallway, past Merith and Fólas with their red cheeks and wide eyes, past the royal guards who spin around and follow her. She can't even storm off alone.

When she closes the door to her chambers, Adaline hurries past Kayla, tears off her dress, and throws on her shorts and shirt from back home. After climbing into bed, Adaline punches her pillow into the shape she wants, slams her cheek into the stuffing, and remembers how she spoke to Ëólas, how he seemed nothing like the person she fell in love with, the person who usually knows her better than anyone.

Her chest convulses as she uses her pillow to stifle her crying. When did he stop trusting her as his partner?

CHAPTER FIVE

A DEAL

When her tears dry, the door creaks open and closes. The sofa in front of the bed catches a belt and a few layers of clothing. The mattress sinks behind her, followed by a long exhale. After lifting the covers, a warm body lies down behind her, and Adaline inhales a faint trace of lavender and pine. She could roll over. She *should* roll over, having never been a fan of the silent treatment, but she's not yet sure what to say that will bridge the gap between them. And she doesn't want to yell at him again, to hear him yell too.

Ëólas rustles the mattress as he shifts onto his side, and Adaline pictures an aerial view of them lying back to back, a chasm between them. If she rolls over now, would he face her?

She takes a shaky breath. Ëólas loops his arm underneath her own and fits his frame against hers, his hand wrapped tightly around her waist. She laces her fingers with his. They lie together for at least ten minutes, releasing the tension that's been crushing their bond, hurting them both physically and emotionally.

He nuzzles his mouth close to her ear and whispers, "I, I've never felt fear before, not like this."

Adaline wriggles backward, pressing herself more closely against him, to feel his warmth and share her own. "You're scared of Āranol?"

"No."

Scared I'm not strong enough to face him?

They hold each other in silence until Adaline wiggles beneath the comforter and turns over. The fear in his golden eyes mirrors when he found her bleeding and broken after she killed her abductor. He'd held her as gently as possible back then, hurrying her to the castle before she passed out. She knew she was safe with him though. She's always known that, even when they fought.

Ëólas brushes his knuckles over her cheek, then drops his hand to her chest, his finger pushing the comforter and her shirt down so he can trace a small circle over her heart. "I don't know what I'm doing. It's my job to protect this city and you. But I'm failing. I don't know where or who our enemies are. They might have already surrounded us, and I won't see them coming. It's like everyone's trying to take you away from me. I don't trust anyone in the city. I don't trust most of the city guards. I don't trust my plans because we have human enemies too, and I can't predict their moves. And despite Alderton and Lameiría lending us aid, any number of those soldiers could secretly serve Ãranol."

His chest deflates from the thoughts plaguing him. "I wish I could lock you in this room until the entire ordeal is over. But you're the queen, and no one can tell you what you can and cannot do. Not even me."

Adaline skates her hand under his arm and presses herself against him, nestling her forehead under his chin. When she speaks, his scent fills her lungs. "It's not your job. It's our job."

"But—"

"No buts, Ëólas. We promised we'd share everything equally."

"We're not equals, my love."

"Ugh." Peeling away from him, Adaline sits up, hugs her knees to her chest, and rubs her forehead with the tips of her fingers. "How can I get through to you on this? I refuse to be your queen first and foremost. With everyone else, I understand that line must exist at some level, but not with you. If I'm queen, you're king, and we're a team. That's it. I won't have it any other way." She punches the mattress as she turns to him. "Or I'll quit."

"You'll quit?" A smile tugs at his cheek.

He thinks I'm joking? "Yes. I'll abdicate."

Sitting up and leaning against the oversized, hand-carved headboard, Ëólas stuffs his pillow behind him and scoots Adaline onto his lap, gripping her knees to tuck her legs beside him. "You can't mean that."

"I do. This," she gestures between the two of them, "comes first. And do you know why? Because with us united, I can focus on giving this city my all and be the queen they deserve. I'm not saying I can't function without you—it's just that I function best *with* you. I mean, have the last few days gone well for you, with pushing me away?"

Ëólas's head falls back, banging the wooden headboard, his dirty-blond hair falling behind his lean, sculpted shoulders. "No. Magnus and the others were ready to throw themselves from the windows."

Adaline bites her lower lip to stop herself from smirking. "So you do fully recognize that you've been an arse?"

He glowers at her but doesn't argue. "I wasn't trying to be. I couldn't…"

He closes his eyes to shut out his thoughts, but Adaline refuses to let him retreat. She kisses his jawline, then skates her lips along his neck. When she suckles his earlobe and his throat rumbles, she asks, "You couldn't what?"

"Indulge myself. With you. Not when I have zero results for my efforts."

She brushes her lips back and forth along the hollow of his neck while she considers her next words. "I'm sure you have some good plans though."

"We do. I just keep questioning everything. Repeatedly. And I," he sighs loudly, "I didn't want to tell you, to make you worry."

Cupping his cheek, Adaline turns his face to make him look at her and places his hand over her heart. "Nothing is worse than you shutting me out. And please remember that when you're depriving yourself, you're depriving me too."

His face contorts with regret. "Merith was right. I have been a terrible husband." Sliding his hand under her T-shirt, Ëólas massages circles along her spine, kneading his apology into her flesh. "I don't like having these—what are they—insecurities?"

Adaline throws her head back and laughs. "Welcome to my world!"

"Thank you," he says sarcastically.

"You know what helps me overcome those?"

"Being impulsive?"

"Being with you."

Skating his hand up her spine, he digs his fingers into the muscles around her neck, riding her shirt up in the process. "Well, that was rather sweet of you."

"It's true. Though, being impulsive helps too."

Now Ëólas laughs, releasing the last of the tension between them. "And what happens when we next disagree, my love?"

"We talk to and listen to each other and find a compromise."

"And if we can't find one?"

She kisses his jawline again. "Then my vote is worth fifty-one percent."

His initial chuckle transitions into a guttural growl. "I, I don't like that."

"Because you're used to being right?"

"Yes."

"Welcome to marriage, my love."

"I fear I'll never be right again."

"Hey!" She thwacks his arm with the back of her hand, then traces her finger down his chest, between his solid pecs, and circles his first ab muscle. Hooking her finger over the waistband of his sweats, the pair he brought back from Maryland, she tugs the elastic. "I've missed you."

"Are you speaking to me or my member?"

"Both." Smiling wickedly, she studies the upward curve of his lips. "Ever heard of makeup sex?"

"No, but I think you should teach me."

Standing up, she shimmies her shorts down her hips, his eyes watching them fall to the floor. She pulls his arm, directing him to sit at the end of the bed, wraps her arms around his neck, and straddles him, her lips and hips hovering just above his. He squeezes her round bottom and yanks her against him, his gaze darkening like a starved animal who selected his next meal. He tilts his face toward hers, but she pulls back and admires his flustered face and pouting lips.

"Are you going to be in meetings all day tomorrow?" she asks.

"No."

She brushes her lips over his. When he opens his mouth to seek her tongue, she draws back. "Will you miss lunch again?"

"No," he says, his voice husky. "Nor dinner. Nor bedtime. Nor—"

Adaline crashes her lips against his, her tongue delving into his mouth, their kisses fierce and ravenous. He moans and slides his hands under her shirt, his fingers dancing over her nipples that turn to pebbles for him. She rocks back and forth along his bulge, her insides flaring as he hardens more. Rising onto her knees, she gives him space to shed his sweats and kick them away, then sits down, slipping his length between her wet folds, and shudders with euphoria that he's come back to her.

Groaning, he tips his head backward and kisses along her neck. His thumb encircles her pearl, making her ready for him. "You did, indeed, miss me," he says, pulling her shirt overhead.

His eyes fall to her chest. Licking his lips, he palms both mounds, pressing them together and then moving them apart while her folds caress and moisten his length. He kisses each nipple, swirling his tongue around the nubs and letting the cool air tickle her.

He suckles her breast again, nibbles her peak between his teeth, and grins when she simultaneously yelps and moans. "I love the size of these," he murmurs. "Because they continuously spill out of my hands, I always have more to tame."

"I'm glad my breasts entertain you." Positioning him against her entrance, Adaline swivels her hips and circles his tip but doesn't let him in. "Are we agreed that we're equals, my love?"

He grips her hips, trying to push his way inside her, but she lifts up, leaving him standing at attention. "Is this how we'll negotiate hence forth?" he growls.

"Maybe."

"You're setting a dangerous precedence here."

"I'm aware." She dips lower, letting his tip enter her an inch, then bobs up, taking away his pleasure. "You didn't answer my question."

"Fine. I agree. But you may regret this, my love. I know how to gain your acquiescence too."

"You can try. But I'm confident I'll win."

"Oh really?"

"Yep." She sits down, permitting his entirety to fill her, to push against her walls, making Ëólas's eyes roll back in his head as he groans. She clenches around him, swirls her hips, and rises only to slam back down and grind on him. She repeats the pattern, riding him and the waves of pressure gathering deep inside her. "We're not going to execute the elf."

"Fine!"

Ëólas's breathing becomes erratic, his fingers digging into her bottom, his cock swelling. She pulls up again but doesn't let him fall out, not all the way. "And we'll plan our schedules together. If we have separate tasks, fine, but we'll share that with each other, *before* those events take place."

"Agreed," he gasps, clasping her hips and tugging her down as he thrusts himself inside her.

She grabs his nape, twisting her fingers into his hair, making him look at her as the friction between them builds, her breasts slapping his chest. A light sheen covers her shoulders and stomach as she pants, "And you'll stop treating me like a fragile doll locked in a dollhouse."

"No," he growls, flipping her onto her back and pushing her to the center of the bed.

He plunges deep inside her, making her arch her spine and lock her ankles around his waist. With his chiseled arms beside her, securing her beneath him, he sucks the hollow of her neck, the tingling sensation setting her skin on fire and driving her to grind her pelvis faster against his. He rises onto his hands and ploughs into her, pounding the headboard into the wall over and over again until she's screaming and so tightly wound that she's about to burst—which is when he pulls out, leaving her throbbing at the edge, trying to pull him back inside.

"I'm going to continue taking every precaution to safeguard you above all else." As he lowers himself onto her, he glides in slow and steady, making her quiver beneath him as he whispers in her ear, "And you're going to let me."

She digs her nails into his upper back, creating crescent moons in his skin. "O-okay. But you'll tell me those plans and earn my consent."

"Deal." Sliding his arms under her back, he crushes himself against her, kisses her passionately, and swallows her moans as he fills her to the brim.

There's no escaping him as she convulses and twitches in his embrace, her mind and body coming undone. He's invaded every inch of her, body and soul, and she wouldn't have it any other way.

"My love?" Ëólas murmurs in her ear.

Lying on her stomach, Adaline buries her face in her pillow. It can't be morning already. Her hand finds Ëólas's face and pushes him away. He chuckles, but when he tries to leave the bed, she latches onto his arm and tugs him around her, turning his naked body into her blanket.

He kisses her earlobe. "And this, my love, is why I hate waking you early."

"What time... What's happening?" she mumbles.

"We're hours from dawn. But Lameiría's troops have arrived. Merith and I are going to greet the generals."

"Oh. 'Kay. I'll come. Just a moment to..." Her words die in her silk pillow as her consciousness drifts away.

"You needn't get up. I've got this. They can wait until the morning to see you."

"Umm-hmm." She hears Ëólas pull on a shirt, but she's asleep within seconds.

When Adaline next wakes up, her eyes fly open, and she sits up with a start. The moonlight casts an eerie bluish-white glow on the furniture and bed. Ëólas hasn't returned yet, and the sheets stick to her clammy skin. Shoving the coverings off her, she gets up and puts on her silk robe. Her chest feels tight, as if she had been sleeping with a boulder on top of her, and her synapses keep misfiring, preventing her nerves from settling. Pacing her chambers doesn't make the discomfort lessen. Her hands won't stop trembling either.

What's going on with me? What is this feeling?

Pausing in front of their fireplace, she pushes the bedroom out of her mind, ignores the soldiers' voices drifting on the wind, and focuses only on the discomfort growing inside the pit of her stomach, where she feels beaten from the inside out. Rather than burying that ache, she closes her eyes and lets the pain flood her so it can pass through her system, so she can let it go. But she can't dislodge the tugging sensation plaguing her abdomen, as if someone's latched onto her intestines and aims to pull them out through her mouth. Unable to breathe properly, she gags and gasps for breath, not sure if she'll suffocate or retch first.

Down the hall, Seira's sudden, shrill screams crawl through Adaline's veins, making her skin prickle and heart race faster. The crickets outside grow louder until all sounds become muffled, and she smells rust. No, blood. When she opens her eyes, her chambers have disappeared, along with the remnants of Seira's frantic cries.

In place of armoires and a smoldering fire, undulating low hills capped with waning moonlight surround Adaline. Tall grass tickles her exposed calves. Neither the castle nor New Leira is visible, not even a flicker of light. Pulling her robe tighter, she shudders in a breeze that carries within its currents someone chanting. A male voice.

That's not Elvish.

Whatever language he's using, the words themselves feel heavy, ancient, and inapposite. A building pressure in her temples pushes her thoughts downward, as though she's sinking into an abyss. Adaline staggers toward the voice, her stomach turning inside out and the wind numbing her limbs. In a few steps, she crests the hill, at the bottom of which sits a lone tent. Pulsing candlelight illuminates the interior. A wedge-like strip of light splayed on the ground marks the tent's entrance to the right.

I, I wasn't trying t-to travel. So how did I... Where am I?

Tripping over her feet, Adaline stumbles forward until dirt scratches her bare toes. She glances around the moors, the low hills all covered in grass. Yet a massive circle of flat, barren earth greets her toes. Pressing her knees together, she squats down and scoops up a handful of dirt. The soil falling between her fingers leaves behind blades of dead grass, shriveled and brittle. When she pokes one, it dissolves into ash.

That's not natural.

Adaline, placing both of her palms on the dirt, tries to ground herself, to tether herself to the earth, but she feels no response. It's like she's knocking on a door but knows no one's home. She tries again, recalling when the street tore itself open to bury her enemy, how the ground felt like an extension of herself, like two friends who could read each other's minds. Here, the ground feels as lifeless as a dead body. Its coldness creeps into her bones, freezing her from the inside out.

Forcing herself to stand, Adaline takes one step into the circle, and her legs collapse beneath her. She falls onto her knees and struggles to hold herself up. The world spins uncontrollably, making her head light and her vision blurry. She squeezes her eyes shut, searching for home, but she cannot feel the doorway to her chambers. Lost and alone, she pushes herself up, her legs wobbling, and drags her feet forward. Her stomach bubbles and burns, and her head spins so much so that she could vomit at any moment.

I just need to see...to know...

When she reaches the dark-blue tent, a male voice fills the canvas interior with a low, gravely chanting. Her fingers shaking violently, Adaline peeks around the right side, hoping to see who might be inside. An elf with silver-streaked light-brown hair towers over five others kneeling side by side, their backs to Adaline. Hooded, black cloaks conceal the first three. Thick leather straps crisscross the other two's backsides, securing their chest plates.

They're soldiers?

Not recognizing their leader, Adaline considers announcing herself, asking for help. Before she can, the elven lord tilts his pewter chalice above one soldier, and a thick red ooze drips into his open mouth.

No, no, no. That can't be... He's not...

When the lord abruptly stops chanting, Adaline releases a deep, silent breath. Her silk robe sticks to her backside. Her limbs tingle awake, her feet prickling as if she has been standing on pins and needles. She takes two steps back, but then the chanting resumes.

And the screaming begins.

The soldier who drank from the chalice releases a never-ending, blood-curdling scream as if someone were drilling a hole into the side of his head. Adaline slams her hands over her ears, trying to shut out that sound. If only she had a sword or dagger, anything to put him out of his misery. She could do that, take a life as an act of mercy. But she doesn't move, much like the other four soldiers who don't so much as squirm or cry out to help their companion.

The soldier continues screaming, his voice turning hoarse and guttural, until he must be empty inside, his body a husk, his soul extracted and sentenced to evaporate into thin air. At his side, his hand turns ashen. His skin puckers and boils, only to collapse in on itself, leaving the length of his arm and his fingers gnarled. His nails grow longer, sharper too, and the elven lord drapes a black cloak around the soldier, covering his face with a hood.

"So faithful," the lord says, his voice almost purring. "Will he live? Wonderful."

Although Adaline doesn't hear anyone reply to the elven lord, he continues talking out loud. "Yes, yes. Rest, indeed. My poor children. They've given up so much. None of this would be necessary if it weren't for her."

Her?

Bile burns Adaline's throat. As the lord tips the chalice over the last soldier's mouth, she backs up, her heart pounding so loudly that she fears the drumbeat will give her away. But the last soldier's screams drown out all other sounds.

Further and further, Adaline drags herself away from the tent, the hard, barren ground scraping her heels. She looks at the moon and silently prays to the fae for help, to stop this madness, to spare these people, to spare herself from having to hear another person scream like a wild animal skinned alive and begging for death.

Stop, stop, stop. Please, for the love of the fae, make it stop.

Again, she covers her ears, her bones rattling, her vision blurring, and her head throbbing. By the time his cries peter into a pitiful whimper, Adaline reaches the edge of the barren circle—at least, she should have. The perimeter has expanded. She needs to crest the hill, but her feet weigh a ton, and her body sags, until the screaming stops abruptly and Adaline's mind clears.

I need to tell Ëólas about this.

With whatever spell has broken, she scurries uphill, each step burning the bottom of her feet. The closer she gets to the grass, the more her nausea fades, but a hissing sound makes her whip around to find the source. From the tent, a silhouette emerges with glowing red eyes. Adaline stops. The acid in her stomach rises, burning her esophagus. She can't move. If she takes another step, she'll throw up her dinner. She'll need an entire box of antacids after this.

The shadow drifts forward, slowly at first, a cloak caught in the wind. Steam curls around the figure, as though the starlight intended to set him on fire, to burn him out of existence. But the silhouette picks up its pace, striding toward her, those red eyes ready to carve out her soul. Adaline's inner voice shouts for her to go back, to go home, to find Ëólas. She opens her mouth to cry out, but her voice catches in her throat; the foul stench of singed flesh wafting toward her makes her stomach spasm, and she dry heaves.

As she stumbles backward and her feet touch the edge of the barren circle's threshold, the shadow runs at her twice as fast as any man, and that angelic feminine voice whispers in her ear, "Focus on your bond, Adaline. Flee this place!"

Those red eyes lunge at her, and every inch of Adaline's body yearns to return to Ëólas, to return to safety. Pressing her hand to her heart, she latches onto the tether between their souls. The figure leaps into the air. Adaline extends her hand and grabs onto Ëólas's arm. She can't see him yet, but she can feel him. And she lets that connection yank her away from the moors, away from the figure extending its sharp nails toward her throat.

Chapter Six

A BIGGER PROBLEM

An instant later, Adaline appears in front of Ëólas among a sea of tents, torches, campfires, and soldiers. Carts and wagons dot the farmers' fields that run the length of New Leira. In the distance, the old palace, the city's skyline, and the castle mark the horizon. A chilly breeze blows across the grass in waves and pushes Adaline's curls off her face. Her hand still grips Ëólas's arm.

His eyes jump to her fingers, then sweep up and down her body, noting her sweaty, thin robe and bare feet. "Adaline?"

She opens her mouth to tell him what happened, but the fresh air dislodges the emotions she had reigned in. Doubling over, she retches, missing his boots within an inch. Ëólas, swinging beside her, pulls back her hair. As she collapses, he catches her around the waist and lays her gently on the ground, her upper body resting on his lap and away from the mess she made. She prefers the stench of vomit to that of burned flesh.

Merith drapes his cloak over her, shielding her from the cold and the soldiers' eyes. "My lady," he whispers, his voice strained with worry.

She lifts her shaking hand and touches Ëólas's cheek. "Sorry to scare you like that."

"What happened?" Ëólas asks. The campfires cast an orange hue over his glossy, anxious eyes.

She shakes her head. Every time she remembers those red eyes and that dead circle, her stomach churns; she risks throwing up again. "I'll tell you in the study."

"You need a bed," Magnus says, emerging from behind a wall of elves trying to give her privacy.

What are you doing out here too? "I need you and everyone else in the study. It's about Morgán." At the mention of his name, she remembers Seira and her screams as Adaline traveled away from her chambers. "Someone needs to check on Seira. Now."

Ëólas doesn't argue. The hushed voices of people giving orders turn into Ëólas and Merith pushing and pulling her body onto a horse. Only when Ëólas wraps his arms around her does she breathe easily, her head resting on his sturdy, warm chest. She fingers the lapel of his long coat. She always loved this one; the gold-embroidered hem brings out his eyes, and the soft navy velvet between her fingers proves she's home and he's real.

As Ëólas tugs the reins, turning his horse toward the castle, Adaline glimpses a tall lady with long strawberry blonde hair pulled up in a high ponytail and wearing Lameiría's leather armor. After issuing orders, the lady mounts a horse beside them.

Sora, you made it! Oh my god. I threw up in front of Ëólas's people. "E-Elves don't vomit, do you?" she asks him.

"Don't fret about that." He kisses the top of her head.

After she enters the study and sits down, Adaline wedges her hands beside her legs to keep herself upright on the gold-brocade sofa beneath the row of stained-glass arched windows. Ëólas drapes his cloak on top of Merith's, tucks Adaline against his side, and rubs her arm to help her stop shaking. With her teeth clattering, Hamon tosses kindling into the fireplace and blows on the embers while Sora and Fólas hover around Ëólas's desk.

Please, don't throw up again.

"What the hell was that all about?" Thoren booms as he slams the door shut.

The look of concern on his ruddy face, on all their faces, makes Adaline wish she could hug each of them. With her friends gathered together, she lets her nerves uncoil, and her body melts against Ëólas's frame. She smiles weakly at them, trying to encourage them to shed the distress that's cinched their faces.

"What happened?" Ëólas asks. "Why are you ill?"

Leaning forward, Adaline looks at the door, praying her cousin might walk into the room at any moment. "Is someone checking on Seira?"

"Yes, my lady." Merith, standing directly in front of her, deepens his scowl, unwilling to be at ease just yet. "I sent four of my best guards. Is she in danger?"

"No. I don't think so." Adaline folds herself against Ëólas's side. "She must have felt what I did."

With his arm wrapped around her shoulders, Ëólas pulls a few strands of hair off her lips. "Which was what?"

"I saw a—I don't even know how to describe it—a creature."

"In our chambers?" Ëólas nods at Merith, who draws his sword and heads for the door with Sora and Fólas behind him.

"No, not in the castle." As Adaline shudders, the cloaks tumble downward, exposing her neckline to the drafty room. She hoists the fabric up to her neck, and Ëólas tucks both layers behind her shoulders. "I traveled. Don't look so crossed, Ëólas. It wasn't voluntary."

Studying her closely, Magnus takes a seat on the sofa next to Ëólas and beside the door. "How can you travel involuntarily?"

Despite her exhaustion, she doesn't miss her friends exchange nervous glances. "Please don't make me sleep with a dagger attached to my thigh."

"We'll discuss that later," Ëólas says. "Please, go on."

Thoren, with a gruff "humph," plods to the long table at the back of the room that holds three rows of goblets and several glass decanters and carafes. After selecting a red-tinted decanter, he yanks out the stopper and pours wine into a goblet. Done, he slams the decanter down on the table.

What's he so upset about? Not my safety. Or is he?

While fidgeting with the hem of Ëólas's cloak, Adaline forces herself to relive what happened. "I woke up feeling anxious, like I knew deep down something was wrong, is wrong. I tried to relax, to make it go away, but—how can I explain this? It was like someone knocked on the door, but I didn't know what a knock was. And the moment I touched the door, someone yanked it open and pulled me through." As Adaline continues, her friends' expressions grow grimmer. "I, I think it was Morgán."

Ëólas sits quietly, his muscles stiffening, while his mind toils away. "Can he do this again?"

"I, I don't think so. I know the feeling now. It's one I'll never forget."

"What does it feel like?" Sora asks.

"Like someone's yanking my intestines out through my throat."

Fólas grimaces. "That's quite visceral."

"It felt visceral." Adaline covers her mouth with her hand, wishing she could erase the putrid taste at the back of her throat.

Thoren grabs two goblets and brings both to Adaline. "Water or wine?"

The acid oak smell of the wine makes her dry heave. "Water, thank you." She takes the cup and sips slowly while Thoren sets the second goblet on Magnus's desk. With her hands trembling and her sweaty back shivering, she splashes several drops from her cup onto her legs. The beads of water roll off the cloaks and drip-drop onto the stone floor, their timing matching Adaline's racing heart. "I've never had the flu, but I imagine it feels like this."

"I'll take you back to our chambers. If you're certain you won't vanish again, this conversation can wait till morning." Ëólas slides his arm behind her back to pick her up, but she arches her spine to get away.

"No. I-I can't sleep. Besides, I have you all here now, and talking's good: It helps me feel better. I just need a moment to wash this taste out of my mouth." *And feel normal again.*

Taking a few sips, she swallows slowly, testing the stability of her stomach. Her insides don't revolt against the water, so that must be a good sign. But everyone's nervous energy gathers like a storm cloud above her head as they watch her every move.

She shifts into the corner of the sofa so she can see Ëólas fully. "Is everything okay with Lameiría's troops? I thought only you and Merith went to greet them. Did something else happen?" *Oh god, please don't tell me we have even more problems.*

Ëólas rests his hand on her knee. "Everything's fine here."

"I invited myself." Magnus scratches his cheek, his finger digging into his dark beard. "I wanted to make certain Lameiría's troops feel safe with my own occupying the fields on the other side of the city."

Thank you, Magnus.

Fólas smirks. "To be fair, Hamon was on his way home when he caught the commotion."

"That's hardly appropriate for her majesty to hear!" Thoren barks.

"Hamon?" Adaline says his name as though she caught him sneaking out the backdoor of someone's home.

A pink flush consumes his cheeks, though that could be from the fire blazing beside him. But as he walks closer to their group, his hands stuffed in his pockets, his face fades from pink to gray. "It's not like that. Besides, shouldn't we discuss the more important matter at hand?"

"Yes, I agree." Sora crosses her arms over her chest and stands beside Merith as if she's already captain of the queen's guard, though Adaline doesn't know if Ëólas told Sora the gig is hers if she wants it. "Please, Your Majesty, where did you travel to? What happened?"

Adaline, swallowing one more trickle of a sip, shakes her head, and her momentary enthusiasm diminishes with the volume of her voice. "I don't know. There were lots of low hills covered with grass—except for where I appeared." She tells them about the barren ground that made her ill, the chanting that drew her toward the tent, the ceremonial pewter chalice. The screaming. And the cloaked figure who chased her.

By the end of her story, Ëólas, leaning forward, dangles his hands between his knees, his hair falling over his shoulders, his eyes staring blankly at the stone floor. No one speaks until someone knocks on the door, making Adaline flinch. But it's a real knock, and she's not choking on her intestines, so everything must be fine.

Merith, sticking his head out the door, speaks to someone in the hallway. When he comes back, his silver puppy-dog eyes fall on Adaline. "Lady Seira won't respond to her lady's maids. She won't move. Won't speak. It's like she's not home anymore. I'm sorry, my lady."

She's catatonic? Adaline stares into the water at the bottom of her goblet that she cups between both hands. "Morgán has broken the laws of nature."

Ëólas rubs his fingers into his furrowed brow and grinds away at the wrinkles. "I was afraid you'd say something like that."

"What exactly does this mean?" Magnus asks.

Adaline swirls her goblet. The water slaps the sides and collapses in on itself, trapped and subdued. The cup's design, the leaves and stems, resemble Morgán's chalice. Only, his held that thick red liquid, thicker than wine. She sets the goblet on the floor. "It means Morgán has magic. Worse, he's abusing the elements, bending and breaking them with blood magic."

Silence and stillness settle throughout the room. Unable to remain sitting, Ëólas meanders toward the fireplace and leans his forearm along the oak mantel. He exhales through his flared nostrils; otherwise, he maintains his typical stoic expression, the one he wears when he's taking in and processing data.

"How could any elf resort to such an atrocity?" Sora sounds as if she might throw up herself.

"I assume that doesn't bode well, then?" Magnus asks quietly.

"No, it doesn't." Ëólas shifts back and forth on his feet. His tone hardens as he scruffs his chin and calculates the exponential new threats—many of which no one here can fathom.

With no one ready to disrupt the gloom that's filled the study, Adaline slides off the sofa, clasping Ëólas's cloak around her neck, draping Merith's over the sofa arm, and moves beside him. The fire flickering near her knees chases away the last of her chills. "Are you okay?"

"No." Ëólas leaves behind his ruminations. "I cannot stand the idea of you alone and defenseless and facing someone so, so—I don't even have a word to describe someone so morally corrupt."

She touches his arm, but he glowers at the fire, unwilling to meet her eyes. Sensing his rising anxiety that he masks too well, she ducks under his arm and pops up between him and the fireplace. As he steps back, she grabs his coat collar, making him look at her. "When I was trying to escape, I couldn't find my way home, but that voice told me to search for our bond. And I felt you, even though I couldn't see you. You were my compass."

Grief and affection collide across his face as his brows wilt and his lips curl into a sweet smile, shattering his neutral façade. He cups her cheeks and studies her face as if to memorize every detail. "I should have been with you."

She nibbles her bottom lip. *Keep me with you—that's what he asked me before we said our vows.*

"I don't think I always can take you with me. But I can promise you something else." She traces the gold embroidery along the hem of his coat, then peers up at him through her lashes. "No matter where I go or what I do, I will never stop fighting to get back to you."

Pulling her into his arms, he presses his lips to her temple, not caring that the others keep darting their eyes away. She locks her arms around his waist and rests her cheek on his chest, ready to end this meeting for now, ready to lie in his arms for the rest of the night, where no monsters can find them. At least not for now.

Neither of them moves until Merith clears his throat and asks, "My lady, do you think you can travel to the same location now?"

Adaline's muscles seize up. "Why?" She steps back, hoping to see Ëólas frowning at Merith.

Instead, Ëólas stares at the swords and daggers that decorate his middle shelves. "Because if Morgán's soldiers are weak and need rest, then the figure rushing at you must have been Morgán. And if you can take me back there, then I can end him."

"What? Are you crazy?" Adaline backs up, nearly tripping over the area rug beneath Ëólas's desk. "I could barely get away the first time. The only reason I did was because I used you like an anchor. What if we're both trapped there next time?"

"The queen is right." Sora moves next to Adaline and shakes her head at Ëólas. "You'd also be leaving her majesty unprotected while you fought Morgán."

And this is why I need more ladies on my council.

"But we can't let this opportunity go to waste, especially with Morgán now using blood magic." Ëólas pauses and looks at Adaline for support. "Is there any way you can travel me there, without you?"

Adaline's jaw falls open. "Do you remember the part about him disfiguring his own soldiers—who are elves?" Those soldiers' screams still haunt the recesses of her mind.

"Can you take us both?" Merith asks.

"The three of us?" Sora adds.

What the fuck? You want me to deliver you all to Morgán on a silver platter? "No!"

"Adaline," Magnus rises from the sofa, "if they can stop Morgán now, that could end this war before it begins. Think of all the soldiers, from Alderton and Lameiría. You could spare thousands of lives tonight."

She can't look him in the eye, can't look any of them in the eye. They haven't seen the loss she has, how her father and Nan mourned their other half every day for the rest of their lives, how her family seems doomed to lose their spouses. She'd do anything to keep Ëólas safe, to keep him with her. If she knew how to fight, to work with the elements, then she'd be a worthy partner at his side. Instead, she'll get him killed. And Morgán knows that, knows how to weaken her family. Because he's succeeded twice already.

But thousands of lives.

Each one belonging to someone else, as a child or parent or spouse.

And she promised she'd protect her people.

They're counting on me.

Adaline nods once. Hugging herself, she turns about until she faces due west, and her mind searches beyond Magnus's shelves and the display holding his long sword, the one with the jewel-encrusted hilt that no one would use in battle.

Can she go back there? Back to the circle of death. Yes. Even now, she can feel the earth Morgán murdered and the surrounding land crying out to her. Maybe that's what drew her to that spot, not Morgán but the earth begging her for help, warning her.

"Yes, I can find my way back." She locks eyes with Ëólas. "But I don't know if I can bring anyone else. I'm still figuring out how my traveling works, and I've only ever taken one person with me."

"We'll take our chances." Ëólas strides toward his shelves and retrieves two swords that he ties to his belt. "If you're no longer feeling ill, please go get dressed—don't forget your sword—and meet me back here."

Adaline hesitates, hoping Merith or Sora will object. When no one speaks up, Adaline sighs. "Can I check on Seira?"

Ëólas nods solemnly. "Of course. But please make haste. Every moment we linger here gives Morgán the advantage."

Without waiting, Adaline hurries to her chambers where she changes into a new pair of black trousers, riding boots, and a form-fitting plum tunic—all while avoiding the mirror and her mother's eyes. She throws on a matching brocade vest too, followed by her belt and sword. From her duffle, she takes out and puts on her zip-up black leather jacket. Last, she slips her dagger into her boot.

Racing down the hall to Seira's doors, Adaline pushes one open and enters. Seira's lady's maids rise from the sofas, their cheeks raw from crying. On the chaise between them, Seira slouches sideways against the backrest, her hands latched around her knees, squeezing her legs to her chest. Her head drapes to the side, her platinum blonde hair falling like a curtain over her face, and she hums a faint yet somehow familiar song.

Adaline crosses the room, past the four-poster birch-wood bed with its sheer lavender curtains and woven-branch frame, and she sits on the edge of the light-cream chaise. After listening to a few beats, Adaline recognizes the melancholy tune of "Over the Rainbow," a song Seira couldn't possibly know.

Unless Seira had traveled to the other world.

How on earth…? Shaking off her confusion, Adaline gently touches Seira's hands. "Tíer Nía? It's me, Adaline."

Seira doesn't move, doesn't stop humming. Adaline brushes Seira's hair behind her shoulder, revealing her dilated grayish purple eyes. The emptiness within them feels all encompassing. Wherever Seira's gone inside her head, Adaline doesn't exist or can't reach.

What happened to you?

Adaline curls her fingers under Seira's hand. "I'll be back soon." *Hopefully with news that you don't have to worry about Morgán again.*

As she leaves Seira's chambers, Adaline squeezes her hands into fists, her entire body heating up as she replays that vacant look on her cousin's face. Her cheeks burn like hot coals ready to burst into flames. Gritting her teeth, Adaline breaks into a run. *Everyone's right. We have to stop Morgán as soon as possible.*

At seeing Adaline sprint into the study, Ëólas breaks away from Merith and Sora. "How's Seira? Any change?"

Adaline shakes her head. "Are you ready?"

"Yes. But are you? How's your stomach?"

"The nausea's gone." She faces due west again, sensing the pull of the moors. But she doesn't take Ëólas's hand. "I, I don't want you to get hurt."

"I handed my lord his first sword when he was five years old," Merith says, moving in front of her. "He didn't earn the title of commander general until he could best me. He'll be fine, my lady."

When I was five, I spent my time frolicking in meadows and talking to birds. Adaline chews the inside of her cheek.

"My love?" Ëólas laces his fingers through hers and kisses the back of her hand. "Our goals are the same. Trust me, as I trust you."

"Deal. But stay close to me, okay?" she says.

"Deal."

With their friends wishing them safe travels, Sora places one hand on Adaline's shoulder, and Merith takes hold of his queen's free hand. Clearing her mind of doubt, Adaline turns all her attention to the earth summoning her like a child crying out for its mother. Grass grows through the floor until the stone vanishes, and the distant hills swallow their friends. The fireplace puffs out of existence, its light and heat lost. But that's not all she left behind.

One hand is empty.

Chapter Seven

A Reunion

Well, shit. Adaline and Ëólas stare at the space where Merith should be. Not feeling Sora's hand either, Adaline twists around to find nothing but a thick fog concealing the moors, blotting out the horizon and anyone cloaked within it.

Double shit.

Should she go back and try again? Was she supposed to be thinking about them too? She's never had to think about bringing Ëólas. *Ugh!How can I fail him at a time like this?*

Ëólas touches his finger to her chin and turns her head to face him. *No,* he mouths. He pushes the corners of her lips upward, smoothing away her frown. Taking her hand, he scans the horizon. If he sees anything with his super elf sight, he doesn't indicate so.

Using her internal nausea gauge, Adaline guides him forward, toward the portion of land that's eerily silent and the surrounding hills that still weep. The stale air rolls between their ankles, the fog so thick that Macbeth's three witches could appear at any moment with their toil and trouble.

Fire burn and cauldron bubble, no thank you.

After a few feet, Adaline's stomach collapses inward. She stops abruptly and kneels down, Ëólas doing the same. Leaning forward, he whispers a few words in Elvish; rather his lips move, but she can't hear or discern a single word. Ëólas hovers his hand above the ground, and the fog parts a few inches, revealing the edge of the dead circle. He touches the dirt and recoils, and his frown sags further.

When they stand, he places one hand on his hilt and the other on Adaline's back, tilts his lips to her ear, and whispers, "The fog...move...I hear..."

Adaline leans backward and shakes her head, pointing to her ears. He makes an oops face and mouths, *Sorry.*

With neither of them willing to draw attention to themselves, he silently pushes on her back, and they hike forward, crossing into the circle. The water Adaline drank earlier turns to acid, and she clamps her mouth shut as if that can prevent her from retching again. Ëólas examines her sour expression, but she keeps walking, descending the hill as quickly as him, both of them wrinkling their noses at the smell of dried blood.

Several yards ahead, a familiar male voice pierces the fog. "You came back."

Adaline clings to Ëólas's hand. *No, not him. Not now.*

His voice sounds the same as it did twenty years ago, when he promised to bring her to her mother. Even though the fog hides him, Adaline's veins sizzle, and her skin radiates so much heat that her leather jacket sticks to her backside. As the fog parts and Āranol's silhouette solidifies, she grabs her hilt and draws the blade upward. But Ëólas pushes her hand down and places himself in front of her, his sword already drawn.

Āranol approaches them slowly, not out of caution but as though trudging through the circle sickens him too. His shoulders hang low, and his labored breaths blast white wisps into the chilly night air. He's always been a convincing actor.

The closer he gets, Adaline squeezes Ëólas's forearm and tries to shove it aside so she can stare Āranol in the face and show him he didn't win, that he'll never win. He's also not as tall as she remembers. He had seemed enormous back then, taller than her father. But Merith could squish Āranol like a toad.

If only Merith were here.

Āranol still favors wearing shades of turquoise and gold, and his light-brown hair falls in layers around his chartreuse eyes. Even though Ëólas angles his blade in front of her, Āranol doesn't draw his own. If she didn't know better, she'd think him a noble knight or prince, given his deliberate movements and confidence. But that's only his arrogance bleeding through. Adaline will never trust that pretty face again.

Fifteen feet away from them, Āranol stops. "We have a—"

Ëólas leaps off the ground so quickly that Adaline's gasp can't catch up with him. She never saw Āranol draw his weapon, but the clang of steel rattles the pebbles at her feet as they roll past her. She's never seen Ëólas fight before, not really. He had been fast during their trainings, but he had held back. Watching him now is like discovering her high school music teacher is actually a virtuoso who performs on the world stage.

Twisting sideways, Ëólas dodges Āranol's thrust and parries his own blade forward, trying to skewer Āranol's abdomen. Whereas Ëólas wields his weapon with grace and precision, Āranol's attacks are brutal and sharp as he hacks at Ëólas. Their speed and ferocity leave her gawking at the two of them until Ëólas's strikes become swifter and more forceful, making Adaline cringe and her chest curl inward.

"Would you pause just a moment?" Āranol hisses.

Ëólas doesn't yield. His strikes push Āranol backward, further away from Adaline. "I will never let you near my family," Ëólas says in between blows.

"Do you always overreact like this?" Āranol sidesteps, saving his arm from being sliced off. "Settle down. We have a bigger issue here."

Wait, what? Adaline rubs her ears. She must have misheard him.

With his unrelenting strikes, Ëólas cleaves the night in half, his cloak and dirty-blond hair fanning out behind him, as he swings his blade at Āranol's neck. Digging his boots into the ground, Ëólas uses both hands to push Āranol's blade downward, toward his artery. Āranol seethes, his knees and arms buckling. But Ëólas's face turns hard, emotionless, unyielding—much like when he viewed her to be the harbinger of death for all elven kind. She wants to scream at him to stop. But how can she reach Ëólas without jeopardizing his safety? And does she travel him back to New Leira without them finding Morgán?

Oh, shit. We forgot about Morgán!

Tearing her eyes away from Ëólas, Adaline scans the horizon quickly, searching for signs of a tent or a pair of red eyes, but the fog blocks her view. She faces a lone breeze that skirts by and begs, "Please, help me see more clearly."

That one current zips off. Just when Adaline thinks it's not coming back, that wisp gathers more. Blending together, the wind stirs the fog around their feet and combs the hillside, rolling the gray clouds aside until Adaline can view the entire dead circle and a few surrounding hills. Nowhere does Adaline see Morgán, his tortured soldiers, or his tent. Once again, the enemy has vanished—because Adaline took too long to get her shit together. And now Ëólas is trying to kill their only clue.

Damn it. Maybe he's just trying to maim him, slow him down, prevent retreat.

Āranol jumps backward, avoiding the tip of Ëólas's blade from slicing his clavicle. "Just hear me out."

Ëólas unsheathes his second sword in a wide arc. "You think I'll trust someone who's been trying to kill my wife?" In one swift movement, he slams his right blade down on Āranol's and uses the second to slice the enemy's thigh.

Snarling, Āranol lunges forward, moving faster than Adaline's seen yet. He ducks under one blade, jumps over the other, and slashes Ëólas's upper arm while kicking him in the gut, sending Ëólas stumbling back several feet. Seeing blood soak through her husband's coat, Adaline screams out and sprints forward. Shoving her hand into her boot, she chucks her dagger at Āranol's face. He hits the blade aside as if she threw a paper plane at him, but her goal wasn't to hurt him, just distract him long enough to reach Ëólas, latch onto his other arm, and hold him back from retaliating before their one lead dies or, worse, Āranol impales the love of her life.

While Adaline holds on to Ëólas, Āranol backs up further, raises his sword in front of his body, and waits for Ëólas's next move. "I thought you might be someone I could reason with."

"This coming from someone who intended to attack my people and slaughter thousands of innocent lives? I cannot reason with the unreasonable." After sheathing one sword, Ëólas peels Adaline's fingers away from his arm, his hand slipping under and around hers. Keeping Āranol within his periphery, Ëólas looks at Adaline, and his ridged jaw and dark eyes soften, the hardened soldier giving way to the loving husband. "I won't let him near you."

"It's you I'm worried about," she says.

"It's only a scratch, my love."

Ãranol rolls his eyes. "Enough already." He puts his sword away, which makes both Adaline and Ëólas glance at each other in confusion. Lifting his hands in surrender, Ãranol limps toward them, his sticky trousers tugging at his five-inch wound. "We have more important—"

"What happened to my mother?" Adaline asks.

Halting mid-step, Ãranol curls his upper lip and stares at her as if she just asked why the sky is blue. "You're still on about that?"

"Are you fucking kidding me?" Adaline lunges forward, only for Ëólas to grab her arm and drag her next to him. "Answer my question! What did you do with my mother?"

"Such vulgarity." Ãranol glances at Ëólas and makes a retching sound. "And you find that attractive?"

"I swear by the fae," Adaline's fists burn as if she holds embers in her palms, "if you don't answer me, I'll—"

"Oh, for creation's sake. Fine, I'll tell you about your mummy—if you agree to hear me out about what really matters here." Ãranol gestures at the barren ground. "Surely, you've noticed the dead earth upon which we're standing."

Faster than anyone can blink, Ëólas lifts his sword and points the tip at Ãranol's throat.

Refusing to wince, Ãranol glares at Ëólas. "She has you wrapped around her little finger, huh?"

Adaline digs her nails into her palms, squeezing her anger between her fingers. She won't let Ãranol get the better of her. "What happened to my mother?"

He rolls his chartreuse eyes, but his gaze falls to the side. "We kept her prisoner for a few years, in case you came back. But you didn't, and she didn't particularly like my father's laws—humans can be so stubborn. She proved harder to break."

Proved. As in past tense. Adaline inhales sharply as the world shifts out from under her. Only Ëólas's steady hand on her arm keeps her oriented, keeps her standing.

"Where is she now?" Ëólas says, his voice low, brittle, and wearing thin.

"She killed herself. A few years ago." Ãranol side-eyes Adaline. "Must have become tired of waiting."

Black specks spread throughout Adaline's vision until Ëólas and Ãranol vanish. She sees only her mother dabbing her paintbrush against the palette resting on her hand, the small dollops of colors smeared into a rainbow. Aurellia's captured their home on canvas. Its careworn front door. The bubblegum-pink azalea bushes out front. The streak of cloud dust across the blue sky. Edwin, approaching from behind, sneaks a kiss onto her cheek. If Poppa disturbed her too much, he'll walk away with a smear of red down the length of his nose and a grin wider than an apple tart.

Adaline tries to swim against the thoughts and emotions flooding her, but she cannot unsee the police truck dragging her father's car out of the river. *You felt her die, didn't you, Poppa?*

"Adaline," Ëólas whispers, taking her hand and holding on fiercely, his sword pressed against Ãranol's throat.

"Will you kill me when I'm unarmed?" Ãranol asks. "Are you not a person of morals?"

Ëólas grinds his teeth. "How dare you speak to me of morals."

"Fixing the world her family broke requires sacrifices—not that you would understand, seeing as how you've completely overlooked her family's heresy." Ãranol glances at Ëólas and Adaline's entwined hands, and his face twists in disgust. "Really?"

My family's heresy? Adaline tugs Ëólas's hand, pulling him back an inch and preventing him from piercing Ãranol's throat, at least for now. *Stay focused, Adaline. Know thy enemy. Grieve later.* "What are you talking about? Your father's betrayal destroyed Aerytol."

"Please," Ãranol scoffs. He gestures at the stars as if calling upon his witnesses. "Your family committed the first betrayal. And my father dedicated his life to sending your lot back to where you belong and undoing the chaos your family caused."

Back to where we belong? England? That can't be right.

His conviction makes Adaline question herself, and the heaviness accumulating in her heart doesn't help. Her thoughts tumble over themselves, making the base of her skull throb. Every second that ticks by, the hope she'd held on to dims, a flame that's running out of wick. How could her mother give up like that, knowing it would kill her father too? *But the wind never found her, never brought back a message.* Nothing about this conversation makes sense.

Ëólas voices the thoughts that she's struggling to form. "What are you talking about? Adaline was born here."

"I don't care where she was born!" Ãranol spits, ignoring Ëólas's blade scratching his skin. A bead of blood dribbles down his neck. "Fae don't belong here."

When Adaline and Ëólas jerk their heads backward, Ãranol observes Adaline like a butterfly he's pinned to the wall. He smirks at Ëólas. "She didn't tell you, did she? How like a fae to omit the truth."

"What truth?" Adaline's voice raises higher than normal.

Ignoring her, Ãranol talks to Ëólas like a friend offering his condolences. "She didn't tell you about her family, that when the fae finished creating our world, one selfish lady broke the law and stayed behind?"

One lady?

Adaline's hand falls away from Ëólas's. Slowly, Ëólas's scowl melts into realization as his brow unfurls, his eyes widen, and his jaw hangs slack.

"Now it makes sense, doesn't it?" Ãranol asks. "Why the elements respond so readily to her. They're like children skipping home to mummy."

The tip of Ëólas's sword drops away. "You're saying that Aeríoléna was—"

No, that can't be. I can't also be part...

"—fae. Correct." Ãranol applauds Ëólas and continues his history lesson, his tone now condescending. "And do you know what happens when you mix immortal and mortal blood? Chaos, that's what. Why do you think the world fell apart?"

While Āranol's claims leave Adaline and Ëólas momentarily immobile, he pushes one side of his long coat behind his hip, rips his dark turquoise tunic at the seam, and uses the dagger tucked under his coat to cut off a long strip of cloth that he wraps around his thigh.

Āranol cinches his makeshift bandage with a tight double knot. "And, as if the world wasn't fragile enough, her grandmother allowed human blood to pervert the family line further." Standing tall, he narrows his yellow-green eyes and waggles his finger at Adaline. "You're trouble, that's what you are. Human aggression and greed mixed with immortal blood? You must be terrifying when you're angry. You'll end us all. Then again, if we're lucky enough, you're a sterile mule, and your line will end with you."

When Ëólas's fist connects with Āranol's nose, a cracking sound echoes across the Wastelands.

Damn. I'm impressed Ëólas didn't kill him. "I still have questions for him."

"I know." Ëólas, shaking out his hand and flexing his fingers, doesn't lift his sword again, but he doesn't sheathe it either.

Hunched over, Āranol cups his nose, but blood seeps through his fingers, falls to the ground, and congeals into shiny, large red beads because the earth refuses to absorb his blood, having had enough already.

"Seriously?" Āranol's hands muffle his voice. "You're still going to worship the Aerytolíans—fae who fell from grace? Oh, she captured you with that pretty package of hers. I get it." He looks Adaline up and down. "Fae are hard to resist after all, even when diluted."

"You'd best shut your mouth," Ëólas growls. "Adaline, don't—"

"Did she seduce you the moment she arrived, with those large doe eyes and her innocent questions? Must have taken hours for her to lure you away from your soul mate and trap you in—"

As Ëólas shifts his shoulders forward like a panther about to pounce, Āranol backs up, raising his bloody hands. Adaline clenches her fists shut like a lid on a grease fire and presses them tightly against her chest. The more Āranol's words echo in her mind, her cheeks burn, and her breaths come and go so quickly that she can't seem to fill her lungs fully.

Oh my god. Did I steal Ëólas? Was he meant for someone else? Did I—

"Adaline, look at me." While Ãranol gestures *don't mind me* and his bloody nasal drip makes him cough, Ëólas wraps his free hand around her waist, closes the distance between them, and leans his forehead against hers, the tip of his sword directed at Ãranol. "Don't you dare let him into your head. His father has lied to him his whole life. He has no idea what he's talking about. Please, look at me, Adaline." Ëólas lets her go and shows her his palm, waiting for her to do the same.

She stares at those long fingers and unwavering hand that's been nothing but kind to her, that's always protected her, even when they didn't get along. They certainly disliked each other in the beginning. She tried to stay away from him, but fate, destiny—whatever's at play—kept drawing them together. When her chest stops heaving, she presses her palm against his.

Ëólas laces his fingers between hers and grips her hand tightly. "I choose you. Do you hear me? I'll always choose you. Human, elf, fae—I don't care. This right here is destiny."

The bond glows brightly between their palms, and Adaline lets that tether, its strength, its undeniable evidence, ease the fear that had been crushing her heart. She takes a deep breath and folds herself against Ëólas's side, his chin nuzzling her temple.

Having pulled out a handkerchief, Ãranol applies pressure to his nose. As his enemies' palms glow like the fusion of two stars, he knits his eyebrows together and looks away, unable to face what he must have considered impossible.

"Is this all you've come to say? To tell us Morgán's twisted view of history?" Ëólas positions himself half in front of Adaline to block her from further onslaught. "If we're done talking, let's resume our fight and end this now."

"Oh, please." Pinching his nose with the handkerchief, Ãranol tilts his head backward. "We wouldn't even be having this fight if she had remained in the Immortal Realms after I banished her there."

"Banished me?" Adaline's voice quivers as her blood boils, but sensing that Ëólas might explode any moment, she grabs the back of his coat and forces herself to keep her voice even. "Is that how you justified trying to kill me?"

Ãranol chuckles twice, even though doing so makes his face twinge. "No one can kill a fae."

"Um, I beg to differ."

"I sent you home."

"I traveled to my father, who rushed his dying child to a hospital where doctors saved my life!"

Ãranol sniffles and tests pulling the handkerchief away from his nose, his eyes refocusing on his bloody hands. "No. It's, it's not the same thing," he mumbles, folding the cloth over a few times and scrubbing his hands as clean as possible.

"As the person who lay dying, I'm telling you otherwise. And even *if* Aeríoléna was fae, I'm still mostly human." *What other bullshit has his father been feeding him?*

"There's no such thing as diluting immortal blood. It's *immortal*."

"Says who? Morgán? If that were true, then I wouldn't have buried my grandmother nine months ago."

Wiping streaks of blood away from his nose, Ãranol presses his mouth into a thin line. But his gaze turns inward. With Ãranol lost in his own thoughts, Ëólas silently moves his blade at an angle and slides one foot back so he's ready to strike the moment Adaline signals she's had enough. But what then? The idea of Ãranol bleeding out on the ground doesn't erase the past, doesn't help them now, doesn't tell them what his army's planning or where to find Morgán. Maybe she could drag him back to New Leira, lock him up for a few decades. Maybe he'll kill himself then too.

"Are we done?" Ëólas asks. "Is there a point to this conversation, or are you going to continue trying to turn me against my wife?"

"You're both so melodramatic." Shaking off his thoughts, Ãranol resumes his agitated tone and points to the edge of the dead circle. "I approached you because," he heaves a loud, grumbled sigh, "I thought maybe you could help."

Adaline touches Ëólas's wrist, silently asking him to give her a moment. "You saw what Morgán did here?"

For the first time since he's shown up, Āranol removes the hatred and sarcasm from his voice, and his gaze falls to the ground. "That person—he's not my father."

Don't let him fool you. "You helped him?"

"No! After we parted ways, I sent my troops ahead to our next destination—"

"Which is?" Ëólas asks.

"None of your business," Āranol snaps. "What does concern you is that after we left, I doubled back. He wasn't acting like himself."

Ëólas squeezes his hilt until his knuckles turn white. "So you watched your father torture his people?"

"It wasn't like that. You have no idea." Āranol cringes as if he too is still trying to run away from that tent. His hands visibly shake at his sides, his blood-stained handkerchief quivering against his good leg. "When the chanting and the screaming started..."

"You could barely move," Adaline whispers, her thoughts scrambling as she remembers those soldiers' cries, at how she couldn't do anything to help them.

Āranol nods, his jowls protruding as he clenches his jaw.

"You saw me," she says.

Āranol stares uphill, where Adaline initially appeared. "I didn't know it was you until you vanished. But yes. And when you did, my father discovered me behind his tent." His shoulders sag, and the flicker of doubt and dark memories cast their shadow over his proud face. "I have never feared my father, save tonight. He looks the same as before, only his eyes have changed; it's like someone else hides behind them. His presence turns my stomach, and a dark aura surrounds him. You sense it, don't you? That's why you came here."

"Yes," Adaline murmurs.

"After you left, my father dragged his volunteers, my friends, into a covered carriage. I do not know if this was some trick of the night, but sometimes, when the shadows shifted beneath their cloaks, their faces seemed to belong to someone, or something, else. Their nails are unnaturally long, their fingers mangled. The mere sight of them unnerved me."

While Ëólas's handsome features condense with concern, Adaline searches for the right words to summarize what she witnessed. "It felt, I don't know, demonic."

"That's a fitting description." Ãranol scrapes his handkerchief along his palm, trying to scrape off the last dried blood to little avail. "My father left without pleasantries, only an order that I stall his escape."

Adaline lifts her hand as if to smack Ãranol across the face or scratch out his eyes. "So that's what you're doing, stalling us, you son of a—"

"No!" He raises his hands in surrender and as shields, his nose continuing to swell. "If I sought only to delay you, I would have continued to engage your," he gulps, "husband in battle. But I yield today. And as much as I despise Aerytolíans, you might be the only one who knows what has become of my father. And how to release him."

Every word from Ãranol seeps into her skin like mud through a white cloth. She looks at Ëólas, at his pensive but alarmed expression. Even he can't conceal his worries now.

Please, universe. Don't make me save Morgán. "It sounded like your father was speaking to someone else in the tent. Do you know who that was?"

"No. Only six occupied that tent. Over the years, I've heard my father receive counsel from someone else, but I have never seen this person enter or leave his chambers."

Okay, he's gone crazy. Granted, I kinda already knew that.

"How many have you in your army?" Ëólas asks.

"A thousand," Ãranol says. "But you already knew that, clever as you are."

"What are you thinking?" Ëólas asks Adaline.

"You've never heard of anything like this before?" Adaline frowns when Ëólas shakes his head. "It sounds familiar. But that's based on myths from, um, back home."

"Maryland?"

"Yeah."

"Keep your armies in Aerytol," Āranol says. "You're going to need everyone at your disposal. I believe he aims to come to you. Look a little relieved, Your Majesty. I do believe we will never see each other again."

Am I really that lucky, that he'll leave me alone? No way. He's a liar. But the gravity of his tone and the hint of a small, sad smile in the corner of his mouth make Adaline replay his words. *Oh no.* "You think your father will kill you?"

Āranol's silence hangs heavily between them. Without ceremony, he backs away one step at a time. His gaze falls once more to Ëólas and Adaline holding hands, then turns his face to the stars, and shakes his head. "Oh, one more thing. I don't know whether this is true, but my father lamented that his new soldiers would never view the night sky again, that the stars had cursed them." Without waiting for a reply, he turns around, exposing his backside to his enemies, and limps away.

Well, that was an anticlimactic reunion. Sort of.

Why would he help us, give us that info? To trick us. To stop us from overtaking Feídra né Morna. Because he doesn't have any hope left.

Adaline's chest heaves. She hadn't thought much about seeing him again, having assumed he'd be one of many soldiers they'd have to battle to free Hell City. Her husband and the royal guards wouldn't have let him near her, even if she had wished to seek him out. Maybe she would have, not to kill him but to confront him because she'd never do anything that would make her like him. No matter the circumstances, she also assumed she'd feel nothing. Not even hatred. And certainly not something bordering on sympathy.

"Morgán will need you at Feídra né Morna," Adaline shouts. "I'm coming for your city, to free all those people."

"So, you are a conqueror," Āranol calls back. The fog swallows his feet, luring him further into its embrace. "How very human of you."

"You don't have to die. You can still think for yourself. Choose your own path." *It doesn't have to be this way.*

He keeps walking, a soldier following orders even though he knows he's lost the war.

"I, I shouldn't let him go." Ëólas's hand twitches in Adaline's, his eyes zeroing in on the same spot Ãranol had once stabbed her. The further Ãranol gets, Ëólas calculates the risks he's taking.

"Are we being foolish here?" she asks.

Ëólas tightens his grip on his hilt. Releasing Adaline's hand, he jerks forward, but this time she's fast enough to block his path.

Touching his cheek, she waits for him to turn away from Ãranol and for his darker thoughts to dim. "Merith might be pissed at us. But not like this. Not right now."

Cupping her hand, he presses her palm against his skin and growls his frustration, his doubt. But he doesn't go after Ãranol. As Adaline retrieves her dagger, the blade abandoned in the dirt, she sorts through Ãranol's words, trying to decipher which were lies. Her mother—she wouldn't. She couldn't.

Before Ãranol drags himself out of the circle and the thicker fog consumes him, Adaline quietly asks, "Tell me, how did my mother die?"

Pausing for only a few seconds, Ãranol turns his head sideways, and the wind delivers his words. "She jumped off the cliff into the ocean. The tide pummeled her to death."

Again, Adaline hears the truck's winch dragging her father's car from the river, the muddy water pouring out the windows, the tires fallen off, the people watching from the roadside. *Both my parents drowned.*

Chapter Eight

MORE TIME

At Ëólas's behest, Adaline travels them to their personal chambers, leaving Ãranol, the moors, and the stench of decay behind. Ëólas sheathes his sword and wraps both arms around Adaline, hugging her close to his chest and inhaling deeply.

She wriggles free, places her dirty dagger on a shelf, and sheds her leather jacket, folding it carefully and hanging it in her armoire next to the new dresses the seamstress has been adding daily. Taking a cloth from the dresser, she dips the silky cotton into the washbasin and wipes her neck. The cool touch against her skin helps her breathe more easily. "I know you're worried about me, but I'm fine. Really. Our friends are waiting for us, and they're probably anxious that we've been gone so long." She tosses the cloth into the empty ceramic bowl and heads toward the doors to their sitting room.

Ëólas doesn't budge. "They can wait a moment longer. We just received a great deal of information, and I'd rather you have time to process that before everyone adds their own thoughts to the equation."

"I don't have time to get distracted, Ëólas. We need to act. Morgán is headed this way, and so are his demonic assassins. That's what they are, right? That's what he's planning?"

Ëólas runs his hand through his hair. When he lets go, the soft layers fall to the left of his part. "Yes, but they won't be here within the hour, so let's step back and figure out what we can trust, given the source of this information."

Adaline puffs out her frustration. Yanking open the door to their sitting room, she calls to the guards posted outside their chambers. "Someone, please go to the study and let Lady Sora and Lord Merith know that we've returned unharm—" She glances at Ëólas's torn sleeve. "That we're safe and will join them shortly. Thank you."

When she shuts the door, she returns to her basin and pours fresh water into the washbowl. "Take off your coat. And your shirt." She wrings out a fresh cloth and storms over to him while he removes his clothes, ignoring his washboard abs and lean shoulders that always try to distract her. Pushing her curls away from her eyes, she studies his arm and dabs the length of the wound. "That's not a scratch," she mutters.

"It doesn't require stitches." If the water or cloth sting, he doesn't let her know as she washes and wraps his bicep, his hair falling to just below his nipples.

"That's what I said when that elf attacked me a few days ago."

"You did require stitches."

Grumbling, she ties the knot to his bandage tighter than necessary. "Have Loríen look at that as soon as possible."

"Yes, my love." When she steps back, Ëólas rubs her arms even though Adaline's too frazzled to stay still. Taking her hand, he kisses the back. "I'm so sorry about Aurellia."

"I'm fine. Really, I am. Don't look at me like that. I mean it. I dealt with my mother's death twenty years ago. Stop with the puppy eyes. I don't have time to break down." She walks over to the window, pushes open the glass pains, and leans her head outside. The wind whips by, shoving her curls to the other side of her head, but the only sounds within the wind are that of the owls keeping watch, the nervous chatter from the elves setting up their campsites, and the distant cry of nature dying. Her head falls to her chest. "Please, I need to be strong right now, and I need you to help me do that."

"Alright. But what about Aeríoléna? Do you think—"

"There's truth in that? I, I don't think so. Morgán must have spread that lie to justify his war." Turning around, she leans against the windowsill and watches his abs disappear under a fresh shirt. "Besides, I certainly don't feel immortal, thank God. That sounds more like a curse than a gift. But I do wonder."

"Wonder what?" He buttons up a light-blue vest.

"That voice I keep hearing—it's not Nan. What if that voice comes from the Immortal Realms?"

"You referred to her once as your guardian angel."

"Yeah. But you know what? In some myths back home, fae are fallen angels. Interesting, huh? But it's not like I have anyone to ask, unless Seira's functioning again and will give me straight answers. All I can do is keep moving forward and try to make the best choice based on the information we do have."

Ëólas laughs once through his nose. "And you thought you weren't ready to be queen," he mutters. "Alright," he holds the door open for her, "we can ponder this fae business another day. I have one more question before we face our friends, though. Do you know what's happened to Morgán?"

Adaline massages the back of her neck as she meanders into the sitting room. She plucks a cushion off the sofa and hugs it to her chest. "I have my suspicions, but I'd rather hear everyone else's thoughts before I continue down the path I'm already on. I know moving this along isn't your favorite method, but I'd rather discuss this as a team, okay?"

When Ëólas extends his hand, she tosses the pillow onto the sofa, and together they hurry to their waiting friends. When they enter the study, Hamon leaps off the sofa, rubbing the sleep from his eyes. Even Magnus and Thoren's eyes have a red tinge to them. Everyone needs a damn good night's sleep. Adaline too. What she wouldn't give for an extra-large cup of coffee right now.

Would it be horribly invasive to introduce coffee beans into this ecosystem?

As soon as the guards close the doors behind them, Merith shifts sideways so that half his body emerges from the dim corner in the back of the room where he must have been brooding. "Why were you gone so long?"

Adaline and Ëólas freeze. Suddenly, letting Āranol go doesn't seem like a good choice.

Crossing his arms over his chest, Ëólas meets everyone's pointed gaze. "We ran into Ãranol."

"He's dead then." Sora slips a book back on Ëólas's shelf, her face gleaming.

"Ah, well," Ëólas oscillates his head from side to side, "not exactly."

"You left him to bleed out?" Thoren asks.

While Ëólas debates his next words, Adaline lifts her chin and steps forward. "We let him go." She drops her chin when everyone's enthusiasm collapses into confusion.

"What? Why would you do that?" Merith glares at them.

"It was more of a conversation," Ëólas says.

Merith arches one eyebrow. "And yet you changed your clothes."

"Ëólas hurt him more. Got him twice!" Adaline rests her hand on his bicep, the one not scratched, and glances at his profile, at his slender nose and high cheekbones and the diamond-shape of his wide jawline. When he turns his golden eyes to her, she smiles. "I really loved when you punched him in the nose. I kinda wish I had done that."

"You can punch him next time."

"Oh good." She props her head on his shoulder. "If there is a next time." *Why am I worried about him? No, that can't be right. I'm worried about what he'll do. That must be it.*

"As adorable as this is," Magnus waves his hand from Adaline to Ëólas, "what exactly transpired after you left?"

After Adaline apologizes for leaving Merith and Sora behind, she and Ëólas relay the night's events, which has Merith look increasingly agitated and everyone else more frightened. They share every detail, except for the part about Adaline's family potentially descending from the fae. Everyone already looks at her with awe because she's Aerytolían. She doesn't need them worshiping her too.

Man, I really am going to have an identity crisis.

"Do you have any clues regarding what Morgán's done to himself and his soldiers?" Merith asks.

Too tired for decorum, Adaline flops down onto the sofa and gestures for everyone else to do the same. No one takes her up on her offer, choosing instead to pace or stare out the window or pour themselves more wine. In one night, Thoren's emptied half the decanters in the study.

Staring at Ëólas and Magnus's sparse bookshelves, Adaline rests her head in her hand as she leans against the sofa arm. "I have my theories. Back home, we have thousands of legends about mythical creatures, including elves. If that one turned out to be true over here, then who's to say the others aren't possible either. Hell, look at Mr. Toad."

"I'd rather not." Ëólas returns both his swords to his display shelves, the scabbards resting top to bottom on a display stand.

Oh, hon. I'd rather not deal with him again either.

"Do we have a plan then, one that doesn't involve letting all our enemies go?" Merith asks like a disappointed father.

Ëólas glares at him but doesn't engage. "I think we should proceed with Adaline's original idea, that we make our way to the Wastelands. Morgán's roughly seven days from New Leira, maybe less, depending on their speed. The quicker we can find him, we can cut him and his assassins off from ever reaching the city."

Sitting up, Adaline looks from Ëólas to Magnus. "I agree, but what if they do show up here? I can't stand the idea of our people, especially the children, witnessing more attacks, and this time we have to deal with actual monsters."

Magnus traces the map laid out on his desk and looks directly at Ëólas. "I'll remain here while you head into the Wastelands. Should conflict arise here, my army will defend the city, and I'll provide temporary sanctuary in Alderton to all of Aerytol's citizens, regardless of species."

Clasping Magnus's forearm, Ëólas also claps him on the shoulder. "Thank you, my friend."

As they shake, Magnus's bright blue eyes light up.

Aww, the bromance is real. "Awesome, we have a plan." Adaline jumps off the sofa. "When do we leave?"

Everyone in the room freezes and turns slowly to stare at her, making her eyes widen and her lips spread into an awkward smile.

Thoren slams his empty goblet on the table. "Who the hell said you're going?"

"Um." She points at herself.

"You may be queen, Your Majesty, but you don't have the skill sets or experience for a war campaign." Using the back of his hand, Thoren wipes red wine away from his mouth and approaches her, his giant size blocking the light from the fireplace. "The battlefield is no place for a lady," he pauses and glances at Sora scowling at him, "er, um, with practically no training. And you, my lady, don't have the stomach for war."

Even though Thoren's sufficiently deflated her confidence to the size of an empty latex balloon, Adaline squares her shoulders and stares him down, hoping her words make her sound sure. "But Morgán is after me. I have to leave the city to draw him out. He'll come to me."

Ëólas hasn't moved a muscle since Adaline's announcement, leaving Magnus to reinforce Thoren's blunt delivery. "All of us want you as far away from him as possible."

Shadows hide the blue undertones of Merith's dark skin, making half of him disappear in the dim corner of the room. His gruff tone and stone-cold silver eyes seal his promise. "We'll kill him before he sets eyes on you."

Adaline worries her bottom lip. She doesn't want to command them. She'd rather they believe in her, trust her, but she's not done much to earn that yet. This is why she has a council, right? To heed their advice. But she can't stay locked up in this castle and separated from Ëólas for months while he fulfills the promise she made to Calvden and the other humans she met in the Wastelands.

While her thoughts race, Ëólas meanders to the bookcase and places his hands on the shelves. She can sense his hesitation. The idea of being separated haunts him too, but he also made her agree to his terms that he's going to safeguard her above all else. He'll never agree to taking her with him, to having her march beside him. They're not equals.

So what's her next plan of action? She could veto his vote or dress up like one of his soldiers. Because that will go over well.

His shoulder blades flex as he presses his palms against the wood shelf. "Adaline should come with us."

What? Adaline's heart speeds up, her chest ready to burst.

"What?" Merith storms into the center of the study. "But the queen lacks training. She's not ready for this."

"I agree with Merith," Sora says. "I promise I'll stay by the queen's side and keep her safe. She can't—"

"You doubt your queen?" Ëólas asks everyone, making them shut their mouths. Pushing off the bookshelf, he strides over to Adaline and exhales loudly through his nostrils, his lips pressed together grimly. He doesn't like this plan; that's evident on his face. But he takes her hand, lacing their fingers together. "You're capable of more than we know."

Adaline wraps her arm around his waist and melts against his chest. *Thank you. I won't let you down. I promise.*

"Besides, we have plenty of time to train." Ëólas smirks when she glances up at him, her lips pinched together in confusion.

"We do?" she asks.

"Yes. We'll return to Maryland. We can spend as much time there as necessary until you're proficient with a sword."

I don't think a sword is my fighting style. And how long constitutes proficient? "Okay."

With their fingers still entwined, Ëólas and Adaline squeeze each other's hand, their version of a handshake. Then Ëólas turns to Magnus. "We will set off tomorrow with a portion of Lameiría's troops. Two thousand suffices to deal with Āranol and Feídra né Morna. They don't have many defenses, and their army's small. We entrust New Leira to you."

"I, I don't think that's a good idea," Adaline says. "Oh, not about Magnus. I trust you completely. I mean taking only elven soldiers. We're going to free humans. No offense, Ëólas, but they need to see humans in a position of power and strength. Elves alone can't be their liberators. Hamon, Fólas, do we have enough city guards to take with us? Are they trained for the battlefield?"

Moving in front of her, Hamon bows his head. "I'd be honored to go with you, my lady."

Magnus shakes his head. "You're an excellent captain, Hamon, which is why we need you and the city guard to do what you do best. Adaline can take a thousand of my soldiers."

Her eyes widen. "Magnus? How can we—"

"I admire the message you want to send, but Aerytol doesn't have the numbers you need, not yet. And given that Morgán loathes humankind, I shudder to think what other plans he may have in store for humanity. You are our first line of defense, my dear. Take a thousand of my men; let them help free their brethren."

"Magnus, you're a gift." Adaline strides forward and hugs his large arm. "Um, just so I know, do we have a second line of defense?"

With a chuckle, Magnus kisses the back of her hand. "Of course. Like Ëólas, I've redirected my best spies to sniffing out Morgán. They'll help us find him first, in case Morgán doesn't go after you directly."

Who are these spies? Eek—how would he go after me indirectly?

Before she can ask, Thoren scratches his beard and yanks out a single hair that he studies and drops on the floor. "We're asking a lot of our soldiers, my lord, expecting Lameiría and Alderton to march together. These people haven't been living side by side in the city, and we're going to just throw them together? Expect them to fight together?"

Magnus pats Adaline's hand resting on the crease of his elbow. "If anyone can bring them together, it's the Queen of Aerytol."

Yeah, okay. No pressure there.

After returning to their chambers and collapsing in bed, Adaline passes out in Ëólas's arms within a matter of seconds. He doesn't let her go until dawn peeks through their curtains a few hours later. Prying her eyes open, Adaline untangles her limbs from Ëólas's even though she's not entirely sure she did sleep. She could swear she closed her eyes only moments ago. They both throw on boots, dark trousers, and tunics, although Adaline requested that hers fit more like a lady's blouse than a baggy undershirt.

On the bed, they layout a set of clothes to change into once they return from Maryland, including additional layers to protect them from the encroaching colder weather. In addition to a cloak, Adaline folds and sets aside the tailcoat from Élara that the seamstress mended. Like Ëólas, she finds a leather knapsack with a drawstring closure and buckled flap on the sofa in the sitting room. She has no idea who provided them, but the timing is spot on. The benefits of being queen, she supposes. Everyone tends to her needs without her having to ask for much. Then again, Ëólas might have made the request.

With Kayla's and Nuríel's help, they pack for the long journey that awaits them, this time having the resources to plan accordingly. Adaline stuffs into her knapsack three of her new trousers and tunics and several socks while Kayla and Nuríel pack additional clothes and luxuries in a trunk that Adaline and Ëólas will have with them until they cross into the Wastelands.

Throughout the preparation, Adaline pauses every now and again to memorize Kayla's face, the forest carved into their wooden headboard, the white ceramic nobs decorated with hand-painted green leaves on the armoire and dressers, the gilded floor-length mirror that would cost a million dollars back home.

She's spent only a few nights in this room. Just when it began to feel like home, she has to leave again for who knows how long. And when they do return, that's only to march off and confront demonic assassins and whatever else Morgán's planning. Will she be a completely different person when she comes back? A well-trained killing machine?

Ëólas enters the room, carrying a heavy, oblong bundle wrapped in several layers of thick canvas. "Training swords," he explains.

Damn, there's really no escaping this.

As the few remaining hours before departure tick by, Adaline and Ëólas privately meet with Fólas and Hamon to ensure everything's in place for the city to carry on and thrive while the queen and king are traveling.

Before the sun peeks above the city's skyline, Adaline watches from the dining hall balcony as the generals direct their troops to line up behind the castle wall, forming five columns for both armies.

Mercia joins her, resting her hands on the balustrade. "I wish you weren't going." She turns her plump red cheeks away from Adaline. "I'm sorry. I shouldn't have—"

"It's okay. I asked you to be honest." Adaline studies Mercia's light-gray eyes that hold back her fears—and her hopes. "I don't know how much time will pass for me before I return, but I'll miss you."

Mercia lurches forward and throws her arms around Adaline, who pats her back. "I promise I'll look after the city."

"And don't be afraid to stand up to your father as my envoy. I entrust this city to you too."

"Oh my. I, um, okay." Mercia beams as they stroll into the dining hall arm in arm, the walls now decorated with new periwinkle and silver Aerytolían banners featuring the same small flower-like stars on Nan's pendant.

Beside them, Adaline spots Jorrel and Merith huddled in the corner, away from everyone else who's gathered to say farewell. "You'll have to let me know what it's like working with Lord Jorrel," she whispers to Mercia. As Éólas's envoy, Adaline still knows little about him. She certainly can't keep referring to him as the panda.

Whatever he's discussing, Jorrel's round facial features shrink with worry. Merith listens intensely but doesn't say much. With Jorrel mid-sentence, Merith finds Adaline's eyes on them. He claps Jorrel's shoulder, says goodbye with a firm nod, and leaves Jorrel staring at his backside. The panda, um, elf tucks his shaggy black hair behind his leaf-shaped ear and fixates his eyes on the scrolls he's carrying as he scurries away, probably to his own office.

Huh. I've never seen those two interact much before.

Adaline turns back to Mercia. "I know you and Jorrel have this. Hamon and Fólas will fill you in on the details as soon as they get back from their rounds."

"What's this now?" Thoren asks, approaching them. "Mercia, what are you doing here?"

Mercia glances at the exit, then faces her father. "I'm here as the queen's envoy." When Thoren's brows turn into storm clouds, she adds, "While we're still in Aerytol, I will assist my friend to the best of my ability."

Attagirl.

Propping his meaty fists on his hips, he glares at Adaline. "This is your doing."

Adaline shrugs. "She's been indispensable to me the last four days." *You really haven't noticed?*

"Hmm. Your mother's looking for you," Thoren tells Mercia. "Make sure you inform her about this."

With a nod from Adaline, Mercia gulps, gathers her skirts, and hurries out of the hall, taking heed not to run. While Ëólas and Magnus finish up their own discussion, Seira sprints through the doors and dashes over to Adaline.

"Seira!" Adaline hugs her tightly. "You're okay?"

Seira blinks rapidly, her periwinkle eyes wild with little-to-no sleep. "Yes, I'm sorry. It's too much sometimes. You already know, don't you?"

Adaline takes Seira's hand in hers. "I know. I, I think you were right about Ãranol, that his path's not decided." *And about Morgán's desperation.* "Tíer Nía, listen, Ëólas is taking me back to Maryland. Is there any chance you can come with me? I," Adaline turns away from Ëólas, Magnus, Sora, Merith, and Thoren gathered in a huddle, and lowers her voice, "I don't know how to use my magic. Can you teach me?"

Seira's pixie-like face wilts, her platinum blonde hair falling in front of her pink cheeks as she lowers her head. "I don't know how to use mine either," she whispers. "I didn't have anyone to teach me, not after—" Her face pales and her eyes dilate, the black orbs consuming all color, but instead of falling in deeper and finishing that thought, she bites her lip hard and tugs Adaline's arm, pulling her closer. "We'll need Cindy."

"Cindy?" Adaline lurches her head backward. "My Cindy?"

"Yes. I keep seeing her using some sort of device that spins rapidly with all these little bottles."

She's seen Cindy in her lab? And she's volunteering this info? "I'll keep that in mind. But, I mean, are you sure?"

Seira nods fervently. "Most definitely. Cindy holds the key to our survival."

Chapter Nine

THE NEW PLAN

Magnus, Merith, and Sora's faces become increasingly transparent until they disappear altogether. The condo takes their place, materializing around Adaline and Ëólas, replacing the Aerytolian banners with white picture frames that decorate the cozy cream-colored walls. The rows of tables bereft of nobles dining and chatting give way to the granite kitchen island and its bay window, and the sky beyond the archways and balcony dim from pale blue to black.

Ëólas lets go of Adaline's waist, walks over to the front door, and flips the lights on, banishing the night in an instant. "Convenient."

"The lights or the traveling?"

"Both." He leans the canvas package against the entryway closet door.

"Mmm." Adaline reaches into the back pocket of her trousers and retrieves her mobile phone. She presses the power button as Ëólas strolls over and stares over her shoulder, his hands wrapping around her waist, his chest warming her back. The phone vibrates awake and blinks to the current time. "Only twenty minutes have passed since we left Nan's house."

"Wait. You mean today is still Sunday? The same Sunday we found that trunk and stone at Arraya's house?"

And when we learned my grandmother was a queen and Cindy's mom said my mother was from Alderton. "Yep."

"But we've been gone six days." After pacing in front of her a few times, Ëólas rubs his finger above his chin as he calculates the same math Adaline just did. "But the two days we spent in Maryland resulted in seconds passing in Gladríen?"

"Uh-huh. And after I spent a month with you, less than two hours passed here."

"So, one month equaled two hours, six days equaled twenty minutes, and two days equaled seconds. The math doesn't make sense."

"Exactly." She clicks her phone off and shoves it back in her pocket. "I guess that's one more thing we should add to my training while here, testing how my traveling works."

"Good idea."

"Okay." Adaline claps her hands on his shoulders. "Here's the plan."

"I'm all ears."

"We're going to pack up some clothes here, buy groceries, and move into Nan's house, or at least spend most of our time there. We'll have space in my dad's gym, um, training room and in the backyard." Thank goodness for the trees that separate their property from the neighbors.

"You're okay with that, moving back there?"

Adaline shrugs, her fingers dipping beneath his collar. "It makes the most sense. And it'll be nice for the house to not be empty anymore." She pecks him on the cheek and strides into her bedroom, where she dives into the back of her closet and pulls out four large rolling suitcases. "Can you grab my laptop from the living room, on my desk?"

"Um, the rectangular metal-like thing that tells you everything?"

"That'd be it."

"Ha! I remembered."

After he places the laptop on the bed, he sits down between it and an open suitcase that Adaline's piled high with sundresses, shorts, and tank tops. During several trips from her dresser to the next suitcase, her phone buzzes with a message from Cindy. Pushing her panties and bras into the crook of one arm, she flips her screen open. "Oh, crap. I forgot Cindy invited us for game night tonight."

"Oh. We should—"

"It's okay. She needs to reschedule." Adaline taps furiously at her screen, her dark-red thong slipping out of the jumble in her arm and fluttering to the ground.

Ëólas picks up the tiny piece of sheer fabric, nods in approval, and takes the bunch from her, placing them in her bag. "Did you tell her about us?"

"Um, not yet. This is her roundabout way of asking for an update. I didn't have enough time, what with going to Nan's and finding her trunk. It's okay though." She clicks her phone off and shoves it into her pocket. "I told her work crap popped up and I'll text her tomorrow. I'm not ready for her to bombard me with questions."

"Did she suggest a new date?"

"Tomorrow. For dinner. I'll message her later with an excuse of some kind."

"Why don't we—"

"Oh, can you grab my shoes from the hallway closet?"

He stares at her thoughtfully for a moment, then disappears from the room. While she's stacking a pile of sweatpants, he returns with his arms full of heels, sneakers, fashion boots, and muddy work boots that he lines up beside her bed. He sits down, and she dashes across the room four more times.

"My love?" He steals her hand before she scurries away again. "We've done enough planning today. And given the lack of sleep you had last night, we should relax now. Properly."

We can relax? "Oh. Um."

Relocating the suitcase to the floor, he pats the bed beside him. Adaline takes a seat next to him and sags with the mattress. If she doesn't pack, then what should she do now? Turning on a movie or reading a book seems like an insult to the people they left behind and the soldiers awaiting their return, awaiting a stronger queen's return. Granted, if she's lucky, not much time will pass for New Leira—even though she could be gone for years.

Ëólas turns sideways so he can measure her reactions. "Think out loud, please?"

The role reversal tugs the corners of her mouth into a half smile. "We left before breakfast."

"We did."

"It's past dinner time here."

"True."

"That's kinda odd, isn't it?"

"A bit." He brushes his arm against hers. "But I like odd. It certainly keeps life interesting."

Thank God for that. "I should get started training."

The loud rumble from the pit of her belly makes Ëólas smirk and drag her into the kitchen. "I don't suppose you have servants?"

"Ha!"

"No worries." He pulls a butcher knife from the knife block and sets it down on the bamboo cutting board. Scanning the countertops, he picks up an apple and rubs his fingers on the wax coating that squeaks and makes him scrutinize the skin up close. "What in the world?"

With a laugh, Adaline opens the fridge and pulls out a carton of eggs. "How about an omelet?"

"Classic in any world."

Adaline jerks up to standing, the carton bobbing in her hand. "Huh."

"What huh?"

"It's just... I know things now that I didn't a few days ago, things that I didn't know I didn't know." She places the eggs on the counter, the corner falling off the edge as she wanders back to the fridge and stares at the shelves, not choosing anything.

"Like what?" He sets down the waxy apple, far away from himself, and pushes the eggs backward.

"Like this world is Earth."

"Aren't all worlds made of earth?"

"No, Earth with a capital E."

He cocks an eyebrow. "Not very original."

"Yeah, but a few days ago I didn't know that the other world is Ellíum. But now I remember that fact, as if I've always known it. I mean, I guess I did, when I was a kid."

From the drawer, she grabs a hair tie and secures her curls in a loose ponytail. Next, she pulls out a second cutting board from the cupboard beside the fridge, lays them on the countertop side by side, and places a stainless-steel mixing bowl in the middle. She sets a large frying pan on top of the gas stove, turning her back to the calendar displaying the last date for the semester.

Grabbing two santoku knives (and putting away the butcher knife), she passes one to Ëólas, along with a green bell pepper that he cuts into cubes. Before Adaline minces the onion, she turns on the Bluetooth speaker and jumps to her Rachel Platten music station. Oh, how she missed the constant stream of music in her home. She rolls her neck and sways from side to side.

I can't believe this is what I'm doing right now. We just left our friends eating their last meal. Well, not their last-last meal. Just their last meal at home for a while. I hope.

Aside from the chopping and sweet, relaxing melody, the condo is quiet for a Sunday night. No guards await them outside. No one's lining up for war, at least not under Adaline's command. No one's going to ask her to make decisions she has zero idea how to answer. No one's going to bow or curtsy or look at her with awe. And no one's going to bring them a hot meal with fresh ingredients, zero preservatives, and no added sugar.

Every so often Adaline uses the back of her sleeve to wipe away her tears.

"My love, what's wrong?" Ëólas rests his hand on hers to halt her chopping.

She looks at him through damp lashes. "Um, onions. When you cut them, they release spores that sting the eyes. Well, human eyes, I guess."

"Fascinating."

Adaline sniffles, drops his bell pepper bits into the frying pan, and passes him her cutting board. "You're responsible for onions from now on."

"Noted." Sliding his cutting board further away from Adaline, Ëólas minces like a professional chef while she sautés the peppers and cracks and whisks the eggs in the mixing bowl.

The crunch of the shell breaking and the yoke oozing makes her skin crawl. "Do elven kings know how to cook?" She blinks her eyes to ease the lingering burning sensation.

Ëólas flips the santoku knife in the air and catches the handle. "Merith taught me when we spent a few years training in the heart of the forest, no assistance allowed. But I don't mind cooking if that's what you mean."

"Good to know. We don't have servants here, so all the cooking's on us."

After Ëólas adds the onion to the frying pan, he hugs her from behind, leans over her shoulder, and watches her add four slices of bread to the toaster, spin dials, and press buttons as she finishes making them breakfast. His grin widens, pushing his chin into the hollow of her neck, when the inside of the toaster glows orange.

Using the spatula, Adaline scrapes along the side of the pan, trying to release the edge of the omelet and not break the whole thing each time Ëólas kisses her neck or slips his hands under the hem of her tunic. "You're frisky this morning. Evening. Whatever."

"Mmm."

With him pressed against her, their hips sway together while she flips the omelet and butters their toast. As she plates their food, she rubs her bottom against his front side, earning a growl from him that makes her giggle and her nether regions tingle. *Maybe we can relax tonight.*

She reaches for the utensil drawer, but the calendar catches her attention again. "Um, so, we have tomorrow to ourselves, but I have to return to campus on Tuesday and face the Grump." *After training tomorrow morning, I could return to the cave site, but how do I cover up the circle's true origins—without sabotaging my team's work?*

"The Grump—that's Ben, your boss?"

"My mentor. Yes." *Ugh.* After Hell City, the thought of calling anyone a mentor makes her want to vomit.

"He sounds pleasant."

"He's all bark and no bite. But I have a lot of explaining to do, leaving our team as I did." Adaline grabs their silverware, the prongs of their forks sticking out of her hand like miniature pitchforks. "Are your clothes packed?"

Ëólas carries their plates to the other side of the kitchen island and sits on the stool next to Adaline. "They're still in the shopping bags."

"Oh, right." She takes a bite of toast, a corner she didn't butter enough, and the bread scratches her throat. "Tomorrow, we need to pop over to the mall. I want a haircut, and you need a mobile phone."

"Whatever for? I have only one person to call here." He pinches her round bottom, making her yelp.

"Yeah, well, you never know. Besides, not having a mobile is just unheard of, even if you don't use it." A sudden image of Ëólas with his own social media accounts pops into her head.

"What's so amusing?"

"Nothing." She reaches for the butter dish on the other side of the counter and slathers the edges of her toast so every bite is salty delicious. "I hope you don't mind the detours, but once we've settled into Nan's, we can start training."

Her mind flashes to her sword jerking into her abductor's torso. The smell of caramelized onions and bell peppers makes her gag. *Stop that, brain. I'm going to be the best student Ëólas has ever had. And I'm going to learn how to control my magic too. No ifs, ands, or buts.*

Ëólas finishes his last bite of eggs, picks up a slice of toast, and rotates it a few times to examine the perfectly even cut. "We should meet Cindy and Dax for game night."

"Oh." Adaline slowly chews her toast until it's mush in her mouth. "We don't have to."

"Why should we cancel?"

"Because we have a full day tomorrow." Pushing half her toast into a corner, Adaline forces a mouthful of eggs into her mouth.

"My love, we can take a day to settle in and see your friends."

"Are you sure?" Adaline swivels in her seat, her knees pressing into his thighs. "I mean, I have so much catching up to do, and—"

"No." He places his hand on her knee, his touch drawing her off her stool until his hand naturally slips between her thighs. "It's not like that."

What's it like then?

With a sigh, he slides off the stool and walks to the sink where he washes his dish, keeping his back to her, while Adaline's breakfast turns cold. Without another word, she goes to him, wraps her hands around his waist, and rests her cheek against his back. Slowly, his muscles warm and release their vice-like grip, and his shoulders fall away from his ears.

What's troubling you? Teaching me? Leaving everyone behind? Being stuck in this world without friends? "If you really want to go, then game night's on."

Ëólas turns off the sink, twists around, and kisses her tenderly. The undulation of his lips mesmerizes her until she forgets why she's nervous to see Cindy again. With no one summoning them with urgent matters, they linger in the kitchen, making out for a long while, savoring each other's taste. He pulls her hair tie away and runs his hands through her curls, his fingers laced through her hair at the nape. The rhythm of his sweet, deep kisses shuts off her mind, her objectives, her worries. Skating her hands up his chest and around his neck, she locks her arms behind him, pushing her leg between his, pulling his thigh between hers. The pulsing between her folds matches her slow heartbeat, and when they finally loosen their hold, just enough that they can see each other clearly without their noses rubbing against the other, Adaline yawns, and Ëólas smiles with amusement.

He slides his hand into hers, and they head to the bedroom, forgetting the dirty dishes for now and moving aside the half-packed suitcases. They toss their clothes aside and climb under the covers with Adaline draping her arm over his torso and settling into the crook of his arm. His shoulder and soft hair make a comfy pillow, and he strokes her arm, helping her muscles relax one by one.

As her consciousness fades, pieces of her conversation with Āranol hum through her thoughts and drag her away from sleep, like her mother jumping into the ocean, or Aeríoléna having to choose between her people and her love, or Adaline potentially having immortal blood. Can the scales still balance if she's part fae? Living forever without Ëólas would be torture. That's why she didn't ask Seira about Aeríoléna. She can't handle one more obstacle right now.

"No more fretting for the rest of the night," Ëólas whispers.

With a kiss on her forehead and Ëólas's caresses along her arm, Adaline falls into a deep sleep that takes her to the edge of a forest. The clouds above smear the sunset into shades of red, orange, and purple. Birds or winged creatures of some sort fly high above. Walking across the field toward the forest, a woman with long raven-black hair spies Adaline. A set of wings rise behind the woman, their iridescence catching the sunlight. Adaline tries to run toward the woman, but every time she fights to move her feet, a sheer curtain falls between them until the woman is only a silhouette.

"Aeríoléna," Adaline shouts, but her voice won't leave her throat. It's trapped inside her like a bubble in the ocean.

As the woman waves to her, Adaline falls through the forest floor and into the sea. She kicks her legs and thrashes her arms against the current that drags her further downward. When her lungs are about to burst, the water in front of her takes the shape of a translucent sprite who blows a bubble of air around Adaline's head. She gasps with relief, her chest heaving.

Then the sprite dissolves, leaving Adaline alone and sinking deeper into the darkness until a whale pushes her through the ocean, past groups of turtles and stingrays and sharks. None of them notice her. The whale nudges her forward with the tip of its chin one last time before swimming away, and Adaline and her bubble drift to the base of a mountain.

Sunlight filters through the water, and from a cliff above, a shadow descends like a bullet into the ocean. Adaline tries to swim upward, but the current pushes her away while the submerged figure flails against the riptide, and the waves pummel her against the base of the cliff.

"Don't hurt her, please," Adaline cries, as her mother drowns. "Help her. Momma, you have to ask the ocean for help."

Her mother stops fighting, but she doesn't ask for help either. Instead, her legs and arms drift lifeless at her sides as she sinks downward, and Adaline drifts further away.

Chapter Ten

GAME NIGHT

Holding the sides of the Catan box, Dax shakes the lid off, letting the bottom with the game pieces drop onto the coffee table. His wide grin takes over his broad face as he connects the blue harbor border, lays out the land tiles, and explains the game to Ëólas. "Okay, so these little buildings are settlements. The bigger ones are cities, and these sticks are roads."

While the guys hover around the coffee table, Cindy stirs the Picadillo in the tall skillet on the stove, and the aroma of sautéed ground beef, potatoes, carrots, and onion fills the small apartment that Cindy and Dax rented in a hurry when they first got back together. The scent of recently minced chili tingles Adaline's nose.

After reducing the stove's heat a tad, Cindy opens the fridge and pulls out two bottles of wine. "Why'd you cut your new mermaid locks?"

"Oh." Adaline pushes her long waves behind her shoulders, the curls at the bottom brushing the small of her back. "It's still long. I just got tired of sitting on my hair all the time."

With a chuckle, Cindy sets the bottles down in front of Adaline on the opposite side of the island counter. As she turns the labels to face her guest, Cindy's eyes drift to her engagement ring, and a goofy-happy smile takes over her face. "Chardonnay or Moscato?"

"Moscato." Adaline opens the light-brown cupboard and takes out four wine glasses.

Yanking a stiff drawer open, Cindy shoves her hand into the back in search of the corkscrew. "So, how'd you two meet?"

This is just like when I first met Sallie. Stay as truthful as possible. "During one of my adventures abroad." Placing the cups on the yellow laminate counter, Adaline rotates her bangle around her wrist and stares at the standard off-white walls. "I showed up at some ancient ruins, and—"

"I thought she was trespassing," Ëólas calls from the adjacent room.

"We fought a lot." Skirting around Cindy in the small L-shaped kitchen, Adaline grabs the glass markers from the junk drawer and writes an A on the base of her glass and an Ë on another. The moldy week-old flowers decaying in the vase on the counter remind her of the dead circle, a memory she promptly pushes out of her mind, especially with her best friend standing opposite her and stealing glances at Adaline's facial expressions.

Staring at the drawings on Catan's resource cards, Ëólas chuckles. "Took us a while to see eye to eye, but she can be very persistent."

"So can you," Adaline calls over her shoulder.

Stabbing the Moscato's cork, Cindy smiles fondly. "When was this?"

"Oh, well," Adaline pretends to struggle with snapping the marker cap back on, "the last time I traveled to the UK was four years ago."

Frowning, Cindy holds the wine bottle at an angle and groans as she twists the screw deeper. "You never mentioned him."

"Ouch." Ëólas winks at Adaline and turns back to Dax, who introduces him to the robber pawn.

"To be fair, he infuriated me for a long while," she says.

"Because she was in denial for a long while."

"Ouch."

Ëólas smirks.

Squeezing himself into the small kitchen, Dax grabs an extra-large bag of Doritos and pretzels from the counter and a stack of napkins. "A woman in denial. Man, I get that. More than you know."

Cindy juts her hip out to the side and gives Dax the stink eye, but he leans sideways and surprises her with a big, loud smooch. Their lip lock transforms Cindy's annoyance into amusement, not that Ëólas sees that part.

Adaline sighs. *Poor hubby. He's going to have to get used to PDA here.*

Ëólas quickly diverts his gaze to the moving boxes stacked in the dining room—the same ten that have sat there for the last few years. But with Cindy and Dax finally engaged, Adaline would bet a hundred dollars that they spent yesterday house hunting.

Escaping back to the living room, Dax sets aside the snacks and explains the game rules in more detail. "For your resource cards, you've got lumber, wool, brick, ore, and grain."

Without warning, Ãranol's words echo in Adaline's mind: *So, you are a conqueror. How very human of you.*

Maybe playing this game wasn't such a good idea. She hadn't stopped to think that maybe it would open old wounds for Ëólas, how human development forced his people into designated kingdoms, but she senses only pleasure from him. When he meets her gaze, his genuine smile makes her heart flutter.

The pop sound of Cindy liberating the wine makes Adaline spin around again. Cindy pours them both a full glass. After they gently clink their glasses to friendship, they take their first sips.

"He's adorable and clearly in love with you." Cindy puts down her drink and rubs the stem between her thumb and finger, making the glass spin. "I can't believe you thought he wasn't interested." With the guys distracted, she rests her arms on the countertop, leans in close, and whispers, "So what happened Saturday night?"

"Saturday night?" *Shit. If we found the stone at Nan's yesterday, then the night before—*

"After you left the restaurant."

"Oh, right. I told him how I felt, and we talked everything through." *Excessively so.*

"And?"

"And what?"

Ëólas picks up a game controller for the first time and pushes the buttons that do nothing right now, leaving him stumped. Adaline bites her lip to stop herself from laughing. *His curiosity is the cutest.* Her eyes trace the lean muscles on his upper back, the way his polo hugs his biceps and torso, showing off the ripples. His black jeans hug his solid bottom too. She'd love to squeeze that ass. She usually does when she's pulling him tighter against her, helping him to dig deeper as he grinds—

Cindy knocks on Adaline's forehead. "Damn, girl. That's one hell of a grin. Share the dirty details."

"Oh, yeah. Well, you know. We talked and," she watches Ëólas from the corner of her eye, "we had the absolute best, mind-blowing sex." As Ëólas fumbles and drops the controller and his cheeks turn beet red, Adaline giggles. "And we decided we'll travel back and forth between our homes so we have the best of both worlds." *Literally.*

"That's amazing, Chica. Congrats! Sooooo, do you think he's the one?"

Adaline bursts out laughing, her thumb fingering the ring she moved to her other hand. "No question about that."

"Aww. Adaline, this is huge!" Cindy bounces on her toes, making her glass wobble, the wine inside slosh around, and the highlights in her shoulder-length brown hair shimmer. "You have to tell me everything."

"Heh. Yeah. I do. I really do. But I think you need to add the tomato puree." With Cindy dashing to the stove, Adaline rotates her ring again. How does she tell Cindy about an entirely different world, that she wasn't even born here, that elves are real and her dad was one, that people are trying to kill her, and that she needs Cindy's help, which might put her in danger? And what's worse, pretty much everyone in Aerytol looks at her with reverence. What if Cindy does too? What if Adaline can't simply be herself in this world either?

Cindy turns the knob down to simmer and furrows her brows as she stirs dinner, her strokes slowing down. "Wait, I don't get it. How's that going to work, traveling back and forth between your homes? Will AU let you take semesters off like that?"

"Oh. Um." Adaline fills her mouth with wine. They haven't thought that part through. If little time passes when they're gone, then to everyone here, it'll seem like Adaline and Ëólas never leave. "I honestly don't know, but we're taking the summer to think things out."

"Huh. Okay." Cindy shrugs and stirs the Picadillo, slowly, thoughtfully, as if she's searching the pot for something hidden beneath the surface. Shaking her head, she stirs more vigorously, rapping the spoon on the side of the pan to fling the sauce off. She turns around, placing her hands on her hips. "Well, keep me posted. But does this mean you're free to be my maid of honor? You'll have to put up with my sisters as junior bridesmaids."

"Absolutely!" Adaline leaps around the counter, and they hug each other fiercely.

When they let go, Cindy cringes and points down the hall, where Ëólas's back disappears into Dax's home office. "Uh-oh, you might want to save your man."

Ha. My elf doesn't know what he's walking into.

Adaline follows behind and peers around the chipped doorframe to watch the guys. Five computer monitors occupy Dax's extra-long desk, behind which two copper and bronze Cameroon elephant masks hang on the mustard-yellow accent wall. Beside his desk, he has a collection of eight short and tall potted plants that make the corner of the room look like a jungle, his favorite being the giant spider plant he's been tending to for nearly fifteen years. On the opposite side of the room, movie posters cover the wall from floor to ceiling, including *The Dark Crystal*, *A New Hope*, and *Labyrinth*.

Oh! Ëólas has to watch Labyrinth!

In the center of the room, Ëólas circles around a long folding table with an open battle map depicting roads, ruins, caves, and secret entrances. The map holds a set of dice and several miniature silver figurines. Ëólas stoops down to eye level and examines the creatures. "What is all of this?"

"This, my friend, is *Dungeons and Dragons*."

"It's warfare? I'm good at warfare."

"Sort of." For the next ten minutes, Dax attempts to explain how the role-playing game works, and the more questions Ëólas asks, the broader Dax smiles.

"Is this the game we're playing later?"

"No, no. I'm in the middle of a long campaign with my friends, so I've left this up for now."

Cindy pops over Adaline's shoulder. "I think Dax just made a new best friend."

Wouldn't that be something, the four of us going on double dates, attending each other's weddings, watching our kids grow up together. Adaline moves her hand to her belly and pushes the word *mule* out of her mind. But how could she raise a child in this world, only to tear them away overnight and tell them they're royalty? She couldn't mislead her kids like that.

In the middle of Dax's explanations, Ëólas walks over to Aragorn's replica sword on the back wall. "May I?"

Dax scratches his short, black curls. "Um, sure."

Oh, honey. That's not real.

Ëólas takes the blade down, examines the pommel, and presses his thumb along the length of the blades. "The edges are dull."

"Yeah. Sharpe blades are illegal in the States."

Ëólas spins the blade a few times from side to side. "Decent balance."

"You know swords?"

"Ah. Yes. My father was a military commander. I spent some time training myself, and my mentor taught me many means of defense, including—"

"Fencing!" The dreamy look on Dax's face looks like he's floating on cloud nine.

Ëólas spots Adaline, who nods encouragingly. "Yes, including fencing."

As Adaline steps away, ready for more wine, she overhears Ëólas ask, "What's this?"

The tone in his voice, the slow cadence and darker note, makes her turn back. In his hand, he holds one of Dax's discarded figurines. His golden eyes darken as he takes in the pointy ears and gnarled, withered hand with elongated nails like claws.

Dax angles toward him and adjusts his glasses. "Ah, that is the vampire elf."

"A what?"

"It's a cursed species that kills nature around it."

Adaline and Ëólas exchange a look. She edges herself further into the room, and Ëólas passes her the figurine. As she studies the clawed hand, the memories of those screaming soldiers come back to her, and all warmth leaves her body.

"Cursed how?" she asks.

"Oh, it's a tragic situation, really. Elves are supposed to look after nature, right? They're a part of it, so when they succumb to evil and embrace death, the world suffers." Dax moves his arms about as he talks, channeling his role as dungeon master to set the stage and add drama to the story. "Their presence alone kills the plants they once loved. They can't even move together in packs because they can't stand to be around so much evil energy."

"What about the stars?" Adaline asks.

"Nah, they can't see those anymore either. Moonlight weakens them. How did you know that?"

"Just a guess." Adaline puts the figure down but can't stop staring at it, at the fangs and those long nails. *We can't possibly base our strategies on a game. And yet, the similarity...*

"What are their weaknesses?" Ëólas asks.

"Oh, um," Dax pulls out his guidebook and flips through the different creatures. "They can't teleport through plants like good elves can."

Ëólas snorts. "That's preposterous."

Dax eyes him for a moment. When Cindy calls him to help set the table, he passes the book to Ëólas and excuses himself. Together, he and Adaline stare at the entry on vampire elves. As Adaline reads the entry aloud, Ëólas moves his hand to her back, lending her his body heat.

Crossing her arms over her chest, Adaline scowls at the pages. "We can't believe any of this. It's a made-up game."

"Indeed. And yet if both elves and vampires are myth here, who's to say only one of us can exist in Ellíum? And didn't you read that vampirism is a disease? Maybe that's something we need to cure."

"Oh shit."

"What?"

"Cindy. She's an immunologist."

"What does that mean?"

"She studies diseases, specifically how to cure them. And before we left, Seira told me we need to bring Cindy back."

Ëólas puts the book down but doesn't peel his eye away from the vampire elf sketch. "We need to tell her sooner than later."

"I know, I know. But not tonight, okay? I need time to figure out how." *And make sure I don't lose my best friend in the process.*

Surely, they can take their time to adjust, to build a life for themselves outside of royal expectations, to rediscover who they are as Adaline and Ëólas, the newlyweds. Given how slowly time will pass in Ellíum, there's no rush, and Adaline could use the break from Ãranol, from running a kingdom, from fighting for her life. She just needs to hide the truth from the person who knows her best. How hard can that be?

Chapter Eleven

THE OFFICE

"Are you sure you want to return to campus today?" Ëólas stares wide-eyed at the multitude of students coming and going as he and Adaline follow the sidewalk away from main campus, the tall, glass dorm building behind them.

"Yes. I just hope the Grump stayed home today to recuperate from the weekend." *And we don't bump into Derek. Any chance I can be that lucky?*

Ëólas stops in front of the pole displaying directional signs with the names of foreign cities and the thousands of miles that separate them from D.C. "And you can just fly there," he mumbles.

Looping her arm around his, Adaline nudges him onward, and they both duck beneath the boughs of a dogwood tree that Adaline prays Facilities Management won't cut down. The grassy areas with benches, the shaded eating areas, and the random bamboo forest behind the Department of Anthropology clash with the sound of traffic rushing by in the distance.

Adaline points ahead to a small, rectangular building tucked away at the back of campus, far beyond the library that caps the quad. Hamilton's brick masonry and squat dormer windows don't match the rest of campus, making the building feel like a Gothic relic and hideaway. "My office is in there."

"Nice." Ëólas nods at the building's circular stone courtyard surrounded with flowers, hedges, and small trees. He follows her through the narrow, arched doorway with its comparatively oversized, white-painted frame.

When they turn down the hallway toward her office, Adaline freezes, causing Ëólas to stumble into her. In front of her door leans her backpack, the one she left behind in the cave when she vanished. She trudges down the hallway, unlocks her door, and yanks her bag inside. The small office, its threadbare carpet, cluttered desk, and chipped bookcase greet her with the warm ambiance of old friends. She smiles the moment she steps inside but shuts the door quietly and stares at her bag.

"Dare I ask?" Ëólas whispers, as if the backpack might contain an enemy.

"The Grump is back. Leaving my bag in the hallway is his way of baiting me into his office and making me sweat."

"Didn't you say he's been understanding?"

"Yes, but that's not like him. He usually rides my ass." When Ëólas's eyebrows hit the ceiling, she clarifies, "Not like that! Ew, gross. He's always been hard on me, but that's because he knows I can rise to the challenge. Gah!" Adaline throws her bag into the corner behind her desk. "I can't lie to his face. I could fake it via text, but the moment he sees me, he'll know I lied about Cindy's mom being injured. How do I explain what happened and why I ditched my team?"

"Tell him the truth?" Ëólas scrunches his nose as he thinks aloud. "If he worked closely with your father, perhaps he already knows, like Cindy's mom."

"How the hell am I supposed to know if he does? I can't just ask him." Adaline nibbles her bottom lip. "Okay, I can handle this. I'll be back in a few minutes. Don't be surprised if you hear us arguing. That's just his way."

Ëólas arches an eyebrow and looks his wife, his queen, up and down. "He has no idea to whom he speaks."

Kissing his cheek, Adaline walks out the door. *I can handle the Grump. I've survived worse. Hell, I even faced Áranol. The Grump is small potatoes.* She pauses outside his door for a moment, shakes her hands loose, and knocks loudly.

"No office hours today," he hollers.

Adaline turns the handle anyway and steps inside, closing the door behind her. Not everyone has to hear this.

"Oh, so your emergency's ended." He doesn't look up from his laptop. The light from his screen illuminates his thick spectacles and bulbous nose.

"It is. Thank you for returning my stuff. I read your email, and it seems the students did really well at the cave site. I look forward to hearing about their findings directly."

The Grump glances at her. Only his eyes move, nothing else. Then he looks down again and resumes typing. His upper lip twitches in an almost snarl. Adaline contemplates leaving his office, but she can't seem to make her feet move; she prefers direct attacks.

With her thumping her toe on his carpet, the Grump stops typing and closes his laptop. "What do you want?"

"I want to know why you've been so supportive."

"Am I not allowed to be? Oh, right. The Grump doesn't do nice." He sits back in his chair and crosses his arms over his round stomach. "You think I don't know what people call me? Not like I care. I am a grump. I own it. How about you? Are you going to own what really happened this weekend?"

Adaline twists her fingers behind her back and tugs a few curls. "Personal stuff. Enormous personal stuff." *Do you know? Should I show you or hide the elf in my office?*

The Grump nods. "Like lying to attend your friend's engagement party?"

Wait, what? How on earth did he hear about that? "It wasn't. I didn't—"

"Look, I know this about you, kid: You were damn determined to put together another expedition to that site even though it proved a waste of time before. You worked your ass off to get the funding and made all these promises about the discoveries you'd make, only to abandon your team not even halfway through day one. Then I had to take the lead and do your job. I'm not being supportive, Adaline. I'm done with you. You let me down, kid. You're not who I thought you were."

The Grump opens his laptop and goes back to work, typing away and pretending like she's not in the room. He's right though; she's not the person he once knew, not anymore.

"Ben, it's not like that."

"Don't care. I have a meeting with the tenure committee next week. That'll be an interesting conversation."

Are you fucking kidding me? He's going to tank my career? How the fuck did he hear about the engagement dinner? It's not like he knows anyone who was—Derek! Oh, that son of a bitch. He's out to ruin me, all because I told him the truth. And doused him with sangria. Adaline clutches her fists. Just the thought of him makes her cheeks burn.

"Damn it, Ben! You know I work my ass off, and I've proven the quality of my research for the last two years, but you're going to throw me under the bus now? You have it all wrong."

He stops typing but doesn't look up. "Convince me otherwise."

"You know what? I'm sick and tired of you having to make everything so damn difficult. My father would be so disappointed in your lack of support." Adaline storms out of Ben's office and down the hallway to her own. As she twists the knob, Ben is right behind her.

"Just because Eddie was a professor here doesn't mean you should get an easy ride." He shoves his glasses up his nose. "I don't support nepotism, Adaline. Your father proved himself here time and time again, and you've only proven that the moment you get your own project, you bail without reason, leaving me to do everything. They were your students, not mine. You let them down."

"I had other things I needed to deal with," she hisses, trying to keep her voice down. "As my colleague, I should be able to count on you."

"Counting on me doesn't mean dumping your workload, team, and project on me. I went there to help you, not to take over. If you want to prove your worth, you better have a damn good excuse ready for the tenure committee. Well, what do you know? I *am* looking out for you after all. I'm giving you a heads up for what's coming."

Adaline glares at the Grump before stepping back into her office and slamming the door in his face, but the Grump doesn't let her have that satisfaction.

"Ow!" His boat shoe stops the door from latching.

Ëólas picks up the letter opener resting on top of her three-tier paper tray. The length and tip of the opener look a lot like a dagger, which Ëólas holds out to her. When she rolls her eyes, he returns the pointy object to her desk and glares at Ben.

Adaline leans her weight into the door, preventing the Grump from pushing his way into her office. "Move your foot. You've said more than enough."

"Look, kid. Give me a legitimate reason why you left, and maybe I'll reconsider."

Adaline furrows her brows and slowly opens her door. "You can't be serious."

"Have I ever been one to joke?"

She huffs in his face. "I can't give you one. It's personal, and that's all there is to it. Either you trust me and my abilities or you don't, and quite frankly I just don't give a damn anymore. I have far more important matters on my plate, and if you tank my career, then I guess I'll just have to start over again in this world."

"In this world?" Ben asks. "That sounds awfully grandiose for you. What could you possibly value more than your work? I thought you lived and breathed for your research."

"That's not what you said a moment ago," Adaline says. "What are you getting at?"

Ben leans against the frame of Adaline's doorway while he stares intensely at her, making her feel exposed. He's studied her a few times like this over the years, as if he's sizing her up. Usually he dismisses his thoughts and goes back to ignoring or pestering her. She steps forward to shut the door again, but Ben pushes it open and walks past her as if to sit down across from her desk. His entire body freezes the moment he sees Ëólas.

Adaline lazily gestures her hand between the two guys. "Ëólas, this is Dr. Ben Larson. Ben, this is Ëólas, my husband."

Ben's thick lenses make his eyes appear ungodly wide and the whites of his eyes as bright as searchlights.

"Okay, fine." Adaline throws her arms up in the air. "I left the cave and met up with Ëólas, and I seized the only opportunity I had to marry him before he went back home." *Technically, that's not a lie.* "Is that a legitimate reason for you?"

Ben crosses his arms over his chest. White tufts of arm hair poke out through the buttonholes of his cuffs. "Did you travel there first, or did he come here on his own?"

Adaline and Ëólas lock eyes with each other, neither sure how to respond. *What if he means traveled here from England? But he didn't hear Ëólas speak yet, I don't think.*

Ben sighs loudly. "Adaline, I worked with your father for twenty years. I know an elf when I see one."

"You're genuine?" Ëólas's ears subtly poke through his dark-blond hair. "What exactly did Edwin tell you?"

"Eddie told me a lot. Come on." Ben finally leaves her office and heads back to his own.

Ëólas's curiosity propels him forward, but he pauses at the door and extends his hand. Adaline grunts her frustration but takes his hand and follows.

First, Cindy's family knows the truth. Now the Grump. But Dad didn't bother to tell me anything, let alone make sure I took self-defense lessons.

Did he blame her after all, for leaving her mother behind, for not taking him back home with her when she was little? Logically, she keeps repeating what everyone else has said, that she was a traumatized child. But Āranol's words keep haunting her, that her mother got tired of waiting. Maybe her father did too. But if that were true, wouldn't he have given her memories back sooner so they could have gone home together—before she was the only one left behind?

Adaline edges into the Grump's office, and he shuts the door quietly behind her. He gestures for both Ëólas and Adaline to sit in front of his desk, in the same black plastic chairs Adaline's sat in numerous times over the past two years to talk about her research goals. And the whole time he kept the truth from her too. Adaline sinks into her seat, her lips pursed together as she bites the inside of her cheek and crosses her arms in front of her chest. Her sneaker kicks the bottom of the Grump's desk.

"Your father started working here because he was trying to find a way home. And to keep everyone else away from the cave." Ben pulls his keys out of his pocket and fumbles for the small silver key for their desk. He squints to make sure he has the right one, then wiggles the key into the lock of his top drawer. "Damn cheap metal piece of shit," he grumbles.

Ëólas leans forward as if to see inside the drawer while Adaline looks out the window. The clouds rolling past cast their shadows on the parking lot below.

"Ah, here we are." The Grump jerks the drawer open and pulls out a large manilla envelope with a wax seal on the twine lock. Then he drops the thick envelope with a loud plop in front of Adaline.

She doesn't touch it. Instead, her eyes dart from the wax seal to the Grump's smile, which looks as peculiar on him as a bird wearing a fedora.

When she doesn't touch it, Ben nudges the envelope toward her. "It's from your father. I promised I'd give this to you when you turned forty, that is, if you still didn't know about that other world and hadn't aged. Why do you think I complain about my joints aching so much? Most humans start complaining around age thirty about their body getting older."

Adaline stares at the envelope as if it'll burst into flames if she touches it. She switches to biting the inside of her other cheek. "What's in it?"

"Financial documents and property listings, stuff that your father acquired over the centuries."

Adaline balks and looks away. Her eyes land on the cobweb beneath Ben's windowsill.

"And a letter," Ben says. "To you."

She shifts her gaze to Ëólas bobbing his head, then to the envelope. Still, she doesn't touch it. "Did he blame me? For not taking him home."

The Grump leans back in his chair and taps the top of his desk a few times as he chooses his next words, another habit Adaline's never seen him exhibit before. "He blamed himself. For not being able to protect the both of you. He carried a lot of guilt and resented the fact that, as your father, he couldn't do half the things you could, which might not make sense to you. Look, in your grandmother's trunk, you'll find a stone—"

"Oh my god, the damn stone." Adaline rises from her chair, drops her hands on the windowsill, and leans her weight into the cool bricks. Below, faculty members park their cars and chat with each other about the morning, smiling most likely about their carefree summer plans. "I already found that rock. On my own. With no help." She glances back at Ëólas and flashes an apologetic half smile. "You know what I mean."

He nods once, his soft gaze telling her he takes no offense. Sitting back, he gives her space to process Ben's news while he takes in every word and assesses all the implications. He'll give her his opinion later.

"Ah." Ben raps his hands on his desk and lifts his bushy eyebrows. "So you know everything then?"

"Know everything?" Adaline mocks. "I know nothing! I don't know how to use magic. It just kinda happens when I need it to. I have an entire kingdom looking at me like I'm my grandmother reincarnate. We have demonic vampire elves planning to attack any moment, and everyone seems to know a lot more about my parents and my family than I do. What the hell exactly is a fae?"

"Sorry, kid. I know nothing about fae. But maybe that letter has your answers. I just know that your father tried to keep you away from that world, and I tried to keep you out of that cave to honor his wishes, but it seems like destiny caught up with you anyway, so take what you've got, and do what you will with it."

Adaline snatches the envelope off his desk, ready to make a mad dash out of this office, but she hesitates at the door. "Does this mean you're not going to rat me out to the tenure committee?"

The Grump chuckles so loudly that his belly bumps against the edge of his desk. "I was trying to force a confession out of you. You're a pain in the ass to read, you know?"

"Yes, I do!" Ëólas says. "Incredibly hard to read, especially when she's in denial and—"

Adaline's glare makes Ëólas clamp his mouth shut. Then he puffs out his cheeks and looks out the window, admiring the different sizes and colors of vehicles that enter the parking lot.

Ben bangs his desk again. "Just like your father, always keeping your thoughts to yourself. Are you renewing your contract for next semester?"

"I, I don't know." Adaline hugs the envelope to her chest. "I'm a queen now. How odd is that? But now that we know I can travel back and forth, I don't want to leave here for good. This world is my home too. I just don't know what role I should play yet."

The Grump slaps his desk. "Good."

"I have no objection to traveling back and forth." Ëólas stands and pushes in his chair, which only thuds into the desk. "And I would very much like to fly in an airplane." He turns to the door, but the Grump snaps his fingers and signals for Ëólas to sit down again. He arches an eyebrow at the old man and grips the back of the chair, unwilling to comply with someone else's orders.

"Keep that door shut," Ben tells Adaline. "Are you two actually married?" When Ëólas and Adaline nod, Ben pulls out a steno pad. "Alright. Name?"

Ëólas and Adaline share a confused glance at each other, but he spells his name aloud.

As the Grump's writing, he asks, "Last name?"

"Of Lameiría. Or son of Élara. We don't use last names."

"Well, that's all fine and dandy, but here we do use last names. So pick one, or do you want to share hers if you're married?"

"What are you doing?" Adaline asks.

The Grump plops the pad onto his desk and glares at them both like they're morons, and that familiar expression makes Adaline feel a little less on edge. "You said you're married, and you plan on sticking around for a while, right? That means he needs identification. So, what last name do you want?"

"Wait, what?" Adaline squeezes the envelope, crushing the sides.

"Your family doesn't age, kiddo. Do you know how many times my family's had to forge documents for yours? How the hell do you think you got your social security number in the first place? I've got this. I just need his info. And a passport photo."

With Adaline's mouth hanging open, Ëólas offers, "Élarason?"

"That's...awkward," the Grump mumbles. "How about Larason? Or Larson. We could be family."

Ëólas angles his head questioningly to the side, probably taking in the Grump's appearance and noting how not alike they are. "Sure. Whatever you recommend."

"You two want a marriage certificate too?"

"Yes," they both say.

Ben scribbles their answers. "Address?"

"Adaline's condo, I suppose."

I guess we can update our addresses later, if we want to.

"Alright. And just so you know, you're from Arraya's hometown in the U.K. Check her trunk for details about that," the Grump says. "Adaline, get him to a Walgreens or whatever and bring me a passport photo, the sooner the better."

So, Ëólas and I can really have a life here too? She scowls at the envelope and peers over the top to watch the Grump scribble more notes. He's always been gruff and standoffish; it's his way of giving his students space to grow on their own terms. And yet he's also known when to step in and lend her a hand when she's needed help, without her having to ask. "Ben, I, thank you."

The Grump waves her off. "Yeah, yeah. I have work to do, so get out. I'll text you when his papers are ready."

Ëólas side-eyes Adaline and mouths, *Is that normal?*

With a nod, she shuts the door behind them while the Grump goes back to typing on his laptop as if he's done nothing more than counsel another of his students.

What world have I returned to?

Chapter Twelve

THE LETTER

When they return to the condo, Adaline flops the unopened envelope onto her desk near the door, hangs her keys on the wall, and collapses on the sofa, her back to the armrest and the papers. Ëólas places her backpack in front of the hallway closet, lifts up her feet, and sits beside her, draping her legs over his lap.

She twists the hem of his shirt sleeve around her finger. "I spoke with Cindy today. She wants to discuss her wedding colors tonight and browse bridesmaid dress ideas online."

Ëólas says nothing as he drills a hole into her soul with his unrelenting gaze.

She angles her face away from him too and faces the flat-screen TV. "I'm not ready. He died before we even had time to talk about what really happened. I mean, I get it, why he and Nan agreed I should give up my memories. I wouldn't want our own child to live with something like that. But he was ready to keep me away from Aerytol. Away from you. Away from my mother. Away from—"

"Creepy vampire-elf assassins?"

Adaline purses her lips, which Ëólas kisses. A brief smile dances across her face before dipping into a frown. She peeks at the envelope. "I think—"

"You need to read this by yourself?"

Adaline nods, pulling her knees into her chest to let him up.

"I respect that." He presses his hands into his thighs, his skinny jeans hugging his ass as he gets up. "I'm going to explore the neighborhood for a while. Does an hour sound good?"

"That would be amazing. Thank you."

"If you need me sooner, just call me." Retrieving the new mobile he forgot on the kitchen counter all day, he tucks it into his back pocket, winks, and disappears out the door.

Adaline looks at the clock on the wall beside her desk, its hanging pendulum ticking back and forth. Knowing Ëólas, he'll return at five fifteen on the nose. Wrapping her arms around her legs curled into her chest, she rests her head on the plump throw pillow she and Nan picked out years ago. Even though Adaline had moved out by then, she still visited Nan's once a week, or her father would show up at her condo Sunday mornings to chat about work while Adaline made breakfast. They planned her future together, a future that revolved around academics and narrowing down her field of research. He sat at her table, scooping the eggs onto his toast before each bite, while Adaline rattled off all the places she wanted to travel to next and explore with only her backpack and laptop. And Eddie insisted she could do anything.

Did he really think my connection to home had died?

Adaline slinks off the sofa and retrieves the envelope, dragging it off her desk as if the papers were made of lead. She fluffs the throw pillows and bunches them up around her before sitting down again. Then she bends the envelope beneath the wax seal until it snaps in half. A few crumbs fall away from the jagged edges. She slides the entire contents out onto the chic cream-colored coffee table and sorts through the various files, including a list of antiquities locked away in storage units around the world. She skims the list, pausing at the Egyptian jewelry entry for 1800-B.C. sea-foam beaded wrist cuffs and brooches. She and Ëólas need to travel next to Egypt so she can hold those items herself—and donate them to Cairo's Egyptian Museum.

Is that why Nan had so many charities, to compensate for the historical items they've hoarded?

From between the folders, an ordinary white envelope falls onto the floor with one word written on the front in her father's cursive: *Adaline*. Carefully, she tucks her finger under the open corner. With each tearing sound, her heart retreats deeper inside.

Unfolding the letter, she takes a deep breath and reads,

My dear Adaline,

I can only imagine how confused you must be at this moment, having just learned the truth about yourself and our family. I am terribly sorry I'm not with you right now to help you through this. But I implore you to listen to your grandmother, seek her guidance, and take comfort in her teachings.

She's far wiser than I ever will be.

I feel selfish asking for your forgiveness, that I was too much of a coward to tell you the truth, but I couldn't bear the thought of destroying the life you've been building here or that you would blame yourself for what happened to your mother.

I have tried my best to give you everything you'll need, to make certain you'll feel as at home as I have in this world, and I pray you'll find peace here as your grandmother and I have.

You will always be my greatest treasure. Being your father, watching you come into your own, gave my life new purpose. You are so strong, my sweet girl, stronger than you know, and I am proud of your achievements thus far. I know you'll do wonders.

Even though I'm gone, I still love this world. Its ups and downs. The way humans rise back up and fight for what's right. Its ingenuity and continuous experimentation. In truth, I have always felt much more human than elf.

But what does being human even mean? To make mistakes?
To learn from our experiences? To try again? To leave the
world a better place for our children? Elf. Human. I see little
difference—especially when both have the chance to thrive.

And that is what I want for you—to thrive. Do not burden yourself
with regrets of the past. My father gave his life to save mine, and
your mother and I were ready to do the same for you. And I will
not stop trying to leave you with a better world.

That is why I could not stay with you any longer. Once I was certain
you had what you needed, I had to return home, alone for now,
because it is my responsibility, and no one else's, to find my wife. I
am certain your mother is alive; I can feel it, Adaline. I will find her,
and together we will end the war that's torn our family asunder.

Should you wish to return home one day, I will do all that I can
to make sure Aerytol and all of Ellíum greets you with peace and
safety.

In the meantime, I implore you to focus on today. Focus on
your own story. Focus on the good you can achieve in this world.
But every now and again, keep your eyes on the horizon toward
tomorrow.

One day, your mother and I will meet you there.

You have my word.

All my love,
Your father

Adaline rereads the letter two more times, then lays it on the coffee table at arms' length and stares at the handwriting, a totem of hope—even though she attended her father's funeral. But this letter sounds like he had a plan, like if he disappeared, it'd be intentional.

Adaline texts the Grump: *When did Dad give you this envelope?*

She waits ten minutes for a reply, her knee thumping up and down as she bites her thumbnail, a nasty habit she gave up fifteen years ago.

Finally, the three dots appear in Ben's chat message. Her knee thumps faster but stops abruptly when his reply pings: *About six months before the accident.*

Adaline chucks her phone to the other side of the sofa.

The accident. What if it wasn't an accident? Nan insisted on a closed casket. What if it was all staged? What if they tricked me into mourning his loss? For two fucking years? Did he leave Nan waiting for his return?

Adaline leans back and closes her eyes.

"My dad might be alive," she whispers into the ether, as if speaking the words aloud would conjure him in front of her.

What if he found mom? What if...

Despite the hope taking root inside her, a heaviness settles on her chest, pushing her down as if to snuff out the world around her. She closes her eyes and breathes steadily, allowing the gates to swing open and for the tumult of emotions to wash over her. But she's careful to make sure she doesn't feel like someone's ripping out her intestines through her throat.

She tightens the muscles in her hands, legs, and feet and releases them one by one. The air conditioner kicking on, the refrigerator humming, the clock ticking behind her all come to a standstill as the world settles into a new layer of quiet, an in between space where time and life slow to a crawl. In this space, Adaline drifts like one hovering on the edge of consciousness, the realm between dreams and reality.

When she opens her eyes, a sheer curtain appears in front of her, draped across the length of the living room, its folds falling through the middle of the coffee table. She slowly turns her head; everything behind her is the same: her cluttered desk, the thick metal front door, the granite kitchen island. But everything behind the curtain, like her TV, is blurry and tinted white. She tries to get up, to push the curtain aside, to better see the woman walking toward her from the other side. Despite the oddity of the situation, the approaching woman and her slender silhouette feel familiar. But Adaline can't lift her limbs. The more she tries, the heavier they become. She moves her mouth but emits no sound as her lips form the name, *Aeríoléna?*

The sound of a key unlocking the front door snaps Adaline back into this time and place. The curtain vanishes as though it had never been there. Then again, maybe it's always there, only hidden from mortals.

Ëólas hangs his keys beside Adaline's, kicks off his suede ankle boots, and sets down on the coffee table a brown paper bag. He glances at the letter but doesn't ask about it and drapes his arm around her, his heat radiating through her clothes and warming her bones. If they were in New Leira, Kayla or Nuríel would have made sure the fireplace was raging, but Adaline's faux electric fireplace positioned beneath the TV is nothing more than an empty black box.

"What's in the bag?" she asks.

He nuzzles her forehead with the side of his cheek. Instead of the letter, he studies her, her body language, her voice, her reactions. "Cheesecake. It's the only thing I know for certain you love."

Adaline takes his other hand and kisses his palm. "Thank you."

"Thank you for filling my pockets with cash."

Adaline smiles briefly. "What flavors did you get?"

"Something chocolaty and something fruity. I just asked for their recommendations. I hope you like them."

"It's cheesecake. It's hard to go wrong."

"Good."

She reaches forward and unfolds the top of the bag. In between retrieving the containers and forks, she hands Ëólas the letter. While he reads it, she pops open the first container and takes a huge forkful of the decadent chocolate brownie crumble slice. She takes two more bites as Ëólas returns the letter and pops open the second container, nudging it toward her so she can take the first bite of that one too. She swallows the strawberry, raspberry, blueberry swirl and groans.

"Which one do you like best?" he asks.

"Fruit. I love fresh fruit mixed with tart cheesy goodness."

Ëólas tries a bite of each. "I have to agree." They take turns between bites until only a few remain. Their forks battle for the last of the fruity cake until Ëólas yields and Adaline plops the whole bite in her mouth, covering her lips so the crumbs don't fall onto the floor.

He finishes the chocolate but kisses Adaline to steal one last taste of strawberry. "So much for dinner. Is cheesecake always so filling?" He leans sideways into the corner of the sofa, and Adaline curls up beside him, wedging herself between the backrest and his torso.

"Always."

They lay there for a while, neither speaking, each drifting in and out of their own thoughts.

"I, I think sometimes I can see into the Immortal Realms. It's like Aeríoléna wants to reach me, or maybe I keep trying to reach her. I'm not sure."

Ëólas strokes her arm.

"My parents might be alive." She feels Ëólas's chin bob on top of her head. "If they are, my dad doesn't want me to find them, but that's bullshit. I'm not just going to wait for them to find me."

Ëólas nods again but still doesn't speak.

"And yet I can't focus on them now. We need to deal with Āranol and Morgán and those demonic elves first."

Ëólas kisses the crown of her head. "If your parents are anything like you, then I have no doubt they're alive. And given our common enemy, perhaps your parents will find us first."

She closes her eyes and tries to slip back into that peaceful trance again, but she twists and twitches next to him, unable to get comfortable. "I'm afraid to hope. How many more times do I have to mourn them?"

He holds her tightly. With his other hand, he pinches the meaty pad of her hand between her thumb and pointer finger. The concentrated pain increases the flow of blood up her arm and eases the tension in her head.

"Better?" Ëólas asks.

"Much."

They sit together in silence until the clock chimes at the top of the hour, prompting Ëólas to announce, "Alright. We're taking a honeymoon."

"What?" Adaline sits up, scrunches her brow, and pokes his belly button. "But I need to train."

"And we will. A lot. And I'll be very strict with you. But not today. And not this week." He pushes Adaline down on the sofa and crawls on top of her, using his knees to push hers apart.

Her breath hitches, and she automatically spreads her legs wider, letting him press fully against her. "Are you teasing me?"

"No, I'm just ensuring that I sway you to agree with me."

"Oh, I see."

"You started this method of negotiations."

"I did. But I think you'll find I'm already amicable to the idea." She unsnaps his jeans, slips her hands under them, and grabs his firm bottom, giving both cheeks a hard squeeze. "But what about our obligations?"

"We're not forsaking them. We're just taking some time to reinforce our bond."

"Reinforce it?"

"Most definitely."

Is that right? For us to have fun? To enjoy some time away and just be happy?

Ëólas nuzzles her neck. "What does your work require of you?"

"I have to finish grading final exams this week, and I don't have classes again until August. I'm supposed to spend this summer writing my next research paper, but now that Beccah's taking the lead on that, I don't expect her to require much of me."

"Ha! There you have it. We need to seize this opportunity, Adaline. Newly married elves typically sequester together for a decade, and we've not had a day to ourselves. We deserve a honeymoon, mé ellador. We need this." He trails his finger between her cleavage, pulling her blouse down, and kisses each mound.

How can she ignore him? She can't pretend as though she doesn't want the same, that she'd rather spend several days in bed with him, their limbs entwined and food delivered. He's right. Even a day wouldn't be enough, and the lack of time together hurts her too, diminishing her reserves to keep pressing forward. If she can't love him thoroughly and without distraction, she might self-combust. "Okay. Let's take that honeymoon. Can we wait to move into Nan's house until after our vacation?"

"Absolutely. We'll be too busy enjoying lots of fruity drinks with umbrellas anyway."

"And lots of sex too."

Ëólas merges his lips with hers, pausing only to say, "I'm going to love this world."

Chapter Thirteen

THE CHALLENGE

Ëólas walks around to the driver's side, opens the door, takes Adaline's hand as she gets out, and closes the door behind her. Holding hands, they join the crowd of people stomping through tall grass, weaving in between parked cars, and heading toward the banner welcoming them to the end of summer county fair.

"Explain this to me one more time." Ëólas takes out his mobile and swipes open their e-tickets. "What about being trapped in a metal object and thrown about is fun?"

"Jeez, when you phrase it like that, it doesn't. Then again..." Adaline hops over a ditch and repositions her purse strap so it crosses her chest diagonally. "You're overthinking this. Just trust me. It'll be fun."

"Mmm. Sure."

Adaline halts and yanks him in front of her, pressing her chest against his, her mounds peeking above her navy-blue tank top. Even though they've stretched their week-long honeymoon into two months of exploration, both in and out of the bedroom, they remain insatiable. No wonder elves sequester for a decade.

She hooks her fingers over the waist of his jeans, locking him in place. "You don't trust me?"

"You mean like in Charlottesville?" His eyes linger on her décolletage. "When you promised a fun nighttime outing and pulled my trunks down in the pool?"

"We were alone. The hotel staff never found out. And I seem to recall you being very happy at the end of that adventure." She drops her eyes toward his cock, which she feels twitch against her at the memory.

But a family hikes past them, and Ëólas takes a respectful step backward. "Mmm-hmm."

"I was right about the dinner and dessert tours in D.C."

"True."

"And the trip to Harpers Ferry." Adaline takes Ëólas's hand and tugs him closer to the entrance.

"Fine."

"C'mon. Turn that frown upside down. Let's enjoy the last hurrah before I go back to work and before you become that stern trainer you keep warning me about."

Ëólas plasters a fake but cute smile on his face and presents the e-tickets at the gate. When they pass under the entry sign, the fair greets them with the typical circus music, the smell of fresh popcorn and roasted nuts, the buzzers announcing the starting and stopping of rides, and the flashing lights. Adaline bounces up and down, but Ëólas turns into a statue, only his eyes moving from side to side, until a man bumps into Ëólas's shoulder and drops his bucket of fries. The grizzly man curses and kicks the bucket but continues on his way, leaving the trash strewn across the ground. People passing by either jump over or pummel the fries into the dirt. As Ëólas's face turns ash gray, Adaline quietly picks up the bucket and tosses it into the nearby trash can.

Gently, she takes Ëólas's hand, quiets her voice, and blocks his line of sight so that he sees only her. "Is it too overstimulating? We can go."

He refocuses his eyes on her and only her. "No." He mechanically moves his hands to her hips and hooks his pointer fingers through the belt loops of her shorts, as if to make certain she won't disappear and leave him stranded. "Thank you. I just need a bit of time to adjust. That's all."

She tugs him toward the exit, but he pulls her back and shakes his head. After taking several deep breaths, he shares a genuine smile. "I trust you. Always."

"Okay, Cindy and Dax are running late, but I told them where to meet us. How about we try a game first?"

When Ëólas nods, they walk past the Tilt-a-Whirl and head toward the carnival games. A mother passing them peels strips of cotton candy off the funnel and passes them to her kids' sticky outstretched hands. Ëólas scrunches his nose at the blue fluff.

Once the family vanishes, Ëólas's golden eyes light up. "Oh, I know this one!" He guides her toward Hit A Can.

Using the cash he withdrew from the ATM this morning, Ëólas passes the cash to the vendor and accepts five balls. On his second pitch, the cans burst apart and clang against the sides of the stall and the ground. He holds the victory of his hunt, a giant orange stuffed bear, in both arms.

"Are you going to carry that for the rest of the day?" Adaline asks.

"Certainly."

After Adaline ruffles the bear's single tuft of hair on top and names him Sir Bearsaac, they continue down the gaming boulevard, taking turns at the water shooters, ring toss, balloon darts, and dunk tank. Adaline gives most of their prizes away to exhausted kids draped over their parents' shoulders.

"Aww, you made my kiddo's day." A young mother hands the stuffed Pikachu to her preschooler.

Hugging the stuffie close to her chest, the little girl with red pigtails and a ketchup-stained T-shirt kisses her new best friend's nose. As they walk away, the crowd quickly swallows them, leaving behind no trace of the little one's laughter or her mother, as if they never existed.

"Ah, there's Dax and Cindy." Ëólas shifts the bear underneath his arm and takes off the wedding ring Adaline bought him last month, a platinum band with entwined leaves etched around the center. He slips it into his front pocket. "Are you all right?"

Turning away from her friends, she nods, switches her ring to the opposite hand, and runs over to hug Cindy.

"Damn!" Dax admires the enormity of the bear. "You're going to put me to shame."

"Nope, no more games." Adaline smiles wickedly at Ëólas. "Let's hit the rides!"

Fifteen minutes later, they climb into their steel dome seat on the Tilt-A-Whirl with Sir Bearsaac protecting Adaline's left side. Opposite them, Cindy and Dax snap a photo of Ëólas and Adaline, and Adaline captures a snapshot of them in return. She stashes her phone away as the ride operator pulls the bar down, locking them in place. Ëólas examines his disabled escape route and tests the stability of the bar that he grips with both hands, while Adaline sits back and rests her palms on her thighs, her hands tapping along with the music. His clenched hands make her chuckle so hard that her ponytail bangs the back of the Tilt-A-Whirl.

The ride jerks to a start and twirls them around, sliding Adaline into Ëólas's side while he holds onto the lap bar for dear life, his hair shielding his face, the muscles in his arms taut, all to save himself from being flattened against the metal seat. Adaline throws her arms overhead and hollers woo-hoo, her ponytail hiding Sir Bearsaac, but Ëólas clamps his eyes and jaw shut. The ride picks up speed, whipping them around, cooling their cheeks, creating a wind tunnel of entertainment, and pitching Adaline's heart sideways.

When Ëólas doesn't crack a smile, she hollers, "I'm sorry, sweetheart. It'll be over soon."

She grips the lap bar and pulls with all her might to peel her body off his, but the increasing speed slams her into Ëólas once again. Because she cannot unglue herself from him, because she cannot spare him, because Ëólas—the mighty commander general and king of Aerytol—resembles a little boy shutting his eyes during the scary parts of the movie, Adaline laughs hysterically, freely, and unabashedly.

"Alright, alright. I can do this!" Ëólas reaches around her and pulls for them both, dragging himself an inch away from the hard metal side.

Together they fight the inertia, Ëólas encouraging them with a grandiose "Heave!" But his hands slip, and he falls backward with Adaline propelled against his chest.

Her wild laughter infects him until he snorts and gives in, relinquishing the bar for good. The ride mashes them together, and Ëólas's booming laughter spins around them, a musical wonder that fills Adaline's heart to the brim.

When the ride slows down, they stay stitched together, laughing in tandem as the other riders and the people strolling past twirl in and out of view. Before they climb out, Cindy snaps another photo.

Once again on stationary ground, Cindy shows them the before and after photos and how the ride pulverized Ëólas's stiff muscles and rigid posture. "Well, he looks like he had fun."

"Oh, let's do the pirate ship next!" Adaline pulls Ëólas after her.

As their group waits in line, his eyes follow the movement of the ship, back and forth, nodding his head as if he's counting. "So round and round wasn't enough?"

With Sir Bearsaac tucked under his arm, he doesn't take his eyes off the ship or the skeleton hanging from the mast, not until the couple in front of them begins making out, their kisses wet and loud. Ëólas arches his eyebrows momentarily, but when the boy grabs the girl's ass, Ëólas blushes and turns his back on them, placing himself between the indecent couple and Adaline.

While Cindy debates wedding favors, Adaline leans her back against Ëólas's chest. *I hope you can loosen up here, my love.*

"No one really keeps the wedding favors, do they?" Cindy asks. "Maybe we should just make a donation in honor of our guests?"

"That's a pleasant idea." Adaline tucks her hands in her back pockets, only to remove one and stroke Ëólas's cock. He flinches, gently grips her wrist, and drags her arm in front of her body, crossing it under her chest where he holds it in place.

He doesn't stand a chance, not while he's holding Sir Bearsaac.

"I'd rather we go with the personalized chocolates idea," Dax says. "I never say no to dessert."

"Oh, that's a good point. I second that." Adaline wiggles her bottom with enthusiasm—and against Ëólas, whose posture and movements have stiffened.

While Adaline nonchalantly tucks her free arm behind her and rubs his cock again, a cold current runs through her body, causing her to shiver despite the sheen of sweat coating her skin. She scans the crowd, but no one stands out to her among the sea of strangers. The carnival is swarming with laughing friends, frisky couples, tired parents, and sugar-hyped kids. Her intestines feel fine too, so why the sudden creep factor?

"What do you think, Adaline?" Cindy asks.

"What? Oh, um, I'm so sorry. My mind wandered. What was the question?"

Cindy scrutinizes her friend from head to toe, giving Dax the chance to tell Ëólas about the new bridge he's designing for work. With the guys distracted, Cindy opens her mouth as if to ask what's wrong, but whatever concerns ran through her head, Cindy must not have found the right words. She changes the subject. "What's it like working with your boyfriend?"

"Nice? We're not working right now though. We're both taking some time off."

"Oh. Okay. Well, when are you going to travel abroad next, to visit his family?" She leans in close and mumbles, "Do his parents know how serious this is?"

"Yeah. Yeah." Adaline bobs her head. "I would say they definitely know that." *Ugh, it's so damn hot. Why didn't I bring refillable water bottles?*

"Do you get along with them?"

"Uh-huh. They're great. Doting, even."

"But you haven't been to the UK in four years?"

Fuck! "It's so hot. My brain is all muddled. Did you make a choice about the wedding favors?"

Cindy crosses her arms over her chest. "No."

The two women stare at each other for a moment before distracting themselves with the signs for funnel cake and crispy chicken tenders. Occasionally, Cindy studies Ëólas as if waiting for another red flag to pop up, but after ten minutes of sweating in line, she redirects her attention to Dax's work story.

Even though Adaline tunes in to the guys' conversation, the hairs on the back of her neck stand up, urging her to search the crowd again, from the slingshot on one end of the fairgrounds to the opposite end of the strip where the teenagers scurry to select their bumper cars. She scans the crowd one more time as she leads Ëólas up the platform and onto the pirate ship, where she swallows that unsettling feeling.

I'm in Maryland, not Aerytol. We're safe here. I'm just on edge because Cindy caught me lying.

To Cindy's credit, she doesn't grill Adaline with more questions. Instead, the four of them enjoy a day of rides, eating, and live musical performances. But Adaline underestimates Ëólas and his reaction to the county fair. Three hours later, after they finished all but one ride, Ëólas tosses Sir Bearsaac to Cindy and pulls Adaline toward the slingshot.

"Oh hell no." Adaline leans back on her heels like brakes.

With both her hands in his, Ëólas walks backward, pulling her inch by inch toward the line. "Oh, come on! Trust me."

"This has nothing to do with trust. There is no way you're going to get me on that thing."

"Just get in line with me, and we'll take a closer look together. I've always wanted to fly." He gives her the puppy dog look she inadvertently taught him when she wanted him to try dipping his fries in his chocolate shake.

"That's not flying, Ëólas. That's being hurled into oblivion, only to freefall and then get hurled upward all over again." Adaline shakes her head venomously and looks to Cindy and Dax for help.

Dax cups his hands over his mouth like a megaphone. "She owes you, man!"

He backs away with Cindy, who's laughing so hard that she almost drops Sir Bearsaac. She might have peed herself too, given the way she's pressing her knees together. Adaline glares at her two best friends, but before she can protest further, Ëólas grabs her hips and hoists her over his shoulder.

"No!" She slaps his back until he puts her down but blocks her exit from the line. "Don't you dare," she hisses, but his wicked smile tricks her into smiling too.

"Do this with me, and I'll concede; I'll try that cotton candy."

"Forget the cotton candy!" Adaline tries to jump out of line, but Ëólas hooks her around the waist.

"They can't force you on the ride. Isn't that what you told me? So just wait with me, unless you think you might change your mind?"

"No way in hell."

"Then stay. I need you for courage." Inflating his cheeks into a grin, he skates his hands down the length of her sides. As the line moves behind her, Ëólas pushes his hips into her, forcing her legs to move backward as he steps forward. He keeps his eyes locked on hers and brushes his lips against her earlobe. "You know you want to," he murmurs.

The heat of those five little words caressing her neck sets her core on fire. With his next step, he wedges his thigh between hers and pushes upward, grinding against her mons until she yields and staggers backward.

"Who are you?" she asks, failing to push the corners of her wide smile downward.

"Did I never tell you what a mischievous child I was?"

"No!"

"Ah, well, let's just say that when given the freedom to do so, I can be quite naughty. And I'm simply employing our favorite negotiations strategy."

Oh my god. What have I unleashed?

The line moves again, and Adaline's feet stumble over each other, her mons anticipating each time he'll sneak in and firmly press her throbbing nub, massaging it subtly but forcefully, the microscopic movements making her heart race and lips moist. He turns her diagonally away from the passing crowd and wedges his thigh between her legs again.

"This is so not fair." Her hips rock against him on their own accord. "I'm going to get you for this, I promise."

"I can't wait," he says, his voice gravelly. He takes a bigger step that lifts her up and brings her down again. "Just ride the high, my love."

With her hand on his chest, she grabs his T-shirt, her nails scratching his skin through the thin fabric. As the pressure between her legs builds, her cheeks flush. Her breath hitches. Her shorts rub her in all the right places. He lowers his cheek beside hers, hiding her from the crowd.

He pushes her up the ramp again, and she buries her face in his neck, inhaling his scent. Letting go of the railing, he grabs her ass with one hand, digs his fingers into her round bottom, and bends his knee. With one long thrust, he grinds the length of his thigh against her and holds her in place as she shudders against him, her gasps swallowed by the ride operator announcing their arrival.

In a daze, Adaline follows Ëólas to her seat, her heart pounding, her legs wobbly. She squirms under the harness, pushing against it to check its security. Their seats dip backward, and the night sky locks into place straight ahead. The clouds have become waves, their silhouettes outlined by moonlight.

"Oh my god, oh my god, oh my god." Adaline grips the harness so tightly that her knuckles burn. "I'm never going to forgive you for—"

Their screams stay behind them as the ride hurls them into the air. The instantaneous launch presses all her organs into her back as if she's fallen into a juicer. The wind presses the sides of her cheeks downward, but her unbridled laughter mingles with Ëólas's so much so that she's not sure where her delirium starts and his ends. Just when she thinks they're about to continue into orbit, the seat flips them over their heads twice, twisting the lights below into a kaleidoscope, until they freefall downward, her organs now jostled loose, and they bounce a few more times on the tension wire.

"That's not so bad," Ëólas says as they dangle over the carnival below.

Able to peel her head away from the headrest, Adaline looks between her feet at the city surrounding them. The flashing fairgrounds, steady stream of headlights, and the lit far-off buildings look like stars, as if the world has flipped upside down. With the wind and the distance hushing the chaos of the world below, the sky feels like another home.

"Now this," Adaline says breathlessly, "is magical."

Ëólas holds her hand, his eyes twinkling with adrenaline. "Will you forgive me?"

"After I get payback, definitely."

The arms of the slingshot slowly rise, lowering them down to reality. When they walk down the platform to the ride's exit, Dax and Cindy run over.

"Dude," Dax shouts, "that looked awful!"

"Your hair's crazy fantastic." Cindy brushes downward the loose strands that have formed a lion's mane around Adaline's hair line.

As the four of them walk to their cars and Dax invites them to Renn Fest next month, Adaline's shoulder blades twitch as if someone were drilling a small hole into her spine. She pauses and looks back at the entrance gates, but the night swallows the carnival bit by bit, concealing within its jaws the lights, the sounds, the smells, and anything else within.

"Are you okay?" Ëólas asks again.

"Yeah, just tired," Adaline says.

They traipse through the tall grass, toward the headlights that chirp and blink every time she presses the lock button on the key fob. With the fun behind them and the darkness ahead, she can't help but wonder if her guilt's caught up with her. During the two months they've been gone, she's popped back to New Leira only four times and only for a moment to make certain time isn't progressing quickly. Knowing Magnus is still eating breakfast has eased both her and Ëólas's fear about not having enough time to train. But removing that pressure spawned a different consequence: Maryland makes hiding too easy.

Chapter Fourteen

A Lesson

Stepping into Nan's grand foyer, Adaline sets down two suitcases and her backpack on the marble flooring. She's still not used to the silence that greets her, but with Ëólas here, that will change again. Taking a deep breath, she rolls her bags to the side and holds the door open as Ëólas carries in six bags of groceries and disappears into the kitchen. She heads back out to grab more items, her life in reverse from the last time her father helped her move her belongings out.

Once they put away the groceries, Adaline leads Ëólas upstairs to the largest guest room. She can't bring him into her childhood room with stuffed animals lining the shelved walls and her pink comforter, and she's not ready to claim one of the master bedrooms as her own. Not even Nan touched Eddie's room.

With alternative music playing in the background, they fill the drawers with their clothes—well, partially. Adaline couldn't bring herself to pack up her entire wardrobe, considering she conveniently didn't have enough boxes. On her nightstand, she sets down a framed selfie of Ëólas hugging her from behind with Great Falls cascading behind them.

Looking at the photo, Adaline glows. *It really was the best summer ever.*

Creating a mirror image, Ëólas walks around the king-sized bed and hugs her from behind. "Did you remember to set aside your work laptop and badge for tomorrow?"

She falls into his warmth and folds her hands over his. "Yep. Thanks for the reminder." Twisting around, she brushes her lips against his. He still tastes like this morning's blueberry muffin.

"Mmm," he growls. "I'd rather have you for lunch."

She playfully thwacks his arm but hugs him tightly around his torso, resting her cheek below his collarbone. Her momentary gaiety slips away like the leaves that will soon fall from the trees.

Pressing his lips to her forehead, he lingers there for a long moment and tucks her hair behind her ear, tracing his finger along the round curve. "How about I go start lunch?"

"Oh. Without me?"

"I think I can manage a salad and turkey sandwich." He locks eyes with her, telling her everything will be okay, that he won't be far away should one of them need the other.

When he leaves, Adaline glances down the hallway, first toward Nan's room and then her dad's. *Left or right?* She already searched Nan's room once, granted not thoroughly, given the doozy she found in that trunk. Running her fingers through her hair, she meanders down the hallway, letting her gut lead the way. Slowly, she pushes the door open and steps inside.

This is just like digging through ruins or a library for information. That's all.

She chooses her dad's desk first, rifling through the papers on top. In the bottom drawer, she pulls out a field guide much like Henry Jones's grail journal, her father having filled the pages with religious artifacts and magical items, some of them grouped according to the elements. Other pages highlight ancient wiccan rituals and natural ingredient combinations with their connections to the six pillars.

Dad's research on how to get home.

She sets that aside and pulls out a second guidebook, but when she flips the cover over, a sketch of her mother's face stares back at her. Adaline sucks in her breath and hugs the book to her chest. After grounding herself, she flips quickly through the book, but every page is another sketch of her mother's face from different angles. Perfect replicas of the woman Adaline left behind. She snaps the book shut, rests her hand on the cover for a few heartbeats, and carefully returns the leather-bound reminder to its resting place inside the drawer.

Rather than unearthing more ghosts, Adaline heads downstairs to the kitchen where Ëólas rinses the lettuce and adds the torn leaves to the salad spinner. She kisses his cheek and goes outside through the backdoor and onto the flagstone patio facing the lake. The buzz of motorboats announces family and friends returning to their docks so they can ignite their grills, and the neighborhood echoes a lyrical laughter that punctuates the end of summer.

Walking over to the flowerbeds, Adaline sits on the retaining wall. The snapdragons are still in full bloom, a rainbow of pinks, yellows, and violets. She brushes her fingers over the petals. Touching her fingertips to the dry soil, she closes her eyes as she searches for the link between her and the earth. In New Leira, the link had been instantaneous—when her life was on the line. She needed only to ask for help.

Stretching her fingers wide, she extends her hand over the soil. "Please?"

Nothing. No bond. No soil rolling over itself. Not even a tingle in her palms.

"Oh, come on. You've got to be in there somewhere." She waves her hand back and forth as if she can magically swish the tether between them into existence. "My name is Adaline, and I'm a half-elf. That sounds weird to say aloud. Whatever. I might also be partially fae." She sounds like she's recording an intro video for a dating website.

Grunting loudly, she drops her hand, her palm hitting the retaining wall with a thump. *What made the difference in New Leira?* Everything happened so quickly; she didn't have time to record the process or analyze the steps.

Rolling her shoulders, she flings her hair behind her back, away from her face. *Okay, you can do this Adaline.*

She tries again, talking to the earth, digging her hands into the garden bed, but the soil remains motionless, a lump of dormant dirt. Maybe she was right; this world lost its connection to the magic of creation. Or maybe her dad was right, that growing up here killed a portion of her elven side. Then again, it could be her fault. Not once in the last two months has she attempted connecting with the elements.

But it's not like she's forgotten her friends or her mission or her duties. She wanted just a bit of time to celebrate her marriage, to focus on the best part of her life right now, to enjoy life. Is it so wrong to allow herself to indulge every now and again? How else is she supposed to find the strength to keep going, especially after all the craziness that happened in Aerytol? She's finally happy again, after spending almost three years mourning her family. No, not family. Mourning strangers who kept secrets. All those garage family jam sessions, late-night stories read aloud, conversations while rolling out pastry dough—those memories feel cheaper now.

They should have trusted me with the truth.

Adaline hangs her head. *Fuck. I have to tell Cindy.*

With a loud huff, she stands up and dusts off her hands. *That's enough, Adaline. Guessing games and berating myself won't help anyone. Deep breath. Exhale slowly. Good.*

She glances at the house's honey-colored stone-built exterior, at Ëólas's silhouette moving back and forth in the kitchen, at the evergreens that have watched over her since the first time she moved here. Last, her eyes fall on the floor-to-ceiling windows that belong to the library.

"Okay," she says to herself, shoving her hands in her pockets.

If her family left her zero information about fae and magic, that's alright. She'll figure this out—because research is her thing.

After lunch, Adaline and Ëólas trot downstairs and stop between two doors opposite each other. Glancing left, Adaline frowns. Ëólas steps forward to open the door, but she takes his wrist, opens the door to the right, and pulls him inside her father's home gym that could house eight cars.

Leaning the canvas-wrapped parcel against the wall, Ëólas flips the switch by the door, and the overhead canned lights blink awake. Across from them and above a workbench, a row of ten hopper windows squeezes daylight into the gigantic room, along with the promise of greenery that awaits them outdoors.

Blue gym mats conceal most of the hardwood floor. A treadmill, rowing machine, elliptical, and other exercise equipment line the wall to their right.

"What is all this?" Ëólas asks.

Adaline explains the bigger equipment first and then points to the free weights. "The kettlebell and dumbbells are for strength training."

Ëólas whistles long and low. "Nice set up."

"Don't you have weights back home?" Adaline waggles her eyebrows at the lean muscles under his shirt.

"I have something similar to the kettlebell, but that's about it. Most of my training included pushups, pull ups, weighted swords, tree climbing."

"I'll have to thank the trees."

To their left, metal cabinets line an entire wall, each containing her father's sporting equipment, power tools, and household maintenance items. Of the seven, two have chunky combination locks.

"Huh." Adaline walks over to a middle cabinet and touches the spin dial. "I don't recall these." She flips up the lock to examine the backside. *At least he got the kind with a master key.*

"Do you know how to open them?" Ëólas unwraps the parcel and rests his collection of swords on the bench next to the water cooler.

Crossing her arms over her chest, she eyes the locks as if they were cockroaches. "I have no idea. But now I'm dying to know what my dad's hidden back there. Probably more secrets."

What's the chance that it's spell books or something?

Adaline grabs the step stool wedged in the corner, climbs up the steps, and feels the top of the cabinets with her fingertips. Finding nothing, she pushes the stool away and lies on her belly, scraping her hand along the underside of the cabinets and floor. Still nothing. When Ëólas angles the cabinet away from the wall, Adaline discovers a key taped to the backside.

"Ha!" She unlocks the first cabinet, her heart tingling and her gut tumbling upside down. Swinging the door open, she scowls at the various hand saws, tile saws, and other sharp equipment a parent might lock up.

How ordinary.

She tries the other cabinet, but the key doesn't work on its lock, so Ëólas moves the cabinets aside again but to no avail.

"Alright. Let me try." Ëólas takes the lock in hand and whispers a few words of Elvish. Nothing happens.

She cocks an eyebrow. "You gonna start teaching me enchantments?"

"Ah, yes." He steps aside, holding the lock out to her. When she takes hold of it, he wraps his fingers around hers. "I wish I had something fancier to offer you, but I'm merely asking the metal to unlatch in Elvish. Repeat after me."

With a perfect pronunciation and the sudden realization that her father taught her some Elvish in Alderton, Adaline repeats, "Elsortá, umné meinar," which literally means *please, unlock metal*. But not even the two of them can convince the lock to give way. "Maybe Dad enchanted it too?"

"Who knows? To be fair though, I'm not particularly effective with metal. I'm better with fibers and wood."

"Huh."

While he tries the enchantment again, Adaline stalks across the room and returns with a fifteen-pound dumbbell.

"Ah." Ëólas accepts her gift and smashes the lock while Adaline stands back and cups her ears. When the lock and metal latch clang to the ground, Ëólas puts down the weight and yanks open the now dented door, revealing a collection of swords that belong on a movie set or in a museum.

"Dang." Adaline aches to touch each one, but not for training purposes. She'd rather catalog and date them.

"Lovely." Ëólas withdraws each one to examine its weight, length, balance, and sharpness. Reaching into the back, he pulls out a thick stick as long as Adaline's arm and hands it to her. "This will be perfect for sparring."

"Won't Merith be offended?" She points at the bench holding the swords from New Leira. "He picked out such a nice collection."

Ëólas shrugs.

She swings the somewhat flexible rattan stick a few times and frowns. "*Now* you're letting me use a practice weapon when you were okay with me accidentally maiming you or myself back in New Leira?"

"We didn't have time for toys back then. You needed to carry weapons on your person immediately, which meant you needed to know how to use them immediately. *Now* that we have time, I can train you properly." Ëólas selects another rattan stick for himself and twirls it beside him, his gaze focused, his tone firm, his muscles flexed. "This is light enough for you to focus on developing muscle memory during sparring. We'll use the steel swords to work on your stances and movements and to build up your strength."

Damn, he's hot in work mode. Taking two steps forward, Adaline rises onto her toes and aims her lips at his.

Before their skin connects, he walks around her and takes five steps back. "First rule in this room, our lips do not touch each other. Anywhere. Even when you're being sweet."

"Pfft, fine." *For the record, rejection hurts no matter the circumstances.* She leans over to pick up her stick, and Ëólas uses his to smack her ass, making her cheeks vibrate and core tingle. With a yelp, she jumps up and jabs the training weapon at his chest. "No frisky hands, um, or sticks either."

Ëólas raises both hands in defeat, his stick pointing at the ceiling. "Fair point."

The chime of Adaline's phone calls a timeout. Hugging the stick beneath her armpit while Ëólas rolls his eyes, she pulls her phone out and checks her texts. "Okay, Cindy and Dax are going to meet us here next weekend, *after* training."

"Is that when you plan to tell her the truth—and that we need her help?"

This weekend. In a few days. The big conversation. Adaline scrunches her nose. "Maybe? We'll see how it goes."

"What about that we're married?" He wiggles his fingers, flashing his wedding band that he never takes off—except for when they hang out with Cindy and Dax.

"Yeah, that will be an interesting conversation. 'Hey, you know how you waited a decade for Dax to propose? Well, I got married in a day.' Cindy will love that."

Putting away the rattan sticks, Ëólas hands Adaline the sword he gave her, chooses one for himself, and backs up to the center of the gym. "Maybe *not* phrase it that way?"

"Probably." She tosses her phone onto the bench by the door, next to Merith's sword collection, and joins Ëólas in the center, the blue mat squelching beneath her bare toes.

Nothing about this is weird or uncomfortable. There's no reason for her chest to feel tight and her eyes to drift toward the exit. She's merely working from home with her husband. They're coworkers, after all. The gym is their shared office. As for this sword, it's nothing more than a dancing prop, and the moves she's about to practice are new choreography. She's good at that. Excellent, actually.

She slides her right foot back and centers her weight between her hips that face forward. Gripping the hilt with one hand, she raises it behind the same shoulder. "First attack, right?"

When Ëólas nods, she swings diagonally across her body, practicing her forehand strike. Without stopping her momentum, she swings the sword beside her, bringing it up and over her opposite shoulder, and cuts diagonally in front of herself again with a backhand strike to complete the X pattern.

Ëólas nods as he walks around her, eyeing her body without a hint of lust. She resets and repeats the same move one hundred times, looking nowhere but ahead and letting her muscles memorize the flow while she resists the urge to elongate her neck and limbs—the opposite of dancing. She needs to ground her weight so she's stable and harder to knock over.

"One more time," Ëólas says, both of them allowing for nothing less than perfection.

He sounds like Ms. Weaver during private ballet lessons. Always one more time. Enhance those lines. Strong arms. Strong legs. But sword practice doesn't care much for elegant lines. Precision, yes. Elegance, not so much. Then again, Ëólas displayed finesse when fighting Āranol.

Huh.

Adaline runs through a few more positions, disconnecting motion from thought, until her growling stomach brings her back to the gym. Even then, they don't stop. Instead of Ëólas fussing over her comfort, he swaps the swords for rattan sticks and positions himself in front of her. He strikes fast and hard. Watching his movements, she anticipates the attack and blocks, but his stick slides down the backside of her own and strikes her shoulder. He yanks upward to soften the blow, but the reed snaps her skin and stings, bringing tears to her eyes.

Damn it. He taught her how to avoid that months ago. But she forgot.

They go again. When Adaline can no longer ignore the small muscle convulsing between her wrist and forearm, Ëólas passes her the steel sword again. She lasts not even five minutes before her perfect stance transforms into mushy arms holding a droopy blade. As her arms drop to her sides, her eyes fall to the blue mat.

"Enough for today." Even at the end, he keeps his tone objective, distant, unfeeling. "We'll focus on those weights tomorrow."

He takes her sword and returns it to the broken cabinet. As they leave the gym, he switches off the lights and shuts the door behind them. Then he places his hand on her damp backside and kisses her cheek. "Much better," he says, his voice soothing.

But a far cry from where I need to be.

She pushes back the thoughts creeping to the forefront of her mind, that she's so damn young and inexperienced and liable to get him killed on the battlefield—for a war she insisted on joining.

In the kitchen, Adaline opens a package of Oreos and stuffs her mouth. Ëólas retrieves glasses from the cupboards and fills both with water from the fridge. Per usual, he whispers his enchantment over the glasses to purify the water. Never mind the fridge's filter. To be fair, the water tastes better when he's done.

I'll ask him to teach me that one later. Then again, it's probably something simple, like water be clean.

After she chuckles to herself, she stares into the bottom of her drink, at the miniature bubbles adhering to the side of the glass. *But I'd need a relationship with water to make it work.*

An image of her mother sinking below the ocean's surface floods her mind.

She looks away from the glass, but her eyes land on the backdoor and the lake in the distance. With a groan, she takes a sip of water, the glass shaking in her exhausted hand. As she tilts her head backward to finish her drink, she can feel Ëólas's warm gaze on her. "What?"

"Nothing." Ëólas kisses her lips, Oreo crumbs and all. "Ooh. May I try one?"

"What's mine is yours and yours is mine." She pushes the package toward him, the plastic crinkling across the countertop.

After he eats one and his eyebrows jump, he takes three more and carries the package into the foyer. She's going to have to warn him against junk food. Then again, his genes might guarantee his own perfect packaging.

Spinning off her stool, she follows him upstairs. "I'm going to take a shower." *Do elves not sweat? I couldn't inherit that?*

They part ways at the top of the stairs. "Okay, I'll be in the den. You mind if I get a head start on *Back to the Future*?"

"Nope. Enjoy."

She pecks him on the cheek and heads to their bedroom where she hops in the shower. As the water cascades down her body, erasing the evidence of today's trials, she presses her forehead against the cool tile and closes her eyes. Quiet moments like these are the worst, when she can't turn off or shut out the voices that haunt her, including her own.

Chapter Fifteen

THE FIRE

After a week of returning to work, Adaline clacks away on her keyboard, pausing in between emails to admire Ëólas, who's leaning back in a chair on the opposite side of her desk, his legs extended in front of him and crossed at the ankles, while he continues reading Geertz's *The Interpretation of Cultures*. Every so often, he furrows his brow and scrunches his nose.

With the semester underway, they've easily fallen into a new routine with Adaline teaching classes, holding office hours, and playing the role of the good professor during the day while Ëólas explores D.C. a little at a time, sits in on different classes and lectures taught by the other professors he's charmed, or keeps her company on campus. In the evening, they return to Nan's house where he drills her for hours until her arms have nothing left to give. His relentless training has also made their love making rather one sided, even though Ëólas insists he's fine doing most of the work while she cries with relief. Granted, he crawls into bed satiated too.

"Alright!" Ëólas suddenly sits up straight. "I can't figure out this word. What's la-oog-ha? La-ow-guh?"

Adaline crinkles her nose. "I have no idea. Spell it?" When he does, she snorts. "That's *laugh*."

Ëólas rests the book on his lap and looks at her with a deadpan stare. "That's utterly preposterous. Why would you ever spell *laff* any other way?"

"I'm sorry. Would you like an etymology lesson? It's rather fascinating, not that it'll help with spelling lessons."

"Next time," he grumbles, burying his nose in the book, determined to press on.

Adaline responds to three more student emails, her forearms still throbbing from last night's lessons. When she scrolls to the top, she has an unopened email from the Grump to the entire department about their findings. She hovers her mouse over the subject line, "Promising results," but doesn't click it.

Ëólas peeks over his book. "You look nervous."

She falls backward into her chair. "A bit. I'm just not sure how we're going to publish a research paper about the cave site while also making sure we shut down access to it."

"Anything we can do?"

"Prove that the dig site comes from another world and that alternate worlds and realms do in fact exist?"

Ëólas arches an eyebrow. "Would we fear an invasion?"

"Maybe. Definitely from the Russians. They like stealing creatures from other worlds. Add *Stranger Things* to your watch list."

Reaching into his back pocket, Ëólas pulls out his mobile and taps away at the screen. "Done."

They snicker at each other and return to their current projects until Ëólas puts the book down. "I can't pretend to read this any longer. Forgive me. I'd find the topic much more stimulating when you speak about it with gusto and passion, particularly when you bounce in your seat and smile oh so adorably."

Adaline chuckles. "I told you this would be boring!"

"I don't care. I love seeing you in your office, staring at that rectangular glowing box, and watching how your facial features change as you're typing. You're entertaining on your own."

"Okay, saying sweet things like that is going to distract me and make this take longer."

"Good."

"Ugh!" Adaline tosses her wallet at Ëólas. "My stomach's growling. Do you mind grabbing me something from the dining hall? It's the same one we went to for coffee this morning. I don't care what you bring back, so long as it has carbs. Lots of carbs."

"Sure. I'd like to try this myself." Ëólas picks up her small purple wallet, pops open the snap, and stares at the colorful plastic cards. "Which one of these has your dining dollars?"

Taking back her wallet, she pulls out the card with AU's blue and red logo and hands it to Ëólas. "You've got this."

When he leaves, she clicks on the Grump's email and reads his assessment of the weekend, which doesn't mention Adaline's absence and focuses on Beccah's soil and mineral findings. Adaline thumps her fingers on her desk while she rereads his email for the fourth time. Unfortunately for the team, they went home frustrated and more confused than ever about the site's inexplicable origins.

Adaline closes her laptop and rotates in her chair so she can look out the window at the small parking lot below and the sidewalks that lead in different directions. The few students and staff walking past her building continue along their own journeys, whether or not they like it. One student seems to have made a wrong turn and spins around a few times before choosing a different direction. Did she choose her destination, or did the curriculum requirements force her to go elsewhere?

A knock on Adaline's open door startles her, and she whirls around, her feet tripping over the chair's wheels. Derek leans against the doorframe, his steel-gray eyes locked on her. She grabs her desk to stop her chair from spinning.

"Hey." He waits for Adaline to speak.

"Hi." She feels like a dog trapped in its kennel. "Um, what's going on?"

"I was passing by. Thought I'd find you here. I just wanted to take the initiative and avoid a future awkward moment on campus." With a sigh, Derek shuffles his feet into her office and takes Ëólas's seat. He slouches in the chair, making the pens sticking out of his front shirt pocket poke his chest, and he thumps his heel on the carpet. "We were colleagues, friends, for years. I hope that's not completely gone."

Adaline bites her bottom lip and drops her shoulders. They had been friends first, even when she was still a student and he was her father's colleague. Their close age had made them fast friends as they discussed ancient history during long lunches, attended guest lectures together, and quoted films they'd rank by historical accuracy and believability. "Thanks, Derek."

God, I really didn't do right by him.

"It's all good." He tosses his hand away as if everything's forgotten, even the sangria that soaked into his favorite shirt. "You're doing okay?"

"I am, thanks." *Aside from the major guilt trip I'm having right now.*

"Good, good. I'm glad." He runs his hand through his dark hair. "I, uh, heard your research didn't go the way you planned. Sorry to hear that."

"It's okay. It all worked out for the best." *For you too. You deserve someone who loves you as much as I love Ëólas.*

"Cool. Well, there we have it: Awkwardness out of the way." He gives her a thumbs up.

When she laughs, he taps his hands on his thighs five times like a drumroll, then pulls himself up to standing. His knee bumps her desk, making her monitor rattle, and the picture of her and Ëólas in front of the Washington Monument falls over the edge and tumbles to the ground.

"Oh, shit. I'm sorry." Derek moves to dash around her desk, but she holds up her hand to stop him.

"It's okay. It's fine." She rests the photo on her desk, face down.

Standing opposite her, he scratches his permanent stubble. "Okay, then. I guess I'll see you around."

"Yeah, see you around." Rising from her chair, Adaline walks him to the door and holds it wide open. *I really hope you find the person meant for you.*

"Can I just ask you something?" When Adaline nods, he rests his hand on the doorknob. "I just, uh, I don't get it. I thought things were finally progressing. And then you cut me out, and I'm sure you have your reasons, but I was just wondering if you could help me understand what I did wrong?"

The door may as well have crushed her heart, until she remembers Derek spooning her, his arms crushing her waist, as he whispered he loved her while she hid her tears in his pillow. He never noticed how hollow she felt, not when those feelings pertained to their relationship. But, like Ëólas said, she's excellent at burying her true feelings.

Beyond the hem of her summer dress, Adaline stares at her toes poking out of her wedge sandals. "You didn't do anything wrong, Derek. I wasn't honest with myself, or you."

Clicking her thumbs together, she tries to ground herself, but the carpet and cement don't respond the way the streets of New Leira do. The building leaves her feeling cold and abandoned, much like how she made Derek feel at the end of their relationship. "I just didn't—"

"Maybe you're not being honest with yourself now?"

As Adaline looks up, Derek pushes the door shut and presses his lips against hers, his hands gripping her bare arms, his stubble scraping her mouth, his peppermint scent clogging her senses. He pushes her backward until her shoulders touch the wall and prods at her lips with the tip of his tongue.

Someone other than Ëólas is kissing me. That thought, repeating a million times a second, locks her muscles in place while her heart speeds up so rapidly that she fears she might explode any second.

Once again, Derek found her weak spot and wormed his way inside. Did she make a mistake and lead him on again? No, damn it. Not once did she tell him she wanted him back, that she loved him. In fact, she told him point blank at the restaurant that it was over; she couldn't have been more direct. But he only ever hears what he wants to hear, and somehow he made her feel sorry for him, as if she were the bad guy. But he's the asshole who's cornered her in her office under the guise of friendship and forced his tongue inside her mouth. Only one person's allowed to touch her intimately. Only one.

You fucking shithead!

Rage and indignation radiate through her veins and down her arms, pooling into her shaking hands. Like a flash fire, her palms ignite their own flames, burning holes through Derek's polo and scorching his chest as she shoves him away. She squeezes her fists shut, and the blaze disappears instantly, while Derek yowls and stumbles backward, crossing his arms over his chest, only to briefly touch his blistering skin and cringe. Singed fabric and flesh fill the office.

He looks down in disbelief, tears staining his cheeks, and Adaline seizes that moment to dash to her desk and grab the letter opener. When his glossy eyes search for the weapon Adaline used to burn him, the ordinary yet sharp object in her hand confuses him.

"Get out of my office!" Gagging at the taste of him on her tongue, she wipes her mouth with the back of her hand, stalks toward him, and raises the letter opener level with this face. "If you ever touch me again, I will cut those lips off your face and shove them down your throat so that you choke on them."

Derek staggers out of her office, his eyes wide, his face pale, his pants wet down the front. He takes one last look at her, as though he just discovered a demon, and bolts down the hallway.

Oh my god. What? How?

She stares at the empty doorway for a long while, waving off a coworker who peeks out of his office to make sure everything's okay. With the adrenaline draining out of her, she backs up until she hits the wall and slides down onto her bottom, the letter opener toppling out of her hand and onto the carpet. She studies her palms, her fingers shaking uncontrollably. The flames are gone, for now.

Ãranol's words careen to the forefront of her mind: *You're trouble, that's what you are. Human aggression mixed with immortal blood? You must be terrifying when you're angry. You'll end us all.*

"Oh god," she whispers to herself. "What have I done?"

Pulling her legs to her chest, she wraps her arms around her shins, locking her dress in place, and buries her head in her knees until the damp fabric clings to her thighs, and a set of warm hands rests on her shoulders.

"Adaline?" Ëólas asks, his voice quiet, cautious.

When she lifts her head, the concern on his face is palpable. Of course he felt her fear, her rage. Did he sense someone else kissing his other half?

"I wanted to kill him." Her voice sounds so small, but she knows Ëólas can hear her. "I was going to. I didn't care."

"Who?"

"Derek."

Ëólas looks behind him. For a body? Getting up, he scans the hallway, left and right, then shuts and locks the door. He crouches beside her, his eyes turning dark yellow and his calm exterior dropping away as he snatches the letter opener like a dagger. "Did he hurt you? I'll kill him myself, I swear. I won't give him the chance to get near you again."

Adaline shakes her head. "It was me. I hurt him."

He glances at the door again. Grinding his teeth, he sets the letter opener on her desk, next to two fresh cups of coffee and four swollen paper bags, and sits down next to her. She folds herself into him, hugging his side, tucking her legs between his, and laying her head beneath his chin. As he rubs circles into her back, her tear falls onto his light-green cotton shirt.

"I'm certain whatever you did, he deserved it," Ëólas whispers.

"No." *Ëólas is willing to kill people who hurt me, but who will stop me from hurting others?* "Don't you see what Āranol was getting at? All those centuries ago, Morgán didn't destroy Aerytol because my dad would fall in love with my mom. He did it to prevent *my* birth. He decimated an entire kingdom, killed all those people, and created the Wastelands because of me. I'm the reason the borders shut down, why you were trapped in Lameiría, why those humans in the Wastelands—"

"Stop." He combs her hair away from her damp cheeks. "You didn't make Morgán do anything. He made those choices. He was—"

"Afraid of me, of what I might do." She shows Ëólas her palms, which have returned to their typical olive hue. "Fire came out of my hands. I, I could have burned Derek alive."

With his mind probably racing, he cups her hand and kisses the palm. "You and I were meant to be. You were meant to be. I don't give a damn what Morgán thinks."

His curse startles her. "Ëólas?"

"Fire isn't evil, Adaline. It warms the home, gives us light, and brings us together." He locks his golden eyes with hers. "Just like you."

She throws her arms around his neck and buries her face in his soft hair, inhaling his scent and letting the ache in her heart dissipate, not completely but enough that she can breathe more easily. *What would I do without you?*

After he holds her for a long time, he helps her pack up her laptop and papers into her satchel. Before they leave her office, he takes her hand and asks, "Would you please tell me one thing? Are you afraid of what Derek will do next?"

She remembers him scrambling away from her, his eyes wide with terror, his khakis stained with urine. "No." *I'm afraid of me.*

A few weeks later, while Ëólas measures dimensions for the gym's new sword cabinet, Adaline meanders into Nan's room. Despite the stacks of books and notes she's collected from her father's and the public library regarding magic from various cultures, she can't ignore the possibility that Nan's room might hold more personal, more specific clues.

Closing the door, Adaline tucks her hands behind her back, her fingers still wrapped around the knob that connects her to the rest of the house. Nan's bed dominates the room, its presence casting a shadow across the length of the floor. She half expects to find Nan in bed, all life drained from her in the night.

Did Nan actually find peace, even though she never had the chance to go home?

Adaline peels her fingers off the satin nickel knob and searches through Nan's dresser under the windows on the opposite side of the room. The drawers screech open, protesting their rights to keep their secrets. After fumbling through Nan's delicates, she takes out each stack of sweaters and feels around, checking the grooves along the back and sides. Not finding anything, she returns the sweaters to their designated spots, except for the white knit cardigan Nan wore during the summer, especially when they took the rowboat out on the lake. The breeze made Nan's cardigan flutter at her sides like flower petals. Adaline's arms slide effortlessly into the soft, light-weight fabric. The bottom drawer contains mostly sleepwear, sweatpants, and a collection of anti-slip socks.

A chime from her phone makes her pause, and her shoulders sag at a lunch invitation from Cindy. Without responding, she puts her phone away. *Later. I promise.*

Next, Adaline checks the closet, scanning the floor, which Nan kept surprisingly clean, and the various decorative boxes on the top shelves. Aside from hats, scarves, belts, and other accessories, one box contains old photographs of Nan and Eddie in the seventies, both sporting bell bottoms and their hair parted down the middle, falling past their waists. The further she digs through the photos, she finds them in London at Trafalgar Square, China at the Great Wall, and Egypt in front of the Great Pyramid. Their clothing changes from bell bottoms to poodle skirts to flapper garb. Adaline sets aside that box, intending to bring it to her room.

Next, she kneels in front of the nightstand. The only items of interest are the crafts Adaline brought home from school, including the butterfly magnet she made with a clothespin, some pipe cleaners, and her face glued onto a red button, her two front teeth missing.

The second nightstand houses a stack of hefty photo albums—one primarily of her and Nan together. She flips through the pages, looking for a letter, a note, a message but finds nothing, only photos of them throughout the years. Adaline picks up the album and photo box, takes one last look at the room, and closes the door behind her.

At least she's not leaving empty-handed.

By the time she steps barefoot onto the patio, lightning bugs blink on and off throughout the backyard. The bench swing creaks as Ëólas rocks back and forth, his long toes pressing into the decking. When Adaline approaches, he halts the bench mid-swing. She sits beside him, and his feet push off again. The phone she gave him rests on the table next to him, face down.

Did he forget to charge it again?

She smiles to herself and leans against him, pulling her legs up onto the bench and tucking them beside her. "Whatcha doing?" she asks quietly so not to disturb the hush of twilight.

"Enjoying a quiet moment." He drapes one arm around her shoulder, allowing her to snuggle closer.

She follows a single firefly, trying to guess the next location in which his light will appear. When he disappears into the darkness of night, she wriggles a few times to get more comfortable. Her arms feel like melted marshmallows from Ëólas's relentless instruction, not that he's indicated if he's disappointed or pleased with her progress.

His hand slides down the length of her arm and falls onto her waist. "What's on your mind?"

She waits for the stars to show themselves, but the city lights illuminate the atmosphere, keeping the stars at bay. "Are you happy here?"

He looks at her but says nothing, which makes Adaline fidget with her nails. Taking her hand, he rubs his thumb over the cuticles she attacked. "I have wanted to travel my entire life. And here I am. In another world. With my other half. I've never been happier. I'm like you, a traveler at heart."

"But you look sad. Or bored."

His laugh makes all the fireflies light up at once, as if they recognize his innate connection to nature. "You're not used to seeing me be still."

"That's true." She takes a portion of his hair and combs her fingers through the silky texture. "I found nothing useful in Nan's room, not even a book of shadows or something."

"What's a book of shadows?"

"A magic book for witches."

"You're not a witch, my love. You're a human-elf-maybe-fae connected to the creation of life."

"Then what's the difference between enchantments and spells?"

Ëólas rocks the bench swing again. "Our enchantments are nothing impressive. They just make life more convenient, but we're limited to evoking one element at a time, should it choose to help us."

That's basically what Élara said. "Like asking the fire to not burn down our treehouse?"

"Mmm-hmm. Or asking our bathwater to remain hot, or the air to not touch our food so it remains fresh, or the earth to increase our crops. Spells are merely a string of more precise words that help us to better connect with the elements, to more accurately convey our intentions."

"But I don't know what words to use."

"Maybe you don't need them, or maybe those words will come to you naturally when the time is right, when you're ready."

Fuck that. "I can't keep relying on instinct. Look what I did to Derek. I terrified him. He saw me across the quad yesterday and knocked over a group of students as he ran away from me."

"I can't pretend I'm disappointed to hear that," Ëólas murmurs. "Look, you have strong instincts. I'm certain you'll figure this out, but I don't think you can force this, my love. I know this pains you, but try to be patient."

Ugh. "Noted." Adaline leaps off the bench, her research-filled notebooks and textbooks calling to her. She should grade papers, but those can wait one more day. "I'll be in the library."

After she kisses him goodnight, she marches into the house. As much as she'd love to stay with him and unwind, she can't go easy on herself, not until she understands her magic, not until she can control her fire. Otherwise, they'll be stuck in limbo forever.

Chapter Sixteen

A Different Angle

Letting go of the world around her, Adaline repeats every move Ëólas has taught her thus far, flowing from thrust to block like she's performing another dance routine. The sword is an extension of herself, a prop she uses to tell a different story that still requires accuracy, timing, and focus. When Ëólas choreographs a new combination, Adaline practices it until her muscles ache so intensely that she can no longer lift her weapon. Then she has him massage away the pain so she can go again. And again. Not because he's pushing her but because she needs to burn away her feelings, her doubt, her frustration.

Her arms are stronger and her self-defense skills more defined, but her magic—zip, zero, zilch. She's struggling to open her chakras, and her yoga instructor says that could take months. Her research into the Chinese wuxing system has been fascinating, especially its focus on the vital essence of an element rather than its physical form and substance, but that hasn't yielded any recordable results. And every spell she tried from *Green-Thumb Magic* failed.

That book was all about tapping into the power of nature with herbs, plants, and crystals—everything that Lorien uses and that I've done, combined. Come on! What the hell's wrong with me?

When she and Ëólas finish sparring, she places the rattan stick on its rack and rotates her arm socket to loosen her stiff muscles. He hands her a damp towel that she drapes around her neck and scrubs the sweat off her face. Before following him upstairs, she pauses in front of the opposite door and stares at the knob. She looks away and takes the stairs two at a time.

After her shower, Adaline plops onto the stool at the kitchen island while Ëólas finishes making fried eggs and beans on toast. He hands her a tall glass of water first, then takes a seat beside her.

As she cuts into the eggs, the golden yolk runs into her toast. "Perfect."

"Hurrah. I've officially perfected my backstory." Despite his sarcasm, he gloats as if he's made a five-course meal.

They eat in silence, concentrating on using the toast to sop up the yolk and their forks to stack the beans, egg whites, and toast with each bite.

When she's finished her dinner, she twirls her fork over her empty plate. "You haven't said anything."

"About what?"

"About how I'm doing."

"Ah." He collects both their plates and puts them in the sink, rinsing the dried yolk off the dishes before it solidifies into glue. After drying his hands, he flips the dish towel decorated with Jack-o'-lanterns and bobblehead witches over his shoulder and leans against the sink, crossing his arms in front of his chest and one ankle over the other.

He looks at Adaline carefully, his lips pursed. "You've surprised me."

She peeks up, studying him through her lashes. "In what way?"

"At how well you remember everything, how quickly you learn, and how precise your movements are. I dare say your technique is flawless. We need to build up your arm strength a bit more, but you already have the skills. I'd swear you had decades of training. You're a natural, my love. You were born for this."

Adaline takes a sip of water, but the liquid balls up in the back of her mouth as if to choke her. Getting up, she opens the fridge and takes out a large stainless-steel bowl of freshly cut mangos, strawberries, and kiwi that she sets on the counter. The bright colors stare back at her, the red juice of the strawberries bleeding into the mango.

Born for this... That should be a good thing. The stronger I get, the more I can help.

After draping the dish towel over the drainboard, Ëólas sits beside her and plucks a slice of kiwi from the bowl. "I don't think we have these in Ellíum. Isn't that interesting, what little differences there are between these two worlds?"

"Yeah." She forces herself to swallow. Her stomach aches for more food, but her throat feels too tight for her to eat anymore.

How is he so calm, so unaffected by what we're doing here, so unbothered that I can't reach the elements here, so accepting of the idea that I could be dangerous?

"Are you alright?" He swivels sideways to get a better look at her.

"I'm fine."

Dragging his arm across the counter, he slides further into her peripheral vision until she finally looks at him. He's arched an eyebrow but waits for her to speak.

"Sorry. Habit." She pushes the fruit away from her and lays her palms on the cool white granite, its black and gold speckles competing for attention under the canned ceiling lights. "I just don't particularly relish the idea that I was born to kill people. It kinda proves Ãranol's point, don't you think? That I'm an agent of chaos."

"There is no way you're here to cause harm, my love."

"You have a biased opinion."

"So does Ãranol." His eyes fall to the chunk of pineapple he's pinched between his fingers, to the red-stained juice dripping down his hand, and the shadows of his unspoken thoughts darken his face. Before Adaline can ask him what's on his mind, he tosses the pineapple into his mouth and flashes her a bright smile. "But I have facts and what I've witnessed firsthand. He has stories, false ones at that."

Adaline sighs. *I'm glad I haven't let Ëólas down with my training, but I can't shake this feeling that I'm making the wrong kind of progress.*

No, no. That's not true. I can't be a burden—not to him, not to anyone. When she peeked in on Magnus this morning, he was halfway through breakfast, but more of the army has lined up—all those soldiers depending on her.

Shake it off, Adaline. "On a happier note, Doña Mariana's invited us for Thanksgiving dinner in a few weeks. I said I'd bake two pumpkin pies."

"Lovely. What's this holiday about? Do the children dress up for this one too?" Reaching into his back pocket, he pulls out his mobile and searches for details.

"Oh." She covers his screen with her hand, pushing his phone onto the counter. "Um, the history behind this holiday is rather controversial," *and may trigger intergenerational trauma for you,* "just so you know. But Cindy's family and I celebrate it like a harvest festival, as a time for family and friends—and a ton of food."

"I love a harvest festival. Are we going to hide pears for Cindy's sisters?"

"Huh?"

"You know, seek the fruit of life? It's a game. Never mind."

Tipping forward onto the edge of her seat, she kisses him tenderly. "We always have room for more traditions. Tell me about it, and I'm sure the girls will love it."

His eyes study her endearingly. "You know, you are extremely kissable. Thought you should know that."

What? Did...did he just use a cheesy pickup line on me? Adaline covers her mouth with her hand but still laughs. "Where did you hear *that?*"

"Yesterday, on campus. What's so funny?"

"Oh god. Be careful around the hormonal students. They'll corrupt you more than I have."

"You can corrupt me whenever you like."

"Except in the gym."

"Except in there." Ëólas waggles his brows, but before he can act on his thoughts, his phone vibrates on the counter, and he checks his messages. "Ah, while you and Cindy discuss bridesmaid details this weekend, Dax wants to play soccer with me. That's a sport, right?"

"Oh, crap. You have a lot of studying to do."

And just like that, her one comment thickens the atmosphere and settles like a boulder between them.

Ëólas scrubs his hand over his face. Resting his elbow on the counter, he massages the side of his head. "Alright. I'll get started on that." Pushing himself away from the counter, he spins around on his stool and slides off, returning the fruit to the fridge.

Adaline stares at his back as he washes the skillet and pot, his shoulder blades flexing as he scrubs vigorously. She loads the dishwasher, keeping her back to him, and they clean the rest of the kitchen in silence, moving around each other and avoiding eye contact.

When she hits the start button on the dishwasher, she hugs him from behind. Old spice has replaced his signature lavender and pine scent. "I'll tell her soon. I promise."

He turns off the water and dries his hands. "I know," he murmurs. Pulling her in front of him, he places his hands on the sink, locking her between his arms. He debates saying more but instead asks, "Are we still on for *A New Hope* tonight?"

"Definitely."

After a quick but firm kiss, he heads into the library to read *To Kill a Mockingbird* or research European football, while Adaline collects Nan's photo album from the counter and tucks it under her arm. Pushing the backdoor open, she steps onto the patio and sits on the swinging bench, pulling her legs onto the cushion and folding them crisscross. The sconces along the back of the house illuminate the flagstones, fighting back the edge of night.

Even though today had been unusually hot for early October, the crisp night air tells a different story, one filled with the smokey scent of a neighbor's firepit, the leaves rustling in the wind, and faint laughter originating from someone else's backyard. And yet the water lapping against the dock reminds Adaline of New Leira, when she'd spend hours at the Rialto Bridge, telling stories and making new friends. She misses home—the one that needs her.

The sudden loud snap of a branch makes Adaline sit up straighter and peer into the darkness beside her house. She holds her breath as she listens carefully. Not hearing anything for a long while, she returns her attention to Nan's collection of photos.

Man, get a grip, Adaline. Stop with the paranoia.

Rocking her torso forward and backward, she gets the swing moving and rests the album on her legs. On the faux-leather plum cover, she traces the embossed cursive capital A. Instead of a baby book, Nan created a collage of Adaline's childhood in Maryland. She's already searched the album from front to back more than once, hoping to find an inscription or clues. She even searched the photos and their backsides with a black light—to no avail.

This time, she flips the cover open with no agenda but to reminisce. The first page contains a random assortment of snapshots: Adaline, age twelve, learning how to row a boat; age seventeen, building a snowman with Cindy and her little sisters; age eight, wearing galoshes up to her armpits as she and her father cast their lines into a river; and age fourteen, stirring Nan's favorite creamy chicken and potato soup.

How odd.

Her grandmother kept her closet floor spotless, her accessories arranged by type, and her shirts and sweaters folded by season—but she put this album together so haphazardly. Was Nan in a hurry? Adaline checks the inside and back cover again, feeling along the edges of the binding, but nothing yields, and the album looks brand new.

Adaline flips to another spread. Like all other pages, Nan didn't bother to group these photos chronologically. Instead, this spread shows Adaline at different ages participating in the spelling bee, playing a game of chess with her father, screaming at a Rubix's cube before she chucked it across the room, navigating a corn maze at Summer's Farm, and climbing through a rope obstacle course in Girl Scouts.

She grouped the photos by elements.

Sure enough, another set of pages includes photos of Adaline learning how to cook ramen noodles over a campfire with her troop, hugging her glowing Jack-o'-lantern with its crooked smile, setting out candles for Cindy's spa birthday party, roasting charred marshmallows over the new firepit her father had brought home, and lighting the yule log with their Christmas stockings moved to opposite ends of the mantel.

Among this collage, one photo doesn't match the vibrancy of the others. It's a terrible picture with most of the background solid black around Adaline's illuminated face, thanks to a candle that's not in the photo. A hurricane had reached Maryland, and most of the state went three days without power. Nan had gathered every candle in the house, which was a lot, and the family spent the night camping out in the library to stay warm and help Adaline beat back her nightmares. In this photo, she sat in the corner of the room, waiting for her father to light the fireplace. Her grandmother sat in front of her, telling Adaline stories about her childhood and the lack of electricity.

"Sometimes," Nan said, "on a cloudy night, the darkness could be so thick that I couldn't see my hand in front of my face."

"Whoa. That was before TV, wasn't it, Nan?"

She threw her head back and chuckled. "Absolutely, my sweet girl. None whatsoever."

"Weren't you scared?"

"Never. You know why?" Nan balanced a small jar containing a votive candle on Adaline's upturned palms. "Because the light that burns inside us never dims. And you, my little firefly, pour passion into everything you do. You have a bright, beautiful light too."

Nan always had a way of making Adaline feel invincible. Brushing her fingers over the photo, she stares at the image a moment longer before flipping the book closed and tucking the memories away for safe keeping.

I certainly was blessed with a happy childhood. But at what cost?

And there it is again, that dull ache that's taken up residence inside her chest. Most of the time, she doesn't notice it, but that ache knocks on the walls and makes itself known every now and again. Only work or Ëólas seems to make it settle down and hush up.

Standing up, Adaline holds the album against her side and massages her chest as she walks to the center of the backyard, where she sits down, extends her legs in front of her, and places her hands and the album on her knees. The waning moonlight casts a silver glow across the horizon, which the lake reflects within its ripples. The trees surrounding the river etch their branches into the sky.

Adaline closes her eyes. Placing her hands on the album, she calls to mind the sacred circle, focusing primarily on fire, wind, water, and air. She inhales deeply and smells the crisp, smokey scent of that far-off firepit, feels a breeze move her hair, hears the lake splash against the dock, and smells Nan's collection of lavender and basil. She also calls upon the mind, body, and soul. The muscles in her arms and legs relax, and she clears her mind.

"Nan, please help me," she whispers.

She sinks deeper into the trance, letting the outdoors fall into the abyss between realms. Keeping her eyes shut, she hears wings flapping overhead, a waterfall gushing in the distance, the grass rustling in the wind, and the sun warming her face. Adaline opens her eyes, and that same translucent curtain blurs the world around her. Behind the curtain, a winged creature with the silhouette of a human sweeps down from the sky and lands close to Adaline. As much as she wants to jump up and pull back the curtain, Adaline stays seated, keeping her hands on her knees.

The winged creature walks closer. "Adaline," she says, with the same ethereal voice Adaline's come to trust, "you're so close. Too close. You must be careful."

Too close?

The more Adaline struggles to hear, the quicker the woman's voice and the curtain fade away, denying her the chance to ask a single question.

"Damn it!" Adaline slams her fist on the grass beside her.

Fine, I'll do it on my own.

Taking a deep breath, Adaline tosses the album aside and lies back, calling to mind her most recent notes on meditation and invoking the elements. She stretches her arms out at her sides, and the slanted beams of moonlight breaking through the clouds illume patches of her skin. The grass prickles her hands and neck. The scent of burnt firewood wafts across the backyard, and small waves announce their arrival as they slap the dock.

The elements in this world can't be dead.

Maybe they've just been on their own for too long. Maybe they can't even recognize an elf or fae. Or maybe they can't comprehend how a fae could also be a human. And an elf. Then again, Āranol could have been lying.

"Ugh," Adaline groans. *Clear your mind, Adaline. I just need to focus on my notes.*

She scrunches her eyes, nose, and mouth and releases them along with all thoughts. Again, she focuses solely on her surroundings. The firepit crackling next door. The breeze tickling the fine hairs on her arms. The river flowing past her house. The smell of fallen leaves. *The last fucking mosquito sucking my blood.* Adaline smacks her arm and kills the parasite, leaving a tinge of blood on her skin.

She lays flat again. *Sun. Water. Grass. Wind.* She repeats these words until her body relaxes and the world fades out of existence.

When she opens her eyes again, Ëólas leans over her, the ends of his dirty-blond hair tickling her neck. Stars twinkle above him. "Ready for bed, my love?"

"I fell asleep," Adaline moans.

"You did."

She sits up and slaps her knees. "Damn it. Why didn't you wake me sooner?"

Taking a seat beside her, Ëólas bends one leg and dangles an arm over his knee. "Because you were tired?"

"But I failed."

"You were training."

"I was napping."

"Maybe don't lay down next time?"

"Ugh." Adaline flops onto her back and stares up at the stars—or the lack thereof, thanks to the hazy yellow radiance of the surrounding city lights.

What's wrong with me?

Crawling on top of her, Ëólas replaces her view of the night sky with his own glowing golden orbs. "I think you've been working diligently but should try approaching these lessons from another angle."

"Oh, really?" She tugs the hem of his slim-fit polo shirt. "Any recommendations?"

"I'm happy to play the instructor again."

With a smirk, Ëólas glides his hands under her knit sweater and pulls it over her head, discarding her clothing beside them. The chilly air makes her nipples rise against her tank top. She reaches for his neck, but he captures her wrists with one hand and holds them in place above her head. The grass tickles her arms, and her heart races as he circles his thumb around her bud, making her anticipate what he'll do next. When she wriggles her bottom, he tears off her tank and her bra. Goosebumps breakout over her skin, but her neck burns with a telltale red flush as the grass blades prickle her backside, making her skin extra sensitive to everything touching her.

"Stay still," he orders, skating his knuckles along the side of her mound. He grazes her bud with his fingertips, teasing it into a hard pebble. When she wriggles again, he pinches and twists her nipple, making her cry out as the tinge of pain radiates down the length of her torso and pools between her legs. "I said stay still."

As he sits back on his knees, the patio lights illuminate her breasts. He skates his palms around her globes and over her abdomen, his featherlight fingers playing games, making her muscles both contract and relax and her longing sink deeper inside her.

He pauses at the button on her jeans. "I think you'll have an easier time connecting with nature if we connect out here."

"That's an excellent theory. We should definitely test that."

"Such an obedient student."

"Most of the time." She lifts her hips, giving him permission to remove her jeans, to see her anticipation for him.

"Mmm. True. We should test that too." He removes each article of clothing, exposing her to the night air and any creatures that may be watching. "Don't move."

He stands up, his eyes never leaving her body as he strips himself. Under the starlight, his skin takes on a cool, dark tone, but his eyes glow darker yellow like the pulsing embers of a fire ready to ignite.

She licks her lips and moves her arms to sit up, to grab him, to taste him, but he shakes his head and clicks his tongue with a tsk-tsk-tsk. "Already not listening. Lie back." He pushes her ankles apart with his foot. "Spread your legs, my love. Let me see you."

A white puff of excitement escapes her mouth. Despite their time together, she blushes as she tilts her knees apart, letting him see what's his and waiting for his body to respond as he watches her. His rising excitement encourages her to spread her thighs even wider.

He strokes himself as he studies her, memorizes her. He arches an eyebrow. "You need to be kinder to yourself too."

She bites her bottom lip, but her cheeks still balloon at the suggestion. Her heart beats faster as she lowers her hand to her folds and massages her bud, her juices gathering for him, waiting for him.

He kneels down in front of her and skates his hands along her inner thighs. "Don't stop," he urges, holding her down as her body writhes. "Faster." While she teases herself, his hands explore her legs, her bottom, her mons, but he doesn't touch the one place she wants him too, the one place aching for him.

His eyes lock with hers as her body heats up, the cold unable to reach her now. The wind curls away from her flesh like rising steam. Her hand works faster, the desire for release growing in her core, building like an inferno that she wants to explode. She chases that feeling, her eyes rolling back in her head just as she climbs higher and higher—only for Ëólas to grab her hand and pull her fingers away. The cold air attacks her bud pulsing furiously.

With her core searing, she glares at him. "What are you doing? I want to finish."

"I know." He flashes a wicked grin. "But it's my turn."

He lowers himself over her, kissing her lips tenderly at first, but their hunger overtakes them quickly. She grabs his neck, lacing her fingers through his hair, and pulls him against her. He kisses her until her moans fill the night air, and neither of them remembers life before this moment. Balancing on his hands, he groans and forces himself to relinquish her swollen lips. Trailing kisses down her neck, he tastes her skin and her tender breasts. As much as he loves showering both of her mounds with affection, his kisses travel further south, blazing a path straight for her core.

The moment his tongue warms her folds, Adaline rolls her head backward into the grass. For a brief second, she prays Cindy's sisters aren't outside, that they don't hear Adaline's panting. She laces her fingers through his hair, his silky locks tangled between her extremities, and holds on as her legs quiver and her bottom rocks back and forth against the grass. Her ragged breaths paint the night sky in shades of gray. Her moans rattle the leaves on the trees. As she grinds harder and his tongue moves faster, she throws her arms out to her sides, and the earth trembles beneath her as she cries out, demanding relief.

When he slides his fingers inside her and drums her favorite spot, she digs her fingers into the ground and gouges the earth with her heels until all her muscles contract and then liquify. Grinning and groaning his delight, he reverses course, kissing his way up her torso, his hands exploring her languid limbs.

He nips her chin, then her jawline, and whispers in her ear, "Gentle or rough, my love?"

Hugging his torso and locking her feet around his knees, she murmurs, "Gentle. At first."

Slowly he enters her, filling her inch by inch, leaving her no space to hide. He rolls his hips deliberately, allowing her to feel his entirety, then thrusts harder, faster, and they cling to each other, their hands roaming and claiming what's theirs. As the grass caresses her skin, as the wind rustles her hair, as the stars burn overhead, and as the water laps the dock in sync with their panting, she clenches around him, and for the first time in her adulthood, Adaline feels like a wild child of nature, delighting in all life has to offer.

Chapter Seventeen

THE BBQ

"So what's the deal?" Cindy grabs three different salad dressings from the fridge, including Adaline's homemade ranch, while attempting to keep her voice neutral. "You're working while he's living here rent free? Is he looking for a job?"

Well, shit. There's an opening to tell the truth, though that's not the note I'd like to start off on. And the chicken is almost done. Bad timing all around. Granted, we've had nothing but bad timing since June.

Adaline pushes the button on the salad spinner, and the basket flings droplets of water onto the clear plastic bowl. "He's building furniture. Your mom saw him sanding our new cabinets in the driveway and asked him to make one for her too. And because she told all her friends, he now has back orders. I think it's a job he really enjoys, and it's a pleasant change of pace for him. He's been working non-stop for, well, a long time."

That's one hundred percent the truth, so please ease up on the suspicion today.

"Huh." Cindy pops the lid off the ranch, dips a carrot, and bites the end off with a sharp snap. She pulverizes the vegetable between her teeth while she stares at Adaline.

Pushing the sleeves of her dark-green cashmere sweater up to her elbows, Adaline drops the lettuce into a large wooden bowl, along with the avocado, tomatoes, and yellow peppers she chopped earlier. Tossing the salad, she looks out the window as Ëólas dribbles the soccer ball around Dax and kicks it into the net she set up last night so he could practice. She always thought he had the build of a footballer. He has the agility and stamina too.

Maybe today's the day, after we eat. What's my lead in? I need to tell you something unbelievable? Maybe.

Cindy finishes her carrot and snaps the container lid shut, bringing Adaline back to reality. "I thought he's an anthropologist. Can he get a job at AU? Is he submitting his resume to other universities?"

"Um." *Man, I wish we had thought of a better cover story.* "He's taking some time to find himself." *Eek. That doesn't sound good.*

"But how's he going to secure a green card without finding a job?"

Shit. "We're just figuring things out as we go."

"But—"

The beeping timer on the stove screeches at Adaline, telling her time's up. "I have to check on the chicken. Come on."

Praying her hands aren't as jittery as she feels, Adaline passes the salad to Cindy, grabs a stack of bowls and plates, and heads outside onto the patio where she already set out potato salad, the steamed green beans Dax grew all summer, dinner rolls, and two bowls of strawberries and blueberries. While Cindy retrieves the silverware caddy and water pitcher, Adaline flips the glazed chicken one last time. Ëólas and Dax jog over and lick their lips at the sight of her taking the meat off the grill.

I'm glad we could get in one last barbeque. Oh, we should plan a camping trip soon! A quiet, distraction-free weekend would provide her and Cindy with massive time to talk about everything. Plus, the escape from work, training, and wasted research would be heavenly. *Yeah, that could work.*

At the edge of the backyard, the wind rocks the tethered paddle boat into the dock, and the ravens circling overhead caw their warnings before diving at the water and flying off with a fish in their talons. Likewise, everyone takes a seat around the glass table and fills their dishes. Even though the temperature dropped this weekend, the sun provides enough warmth for them to enjoy an early-fall dinner outside among the crimson and burnt orange foliage.

Reaching for the drumstick, Dax tears into the meat and hums his approval. "Damn, Ëólas is fast out there. You play cricket too?"

While Ëólas takes a long sip of water to hide his confusion, Adaline rolls her eyes at Dax. "He doesn't play every stereotypical British sport."

Ëólas nods. "Sorry to disappoint."

"Nah, it's okay," Dax says. "I never understood the appeal anyway."

Cindy pushes her green beans around her plate, letting the steam escape and evaporate in front of her face. "When will you publish your next paper?"

"Um, I'm not sure." Adaline eyes her chicken breast as if it were about to rise off her plate and choke her. "I need to choose a new research topic."

As Cindy lays down her fork, the metal clangs against the glass table. "So you're giving up on the cave altogether? But you said it's Maryland's greatest mystery, our own Sphinx with hidden info that could change history. I don't understand why you're just giving that up."

Clenching her teeth, Adaline shrugs and picks at her chicken, avoiding Cindy's persistent gaze.

What the fuck, Cindy? I didn't realize you've gotten this suspicious. Do I really seem that different to you?

Probably.

After all, how could Adaline come back from New Leira and not seem different? Plus, she's never kept secrets from Cindy. She must sense that too because she has always been the person Adaline ran to for support, for the big things she wasn't ready to discuss with Dad or Nan. Neither of them could explain how to navigate elementary school and the popular crowd—Adaline needed Cindy for that, just like when Adaline debated losing her virginity and giving up dancing. Of course, she never hesitated to return the favor. Even after Cindy and Dax found solid ground, she and Cindy still needed those regular, deep conversations that relieve the soul, reinforce their sisterhood, and validate their experiences. But they haven't had a single, genuine conversation since Adaline came home in June.

So much has changed already. Can't I keep one thing the same? And what if Cindy freaks out about me being a queen from another world and a half-elf? Ugh,

I hate that description. Demi-elf? Maybe-fae? Primarily human? They all sound ridiculous.

When Adaline jumps back into the group conversation, Dax answers Ëólas's questions about what it means to be a civil engineer, and she inserts a word here and there to prove she's listening. At some point, Dax shifts the topic to house hunting and lists his must-haves, but the only image that pierces Adaline's thoughts is a massive backyard so he can build a greenhouse. Cindy doesn't contribute much small talk either.

So much for that camping trip. Okay, I can do this. Later. When it's just the two of us. I'll just get her drunk first. Or at least butter her up. "How's the wedding preparations coming along? Did you decide on which flowers you're going with?"

Cindy picks up her dinner roll and tears off an enormous chunk while giving Adaline the stink eye. "Please, I've been planning this wedding for the last five years. You know I want orchids. I'd rather learn more about you two."

Of course you do. But I don't want to do this right now.

Dax dumps a scoop of potato salad onto his plate. "Great point. Ëólas, here's an important question for you: DCU or MCU?

While Ëólas taps his chin and pretends to give this question a lot of thought, Adaline chokes down her water so she can answer for him. "Ëólas's family watched little TV when he was growing up." *Yep, stick to the truth.* "They read a lot, but TV wasn't their thing, so I've been educating him."

"Yes!" Ëólas points back at the house, his voice sounding much more cheerful and like himself. "Tonight we're watching *Return of the Jedi*."

Adaline shakes her head. "No, we're not. We're going to jump back to episode one."

Dax lifts his glass and cheers Adaline. "The Machete Order. Nice!"

"Wait." Ëólas shifts sideways to better see Adaline. "You had me watch episodes four and five, only for us to now watch one?"

"Yep."

"So I have to wait to find out if Vader really is Luke's father?"

Dax puts down his glass so quickly that his water splashes onto the table. "Damn, man. I didn't think there was a person still alive on this planet who doesn't already know that. Where are you from again?"

"Heh." Ëólas rattles off the same story Adaline taught him the night of the engagement party. "A small town between Wales and England. It's not even on the map."

Yep, nothing about that sounds robotic.

Narrowing her eyes, Cindy leans forward until her breasts push her plate into Adaline's. "And that's where you two met, in the UK?"

"Um." *Not quite.*

"Yes," Ëólas says for her.

Cindy nods as if she's on the verge of proving a hypothesis. "Which was four years ago? When you fought and didn't like each other?"

Adaline tries to bob her head, but her neck won't budge.

Thankfully, Ëólas says, "Exactly."

"So, what led to you finally becoming friends?" Cindy asks.

Don't say it. "He saved me." *Damn it.*

"Saved you from what?" Cindy's analytical eyes dart between the two of them.

Ëólas lifts his glass only to realize it's empty. "Um, from some scoundrels who snuck into the ruins and weren't very gentleman—"

Adaline stomps on Ëólas's foot. *No, no, no. Don't tell her that.*

"What the hell?" Cindy shouts, her eyebrows shooting upward.

Leaving his scoop of potato salad hovering in front of his mouth, Dax freezes, looks from Ëólas to Adaline, and sits up straight, dropping his easy-going charm as if he's about to defend his friend and murder someone. "When was this? Adaline, what happened?"

She opens her mouth, but her tongue feels three times its normal size. She didn't expect them to grill her, not like this, not right now.

How do I get out of this? I can't lie to them. I can't lie, period.

"Oh my god." Adaline jumps up out of her seat. "Something just occurred to me. Ëólas, let's go check on dessert." She flees from the table and hurries into the kitchen, shutting the door behind Ëólas.

He leans against the island and hunches his shoulders. "Sorry, I'm terrible at this. I don't know how to answer their—"

"No, it's not you. It's me. I can't lie to Cindy."

"I know. You're a terrible liar."

"No. I mean, yes. But it's more than that. I've *never* been able to lie. Ever."

"And?"

"That's a typical characteristic of fae. My father once said that because fae can be so irresistible, they can't lie." *Ew. I didn't mean to imply I'm irresistible.* Adaline mentally gags at the idea. "Doesn't that confirm Ãranol's accusations?"

"What, that you're irresistible? I already knew that." He steps forward to kiss the BBQ sauce off her bottom lip.

"Ëólas, I'm being serious here!" She sidesteps around him and hugs her belly.

"Alright, alright. Let's test this theory. What might you want to lie to me about?"

She blinks three times. "Nothing. We have open communication."

"Hmm." He stares at the ceiling, then arches an eyebrow. "Do you find Magnus attractive?"

She gawks at him for a moment and then tosses her hands in the air. "Yes. He's very handsome." When Ëólas sucks his lips inward, she looks at him as if she were lecturing that one student who insists on asking the most asinine questions. "Please, I can be objective about beauty and not want to jump his bones. You know that."

Ëólas shrugs. "Yes, I agree. He is a rather handsome fellow. Hey, I can be objective too. Okay, what about—Ah!" He claps his hands together and stares into her eyes. "Are you pleased with your training?"

"Mmm-hmm." Backing away from him, Adaline picks up the sponge, turns on the faucet, and starts scrubbing the cutting board. "It's going fine."

"Fine?"

"I, um, yeah. It's—Can we focus on what matters right now?" She scrapes at a piece of potato skin that glued itself to the bamboo cutting board. "If I'm part fae, what does that mean for our world, for Ellíum?"

"I see. So that's your attempt at lying—you avoid the topic."

"Ëólas, please focus."

"Oh, I am very focused." He lingers behind her, his nearness making her shoulders rise closer to her ears. "What about your training bothers you?"

She turns off the water, dries her hands, and swivels toward the coffee machine in search of the mail pile. She's been meaning to sort through and toss out the junk, only she can't find the mound of flyers, coupons, and envelopes. "Where's the mail?"

"Adaline."

"Really. Where's the mail pile? Wasn't it here this morning?" *Ëólas doesn't touch the mail.*

"Please look at me."

She faces him, but her eyes quickly drift to the hem of her sweater, which she twists around her thumb. How can she share what a mess she is? That she's confused about everything. That she's afraid to go home. That she's not sure which would be worse, finding out with absolute certainty that her parents are dead or that they've been waiting for her—or forgot her.

And what if she fails her people? What if she can't pay back fate? Sometimes, when Ëólas is sleeping or walking into the room, she can't believe she got what she wanted most of all. When they're not training, she almost fools herself into believing they're a normal couple—just a husband and wife building a life together. Not a queen and king with the safety of thousands at stake. The longer they're here, the less real New Leira feels. And yet, in her dreams, she can hear home calling to her.

God, I don't want him to think I can't handle this.

Pushing a loose curl behind her ear, Ëólas steps closer and tips her chin upward until their eyes meet. "What's going on inside that head of yours?"

"I. It's just. I don't." She bites her lip, then takes a deep breath. "Sometimes, it all just feels like too much, too big. And I don't know what I'm doing." *And I don't deserve you.*

Resting his hands on her shoulders, Ëólas tilts forward, presses his forehead against hers, and whispers, "For me too."

She snaps her eyes to his. "What? You mean living here and pretending—"

"No. I mean everything. Being king before I was ready. Protecting our people. Not letting you down. And I'm angry at myself for not being much help with the elements. You married an elf who's useless to you in that regard."

Holy shit. He has insecurities? Holding him close, she exhales some of the tension she's been hoarding since August. "You don't know how much I needed to hear that."

"Really?"

"I'm terrified of letting you down too."

He rubs his hands along her back, kneading her muscles into letting down their guard, and brushes his lips against hers. "My love, you continue to astonish and inspire me."

"Damn. You're amazing." As he gazes at her lovingly, as if she could never mess up so badly that he'd turn his back on her, the coil that's been twisting tighter and tighter around her chest begins to unknot, giving her room to breathe. "Okay, I'm ready to tell Cindy."

"You need me to distract Dax?"

"Can you? For a bit? I need to talk to her first."

"Absolutely. He wants to take me to a shop that sells something called comics."

Chapter Eighteen

THE RUM

With the kitchen clean, the guys head out the door, Dax pulling his car keys out of his pocket as he explains to Ëólas the concept of mutants. Cindy puts the last leftover in the fridge, closes the door, and reaches for the heavy cast-iron kettle. She fills it with water, keeping her back to Adaline, who once again feels like she might throw up. The acid in her stomach churns as she chooses her next words. Once Cindy knows the truth, Adaline won't have anyone left within her close circle who sees only Adaline—not the tragedy, not the trauma, not the expectations that go with her title.

Be brave.

As Cindy places the kettle on the stove, Adaline nods once to herself and steps forward. "Hey, can we talk? I, I really need to tell you something."

Her hand halts a few inches from the knob. Slowly, Cindy turns around. "Thank God." She gestures at the fridge. "Do we need pints of ice cream?"

The corner of Adaline's mouth jerks upward. "No. Well, maybe. Actually, I think it's time to break out Dad's rum."

"Oh shit."

Three minutes later, Cindy and Adaline walk into the living room where they slump down on Nan's gray sofa. Adaline places on the coffee table a tall bottle of dark-amber Stroh 80 rum and two shot glasses.

The diamond on Cindy's finger sparkles like a disco ball under the ceiling lights. "What's going on, Chica?"

Using her thumb, Adaline spins her wedding band, on the wrong hand, back and forth. Cindy glances at the delicate ring, at the diamond surrounded by petals, and flicks her eyes at Adaline's.

She fills the shot glasses and hands both to Cindy. "Trust me."

"Oh god," Cindy mumbles, downing both. Her arms tremble from the potent shock to her system. "Alright, what's up?"

"Okay, everything I'm about to say is going to sound crazy, but before you try to commit me to a mental hospital, please hear me out until the end."

Cindy leans against the backrest. "Whoa. That's quite the set up. Alright, I won't call 9-1-1 until you're done. Now spill the beans. You're freaking me out."

Standing up, Adaline paces in front of the fireplace and attempts to word-vomit the entire story in less than ten minutes. "When I was alone at the dig site, I traveled to another world. Like another realm or planet or universe; I'm still not sure about that yet. But in this world, elves exist, and they have a difficult history with humans. So, when I showed up in the middle of these ruins, Ëólas, who's an elf, a real-life elf—he and I didn't get along so well at first."

While Adaline explains about the Neutral Territory, Cindy's face scrunches up more and more. She curls into the sofa, and when Adaline says she lived in this other world for an entire month, Cindy takes out her phone and hugs it to her chest. "Keep going. Finish your story."

Adaline resumes pacing to avoid eye contact. "Anyway, a group of people kept attacking the city, and we couldn't figure out who they were. But when I was abducted—"

"Wait, what?" Cindy pops up, her legs falling off the sofa. "Someone attacked you?"

"No, it's okay." She waves her hands to stop Cindy from searching Adaline's head for injuries or signs of delirium. "I killed him. Well, I didn't kill him on my own. A tree helped me."

"Naturally." Sinking into the sofa, Cindy shields herself with her knees, and her brow settles into a twisted knot of confusion.

Before Cindy calls the cops or hospital, Adaline relays everything that happened over the last few months, including that Nan used to be a queen and that Adaline is one now, at which point Cindy grabs the rum and pours herself two more shots.

When Adaline finishes, she collapses on the second sofa opposite Cindy and reluctantly adds, "Um, and your mom and abuela know all this. Apparently, our families have been friends for hundreds of years."

Cindy hands the last shot to Adaline, who downs it in one gulp. "Is that the end?" Cindy asks, her voice scratchy and raw from too much alcohol.

Adaline stares at her empty shot glass. "Nope. My dad might still be alive. He left me a letter that he planned to go home, without me, and find my mom."

"Whoa."

Running her hands through her hair, Adaline hunches over to hide her face. She doesn't want to cry, but her tears won't listen; they trickle down her cheeks, falling onto her jeans. The dark patch grows bigger.

Instead of reaching for her phone, Cindy moves next to Adaline, wraps an arm around her, and lays her head against Adaline's temple. "Okay, as much as I'd love to call 9-1-1 right now, I see how upset you are, so let me ask you this first: You said you need my help. How? Why?"

"Honestly, I don't know." Wiping her cheeks, Adaline sits up. "Seira said you are vital to our survival."

Cindy stands up slowly, cautiously, as if any sudden movement might make Adaline come undone. She slips her hands into her back pockets, her thumbs sticking out, and purses her lips. "Okay. What do you need from me?"

Adaline drops her hands between her knees and stares at Cindy. "Seriously?"

"Absolutely."

"I, I don't even know. Seira struggles to stay in the moment. I think her visions overwhelm her, so I don't get clear details. But when Ëólas and I return to New Leira, we might need you at some point. I mean, you don't have to come with us. Or maybe you could for like a day or so, if you're willing. But I'd bring you back super fast and—"

"Wait, you mean you can take me to this imag—um, other world?"

Adaline turns her palms toward the ceiling in an I-don't-know gesture. "Maybe? I've traveled with only my dad and Ëólas so far, but given how close you and I are, I think I can bring you too."

"Okay. Sure. Why not?" Cindy pulls her hands out of her pockets and nods like a bobblehead. "Why don't you take me there right now, you know, just so I can see this place for myself?"

"You really mean that?"

"You're my sister, Chica. Whatever you're going through, I'll be right beside you. I'll help you through this. I promise."

Oh Cindy, you totally think I'm bonkers, but you have no idea how much I love you for saying that.

Adaline jumps up. As they hug each other, she recalls the moments that cemented their friendship—when they broke into and explored the abandoned haunted house at the end of the street and then outran the police, when Cindy tackled prima donna Nicole for calling Adaline a slut, when Cindy confessed that she caught her father in bed with another woman, and when Adaline moved in with Cindy for three months to help her cope after Dax's mom destroyed their relationship the first time round.

Pulling Cindy into another world isn't as effortless as taking Ëólas. This time, it's like Adaline's the end of a piece of thread, and she's trying to float through the eye of a needle, but her vision is blurry, so multiple holes overlap each other with only one being real. But knowing Seira saw Cindy in New Leira helps Adaline to trust herself and float through the right hole.

Holding on to the thread between her and Cindy, Adaline tugs her best friend through the threshold between worlds. In an instant, the living room fades from view. The balcony off the castle's dining hall solidifies around them, along with the distant soldiers lined up and waiting for their commanders.

Cindy shivers violently a few times, but she doesn't cry out in pain or protest, at least not until she opens her eyes and screams, "Holy fucking shit balls!"

"Well, that's quite the hello." Seira walks through the archway, her small hands clasped together in front of her light-blue dress that hugs her chest and hips and then cascades to the floor. The sunlight bounces off a mirror inside, casting a halo around her platinum blonde hair that's parted around her ears, revealing their sweet, pointy tips.

Lifting one hand to cover her lips, Seira chuckles. "She has just as foul a mouth as you. No wonder you're so close."

"Seira!" Adaline rushes forward, hugs her tightly, and peeks over Seira's shoulders to find servers taking away Magnus's and Thoren's breakfasts and Sora and Merith chatting near the doors. With no one else on the balcony, Adaline looks into her cousin's periwinkle eyes. "Seira, are we, is our family, was Aeríoléna—" She mouths the last word, *fae?*

"Of course." With a shrug, she steps around Adaline and flits next to Cindy. "I'm delighted to meet you. We're going to be good friends, I promise."

"Okay," Cindy croaks, her eyes taking in Seira's fairy-princess appearance. *Oh my god. I'm a magical mutt.*

"But your hair is much too short." Seira pinches the end of Cindy's bob and lifts the tips closer to her lips.

"No, no!" Shaking off her shock, Adaline reaches for Seira's hand and gently pulls her away. "Cindy likes short hair. No enchantments necessary."

"Yeah. I'm good, thanks." Cindy glances at Adaline. "Magical hair extensions, huh?"

"I wasn't lying." Turning to Seira, Adaline pats her cousin's hand. "We just popped in so I could prove to Cindy that I'm not crazy."

"Oh, I know," Seira says. "I wanted to be here to say hello. My timing usually isn't so accurate."

Looking pleased with herself, Seira waves goodbye as Adaline takes hold of Cindy's hand and Seira fades into nothingness. The living room returns exactly as they left it.

"Holy shit!" Cindy presses her steepled fingers against her mouth. "I really thought Ëólas had drugged you, or you were having a psychotic breakdown." Shoving her hands into her back pockets, she paces between the sofas. "Damn. Wow. This is incredible. Dax is going to lose his mind."

"I know." Adaline drops onto the sofa and stares through the rum bottle. "It's like a fairy tale story with magic spells, a prince in disguise, and a beast hiding in the shadows. Only, this is real life—my life. And it's both magnificent and dangerous."

Cindy halts, sinks next to her best friend, and clasps Adaline's hand. "You know I'm here for you, right?"

"Yeah, I do. But I don't know what I'm doing. My people need me to figure out my magic, but my family left me zero clues, and all my research has proven a waste of time."

"Well, research is definitely something I can help with."

The two girls fall back against the sofa, and Adaline starts her story over from the beginning, this time going into detail about how Ëólas found her drunk at the tavern; how much Hamon reminds Adaline of Westley and when he finally said, "As you wish;" how tall the trees grow in Lameiría, creating their own green sky; and how Cindy gave Adaline the courage to tell Ëólas the truth that she was in love with him. They talk for hours, lounging on the sofa arm in arm, their feet on the coffee table, paying no attention to when day turns into night. By the time Adaline demonstrates Ëólas's scream when he discovered porn on his mobile, the guys come home, pop their heads into the living room, and find Adaline and Cindy laughing so hard that they fall off the sofa, bump the coffee table, and knock over the shot glasses.

"Well," Ëólas says, "I suppose the conversation went well?" He lays a stack of X-Men comics on top of the black upright piano next to the open archway.

Adaline blows him a kiss, but Cindy leaps off the sofa, trips over Adaline's foot, and tosses her arms around Ëólas's neck, making Dax step aside and say, "Huh?"

"Congratulations!" Cindy thumps his back three times. After they all take a seat, one couple per sofa, Cindy crosses her legs and shakes a finger at Ëólas. "I'm pissed I didn't get to be her matron of honor though."

"What?" Dax screeches, looking from Cindy to Ëólas. "What the hell did I miss?"

Adaline elbows Ëólas. "Would you like to tell him?"

"Oh, yes please!" Ëólas clears his throat, locks eyes with Dax, and sums up everything Adaline and Cindy discussed over the last five hours in as few sentences as possible. "I'm not from Britain. I'm an elf from another world. These aren't contact lenses; I still haven't learned what that means. My mother is Queen Élara of Lameiría, and I've taken Adaline as my bride, although we now rule another kingdom that she inherited from her grandmother, and we have demonic vampire elves trying to kill us and eradicate our people."

While Dax's eyes skitter from Ëólas to Adaline to Cindy, a huge grin spreads across his face. "You're pulling my leg."

"Oh, will this help?" Adaline pops back to her chambers in New Leira and searches for something other-worldly to show Dax. Settling for yet another of Ëólas's long yet slightly curved swords, she holds the blade in front of her body and pops back into Nan's living room behind Ëólas.

Dax leaps out of his seat and waves his hands as if he's about to karate chop someone. "What the fuck? Where the hell did you get that from? How'd you do that?"

"Dax, chill!" Cindy yanks his hand, urging him to sit next to her. "It's okay. Adaline just traveled to New Leira. I saw it with my own eyes—a medieval castle made of white stone, purple and silver tapestries, men in armor lining up outside the castle wall, and a king and a knight finishing breakfast. She brought me there for a little bit."

"I wouldn't call Thoren a knight, but close enough," Adaline mutters, leaning Ëólas's sword against the upright piano.

"You could travel with Cindy?" Ëólas kisses Adaline's cheek when she sits next to him. "Well done, my love."

"Wait, wait, wait. You're telling me that everything Ëólas just said is true?" Dax asks.

Cindy pats his knee. "Yes, Babe."

"Holy shit!" As Dax stares at Ëólas, at those golden eyes and pointy ears, Dax's grin stretches from ear to ear as if he just discovered that he's befriended Mark Hamill or Orlando Bloom. "Dude, please tell me we can spar together."

Chapter Nineteen

THE SCIENTIST

Adaline and Ëólas pause at the edge of the street as traffic slows in front of them. As soon as a double-decker bus pushes the rest of the cars out of the way, they cross the street and enter the square. Tourists and locals cross paths under a semi-cloudy late-November sky. Adaline pulls her peacoat tighter, shielding her neck from the blistering wind. Ëólas hugs her around her shoulders, his dark-blond hair billowing behind him. They stop in front of a bronze lion, their knees against the low fountain wall. The beast gazes onward, his mouth agape and his heavy brows adding an air of wisdom to his noble face.

"He's regal." Ëólas pulls out his mobile and snaps a photo. They turn around, and he lifts his phone with one hand. Huddled together, he snaps a second photo with the lion above their heads.

With their evidence recorded, they leave the square and find two tall buildings they can slip between. Ëólas takes her hand, and Adaline conjures Nan's library—only she doesn't travel instantly. Instead, she slows down the urge to travel, quieting her beating heart and extending her breaths as she focuses not on the destination but on that needle-like hole between worlds until the entry point grows to the size of a doorway that overlaps her view of the street entrance and the Londoners walking by.

Beyond the silver curtain separating worlds, a semitransparent Cindy waits in front of a large desk, and Dax admires the American revolution saber and black leather scabbard hanging above the fireplace mantel. With her fingers entwined with Ëólas's, Adaline guides him forward. When they cross the threshold, the pedestrians never notice their two illegal visitors disappear. Seconds later, Adaline and Ëólas appear inside the library with floor-to-ceiling bookshelves and windows surrounding them.

"How'd it go?" Cindy picks up the notes she left on the desk.

Holding up his phone, Ëólas shows her and Dax the selfie from Trafalgar Square.

"That's fucking awesome," Dax says. "Do Rome next."

While Adaline chuckles, Cindy backtracks to the desk and spins her laptop around, showing everyone her screen. "Not a bad idea, Dax. Now that Adaline's consistently traveled to familiar locations several times, let's try taking this to the next level." Opening her browser, she loads a street map of a random Italian village in the heart of Tuscany. "You haven't been here, right? Cool. What if I pull up the street view? Take a good look. Can you travel there now?"

Adaline memorizes the view. Turning away from the laptop, she visualizes the street; the rows of short, bushy olive trees; the limestone building in the distance with its terracotta roof tiles; and the skinny, towering cypress trees dotting the horizon. But nothing of her current surroundings billows, buckles, or dissolves.

Tilting her head to the side, Adaline grumbles and tries again, slowing her thoughts and visualizing that same needle-like hole she first conjured with Cindy. A tiny puncture appears in the middle of the room, a blurry black dot so small that it could be a speck of dust floating in midair. She takes a step closer and squints, trying with her mind to jiggle it open, make it wider, and visualize it becoming the size of a door. But the dot doesn't budge. She pokes the hole, but her finger passes through the speck as if the hole exists on a different frequency. When she drops her hand, the hole disappears. "That's just rude."

"See something?" Ëólas asks.

"I thought maybe, but no."

Cindy uncaps her pen and grabs her clipboard so she can take notes. "Interesting. Explain what happened." As Adaline relays what she saw and felt, Cindy records the details, her pen moving swiftly across the page the entire time. "Okay, you still can't travel to places you've never been before, even if you have an image. But we don't know how old that street view is, so that's another variable we'll have to test."

"Wait, that's not accurate." Ëólas, pushing the laptop aside, sits on the edge of the desk and casually crosses his arms over his chest, his dark-blue mesh-knit sweater showing off the curve of his muscular arms. "She took us to Feídra né Morna, and she'd never been there before."

"Huh." Dax rests his forearms on the back of the leather chair beside the enormous fireplace. "Are you sure?"

"Absolutely. One doesn't forget Hell City easily," Adaline says. "Besides, that's where they most likely kept my mother prisoner, before, you know."

Cindy taps her chin with her pen. "Maybe you could travel there because of your connection to your mother?"

"But she wasn't there, not when I was."

Cindy scoffs. "Said Ãranol. Yeah, like I'll trust the word of the guy who tried to kill you."

"He wasn't lying," Adaline murmurs. *How do I explain my gut reactions to a scientist?* "I just know. I could feel it."

"Oh, hey!" Dax says, drawing their attention. "She also traveled to Morgán on her own. She hadn't been there either."

Man, he's a good listener. "But that was like intercepting a call. He caught me on the line and pulled me through. Or the earth did. Honestly, I'm not sure about that one either."

Just the memory makes Adaline shiver. While her friends share their theories, she meanders toward the window, leaning against the frame, and stares at the evergreens touching the bright, blue mid-day sky. She exhales deeply, but her spine tingles one ripple at a time, crawling up her back. She rubs her arms and squints at the trees, half expecting to find Morgán standing between the branches, watching her every move. Of course he doesn't, but the creep factor making her skin crawl won't abate.

Morgán isn't here. Calm down.

Urging the sludge in her stomach to settle, she turns toward the people she loves, the people who never cease to amaze her with their support and enthusiasm.

"That's a pretty big stack of notes." Ëólas juts his chin in Cindy's direction. "What have you discovered?"

Cindy passes the bottom printed packet to Ëólas. "I've been tracking the conditions and limitations of Adaline's traveling, as well as every time she pops back to New Leira, how long she's there, and how long she's gone here. We've also been charting her observations, emotional and physical, and any changes she notices."

He flips through the pages, glancing at the columns, rows, pie charts, and line graphs. "Huh. And?"

Dax moves next to Ëólas and glances over his shoulder. "I thought you two were crafting save-the-date cards."

"We've been doing that too, Babe," Cindy says. "Over the last five weeks, I've also tracked Adaline traveling to New Leira at different intervals, from seconds, to minutes, to hours, to days. The last row shows the difference two weeks made."

"That's very thorough of you." Returning the packet to Cindy, Ëólas looks at her with a new level of respect. "What have you learned?"

Adaline steps away from the window. "It's hard to explain."

"Use the rubber band analogy," Cindy says. "That one works well."

"Right. My connection to the world I leave behind feels like a rubber band." Adaline opens the top desk drawer, pulls out a pen and an elastic band, and marks two dots side by side on the elastic. "See how easy it would be to jump from one dot to the next?"

After Ëólas and Dax nod, she slowly stretches the elastic, pulling one dot further away from the other. "The longer I'm away, the harder it is for me to jump back into the exact moment I left. So, we think that after Nan sealed away my memories and I stopped traveling to Alderton, the rubber band kept expanding until," the elastic snaps in half, "the connection broke. And that's why twenty years passed equally in both worlds." She tosses the elastic into the trash can beside the desk and rests the pen next to the laptop.

Cindy lifts her finger to interject. "Well, to be more accurate, about twenty-*one* years passed in Maryland, so it took some time for the connection to break. We're still testing when that might occur again, but we won't know until Adaline's been away for longer periods of time—which isn't an option now."

"Right." Dax nods along while he drifts back toward the saber above the fireplace, his fingers twitching to hold it. "Because you don't want your army to leave without you. Oh, wait—so that's why almost five hundred years passed in both worlds after Adaline's grandmother came here."

Cindy touches her finger to her nose. "Exactly."

"Wow," Ëólas says. "I'm impressed."

"Just think how much more data I would have if someone had confided in me earlier." Flipping her laptop closed, Cindy drops her clipboard on top with a thud.

"For the tenth time, I'm sorry." Adaline throws her arms up in the air. "I was afraid things would change between us."

Cindy juts her hip out to the side and fixes her gaze on Adaline. "Please. You're married now; I will be next year, and we're going to soon want kids. Of course, things will change. But you'll always be my chosen sister."

"Back at you." With a sheepish smile, Adaline lifts her fist, which Cindy bumps.

"Okay, let's move on to our next course of action." Cindy points at the desk chair. "Ëólas, sit down. I need your blood."

"What now?" Like a meerkat, he hurries away from the desk and the black bag next to the chair and hides behind his wife.

Adaline pats his arm. "I'll go first." Taking a seat, she rolls up her sleeve. When Cindy reaches into her bag and pulls out the needle, Adaline waves her hand to redirect Ëólas's eyes from the pointy tip and stop him from cringing. "Hey, it's best to not watch."

After Cindy draws several vials of blood and Adaline gets up, Cindy pats the empty chair. "Your turn, Your Highness."

Ëólas gives her a deadpan stare as he drops into the seat and yanks his sleeve up. Turning away from the needle, he pulls the quarter zipper of his sweater upward and downward. When the zipper jams halfway, Adaline offers her hand, which he squeezes as Cindy punctures his skin. "Actually, you address a queen and king as Your Majesty, though elves don't use those honorifics often. We don't—"

"There." Cindy holds the needle steady against Ëólas's inner elbow while she attaches the first vial. "The hard part is already done, *Your Majesty*. With your sample, I'll be able to identify the baseline for elven blood, that is, what's normal for your people. I'll also need a sample from the vampire elves—um, is that what we're calling them?"

"Thanks to Dax, yes. At least for now." Ëólas watches Cindy swap vials and fill another test tube.

"I'm glad my hobbies can help," Dax says.

Cindy winks at Dax and turns back to Ëólas. "Okay, so your job is to bring me a sample of vampire-elf blood. Once I can isolate the delta, er, um, the differences, I can test how our current medications respond to the infection."

When Cindy pulls out the needle and applies a band-aid to Ëólas's arm, he rests his hand on top of hers to hold her attention. "Thank you. Immensely. We're fortunate to have your help."

"Well, I'm glad you feel that way, because you might not like this next part." Cindy peels off her latex gloves while looking at all three of them. "In order to get a true baseline, I need more than just Ëólas's blood. I need at least thirty volunteers to run a control sample."

"Wait, wait, wait." Dax indicates a timeout with his hands. "Babe, are you saying what I think you're saying?"

Cindy deposits her trash in the mini orange hazardous waste bag she brought from work. "I need to stay in New Leira for a while, not just a day or two."

Dax pumps his fist beside him. "Yes! Can I come too?"

"No!" Adaline says, not believing her friends' reactions, especially given how much Dax knows about vampire elves. "I'm not putting either of you in danger. I mean, I'd love to have you visit—after we've dealt with these demonic elves and Morgán isn't a threat anymore. But until then, no way. If he ever found out that

I have someone who might undo whatever he's done to his soldiers, he'd target you too."

"And you think I'm okay with you vanishing to another world to fight these demonic creatures who might be infectious? Screw that, Adaline! I'm the only one qualified here to do this research. And with point-of-care testing, I can run rapid clinical testing on site. I'll bring a portable power generator. Hell, I'll bring three. And my piccolo."

Adaline massages her temples. "I assume you don't mean the musical instrument."

"No, it's a portable diagnostic analyzer."

Adaline looks to Ëólas, expecting him to object just as loudly. "You agree with me, right? She can't go."

Pursing his lips like a duck, Ëólas rocks back and forth on his feet, pauses, and flashes his apologetic smile. "I assumed she would come with us."

"But she can't defend herself." *Am I really the only person who sees the problem here?*

Cindy raises her hand hesitantly. "Um, that's not entirely true." She scrunches her face, lowers her voice, and hedges her words as she confesses, "I sorta, kinda know how to fight."

"What?" Adaline racks her brain, trying to recall if Cindy ever mentioned over the years taking self-defense lessons. Coming up with nothing, she stalks toward her best friend—who swears she's never kept secrets from Adaline.

Before Adaline can utter a single word, Dax walks over to Cindy and gazes at her with pride. "If you're talking about sword fighting, Cindy can hold her own."

Adaline's voice jumps ten octaves higher than usual. "Why do you know how to use a sword?" *You've never been into the whole Renaissance Fair scene.*

"When Dax and I were on the fence about getting back together again," Cindy exhales, "I joined his LARPers' guild. Made my own costume. You know, couples who exercise together…"

Adaline's face turns into a blank canvas. *Holy shit. She really wanted Dax back.* But Cindy's experience couldn't have prepared her for life-and-death situations. "Those are fake swords, Cindy. They're not even sharp."

"Yeah, but I didn't want to show up like an idiot, so I got lessons beforehand."
Oh hell no. "From whom?"

"Your dad," Cindy winces. "While you were at dance class, Mr. Yates taught me how to use a long sword and daggers and…"

Adaline sucks her bottom lip into her mouth while she throws her head back and stares at the ceiling. Before saying something she might regret, she walks out of the library and through the living room but hears Ëólas quietly ask, "How did he train you?" Crossing the foyer, she makes her way into the kitchen where she fills a tall glass with tap water, turning off the faucet only when the cold liquid overflows into the sink. She takes one sip, but the glass slips from her hand and shatters into a million pieces against the basin.

She doesn't have to turn around to know Cindy's standing in the archway. "Why didn't he teach me some kind of self-defense, knowing I'd most likely go home one day? Why? Why didn't he tell me his plans, that he…"

Cindy silently crosses the kitchen and hugs Adaline around her shoulders. Hanging one hand from Cindy's forearm, Adaline tilts her head against Cindy's, and they stare at the broken pieces together, until Adaline wipes away a rogue tear and Cindy grabs the dustpan from under the sink. While Adaline tosses out the big chunks, Cindy sweeps up the remains.

"You know, I asked him if he ever taught you." After returning the dustpan, Cindy shuts the cupboard door and faces Adaline. "He said you and pointy objects don't do so well together. Remember the pumpkin carving incident?"

Despite the grief weighing her down, Adaline bursts out laughing. They both do.

"I was eight years old! What was he thinking, giving me such a sharp knife?"

"Hey, you still won first place for the most gruesome, bloody Jack-o'-lantern."

Even though the humor is short-lived, Adaline holds on to the feeling behind it. Taking a deep breath, Adaline asks, "How long did Dad teach you?"

"About three years." Cindy click-clacks her short French-tip acrylic nails against each other. "It kinda became our thing."

Of course he'd help her out. Adaline can see Eddie inviting Cindy into the gym room and teaching her how to fight—not for Dax but for herself, helping her to rebuild the pieces that broke after she caught her father cheating, after Dax refused to stand up to his mother, after Cindy left him. While her mom became a surrogate mother to Adaline, Eddie was a father to Cindy. That's part of what makes them sisters.

"That's pretty badass," Adaline says.

"Yeah, well, I had to work hard to make sure Dax never won."

"Hell yeah." Adaline smirks. "So, are you going to tell me about your LARPer persona? You're an alchemist, aren't you?"

"Damn, you know me too well."

When Ëólas and Dax appear in the archway, Cindy waves the guys over and returns to all seriousness as she faces Adaline and uses her don't-fuck-with-me tone. "Look, whether or not you like it, I'll need time to collect and analyze the samples, research and study medicine in your world, and test potential treatment options. You need to take me there. Besides, it's not like anyone here will know we're gone."

Adaline clamps down on the pressure point next to her thumb. "If you come with us, you'll be stuck in New Leira for at least two months while Ëólas and I are in the Wastelands. You'll be on your own."

"Well," Ëólas shoves his hands into his pockets, "not alone. Magnus and Seira will look after them."

Adaline glares at him but hangs her head in defeat. "Okay, okay. I'll take you both."

"Man, this is going to be epic!" As quickly as Dax's face lights up, concern clouds his joy. "Wait, is this wise?"

"Finally!" Adaline says. "You get the danger. What if these demonic—"

"Nah!" Dax shoos away her words. "Not about the vampire elves. Is it wise for a Latina and a Black man to travel back in time or visit this ancient world or whatever?"

"Ah, I see." Ëólas claps Dax's shoulder. "In Ellíum, people will treat you unfairly because of your species."

"And we'll have your back no matter what," Adaline says.

"Cool, cool." Dax rubs his hands together as he plans his vacation itinerary. "When do we leave?"

Um, not until I get my shit together and I can fight as well as Ëólas? Crap, we're never going home.

Chapter Twenty

THE PEAR

Ëólas whips his sword downward. The reverberation of his blade clanging against Adaline's shakes her arms and adds pressure to her throbbing wrist. The small muscle connecting her hand and arm feels ten times its size and as if it could burst at any moment. But Adaline keeps her mouth shut, and Ëólas increases the strength of his strikes, lunging at her and pushing her backward. She catches each of his blows in time, calculating his next moves, watching each twitch of his arm and leg muscles. He doesn't relent as he continues to attack her, forcing her to the edge.

But he's still not moving as quickly as he did with Āranol.

As that asshole's smug face flashes in her mind, Ëólas's sword slides down the flat side of her blade and strikes her arm. She winces and jumps back. If their weapons were sharp, she'd be bleeding profusely and need stitches. Instead, she'll have a black and blue for at least a week, which will make him frown every time he sees it.

Damn it.

With a scowl, Ëólas strikes again. "You're distracted."

"Sorry."

"Don't be sorry. Stay focused." Their blades lock, and he shoves her backward. "Nothing exists outside this fight and what might happen around you."

"I know." *Even though I'll never be as fast as him or any other elf who's wielded a sword for hundreds of years.*

"Prove it."

Ducking under his next attack, Adaline spins away from the wall and swings at his feet, which he easily dodges. When he swipes his sword toward her gut, she catches his blade with her hilt at the last second, but her wrist, rotated at an uncomfortable angle, wobbles to push him off. Her arm gives out, and his blade twists around hers.

At the last second, he slows the tip of his sword so he only taps her gut. He exhales loudly and turns his back on her as he walks to the center of the mat so they can start again from the top.

Adaline crushes the hilt of her sword in her fist. *So much for being a fucking natural. I hate this.* She imagines throwing it across the room or burning the metal until it liquifies into a useless puddle. They've been at this every day for three months, but she already knows with absolute certainty that she'll never have his reflexes, not with a blade. *This is pointless.*

"Again," he says, resetting his stance.

"I'm ready." She faces him, takes a deep breath, and raises her sword in front of her body. This time, she strikes first, leaping forward and aiming for his head, knowing full well he'll swat her away like a fly. Which he does. Again.

Before she can breathe, he comes at her harder, faster. *Has he forgotten whom he's fighting?* He picks up his pace, making her dizzy as her eyes dart from his feet to his hips to his arms, trying to read his body movements, trying to block him. Her eyes can't keep up with her body, and her limbs go stiff. He knocks her sword out of her hand, sending her blade flying across the room and clanging under the dumbbells.

Not quite the way she wanted to throw her sword.

"Where's your head at, Adaline? You're better than this."

"Maybe I'm not."

"I know you are. I've seen it. Let's go again."

She turns her back to him to retrieve her sword, but she stares at the door. If only she could flip him off and run outside. She needs fresh air. But if she gave up, he'd be beyond disappointed in her.

"Come on, Adaline."

She doesn't have to look behind her to know he's already in position. "I just need a moment."

"Your enemy won't give you a moment."

"You're not my enemy. You're my husband."

"Not in this room."

The words *fuck you* sit on the edge of her tongue. She stalks over to grab her sword. Later, he'll speak to her with a softer voice. He'll hold her close, roam her body, show her how much he's holding back his own desires, how much this hurts him too. Later, they'll be themselves again.

"Let's go, Adaline."

Later, she won't want to scream at him. At herself.

Stooping down, she retrieves her sword and moves to the center of the room. *I have to be strong. I can control my emotions. I'm in charge. Deep breath in. Deep breath out.*

The moment she lifts her sword, he attacks again, all love and adoration gone from his face. She hesitates, leaving her side exposed. As his blade stings her ribs, Ëólas and the gym vanish. In place of ceiling lights, stars twinkle overhead. Across the backyard covered in leaves, the kitchen and dining room lights offer a warm glow to guide her home.

"Shit." Clutching her sword, she crosses the dock, the boards squeaking under her feet. *At least I didn't travel into the lake.*

"Adaline?" Ëólas's panicked voice shouts throughout the house.

"I'm here," she hollers as she shuts the backdoor.

When he appears in the kitchen, he's still in teacher mode. "What was that?"

"Instinct, sorry. I'm ready to go again."

She heads for the stairs, but he blocks her path. Instead of furious, he looks almost...elated? "Can you do that again, travel in the middle of a fight to change your position, but before I can land a blow?"

"I, I don't know." *I never considered that before.* "Maybe."

"Let's try that then. Come on."

She watches him jog downstairs but doesn't follow. "I'm fine. Perfectly fine," she whispers to herself. She wipes away a tear and heads downstairs. *I won't be a liability in the field.*

Leaning against the wall, Ëólas waits for her outside the gym. "What's wrong?"

She shakes her head, walks into the room, and heads for the center mat. She flexes her arms and neck, widens her stance, bends her knees, and lifts her sword. *Focus. Right here. Right now. Nothing else matters.*

Grinding his jaw, Ëólas stands in front of her and heaves his blade upward, his arm sagging as if the sword's weight has increased tenfold. He doesn't advance, only watches her face. She tightens and loosens her grip on her hilt, turning off the part of her brain that registers the pain radiating from her wrist. She forces herself to hold her position while she waits for the telltale sign that will give away his first attack. But he doesn't strike. His resolve wavers, his eyes flickering between what he knows from his own training, what he foresees in their future, and what he feels right now.

She hardens her heart and braces herself for the onslaught that will soon follow. *Why isn't he attacking? Is he testing to see if I'll strike first? I don't want to be on the offense. I don't want to do this at all. I hate this thing in my hand. Shut up, Adaline. Focus. I don't have a choice anymore.*

Ëólas finally moves, only instead of lunging forward, he lowers his sword to the ground. His eyes fall to the mat, and he sits down, crossing his legs and lowering his face to hide his expression.

Adaline lays her weapon down, kneels beside him, and drapes her arm over his back. He still doesn't move, probably because he's too busy calculating all the possible consequences of him going easy on her. When her legs begin to fall asleep beneath her bottom, she lets go and rises onto her knees. Before she can attempt to stand up, he hooks his arm around her waist and swivels her onto his lap, tucking her head beneath his chin. She hugs his arm.

"You're the professor," he says. "What do you do when your students are struggling?"

She hugs his arm more tightly. "I try another method until I find one that yields better results."

"Alright. Let's try something different."

She wants to tell him no, that she'll keep going, but one look at him tells her they both need time to rethink their plan. At least he can't vanish on his own and go find Morgán without her, even though she knows that's what he'd rather do.

A stack of papers slips out from Adaline's arms, scattering essays across her office floor.

"Shit." She stoops down to pick up her student's essays, flipping the papers over the staples so the pages lie flat again, and accepts the three Ben collected while he groaned about his knee. "Thanks. What's up, Ben?"

After arching his back to stretch his spine, he shuts the door to her office. "We need to figure out what to do about the cave site. With your father gone and you not beholden to it, I could have it destroyed."

"Destroy the sacred circle?" Adaline envisions Ëólas clutching his heart. "No, we can't do that."

"Well, I can't promise Beccah's paper won't draw more attention, despite the additions I made to her samples."

"Ben!"

"What? I made Eddie a promise."

Adaline takes off her peacoat, hangs it on the wall hook, and untwists the sleeves of her burnt-orange open-front sweater. "Let me discuss this with Ëólas. We'll figure something out."

"Is he still taking furniture orders? I could use a trunk-like coffee table in my family room."

"I'll ask him, but he has his hands full at the moment. He's making hope chests for Cindy's sisters for Christmas."

"Aww, he's a Christmas el—"

"Don't say it. He'll never make you that trunk."

Ben lifts his hands in surrender and backs out of her office. "Have a good weekend, kid. Oh, I'm out Monday, so let's discuss this Tuesday at 10:30."

Adaline's only reply is a salute. Once he's gone, she turns on her computer monitor, unlocks the screen, and grabs her notepad. *Ten thirty, ten thirty, ten thirty.* While her Inbox loads, she reaches toward the mug holding her favorite pen, the one with the built-in fidget spinner that twirls ballet slippers on top. But her hand stops mid-way; of course the pen's not where she needs it.

Getting out her mobile, she pulls up Ëólas's contact info and hits the speed dial button. As the phone rings, she lifts stacks of papers and pushes aside books in search of that pen.

"Hello, my love," Ëólas answers.

"Hey." She sets down the papers and turns toward the speaker. "My students are panicking over choosing their final projects, so I extended my office hours today. I'm sorry, but I'll be home late. I can have dinner ready at six, and, um, if you want, I could be ready for training at seven."

She bites her lip as she waits for his response—while also lifting her satchel and checking her drawers. During the last week, he's binge watched training tutorials online and not once mentioned when they'll resume lessons. He's not been moody, but he has retreated into that head of his, ruminating over God knows what.

"Don't worry about dinner." His voice gives away zero signs of agitation.

"Oh." She shuts the desk drawer and sits back in her chair. "Are you sure? I don't mind—"

"It's okay. I've got it covered."

Placing her arms on both sides of the phone, Adaline slouches and stares at Ëólas's contact picture, at the joy on his face as he stood outside the botanic garden. "Okay then. Thanks for understanding."

"Of course. Do you...think we're ready to try training again? I have an idea."

A student knocks on her doorframe and waves hello. Adaline holds up one finger, and the student disappears to wait outside. She takes her phone off speaker and presses it to her ear. "Yes, absolutely."

"Good. I'll see you at five then." He hangs up before she can ask what he has in mind.

Before calling her student into her office, Adaline rests her head on her desk. Next semester, she'll definitely lighten her load.

After teaching one more class and meeting with students one on one, Adaline grabs her laptop and coat, locks up her office, and makes her way past the dorms and through the main campus quad. Her peacoat flaps at her sides, the temperature not yet cold enough to require bundling up. As she stuffs her hands into her pockets to fish out her car keys, her shoulder blades twitch and contract, and her neck spasms as if someone is breathing over her shoulder. She shivers, dropping her keys in her pocket, and rubs her arms to grind away her goosebumps, but more pop up.

She halts mid-step, about-faces, and collides into a group of students. Using her shoulder bag as a shield, she apologizes profusely and steps off to the side, letting the kids pass. Their vivacious chatter makes her laugh at herself. Shaking off her paranoia, she fishes around her pocket for her keys.

Maybe she's getting restless to go home—to New Leira. She thought being away for a while wouldn't be that hard. But she misses everyone. And whenever she peeks in on them, she feels less connected to her friends who seem almost frozen in time. It doesn't help that Ëólas won't estimate when they should head back. Or that she's made zero progress on this whole magic thing, even with Cindy's help. Adaline's also run out of rooms to search in Nan's house. Her house.

With her keys in hand, she straightens her back, and her eyes lock with Derek's, even though he's coming out of a building on the other side of the quad. He stops on the top step. His face pales. He glances around and scurries back inside, pushing two students out of the way.

Yep, I scared the crap out of him.

When she gets home, she does a double take to make sure she's walked into the right house. Sleeping bags, tents, the old cooking plastic tote box, two duffle bags, and a water cooler crowd the grand foyer, creating an obstacle course for her to maneuver.

Um…what is going on?

While staring at the camping equipment, she hangs up her coat, leans her satchel against the wall, and checks the ceramic bowl on the console table. Ëólas's keys are missing. She touches his stack of books like a totem and meanders into the kitchen where two warm loaves of bread rest under a towel. The morning dishes are cleaned and back in the cabinets, and the oven clock counts down six remaining minutes. When Adaline flips on the oven light, she finds a tenderloin roasting in a cast-iron skillet.

Damn, I've got it good.

She pulls out her phone to text Ëólas when the front door opens and closes.

"My love?" Ëólas calls.

"In the kitchen." She turns off the oven light and walks around the island.

"Right on time, I see."

She hears him toss his keys and Metro card into the ceramic bowl.

"I try." She heads for the foyer, refraining from tearing off a piece of bread. "Dare I ask what's with all the camp—Oh my god!" Adaline shrieks and cups her hands over her mouth.

Sporting the mocha mock-neck sweater he bought last weekend from Banana Republic, his new favorite store, Ëólas stands perfectly still while he watches her reaction. She inches closer and rests her palms on his chest, the ribbed texture of the wool tingling her skin as she skates her hands toward his shoulders, where his long dirty-blond hair used to fall.

She slides her hands up his neck and combs her fingers through his hair. As she pulls her hands away, the layers fall along the sides of his face, the soft fringe ending just below his cheekbones. She takes a deep breath and walks around him, teasing the back of his hair and the last layers trimmed to align with his nape.

When she stands in front of him again, her whole face smiles. "Holy shit."

He smirks and tugs her forward into a hug. "You like it?"

"Do you?" Unable to look away, her eyes follow how his hair frames his face and accentuates his jawline, which she kisses the length of.

"I do. Very much so. I'd been pondering cutting it for a while now."

"Wow." Stretching up on her tiptoes, she circles her hands around his neck and nibbles his bottom lip, sucking it into her mouth.

Groaning, he grips her bottom and presses himself against her, showing her just how pleased her reaction has made him. "I'm glad you like it too."

She chuckles, drops her hands to his chest, and nods toward the grand foyer, her eyes not relinquishing her new view of him. "So, what does the haircut have to do with the camping stuff? Did I miss something?"

"No, I did."

"Huh?"

The oven timer beeps, and Ëólas takes her hand in his. "Come on." He leads her into the kitchen where he grabs the potholders, turns off the timer, and pulls the tenderloin out of the oven, the juices sizzling around the herb-encrusted roast. Adaline inhales scents of cardamum, cinnamon, cumin, and cloves.

The sight of him wearing Nan's potholders and cooking meals makes Adaline's heart ache, but in a good way. "That smells amazing. Thank you for making dinner."

"You're welcome." When he's done tenting the roast with a loose piece of tinfoil, he hooks his hands around Adaline's waist. "I used the credit card."

"Okay."

"I booked us a camping site about two hours from here."

"For when?" She wriggles in his arms.

"This weekend," he says, not letting her escape. "I made dinner so we can hit the road as soon as possible. I'll even drive us there, if I must."

"You don't have a license."

"The plastic card in my wallet says otherwise."

"You know what I mean. Besides, what about—" She can't bring herself to argue with him; those golden eyes reflect nothing but care and concern. "Why?"

"Because you're overthinking everything, from training with me, to scrutinizing that photo album, to burying yourself within those magic books. Hence, I'm stealing you away for the weekend, away from your mobile phone—don't fret, we'll leave them in the car—and we're going to disappear into the forest where I'll show you what it feels like to be timeless. Deep breath."

Her gaze dashes from his hair to the roast to the clean kitchen. He's not once complained about fitting into her life. He's gone above and beyond for her yet again.

She taps his chest like a slow drumbeat. *My students can deal with getting their papers back a bit late.* "Okay, let's do this."

Adaline drags her red camping chair closer to the crackling fire that paints the tips of her Timberlands and Ëólas's suede boots orange. With the sun having set, a cool November gust nips her nose, a sure sign that colder weather lurks around the corner. She leans forward, rubs her hands together, and holds them up to the flames. Her palms pulse like when she burned Derek, but this tingling sensation is natural, cozy even.

Ëólas, immune to changes in the weather, reclines in his chair, his elbows dangling over the sides of the canvas armrests. While he meditates or zones out in front of the fire, Adaline bobs her head and waits for this so-called peace to snuff out her racing thoughts.

She drums her fingers on her thighs, her digits desperate for something to fiddle with, to occupy her mind. "Did you bring cards or something?"

"Or something." He heads to the car where he pulls a long, narrow black package out of the trunk.

Are we training out here?

When he emerges from the shadows, he's carrying a guitar case and Eddie's steel tongue drum, which Ëólas sets on the dirt. He passes Adaline her acoustic guitar as she slides off her chair, and her rump hits the ground. Crossing his legs under each other, Ëólas sets the drum in front of him. The metallic green looks like a space-age turtle shell.

"You know how to use that?" she asks.

"Of course. I watched a YouTube video."

Éólas taps around the drum, creating a light, lingering harmony that resonates inside Adaline's body. As he circles around the instrument, he plays notes faster, using his fingers, the side of his thumb, and the heel of his hand. Each musical chime along the pentatonic scale overlaps with the previous one, letting the song build momentum and banish her thoughts one at a time.

Then he slows down and sings, and his soothing voice summons the long-lost piece of herself she set aside nearly a decade ago, the version she didn't think she needed anymore, that she had to put away when she grew up. Picking up her guitar, Adaline strums chords, merging her song with his, letting him lead but filling in the notes to create a more robust and enchanting melody that fills the campsite. They spend the weekend making music together, a blend of old and new, of this world and the other, and telling stories. He also brought UNO and Catan, and they take several hikes deeper into the woods.

When they crawl into their tent on the second night, they zip away the outside world and make love. With their legs and arms entangled, Adaline drifts off to sleep, her head on his chest and her soul content.

In her dreams, she strolls through the forest, her dark-periwinkle gown gliding over the fallen leaves but not disturbing their final resting place. The crisp air fills her lungs, and woodland creatures bow their heads as she passes. The further she descends into the forest, the trees grow taller, stretching from their roots until their boughs scrape against the bottom of heaven. At the edge of the forest, a lake glistens, reflecting pastel shades of red, orange, and gold.

Near the water's edge, a tree with an inch-wide curved arch chiseled into its trunk hums elevator music. For a second, a flash of white light illuminates the archway. Then the tree dings, and the trunk slides open, revealing the interior of an elevator. An elderly woman with short hair and sagging skin exits the tree and walks across the lake to a cabin the size of a thimble in the distance. When the tree dings again, a young man steps out and hikes into the forest. More people arrive through the doorway, each choosing different paths, but all exude a similar tranquility that must come from living in the Immortal Realms.

With no desire to wander away or busy herself elsewhere, Adaline waits patiently at the base of the tree.

"Are you lost, dear?" an old man asks her.

"No, I'm okay, thank you. I'm waiting for someone."

He tips his fedora, revealing a bald patch on the crown of his head, and walks along the shoreline until he vanishes into the horizon.

The next time the tree dings, the elderly woman who emerges has silver hair twisted into a bun, warm brown eyes, and that same heart-shaped face that makes Adaline want to hug her.

She came.

Adaline hurries over, her eyes brimming with tears. "I've missed you."

"Oh, my sweet girl." Nan hugs Adaline close to her breast, and the pressure of that embrace wraps around Adaline's heart, telling her this moment must be real. "I'm always here," Nan whispers.

When they let go, Nan loops her arm through Adaline's and holds on tightly as they stroll through the forest. Adaline's gown shrinks around her legs until the top becomes a blouse, and she's wearing Timberlands and jeans. Nan pulls her purple cardigan shut over her floral knee-length dress.

Even though Adaline's content to walk side by side with Nan with no destination in sight, something in the back of her mind tells her they have little time. "Nan, I can't connect with the elements like I used to."

She nods her head. A gray strand comes loose, and she tucks it behind her ear that doesn't look entirely round anymore but also not as pointy as Ëólas's. "I know."

"Why didn't you leave me any instructions or notes?"

Nan chuckles so heartily that Adaline can't help but smile too. "Does an apprentice leave notes for her mentor?"

Adaline pauses, pulling on Nan's elbow. "Huh?"

Instead of elaborating on that idea, Nan pushes Adaline's hair over her shoulder and pinches her chin. "We don't leave behind spell books or run magic schools to channel our abilities. Our connection to nature is personal and runs deep, sweet girl. For our family, it flows through our blood."

"But—"

"No buts, Adaline. You've been trying to control your abilities, but we can no more control nature than we can control others. Morgán is trying, and for that he'll live a cursed life. But for you, for me, we interact with the elements just as we do with the people who pass through our lives. With patience and an open heart, we can befriend the elements while guiding them, nurturing them, healing them."

They continue walking until Nan stops in front of a small pear tree in the middle of the woods, its green fruit glowing as they hang low from the boughs. She plucks a pear and places it in Adaline's upturned palms. "But here's the secret most forget—humans and elves alike. We are a force of nature too, sweet girl. The elements live inside us because they're a part of us, from every breath we take, to the water in our bodies, to the dirt from which we were born, to the fire that burns deep in our soul. That's why we complete the sacred circle; the relationship between us and nature is symbiotic."

Adaline lifts the pear into the air, and the stem reattaches to the tree. "Connecting with the elements was so easy when I was a child. It's just not the same."

"You're not the same, and that's okay."

When Adaline turns around to face Nan, the woman looking back at her is the same, only instead of silver hair restrained in a bun, dark-brown hair flows down her back to her calves, the ends twisting into loose curls. The brown in her irises washes away until the periwinkle underneath shines through, and her ears elongate into those sweet points like Seira's while her skin gleams with the perfection of youth. The confidence that radiates from her could blind Adaline, but she keeps her aura soft, inviting, a warm embrace for anyone who beholds her. And yet, Adaline still sees the grandmother who taught her how to bake tarts and command an audience.

If only Adaline had the same level of confidence. "Nan, please, what am I doing wrong? Our people need me. I can't let them down."

Touching her fingers to Adaline's chin, Nan tilts her granddaughter's head up. "We use our mind and soul to connect with the elements, and our bodies channel that energy. All three must be in balance. Too much mind, and we logic away that connection. Too much soul, and our abilities become unwieldy. If our bodies are weak, then so too is the connection.”

“I have too much mind.”

“And Seira has too much soul.”

“I, I don’t know how to fix that. I’m an academic at heart, Nan. I—”

Nan crosses her arms over her chest and chuckles again, the melody uplifting and encouraging. “You said the answer yourself. Heart.” She places her hand over Adaline’s chest. “Above all else, filter everything through the heart.”

When Adaline exhales, they’re in front of the elevator again. *Didn’t I have other things I wanted to ask Nan? What were they?*

She throws her arms around Nan, who squeezes her tightly in return. All too soon, the elevator chimes, and Adaline clings to her grandmother, praying she can hold on a little longer, but she’s not a goddess. She can’t bring back the dead.

“Adaline,” Nan whispers, “our family’s magic has been dwindling. Magic is in a constant state of flux, but elves tend to be stagnant.” She pulls back and caresses Adaline’s cheek. “Adding the continuous evolution of humankind to our family created balance again. Your humanity isn’t your weakness, sweet girl. It’s your strength.”

The elevator door opens, and Nan and the forest vanish as Adaline opens her eyes. Staring at the tent’s ceiling, she remains silent so she doesn’t wake Ëólas. She needs time to replay that dream, to remember what Nan said. Also, she’s not ready to shed the tranquility Nan shared or lose the pressure of Nan’s hug that’s still wrapped around her heart.

Chapter Twenty-One

DIFFERENT METHODS

"Who thought adding lights to a tree, without the aid of an enchantment, was a wise idea?" Ëólas untangles himself from a strand of white Christmas lights wrapped around his arm and deposits the excess on the foyer floor. "Also, if this belongs on the tree, then why did we add them to the stairs?"

"Because it's not Christmas without every room in the house decorated?"

Adaline pecks his cheek and collects the leftover strands, dumping them back in the totes that line the foyer. After dimming the ceiling lights, she plugs in the finished décor. A soft glow, entwined with garland, curves up the banister and adorns every archway, turning the foyer into an enchanted echo of Lameiría.

"Well, isn't that pretty." He slips his hand into her back pocket and kisses her temple. "Wait, did you say every room?"

She thwacks his abs. "Go finish those presents of yours. I'll be ready for training in about two hours."

As Adaline digs through the totes for the outlet timer, Ëólas heads downstairs to the gym where he's pulled Eddie's workbench away from the wall. For months now, he's been toiling away in that room, using his hands not only to swing swords but also to carve, sand, and paint wood. This week, he needs to finish staining the three hope chests—or treasure chests, as Adaline calls them—for Cindy's sisters.

Left alone to prepare final exams, Adaline gives up on the timer and stares at the dull star that lies dormant in her hand. Without its warm inner glow, the plastic looks cheap, cold, and ordinary. She rests the tree topper on a box of ornaments and heads downstairs, her feet leading her where her heart has resisted going since they moved into this house. She pauses in front of the door opposite the gym and places her hand on the knob. Even the chill of the metal on her hand feels foreign.

Filter everything through the heart.

With Ëólas, that's easy. But if Loríen saw Adaline today, she'd say the same thing she did all those months ago in her shop: *The energy around your heart is blocked. You have been suppressing too much, and that puts you in danger.*

Loríen was right. Adaline had been suppressing a lot back then. She still is.

Time to be honest, Adaline.

Releasing a slow exhale, she pushes the door open and steps inside. When she flips the lights on, the mirrors along the long wall shudder alive as they reflect the sofa, stereo, wardrobe, and minifridge opposite them. Adaline trails her fingers over the pink slippers hanging near the door, each pair a different size to mark the years, their dangling ribbons covered with dust.

Opening the wardrobe, she pushes aside the bodysuits hanging on the rack until she finds a black one that can fit a grown woman's body. She drapes it carefully over her torso to assess the size, along with a sheer white wrap for a skirt, and changes her clothes. The bodysuit and wrap fit as well as they did on her twentieth birthday. Without facing the mirror, she pulls her hair up into a large bun, tucking away the loose strands with precision and far more Bobby pins than before Seira's miracle-grow hair spell.

From a shelf, she pulls out her favorite pair of slippers and hugs them to her chest.

Sitting on the sofa, she slips her feet into the cotton interior, her fingers trembling, yet her toes slide effortlessly into their designated home. The canvas hugs her high arches like an old friend. Rising, she glides one foot forward and then the next. With the outfit complete, she lifts her eyes and peers into the mirror.

Does the woman looking back at her know how much has changed, or is her reflection limited to waiting for the next dance so she may come alive again?

Not sure what Adaline expects to happen in here, she rummages through her music collection and finds a song from years ago, one she used during a high school solo performance. She cues the music, turning up the volume to drown out any thoughts that might try to puncture this moment. When the whimsical, smooth music begins, she rises onto the balls of her feet, engaging her core and buttocks and pulling her body into a lean, straight line as if she is a conduit between the earth and sky. In that one move, everything clicks into place.

Rather than pushing her feet into the ground and thrusting her limbs into sharp defensive and offensive reactions, she enters a rhythm of continuous motion where her body flows from one position to the next. Long and fluid, her muscles know when to slow down and speed up, when to allow her energy to grow and expand and then softly contract and relax, returning to her center. Her heart races with jubilation when her legs reach outward and spin her about and when her arms sweep upward and drift back down, the movements appearing effortless.

Few people know the immense strength required to demonstrate such gentleness.

Her smile grows wider, and the music grows louder, faster. Using the entire room, she tells her own story as she leaps and tumbles and rises again. The music's fierce tempo and unabashed freedom breathes through her, and she keeps going, keeps flowing, keeps extending her reach.

Why did I shut away this part of myself for so long?

She recognizes the person in the mirror now, the dancer with the flushed cheeks, long legs, and a steel core. She sees glimpses of the queen too, the one who looks confident, capable, and comfortable in her element. Once the music stops, the uncertainty will come back. But maybe that's okay. Maybe it's okay that she wants to stay in this world and return home. She can be more than one thing. The dancer and the fighter. The queen and the explorer. The peacemaker and the protector.

She can also be the daughter who feels left behind. Yes, left behind. And forgotten. Maybe she needs to own her anger too, because lying to herself is the real threat. Her father had been her shield, her teacher, her best friend—the person she emulated. And he left her—either by accident or by choice—but he left her, nonetheless, before they could reconcile the past, before they could truly know each other.

After the music releases its last burst of emotion, the melody steadily assumes a softer cadence, one that releases all tension and quiets the mind until Adaline's heartbeat and the music fall into alignment. When the song clicks off, she approaches the mirror and touches her reflection's flaming cheeks.

And you, my little firefly, Nan had once said, *pour passion into everything you do.*

"Passion," Adaline whispers to herself.

What did she read about fire according to the wuxing system? That the essence of fire is warmth, creativity, and enthusiasm. Its innate purpose is neither chaos, nor danger, nor to be used as a weapon.

Just like Ëólas said. *Fire isn't evil, Adaline. It warms the home, gives us light, and brings us together. Just like you.*

Lifting her palm closer to her face, she says to herself, "It's okay. You can come out."

A small flame flares awake on Adaline's palm. She turns her hand over, and the flame dances across her knuckles. She opens her other palm, and the flame leaps like a ballerina onto the center of her other hand. "Huh. What d'you know."

The flame flickers and shrinks, already exhausted, so she closes her fist, and the flame goes out—no, goes inward. Returning to the stereo, she searches for a different song, pauses, and tilts her head backward to where her memories reside. She can see them again, the days upon days when she lived in this room, emerging only for school and meals and family jam sessions.

She lets herself be herself without the pressure of having to prove anything to her colleagues or her subjects or her husband. Instead, she's just Adaline, song after song, from classical ballet to contemporary to freestyling whatever flows through her.

During the last dance, a pair of golden eyes appear in the mirror. When the music concludes, Ëólas looks at her as if she's the most magical being he's ever encountered. "I could watch you for decades."

The corners of her mouth perk up. Grabbing a towel from the wardrobe, she tosses it around her neck and walks over to him. "Once upon a time, all I did was dance."

"Hmph." He nods to himself. "It makes so much more sense now."

"What does?"

"How technical your dancing is here."

"Meaning?" She opens the minifridge next to the wardrobe and finds a water bottle still waiting for her. Twisting the cap off, she guzzles half the bottle.

"Those dance lessons taught you discipline and dedication. They built up your strength, your endurance, your precision. Your grace. Your ability to mimic my moves so accurately. You thought your father left you unprepared, but that's not true. He made sure you had the skills needed. He just let you choose the method."

Adaline faces her reflection and the remnants of the queen that remain within those long lines. "I suppose you're right."

She shows him her palm, shows him the flame she can conjure from within, its light illuminating his delight. He cups his hand under hers, waves his other over the flame's dark-orange tip, and laughs as the light flickers and tickles his skin. Even though the flame remains small, they take comfort in knowing it's a start.

The snap of the rattan stick against Adaline's forearm echoes in the gym. Wincing, she rubs her fifth welt in the last ten minutes. *Maybe wearing a tank top wasn't the best choice. I could have turned off the heater while we're down here.*

"Again." Ëólas doesn't bark his orders, but his tone reveals his frustration. "Reset."

She lifts her stupid stick in front of her body. While Ëólas contemplates his next strike, she yells at herself to just move her body to the spot behind him. That's all. A simple jump. That would be so much easier if she just moved her damn feet. But that's not the goal today. It hasn't been the goal all week. They're here to weaponize her traveling, to give her the upper hand with—snap! "Ouch!"

The rattan stick tagged her thigh in the blink of an eye, which she would have seen coming if she had been studying his muscle movements instead of the dead space behind him.

"This isn't working." She hobbles away, massaging the heel of her palm into her tender flesh.

Instead of issuing yet another pointless "Again," Ëólas drops his stick, runs his hands through his shorter hair, and paces around the mat.

I'm sorry I suck at this. I'll—

"Alright." Ëólas faces her, nodding his head to himself, and kicks the stick off the mat. "If dancing has helped your magic more than those research books, let's try something else here too." Grabbing the hem of his shirt, he rips his polo over his head and tosses it onto the floor. "I want to clarify that I've never had anyone train me in this matter." He unzips his jeans and yanks them off, chucking them into the corner, along with his silky drawstring boxers from Lameiría that he still prefers.

Hey now, what? Adaline ogles his lean muscles, the ladder between his pecs, and that glorious V that leads to her favorite toy. "Um, I love the view, but what's going on? Should I?" She points to her shirt.

"No, you're good. Here's the deal."

Deal me in. Wait—I'm not allowed to touch him in this room. What's he doing?

"You aren't allowed to touch me in any conceivable way throughout this entire house, unless you catch me off guard through traveling."

"Come again?"

"Nope. No coming. No showering together. No snuggling for movies. No sleeping in the same bed. No nothing. Unless you travel in the same room and surprise me." He crosses his arms over his bare chest and shifts from side to side, his cock dangling like a carrot. "Nothing? Okay. I'll go make a snack." He does an about-face, flashing his rock-hard glutes, and leaves the gym.

Adaline stares at the doorway and his discarded clothes. *Did he just take away my one source of stress relief?* Flinging the rattan stick at the wall, Adaline curls her lips upward and dashes out the door, taking two steps at a time. Peeking around the archway to the kitchen, she spies Ëólas opening a package of Oreos.

The harder she focuses on the space behind him, the more her eyesight blurs and the pressure in her head builds until her ears pop.

Why is traveling big distances easier? Adaline tilts her head to the side and thinks back to her dream walk with Nan. *Because I have too much mind. With big jumps, I can't be so logical. Seeing where I want to go has been messing with me because, logically, I should just freaking walk there. But if I walk there, I can't pinch that tushy. Okay, game on.*

Leaning against the foyer wall, Adaline stops thinking. She lets go of the hows and whys and under which circumstances. Instead, she places her hand over her heart as if to touch the part of Ëólas's soul that he shared with her. Within the blink of an eye, she travels, appearing in the kitchen behind the countertop—*Woo-hoo*—and reaches forward to pinch nothing but air. *Wait, what?* The open package of cookies sits on the granite in front of her, but Ëólas is gone.

"You'll have to be faster than that," he says, resting his forearm on a dining room chair. "Also, you didn't travel within the same room." He saunters through the kitchen and heads for the staircase. "I'll go pop in a movie. See you later."

"Oh, hell no."

She runs after him, and he sprints into the living room, then the library. They race throughout the house, him sidestepping out of her embrace and stroking himself to tease her. Unfortunately, because she has to stand still to travel, he uses that pause to escape her. Also, her laughter gives away her location every time, but she soon uses that to her advantage. As he's running upstairs, she travels from the foyer to the top of the landing. Upon hearing her snort out loud at the sight of his cock bouncing upstairs, he about-faces. When she travels to the bottom of the stairs and aims to smack his bum, she succeeds at surprising him, especially as he turns around, and her palm collides with his balls.

"Oh my god!" Adaline cries, clapping her hands over her mouth.

Ëólas's eyes enlarge three sizes as his face turns pale, and he crumbles into a ball, his ass sliding down the last three steps. "Ouch. I don't have padding." Sucking his lips inward, he holds up one hand to tell her he's peachy while the other cradles his member, and he rocks back and forth.

"I'm so, so, so sorry." She runs into the living room, grabs the Star Wars throw blanket off the sofa, knocking Sir Bearsaac to the floor, and gently lays the blanket over his nakedness to offer him some form of comfort.

Leaning against the stairs, he squeaks, "I knew you could do it."

Chapter Twenty-Two

A Conundrum

"Adaline," Ëólas whispers in her ear.

She rolls onto her back and tries to mumble that it's still dark outside, but his hand over her mouth cuts off her words.

"Someone's in the house," he says so quietly that she almost thinks she's dreaming, or rather having a nightmare. "Stay quiet." Soundlessly, he slides off the mattress and tiptoes toward the bedroom door.

Adaline can't hear anything. The house is as silent as ever, minus the occasional moan of the heater turning on. She sits up in bed, drags her legs away from the cozy warm sheets, and places her feet on the chilly hardwood floor, her toes curling from the sudden assault. The moment she stands and puts her weight on the boards, they creak, just once, but enough for Ëólas to spin around and flail his hand in the air, telling her to stay put. She freezes, and the overbearing silence permeates every corner of the room. In the dark, the shadows dance and jump across the furniture, tricking her into seeing a threat that's not there.

But then the stairs creak, and her blood turns cold.

Without so much as a rasp of breath, Ëólas puts on his sweatpants, tosses her a nightgown, and goes into the bathroom where he fades into the background. After she shimmies into the black silk nightgown that looks more like a low-cut slip dress, she looks from the mattress to the bathroom. Should she get back in bed or try to tiptoe across the floor like a ghost? If only she had Ëólas's and Seira's ability to appear and disappear without a sound.

Who could be in the house?

As Adaline's about to sink onto the bed, her knees growing stiff from the half turn she'd solidified into five minutes ago, she watches the doorknob turn. Silently, the door cracks open. Fingers encased in a black glove wrap around the door and push it further open in a small arch.

The urge to scream balloons inside Adaline's throat, but she can't jeopardize whatever Ëólas has planned. She scans the room for a weapon, but the only objects next to her are a pillow, her mobile phone—which she now realizes she should have used to call the police five minutes ago—and a lamp that's plugged into the wall. No chance she could pick that thing up and hurl it fast enough to stop whoever lurks in the hallway.

When the door stops moving, a man's nose appears first, followed by long, parted bangs that conceal the intruder's face until he peeks further into the room, and Derek's steel-gray eyes fall on the empty bed. His gaze immediately finds Adaline's.

Why is my ex in my house? And how did he know which guestroom to find us in? Oh my god, he's monster hunting, isn't he?

As he raises his arm and points the barrel of a handgun at her, she recalls every moment during the last few months when he ran away from her. Then again, what about all the times she felt watched. Had that been Derek all along? But she's supposed to be safe here. In this world. With no demonic elves trying to kill her.

Derek cocks the gun, and she raises her hands. In an instant, she sees her father biting into the waffles she made one morning and his voice, full of pride, telling her that she'll rule the anthropology department in less than a decade because she has so much more to achieve, so much untapped potential. Nan, sitting on her front steps, adheres a Band-Aid to Adaline's skinned knee while encouraging her to get back up and try again, to never give in to fear or doubt because then those emotions will control her, rather than her being in control of her life. Her mother paints a seascape with a small boat near a dock, and Adaline can't tell if the rowers are leaving or coming home. Seira cuddles next to her in bed, holding her hand and falling asleep with a single tear in the corner of her eye but a smile on her face. Cindy walks beside her as they hop off the school bus and laugh at the popular kids who think they're so cool when they're really the most terrified of them all. And Ëólas nuzzles his forehead against hers as he confesses that he's never loved anyone as much as he loves her.

Derek takes one step inside the room and looks her dead in the eyes. "Where is he?"

She furrows her brow. "What?"

"Don't play dumb. You know who I mean. Where is he?"

Oh my god, does Ëólas know about guns? Maybe if she can buy time, she can convince Derek to stop this. They were friends once upon a time. "Why?"

"Seriously?" He twists his face into a knot, his lips curling upward, and his eyebrow twitching downward. He straightens his arm as he takes one more step forward.

"Are you going to kill us? That's it? And then what?"

"I'm not going to kill you. Not you."

Ëólas. No. Never. Her palms throbbing, she clenches her fists and slowly walks around the bed, the gun following her every step. "Why are you doing this?"

"Why? Are you serious? You have no idea how long I waited, how long I sought the right opportunity to get you to notice me, to see me as more than a friend. I tried to become what you needed, and it worked too, until that freak showed up."

She stops eight feet in front of him while he steps to the right, almost aligning his back with the bathroom door. A shadow blocks the mirror above the sink from reflecting her silhouette, but Ëólas doesn't tackle Derek. Why? Because he's pointing a gun at Adaline?

What should I do? "So, you're here to kill him, and you think I'll just go home with you?"

"I'm not giving you a choice." Lifting the gun higher, Derek aligns his eye with the square rear notch. "You are mine, even if I have to nurse you back to health myself. It's not that different from how I cared for you after Arraya's funeral. Now, where is he?"

Like I'd ever let you hurt him. She brushes her hair behind her shoulder, and the moment Derek's gleaming eyes drift to her décolletage, she vanishes. Reappearing beside Ëólas, she reaches for his hand. But as Derek shouts profanities and looks frantically around the room, Ёólas dashes out of the bathroom and twists Derek's arm up in the air. He fires the gun, and a piece of ceiling crashes to the floor, scattering shards of plaster and dust across the bed.

With his gun forced toward the ceiling, Derek uses his free hand to swing at Ёólas's face, only to miss as Ёólas steps aside and Derek falls forward. Spotting Adaline in the bathroom, Derek aims the gun at her, but Ёólas tackles him to the ground. When Derek hits the floor, the gun goes off, firing a bullet that grazes Adaline's lower leg, slicing her flesh, and pierces the vanity cabinet. The wooden door splinters around the large hole.

Holy shit! Fuck, that burns!

As the guys wrestle and punch each other, she snatches a hand towel, applies pressure, and limps out of the bathroom. Blood drips down her leg, and she curses herself for standing off to the side like Buttercup did when she let Westley fight the R.O.U.S.s alone. But how does she insert herself between Derek and Ёólas? How does she hurt one and not the other? Before her brain can formulate a plan, Derek uses both feet to kick Ёólas off him and jumps up to standing, his eyes glowing with triumph, until Ёólas socks Derek in the ribs. Doubling over, he falls onto his knees, and Ёólas tears the gun out of his hand. Derek, gasping for breath, drops onto his hands.

Backing away from him, Ёólas holds the gun upside down by the trigger guard, his chest heaving up and down more so from fury than exertion. "What do I do with this?" he asks Adaline, his eyes darting to her bloody leg.

She hobbles toward him. "It's nothing serious, just a laceration. Put the gun over there." She points to the dresser on her side of the room, far away from Derek. "I guess I should call the cops?"

As she stumbles around the bed to grab her mobile, Derek pops up with a smaller pistol. Faster than half a breath, his hand swings in an arch toward Ёólas's chest, and Derek curls his lips into a gleeful grin. He aligns his eye with the notch, and his finger tightens around the trigger.

Adaline raises her palm. Even though her screams remain lodged in the back of her throat, her hand glows bright crimson. Derek's eyes flash red like in old photographs, like Morgán's eyes did, but before Derek squeezes the trigger, flames like a blowtorch leap out of Adaline's hand, arching over the mattress and into his face.

Firing the gun, Derek falls backward, escaping the flames and his bullet shattering the mirror hanging over the dresser. Ëólas body slams into Derek, and as they topple to the floor, the pistol skates across the room.

You fucking son of a bitch! Adaline dives over the bed, leaving a smear of blood across the sheets, grabs both their arms, and travels into the castle dining hall. As always, she brings Ëólas instantaneously. With Derek, however, he tries to tear himself free, but she refuses to let him threaten Ëólas again and drags his two-hundred-pound ass through the threshold. When Derek appears in the dining hall, Adaline falls backward onto her bottom, her legs and arms wobbly like Jell-O, while Derek lunges at Ëólas yet again and reaches for his throat.

Servers drop their trays, spilling dirty spoons and plates on the stone floor. Seconds later, Merith grabs a fistful of Derek's dark hair, yanking him away from Ëólas, while Sora helps Adaline to her feet, yells for someone to bring strips of linen and water, and wraps her cloak around Adaline's skimpy clothing.

Trying to pry Merith's hands loose, Derek yelps and shouts, "Get off me, you piece of shi—What the fuck?" He scans the room with wide eyes as if he were tripping on acid.

Merith throws Derek toward Fólas, who thrusts his sword at the cowering man's abdomen.

"Stop!" Adaline shouts. "We can't kill him."

Staring at the sword hovering over his naval, Derek crawls backward. "What the. How the. Where the fuck am I?" When Thoren slams his sword behind Derek, pinning the sleeve of his leather coat to the floor, he stops slinking away.

Magnus glances from Adaline dripping blood on the floor to Ëólas wearing nothing more than sweatpants. "Dare I ask what happened?"

"He tried to kill Ëólas," Adaline says, pinching Sora's cloak shut.

His lips curling into a snarl, Merith unsheathes his sword and lifts his blade to decapitate Derek, who can do nothing else but stare at the sleek, thin steel.

With a reluctant growl, Ëólas blocks Merith's path. "As much as I loathe stopping you, we can't kill him. The authorities in Maryland will start asking questions, and I don't want that hassle for Adaline."

Leaving his friend to fume and stare down Derek, Ëólas hurries to Adaline's side, his eyes horrified at the streaks of blood running down her leg. "Are you alright?" He angles himself to shield her from the guys' view and pushes aside the cloak to study the gash.

"It looks worse than it is. What about you?" She skims her hands over his torso and arms. Not seeing a scratch, she exhales her relief.

"My lady?" Sora, accepting a bowl of water and a clean cloth from a server, kneels down beside Adaline. Quickly but gently, she washes Adaline's leg and the diluted blood pooling around her toes. "I don't think you'll need stitches."

Thank God. "See, Ëólas. It's not so bad."

"Where the hell am I?" Derek asks. "How did I get here? Who the fuck are these—"

"Shut it!" Thoren turns his blade a quarter of an inch so the sharp edge slices into Derek's forearm.

"Thoren!" Adaline says.

"My hand slipped," he grumbles.

Ignoring Derek's yowling, Sora dips her fingers into a pouch tied to her belt and pulls out a clump of dark green muck that she smears into the wound. "If we can't execute him, then what are we to do with him?"

Derek's mouth hangs open, revealing his red-stained teeth. "Execute?" he whimpers, clutching his bleeding arm.

"Oh my god." As the medicine numbs her leg, a chill spreads throughout Adaline's body. "I, I don't know. With him trying to kill Ëólas, I didn't have time to think this through."

She just kidnapped Derek and, worse, revealed her abilities to him. What might he do if she lets him go or turns him into the authorities? Maybe the cops would think he's insane if he raved about another world and a girl who shoots fire out of her hands, but can she take that risk? And if the cops do book him for attempted murder, how long of a sentence would he get? And what if that investigation reveals Ëólas's fake papers? Maybe Ben knows what to do?

Adaline flinches as Sora ties a bandage around her calf. *Ugh. As if we don't have enough going on with Morgán and his demonic elves. Oh shit—Morgán!* "Ëólas, did you notice when Derek's eyes flashed red?"

"Like Morgán's?" Ëólas shakes his head. "Are you sure?"

Merith yanks Derek up by the collar of his coat and examines him. "He looks ordinary to me." Ordering two royal guards to hold Derek still, Merith searches for weapons. Aside from a set of apartment keys and a wallet, he finds only one item in Derek's inner coat pocket—a purple pen that Merith passes to Adaline.

She spins the fidget ball built into the pen's clip, and the ballet slippers on top turn around. *What the hell?*

"Get away from me," Derek yells in Merith's face as he continues his search, turning Derek's pockets inside out. "Let me go, you fucking freak."

Merith punches Derek in the mouth, snapping his head backward.

The spatter of blood makes Adaline gasp. "Merith!"

"He's alive," Merith says.

Ëólas shrugs. "We need some time to think this through. For now, take him to the dungeons."

"What?" Derek spits blood on the floor. "You're joking." For five seconds, he laughs nervously, but when Merith orders the royal guards to drag him away, Derek shouts, "You can't do this. I have rights. I want my lawyer."

"Ugh. Ëólas, he's right." Adaline grabs his hand. "I mean, we can't go back to Maryland without him. People will eventually know he's missing."

Magnus puffs out his chest as he looks down on Derek. "Consider imprisonment a mercy, Adaline, because according to my law, he should be executed."

"Lameiría's laws dictate the same," Sora says, washing her hands in a clean bowl.

"Well," Adaline waves her pen about like a scepter, "we're in Aerytol, and that law's changing. As of right now."

"But Aerytol's why we made those laws in the first place!" Merith says.

"We're not executing prisoners. Ever. End of discussion." Adaline squeezes Ëólas's hand, signaling him to back her up, but the most she gets from him is a half-assed nod.

Merith lowers his gaze to the floor and pouts. "Yes, my queen."

"Queen?" Derek glances around as if waiting for the hidden cameras to pop out. "You're fucking kidding me, right?"

"No one said you can speak." Merith punches Derek's mouth again.

"Merith!"

"He's still alive."

Adaline shakes her head. *I never should have brought him here.*

Ëólas moves his hand to the small of Adaline's back. "We'll figure out what to do with him later. Right now, we should speak with Cindy and Dax. If we can't go home, then we need them here."

"Hey, dickwad," Derek says. "Let's you and me settle this now, huh?"

Ëólas ignores him and displays that neutral façade, but the severity of his expression makes Adaline shrink inward. "Can you bring Cindy and Dax too?"

"Yeah, I can—"

"Hey, pretty boy. Did you hear me? You and me—winner gets Adaline."

"Are you crazy? I married him." Adaline points the pen at her ring. "What about 'it's over' don't you understand, Derek?"

"The 'over' part," Ëólas mutters.

"Oooh, I see," Magnus says. "Yeah, I'd execute him."

"It's not over. No way in hell," Derek screams as Ëólas waves him away and the royal guards drag him toward the doors. "You're mine, you hear me. You're fucking mine, Adaline. Just you wait, Ëólas. You may think you have her now, but I had her first. Oh, I had her good. And I'll have her—"

In three strides, Ëólas punches Derek in the mouth so hard that his jaw cracks and hangs at an awkward angle. With Merith and Sora beaming, Ëólas returns to Adaline, who's covering her mouth with her hand. He grips her fingers and kisses her knuckles. "You said it first—he's an asshole."

"Yes, but a broken jaw?" she asks.

"I would have ordered Thoren to behead him," Magnus says, as if he were discussing his weekend plans.

"Make sure a healer attends to him. Tomorrow," Ëólas tells the royal guards.

"Ëólas!" Adaline steps around him and tells her guards, "Make sure someone tends to him immediately. That's an order." *I give orders now? How weird is that?* "He's in custody, and I need him in one piece when we figure out how to send him home and get him to leave us alone." As the guards drag Derek whimpering out of the hall, she turns her back to him, tucks the pen behind her ear, and moves closer to Ëólas, resting her hands on his waist. "I can't believe he tried to kill us. What was he thinking?"

She dips her forehead onto his chest while Ëólas hugs her around Sora's cloak. "I didn't think he'd ever... I scared him, Ëólas. What would possess him to—" *Possess him. No, it can't be. But his eyes. Ëólas didn't see that though. I could have imagined that. Or maybe I saw the reflection of my glowing hands in his eyes.*

Ëólas nudges her forehead with his chin, urging her to look up at him. "Thank you for saving my life. With the fire. That was something else."

The corners of her mouth turn upward. Her hands tremble against his bare chest, at the thought of what could have happened. She rises on her toes and tilts her lips toward him, but his red cheeks remind her of the several guards and friends around them, and she deflates onto her heels. *I can deal with hugs and hand holding all day, so long as we have time to ourselves at night.*

He looks at her with a similar longing, as if he finally understands the limitations this world places upon them and their interactions. He frowns, and his eyes darken. "Let's go back for Cindy and Dax."

Adaline nods and looks at Magnus and the others. "We'll be right back. Um, Sora, I'll return your cloak in a moment, thank you." Staying in Ëólas's embrace, Adaline pulls him into their bedroom with the blood-smeared sheets, the shattered mirror, and the hole in the ceiling. "Damn, how are we going to—"

Ëólas locks his lips with hers, pulling her closer until she has no choice but to free her arms crushed against his chest, hook her hands around his neck, and wrap her legs around him. Grabbing her bottom, he sits down on the corner of the bed, unhooks Sora's cloak so it falls away, and slides his hands under her nightgown and up her back. If it were possible for them to be any closer, they would be. When their lips part, they hug each other, her inhaling his Old Spice scent and him burying his mouth against her neck.

After several moments, Adaline attempts to break the silence. "No one noticed your haircut."

His chest shakes as he laughs, and his words rumble in the hollow of her neck. "They had enough else to shock them."

He leans back and cups her cheek, revealing his shaking hand. He rakes his eyes over her body, double checking her arms, her legs, her torso, her face. Then he nods, not needing to say anything more on the subject.

When she slides off him, they change the sheets on the bed. Ëólas fetches a dustpan and trash bag, and Adaline checks all the windows and doors. The house is still locked up tight.

How did he get inside? He might have known about the hide-a-key in the garden. *Did he lock the door behind him?*

After turning off the outside Christmas lights, she peers out the narrow window next to the front door and searches the shadows for a set of glowing red eyes. *That's just not possible. I'm the traveler.*

She climbs the staircase, her fingers trailing over the garland wrapped around the banister, and heads toward her room, all the while reminding herself over and over again that Morgán can't come here. But that doesn't comfort her anymore, because as Adaline and Ëólas go to sleep that night, holding each other tightly, they both know that, come morning, they won't return to Maryland, not really and not for a long time.

CHAPTER TWENTY-THREE

THE TROOPS

"Sorry we woke you at five in the morning." Adaline accepts a cup of coffee from Cindy and takes a long sip, letting it warm her from the inside out.

"Don't worry about it. Dax and I called out sick for a few days, so we're ready to go." Cradling a jumbo coffee mug in both hands, Cindy takes a seat next to Adaline while Dax rolls four large suitcases out of the bedroom and parks them in the living room. When he dashes into his office to say goodbye to his plants, Cindy leans in close and lowers her voice. "But are you okay, I mean, really?"

"Yeah. I know it's crazy, but I'm pissed off more than anything." Drinking her coffee, she drums her fingers on her elven leather trousers, which are surprisingly comfy and breathable. "He couldn't attack after Christmas break? We had plans to see the National Zoo lights this weekend, and I bought hot cocoa bombs as a treat. I have a whole prime rib dinner planned. I haven't finished wrapping presents, and now all that's going to have to wait until after we deal with demonic vampire elves and invade Hell City and start a war and all this scary crap."

"I'm angry too." Ëólas, already wearing his traveling clothes, sits on the sofa armrest beside Adaline, his black leather trousers hugging his legs tightly and yet bending easily. His fitted navy jacket, made from boiled leather, drapes over both sides of his legs, revealing his light-blue silk tunic and its hand-stitched gold embroidery that displays autumn leaves swirling in the wind. Running his finger along the rim of her ear, he brushes a few curly strands aside and kisses her temple. "But we'll still have a jolly Christmas. Eventually."

"A happy Christmas," Adaline murmurs. Holding her mug in one hand, she gulps down the rest of her coffee while she fidgets with the last button of the tailcoat Élara gifted her.

"Ah, yes. A happy Christmas. And we have a few holidays coming up back home too. We should return from the Wastelands in time for the harvest festival, and there's Tínara Festivus."

Adaline twists sideways and leans her head against his torso, her long French braid falling off her shoulder and behind her back. "I haven't celebrated Tínara Festivus since I was a little girl."

Leaning over, Ëólas dips down for a second kiss. "Alright, let's get this show on the road."

"Look at you using colloquialisms." Setting the coffee mug in the sink, Adaline takes Ëólas's hand and pulls him through instantly.

Leaving him momentarily with Magnus, she pops back over for Cindy, carrying her analyzer and generators concealed in suitcases. Pulling Cindy through proves just as easy as last time. With Dax the only one left, she grabs his hand. "Okay, you ready for this?"

"Hell yes. Look what I'm bringing." He pulls out of his denim pocket the *Dungeons and Dragons'* figurine he bought to represent his character, a ranger he named Guardián del Bosque. "I thought if I'm going on this huge adventure, it doesn't hurt to take something for luck, you know? It's probably stupid, but Bosque belongs in your world, and he hasn't let me down yet."

"He's a good choice." *I love your enthusiasm, Dax. Hell, I felt much the same way when I first arrived in New Leira—when I wasn't panicking about how to get home.* "Hey, thanks again for agreeing to all of this."

"I wouldn't miss it. Alright, beam me up, Scotty." Squeezing Adaline's hand, Dax shuffles from side to side, his feet itching to touch castle grounds. When the dining hall solidifies around him, along with a small group of people wearing leather armor over Renaissance-like clothing, Dax drops Adaline's hand and stares awestruck at them, then the torches, the tapestries, and the vaulted stone ceiling.

"And this must be Dax." Magnus releases Cindy's hand, which he most likely just kissed, to clasp Dax's arm. His bright blue eyes take in every detail of Dax's clothing, from the white high-top sneakers to the graphic T-shirt. "A pleasure to meet another of Adaline's friends. I've arranged for clothing to be delivered to your chambers, should you wish to change."

"Oh wow. I mean, yes. Thank you, Your Majesty." Dax simultaneously shakes the king's forearm, bows deeply, and crosses his other arm over his shirt that reads *Goonies Never Say Die*.

"It's no trouble at all. Excuse us for a moment though." Leaving Dax and Cindy to take in their surroundings, Magnus ushers Adaline and Ëólas to a group of five men loitering near the curved head dining table. He signals for the tallest man to step forward, his shaggy dark-gray hair tied back in a man bun and his face weathered from too much camping. "I'd like to introduce Lord Daven, who will oversee my men."

Like most of Magnus's soldiers, Daven's clothing comprises layers of burgundy and gold, although extra-thick leather armor conceals most of the fabric. Grape vines decorate his wide, heavy belt buckle, and the ornate leather laces running up the length of his jacket sleeves reveal his high station among Magnus's court. In addition to crow's feet framing his light-blue eyes, Daven's short, peppered beard doesn't quite hide the dimple to the left of his mouth. His resigned face gives Adaline the impression that he's not particularly loquacious.

Adaline bows her head. "Thank you for your help, Lord Daven."

"Your Majesty." He returns a curt nod and gestures to the four men behind him. "These are my generals who will assist us throughout this campaign."

As Daven introduces each lord, they bow their heads in turn but from afar, none of them wanting to leave the safety of their peers. Each lord also casts wary glances at Merith and Sora, who have drifted to the opposite side of the room. And yet Magnus purposefully chose Daven and these generals because of their proximity to Aerytol, hoping that would make this collaboration go smoother.

This will be interesting.

Among the four generals, one name in particular catches Adaline's attention. "Lord Bodlin, you oversee the eastern county in the northern most province, don't you?"

The beady-eyed lord sucks his belly in two inches. "Yes, Your Majesty. That's correct."

Adaline nods to herself, flashes him a half smile, and turns away as she tries to disregard the awkward sense of irony. When Ëólas asks her what's wrong, she glances over her shoulder to make sure the lords aren't watching her. With them talking among themselves, she whispers, "It's nothing. It's just that Bodlin—he's the lord of Meadowbrook. My father used to pay him tribute. It's just kinda weird, that's all."

"Was he a good lord?" Ëólas asks.

"I don't know much about him, just the name."

Shedding the reminder of how far she's come since being a shepherd's daughter, Adaline hooks her arm around Ëólas's, signals with her finger for Cindy and Dax to wait a moment longer, and walks to the other side of the hall where Merith and Sora wait for their queen and king. Once again, the people have divided themselves, with humans on one side and elves on the other. Even Cindy and Dax have gravitated toward the side with humans, even though they have been trying to blend into the background by hiding their luggage behind their backs and Cindy zipping her puffer jacket shut to conceal her T-shirt and half of her skinny jeans.

When Ëólas stops in front of Merith, Adaline greets Sora with a hug. Surprised, Sora stammers hello but quickly sheds her stern warrior face for that of a friend. Per usual, she wears her strawberry-blonde hair in a high ponytail that extends past her bottom. Like Merith, her leather armor bears the embossed insignia of Lameiría's tree of life with three stars above the massive boughs, and her clothing combines shades of sage green and navy blue.

Stepping back, Adaline drops her hands to rest on Sora's arms. "With all the commotion upon your arrival, we didn't have a chance to talk. Did Ëólas mention that I'd like you to lead my guard?"

Sora blinks a few times and glances at Merith and Ëólas as if to verify that they won't object. "Are you certain, my lady? We only just met. Do you not trust anyone more?"

"I trust *you*—and I need more strong ladies to help me keep these guys in check. Plus, you come highly recommended."

"I—yes, I accept. I give you my solemn oath to serve and protect you, my queen."

"Thank you." Bouncing on her toes, Adaline hugs her new captain again, and this time Sora pats the queen's back like a sister placating a younger sibling.

"Best get used to that," Merith mumbles, his eyes twinkling with amusement.

Adaline sneers at him and turns to Sora. "You realize that, as captain of the queen's guard, you'll have to work with Merith—as his equal."

Sora flashes him a wicked grin. "Oh, this will be fun."

"Okay, okay," Ëólas says. "You and Merith can antagonize each other later. I need to update Adaline about our change of plans before we depart."

Shit. That sounds ominous. "What's going on?"

Facing his wife, Ëólas peers into her eyes and takes hold of her hand. "While Merith and Sora will lead the royal guard, four generals volunteered to lead a thousand soldiers from Lameiría."

"Okay. And?"

"Well, the generals have come to introduce themselves." Ëólas tilts forward, his lips grazing her ear, as he whispers, "If you're not comfortable with this, pinch my arm, and I'll assign someone else."

"Huh? Why would I not feel comf—"

Lameiría's generals enter the dining hall—one being the same elf who volunteered to help her defend Aerytol after the water sprites displayed her memories in Gladríen's amphitheater. She vaguely remembers the two in the back, but the first general, the one leading them toward Adaline, is none other than Ëólas's curmudgeon of a grandfather.

Holy shit. Elashor!

With his personal Secret Service behind the generals, Elashor strides across the room to Ëólas and Adaline, but instead of addressing his grandson, he bows his head to Adaline, keeping his hands firmly at his sides. The dark streaks in his silver hair shimmer under the torchlight, and faint blue veins pulse beneath his thin yet unblemished skin. "My lady, I can only imagine your confusion at my presence."

You think? Last time Adaline saw him, the people of Lameiría were bowing to her, but Elashor had ominously disappeared. *I thought he hated me. What's he doing here?* "A bit, but it's good to see you." *I mean, we are family now. I hope we can get along.*

His brow wrinkles in confusion. "I, um, thank you." He scans Ëólas and puzzles over his shorter hair. "You look well."

Still holding Adaline's hand, Ëólas sidesteps closer to her. "I am."

Elashor, with his mouth twitching, turns to Adaline. "Your grandfather was like a brother to me. I'd known Erol since I was a lad."

"Oh." *I had no idea.*

"I came here because," he straightens his back, "I could not help my friend save his land, but I can help his granddaughter. If you'll have me."

Adaline studies Ëólas's face; he doesn't give away his feelings, but the pulse between their hands tells her that he trusts her decision. She lets go of Ëólas and takes a big step forward. "I'm grateful for the help, thank you."

Elashor's arms relax a tad, no longer glued to the side of his body, and he bows once more, a little deeper too. "Then consider me at your disposal, Queen Adaline. I am here to execute your orders through command of my troops; I give you my word I will not interfere."

"Thank you, but I wonder..." She nibbles her bottom lip. "I don't know much about Erol, except that he had a strong connection to the earth and an inquisitive mind. Would you tell me about him?"

A glossy sheen coats Elashor's eyes, but his flat tone conceals all emotion. "I haven't spoken of Arraya and Erol in centuries. But I will try. For you."

Adaline reaches out to him. Realizing he might recoil at her touch, she instead clasps her hands in front of her. "Thank you. I'd appreciate that."

As soon as introductions conclude, Ëólas dismisses Elashor and the other generals, telling them to wait outside with the troops, and moves his hand to

Adaline's back. "Why don't you take a few minutes to help Cindy and Dax settle in while Merith and I oversee the last inspections? We'll wait for you at the front."

When they leave the hall to finalize the army's departure, Magnus promises Adaline that he'll ensure Cindy and Dax feel at home in New Leira. Adaline then quickly shows her friends to their chambers, the wheels of their luggage squeaking down the corridor to the human side of the castle, with Sora following behind them all.

Mercia greets them at the doors to their suite and ushers them into the lush sitting room. "I'm so pleased to meet you both. As the queen's envoy, I will assist you in any way possible."

"Thank you, Mercia." Adaline kisses her cheek, tells her to join her father on the balcony for the final send-off, and shuts the door, knowing Sora and the royal guard won't move a muscle until she leaves Cindy's chambers.

While Dax examines the authenticity of everything in their room, from the chestnut canopy bed, to the fireplace doors' filigree pattern, to the water closet that dumps their waste into the river, Adaline pulls Cindy aside. "Are you sure you're going to be okay here? I mean, what if something happens to me? You'll be stranded in this world."

Cindy rolls her suitcase into a corner and pushes down the handle. "Look, if shit gets too scary for you, I expect you and Ëólas to pop right back here. So don't worry about us. We'll be fine."

"But—"

"No buts. You can't keep worrying about this, okay? I need you to focus while you're out there so I can do my job over here. I've got my generators and mobile lab. Just get me a blood sample from those vampire elves as soon as possible, and it'll be all good."

Yeah, because I'm eager to see them again. "But I don't know how long I'll be gone."

Adaline could grab both her friends, take them home right now, and bring them back only after she gets that blood sample—which Cindy won't be ready for. And that could hinder Cindy's chances of saving the vampire elves. But how does Adaline help the people who will most likely try to kill her? And why does that also have to increase Cindy's chances of becoming a target too? *Damn it.* Maybe Adaline can think of another option—in the next two minutes.

"Adaline, chill," Cindy says. "Being here one month equals a couple of hours lost back home, right? Even if you're gone, say, four months, we'll lose maybe a day in Maryland. Dax and I have got that covered, and you've got an army to lead. Go. Be a queen. Trust me to do my job here."

Adaline hugs Cindy tightly. "I don't know how to thank you."

"I mean," leaning back so she can look Adaline in the eyes, Cindy tilts her head from side to side, "if you want to lend me a real tiara to go with my wedding dress, we can call this even."

"Deal. But it won't be a borrow."

"Sweet!"

"How about a custom-designed wedding dress to go with it? I can ask the royal seamstress to make it."

"Oh my god!" Cindy pushes her fist into her mouth to stop herself from squealing as she rapidly nods her head.

"Consider it done. Seira will love helping you with that too."

After hugging Cindy and Dax one more time, Adaline walks them to the door, ready to direct her friends to the send-off balcony, but halts and reduces her voice to a whisper. "Oh, try to limit your tech in Magnus's presence—and any other humans, for that matter, but especially Magnus. I'd like to avoid prematurely jumpstarting the Scientific Revolution here."

Cindy pulls down her sleeve to cover her smartwatch. "I'll do my best."

Chapter Twenty-Four

A Clever Way

After several more hugs, a few speeches, and a resounding cheer, Adaline and Ëólas mount their horses at the head of the army. With Daven and his generals to her right, Ëólas and his generals to her left, and Sora and Merith directly behind their monarchs, Adaline gulps once and then gently squeezes her calves until her horse, Conleth, walks forward, signaling the start of their march across the fields of Aerytol to stop Morgán and free Feídra né Morna.

The two-thousand soldiers, also divided in half, follow on foot behind their commanders. Among the sea of navy and burgundy, Adaline and Ëólas wear dark-purple armor. Someone stayed up all night dying the leather and embossing their chest plates with the six elements: Fire, rising out of a lake, grows into the tree of life with whisps of wind brushing the leaves sideways so they form a maze. Like Lameiría's armor, three stars overlook the crest, each resembling the Purple Stardust wildflowers that grow throughout Aerytol and representing the souls of Aeríoléna, Tólen, and the current reigning Aerytolían monarch.

Everyone carries their personal effects in leather knapsacks, but the campaign also includes horse-drawn wagons hauling food and camping supplies—along with the additional trunks, carpets, and furs Adaline's lady's maids packed for their queen and king.

Please, don't let this be a mistake.

As if hearing her, Nan's necklace vibrates the buttoned pocket along Adaline's thigh, where she placed the original family crest after enfolding it in a handkerchief. She hasn't yet touched the metal, not sure she wants to discover what Ëólas meant when he warned that Aerytolíans have an obvious, unique reaction to purified Aerylite. Regardless, Dax inspired her to pack the necklace for luck.

Please help every soldier return home safely.

After about two miles of marching, Adaline and Ëólas dismount their horses, along with the captains and generals, and hold on to the reins of their steeds as they continue on foot. To not exhaust the horses too soon, the generals use their steeds only when they need to see further ahead, issue orders, or view the army behind them. Thankfully, they're walking at a normal pace, not doubling their speed and distance to save Adaline from starving to death.

For their first day, they couldn't have wished for better weather or more beautiful scenery. Nature escorts them with the glistening river to their left, the gigantic birds cawing ahead, the forest saturated with autumn foliage to their right, and the cool sun marching upward behind them. Billowing in the breeze, the purple wildflowers, a symbol of Nan's blessing, cover every inch of the grassy fields.

Despite the cheerful surroundings, the soldiers keep small talk to a minimum. Every so often, conversation from the humans drifts forward, thanks to the wind's need to spread gossip. The murmurs reveal thoughts mostly about home and people left behind and Magnus handing them over to fight for an elven queen and king.

Apparently, I'm more of an elf now. 'Cause that's not weird.

Adaline rubs the bridge of Conleth's nose, the same honey-colored steed she feared to ride before getting her memories back. On the other side of Conleth, Daven guides his own black stallion forward.

"So, Daven," Adaline peeks over the base of her horse's neck, "how long have you served in Magnus's army?"

He keeps his light-blue eyes fixed on the horizon. "Since his coronation, my lady."

"Oh, wow. You know him well then?"

He nods but doesn't add more to the conversation.

Instead of crickets, Adaline hears only hooves and feet trampling the fields, along with a few grunts and guttural chuckles. "Well, we're fortunate to have your help." *Ugh. I sound like an awkward teenager.*

"I don't question my king," Daven says.

Translation: You don't want to be here. Well, crap.

Ëólas subtly shakes his head as if warning her not to bother with small talk. She elbows him in the ribs, even though Ëólas has a point. Making friends with a seasoned warrior isn't something she's studied. What would Daven rather talk about? Fighting methodology, the family he left behind, how he lost his pinky?

Maybe a happier topic like—Oh. "Where were you born?"

"At my father's estate."

Adaline racks her brain, tapping into memories from long ago. "The late Duke Dorven?"

Daven twists his head to eye her properly. "Yes. How did you know?"

"I've not been there, if that's what you're wondering. My father and uncles used to pay tribute to Lord Bodlin. During their travels to the capital to trade wool and sheepskin, they passed by your estate." *Not that Uncle Jamie enjoyed having Dad go with them. Over the years, they had countless silent glaring contests.*

Poor Uncle Jamie. It's not like he knew the truth about their family. I wonder if he's okay.

"I heard rumors that you have family from Alderton," Daven says.

Adaline's horse neighs and brushes up beside her. Combing aside Conleth's chocolate mane, she scratches his ear. "I was born and raised in Meadowbrook." *Is he familiar with all the lands he's leased to Bodlin? What's the chance he might know my family?* "Have you been there?"

Daven grunts once, which Adaline interprets to mean *yes.* "A few times when I toured Lord Bodlin's county. A handful of the soldiers he brought me come from that region." He tosses his thumb at the men behind him.

Whoa. Adaline looks over her shoulder at the sea of hairy, brawny soldiers walking in rows as they travel further away from home. *Someone could know my cousins. I might even have family behind me. But would they want to associate with me?*

Ëólas briefly brushes his pinky against Adaline's, letting her know he understands her conflicted emotions.

Lost in her own thoughts, she leaves Daven alone for a while, but the lack of conversation throughout the morning wears away at Adaline's spirits. No one should have to spend hours ruminating over what awaits them and stressing over the potential enemies walking beside them. If only Magnus could have come too. Then his men would have seen how easily he gets along with Ëólas and Adaline. Maybe that could have eased the tension bubbling like a tar pit around them. She's going to need more than stories to help bring this group together.

Then again, stories might be all I have. Hmm, I must know some movies or books that deal with war. Saving Private Ryan? Forest Gump? Tropic Thunder?

Then again, maybe this group would prefer stories not related to war.

When Adaline sighs after the first few hours, Ëólas pokes her side. "Bored already?"

She chews the inside of her cheek. "I just wish we had music or something. Are we going to walk in silence the entire way?"

"Well, we'd usually sing songs of elves past, but my people don't wish to annoy Alderton."

Hmm. Adaline peers over Conleth's saddle to study Daven's face. He gives no indication of whether that would be true. "Maybe a story then?"

"What do you have in mind?" Ëólas asks.

The first stories that pop into her head are *Macbeth* and *A Midsummer Night's Dream*, but tales about a general murdering his king and a fairy queen falling in love with a human turned into a donkey don't seem like the right fit for this audience. God forbid she encourages rebellion or insults the fae.

Maybe something about sharing? "Ah, yes. How about *Stone Soup*?"

When no one asks her to stay silent, Adaline gives storytelling a try, albeit with a few alterations to better fit this audience. "Once upon a time, in days of old, when the world was new," she begins, combining the oral traditions of humans and elves, "a group of travelers arrived at a village, and they carried nothing more than an enormous cauldron. When they asked for help, everyone in the village insisted they had no food to spare. Disheartened, the travelers went to the river, filled their massive pot with water, and placed it on a large fire. Then the travelers dropped a stone into the pot."

"A stone?" Daven mumbles. "Ridiculous." But he turns his head ever so slightly to hear her better.

Elashor leans forward to see around Ëólas. "How could they hope to sustain themselves with a stone?"

Ëólas and Adaline exchange a knowing look.

Curiosity wins again. "Well, one villager wondered the same thing, so he asked the travelers what they were doing. They explained they were making stone soup, which the king himself requested twenty times last season, and that they'd be happy to share their meal with the village, but sadly the soup wouldn't taste as good without salt and pepper. The villager, still insisting that he had little food, said he could spare some salt and pepper, and so he added them to the pot."

Daven laughs out loud. "Idiot."

"Is he?" Adaline asks. "Or was the villager cautious because no one offered to help him before?"

When Daven reverts to his taciturn demeanor, Adaline continues. "Another villager asked about their meal, and the travelers offered to share their famous soup that won first prize in a neighboring village, although they used a large soup bone back then. Alas, this soup would have to do without. Well, the villager insisted that *this* soup should have an old soup bone too, so he fetched them one and tossed it into the pot—even though he had little food to spare."

When Adaline finishes the story, Lord Bodlin grumbles, "Humph. So the travelers tricked the villagers into giving up the little food they had. The villagers should have run them out of town."

Adaline oscillates her head back and forth. "That's one way to look at it."

"How do you see it, my queen?" Sora asks from behind Adaline.

"Well, the travelers could have attacked the villagers and kept the food for themselves. Instead, they fetched the water, did all the cooking, and shared the meal with everyone, so I think they found a clever way to teach the villagers that everyone benefits when they work together."

"Hmm" is the most Adaline gets from Daven, but it's a start—at least, Adaline hopes so. She'll take any win she can right now, including the look of admiration Ëólas shows her that keeps her going for the rest of the morning.

At lunch, Daven and his lords disappear to check on their men, leaving Adaline and Ëólas to eat a delectable assortment of cured meat and fresh bread with the royal guard forming a wide protective circle around their queen and king. Although, she's uncertain whether her guard is shielding her from Morgán or from Alderton's troops.

Tearing into a stick of cured beef, Adaline cranes her neck and scans the unfamiliar faces of the guard, a few of whom are human. When she spies Tumin and Moren, the guards Hamon and Ëólas originally assigned to her after that fake guard abducted her, she perks up and calls their names while waving eagerly at them. With crimson faces, they wiggle their fingers *hello* and shrink under the stares of their peers.

Eek. I hope the guard doesn't think I'm playing favorites.

Having chosen to skip lunch, Merith steps through the circle and points at Adaline's sword lying beside her. "If you're done eating, my queen, then I request your presence in the field."

Sitting across from her, Ëólas swallows a sip of water, his arms dangling over his knees, his hands holding a leather bladder. "Leave her be, Merith."

"What? Why?" Adaline asks them.

Ëólas shoves the cork into his bladder. "He wants to test your skills with a sword, which isn't necessary."

Training. In the open. In front of all these soldiers. Oh god. Adaline stuffs the last three bites of her bread in her mouth and guzzles her own water.

Emerging from behind Adaline, Sora walks up to Ëólas and scowls at him. "You are mistaken, my lord. We're testing your teachings. I won't have my queen exposed."

"That doesn't make me feel better," Adaline mumbles. When Ëólas rises and protests, Adaline lifts her hand to cut him off. "It's fine. I'll put on my big girl pants. Let's do this."

"That's the spirit," Sora says.

Telling herself to calm down and relax, Adaline rolls onto her hands and knees, stands up, and marches away from the soldiers resting and the horses grazing, her bladder thumping her hip. When she's far enough away that the soldiers are the size of quarters, she faces Sora and Merith—and glares at Ëólas standing beside them, as well as the royal guard lined up behind him.

She shoos her hand at Ëólas as if he were a fly. "No, no. Go away. And take the guard with you."

"What?" Ëólas points at his chest. "Why?"

"Because I'm nervous enough as it is. I don't need more than two people judging me."

Ëólas runs his hands through his hair, the layers falling against his cheeks and the tips pointing at his cute, pursed lips she hasn't been able to taste all day. "Fine. We won't watch you." He does an about-face and instructs the guards to do the same. "I'm not moving," he calls from over his shoulder.

Resisting the urge to throw her bladder at him, Adaline clicks her tongue, counting only two seconds until Merith barks at her to draw her sword. Every bone in her body wants to mount Conleth and get the troops marching again, but Merith's stern expression tells her to stop stalling.

Moving to the side, Sora stands between Merith and Adaline. "I'm going to observe this time so I know what to work on with you tonight."

As Adaline rolls her eyes, Merith draws his sword and strikes before she can grab her hilt.

Dodging left, Adaline hits the ground, scurries away like a mouse, and pops back up. Unsheathing her weapon, she backs away from Merith. "You couldn't have given me a moment to get ready?"

"Your enemies won't give you a moment. Less talking, Your Majesty."

"I prefer being called Adaline."

Merith charges again, but this time Adaline follows his muscle movements and lifts her blade across her body in time to stop him from striking her. *Holy shit! What if I didn't block him in time? What's he—*

Merith's repeated assaults don't give Adaline time to think. When she miscalculates and his sword speeds toward her arm, Merith jerks the blade to a stop before slicing her limb off.

From the sidelines, Sora frowns, and Merith's only comment is a loud "hmm."

"I, I'll go again." Adaline slides her feet apart and lifts her sword at the ready. *Okay, okay. I can do this. Time to surprise his ass by traveling.*

Only, the energy vibrating throughout her body as she tries to escape Merith's endless assaults differs significantly from what she felt when she chased her naked husband throughout the house. Traveling doesn't come naturally when she's the prey.

Because fear weakens us? That's just bullshit. Being fearless is impossible.

Within fifteen strikes, Merith's blade careens toward Adaline's neck. Turning off her mind, she travels behind him and taps the flat side of her blade to his shoulder, officially winning their fourth round. Spinning about, Merith stares at her for a long second, until he drops his grin and resumes his relentless attacks for twenty more minutes that feel like two hours.

A few humans pop up to watch her. Soon, elves do too, despite the royal guard forming a living barrier. Worse, the gap between both sides is more noticeable from here. Not even Daven could break bread with her and Ëólas. How could she think one story might bring them together? And now Merith's helping to prove her lack of qualifications in front of everyone.

I mean, it's not like they know about my fire power, but I certainly can't risk setting the fields on fire to earn their admiration—or terror.

Yeah, that's the last thing she needs: Burning Feídra né Morna to the ground would give Ãranol the perfect reason to rally everyone in this world to his crusade and kill her. She needs to find another way, a cleverer way, to teach both sides that everyone benefits when they work together. But how? What can one person do to get through centuries of animosity and lies?

As they walk back to the army, Sora and Merith remain silent. Adaline keeps her head down, her legs sweeping through the tall grass, the wildflowers leaning aside to make way, and her mind racing with methods to unite this army before Morgán tears them all down.

I can't let one session with Merith discourage me. My skills with a sword are what they are right now. That doesn't change the fact that this army needs me, just like Magnus said.

Upon rejoining the others, Merith picks up his knapsack, hoists it onto his shoulders, and splits Adaline's confidence down the center as he glares at Ëólas. "I should have gone with you."

CHAPTER TWENTY-FIVE

THE FIELDS OF ÆRYTOL

As they continue their journey westward, Merith and Ëólas drift further to the left to talk among themselves, leaving Sora to walk beside Adaline and plan an after-dinner routine they can implement starting tonight. Because walking all day isn't enough exercise. Still, Adaline mentally yells at herself to pay attention, even though she spends half the time stealing glances at the guys throwing their hands about as they silently argue.

Maybe they're Italian elves?

Lost in her thoughts, Adaline cuts Sora off mid-sentence, discussing something about deception strikes, and blurts out, "Was I really that bad?"

Jerking her chin backward, Sora shakes her head, flapping her ponytail behind her. "What? No, my lady. You just..."

"Just what?"

Sora readjusts her knapsack to delay her reply. "You've done exceptionally well for someone who trained for only six months."

"Four months," Adaline mumbles. *Shit!* She bites her tongue and curses herself as Merith snaps his head in her direction, fumes through his nostrils, and laces into Ëólas again. *Oops.* "Then why's Merith so mad at me?"

"He's not, my lady. Your traveling skills thoroughly impressed the both of us."

Could have fooled me. "But?"

"But Merith and I thought you'd come back after years of training, not a few months."

"Yeah, well, I botched that up when I brought Derek here." *I wonder how he's managing in the dungeons. And how Cindy and Dax are doing with settling in and collecting those blood samples.* "That's my fault. Merith shouldn't be yelling at Ëólas over that."

Sora places her hand on Adaline's shoulder. "He's only worried about you. We both are. Everyone here would feel much better if they knew you'd travel back to the castle if the situation turns dire."

Translation: They don't actually need me. Cool.

With that thought stuck on repeat in Adaline's mind, the sun begins its descent on day one, its rays casting an orange hue over the horizon and painting the sky above deep shades of gold and crimson. In the distance to her right, Adaline spies a collection of collapsed buildings, the first she's seen during their westward trek.

Tapping Sora's arm to get her attention, Adaline points toward the ruins. "What are those?"

"A village or, rather, what's left of one."

"Are there a lot like this?"

As she takes in the evidence of Aerytol's demise, Sora's placid expression collapses under a fallen brow, tense eyes, and pursed lips. "Yes. Many."

So ghost towns litter the fields of Aerytol. Focusing straight ahead, Adaline tries not to think about the crumbled homes, the crumbled lives, the crumbled families, but her eyes drift to the right. Behind her, the elves aren't the only ones walking solemnly; neither Daven nor his men peek at the village. *But ignoring the past doesn't erase it.*

Her gut twists and turns toward the broken buildings dotting the horizon, the remnants of the past that set her on this path. She can't pass this up. "I need to go there."

"What? No," Elashor protests from beside Sora. "What's lost is lost. No one needs to revisit the past."

You have no idea what I do for a living.

Ëólas snaps at Merith, "That's enough," and cuts across the front of their line. Next to Adaline, he asks, "Are you sure, my love?"

She nods firmly. "Yes."

Mirroring her determination, he directs Daven and all the generals to spread the word that they should set up camp for the night. Afterward, Adaline and Ëólas mount their horses, along with their captains and twenty members of the royal guard, and they trot toward the village. From among the soldiers dropping their packs, Elashor jumps onto his saddle and gallops to catch up with Adaline's group.

I thought he didn't want to come?

Less than ten minutes later, they reach the ghost town, pulling on the reins until the horses slow down and walk into the village. In the five hundred years that have passed, grass and wild flora cover the rubble, creating a green landscape that's burying the remains. Fallen walls reveal moss-covered stone floors, broken clay pots, and decayed wooden furniture that rotted in the rain.

The foundational outlines and square footage of the smaller homes resemble the layout of Adaline's childhood home. Passing her reins to Ëólas, she dismounts and rests her hand on top of a crumpled stone wall that reaches her waist. The wooden trim that disintegrates at her touch could have once been the ledge of a window that overlooked a busy street. Who lived here all those centuries ago? Did this home belong to an elf or a human, and under what circumstances did their lives end?

With the guards eyeballing every surface as if goblins might emerge any moment, she walks through a gap in the foundation where the front door most likely once stood, the mossy floor quieting her footfalls so she doesn't disturb the dead. Meandering into the largest room, she crouches down and brushes aside dirt and splintered wood that could have belonged to a kitchen table or cabinets. Among the sediment, a mostly submerged thimble catches the fading rays of sunlight. Adaline, digging the thimble free, picks up the small metal cap and sets it on the tip of her finger. If she were back home, she'd catalog her finding and drop it into a plastic bag. Instead, she stands up and pockets the totem.

She turns around to face her husband, her friends, and her guards. "Why did this happen?"

Ëólas looks from building to building, not shying away from his family's history. "After the queen's fall, Lameiría and Alderton engaged in a fifteen-year war."

"But why did the war reach all the way out here too? You said Nan cast a spell of hope, inlūmras né leira. I thought people felt that."

Elashor slips off his horse and walks up to her, his face grave and movements stilted. "Many did. But I did not. I would not yield my search for Arraya, and I showed the humans no mercy. This," he waves his hand around, his eyes taking in the scope of devastation perhaps for the first time, and drops his voice, "this is my doing."

So Morgán started this war, and you perpetuated it.

Resting her hands on her chest, Adaline breathes slowly, deeply, so she can keep her tears at bay. This land has soaked up enough pain; she doesn't want to feed it more grief. And Elashor's not the only person responsible for this destruction. "Nan should have found a way to come home sooner. She could have stopped this. She could have—"

"Gone to the humans who thought she wanted to enslave them?" Ëólas asks.

"Trusted her own kind who betrayed her?" Sora adds.

Elashor hangs his head in defeat. "If she witnessed Erol's death... I do not know many who could overcome that. I could not." Returning to his horse's side, he takes the reins and walks out of the village, his feet trampling over history.

Adaline avoids looking directly at Ëólas, her hand sliding up to her neck, and scans her surroundings once more. *This all started with one lie, and Morgán has had almost five hundred years to spread more.* "May I have a few moments, please?"

Merith and Sora shake their heads no, but Ëólas tugs his reins, turning his horse around.

"Give her space." Ëólas leads the others to the village entrance a few buildings away but keeps her within sight.

You get me. Thank you.

Without the guards' anxiety and Elashor's guilt flooding her, Adaline kneels in front of the house's foundation, fanning her tailcoat around her feet. Dank air settles on her face and hands, numbing her skin. Pulling off her fingerless gloves, she runs her palms through the tall grass and wildflowers, searching for the spell of hope Nan cast, the one that sent her to another world to preserve destiny's design. As the sun sinks overhead and dusk falls across the ruins, Adaline silently thanks the twilight for limiting her distractions and helping her turn inward.

Filter everything through the heart.

While the stars lay claim to the sky, Adaline pushes the grass aside, rests her hands on the ground, and leans forward, not quite far enough into child's pose but enough to elongate her spine and stretch her arms, her chest plate lifting away from her stomach. Her braid falls to the side, its tip laying on the dirt. When the wind ceases, she exhales the darkness that has been pressing down on her since they left New Leira and breathes in light, letting its golden touch travel through her veins and chest, letting it wash away the negative thoughts that make her feel small. She digs her fingertips into the cold earth, its soil hardened, and imagines that golden light spreading away from her like an underground network of roots that touches every blade of grass and every soul buried here.

The current of hope, concealed under centuries of silt, pulses beneath Adaline's palms, making her skin prickle and her heart leap. *There you are, inlūmras né leira.*

She latches onto that undercurrent and whispers, "I'm sorry you suffered so much. Your story won't be forgotten, I promise. Please find peace now. Help me bless this land. Help Aerytol and all those who set foot here to heal."

The earth around her fingers relaxes, releasing its cold hold. Warmth travels up her arms and blankets her chest, comforting her from the inside out.

"Thank you." She sits up, folds her hands in her lap, and inhales one more time, her entire body relaxed like at the end of a yoga class. Rising to her feet, she dusts off her knees and takes one last look at the ruins, imagining the homes rebuilt, kids running in the streets, horses traveling in and out of town, and elves and humans celebrating the harvest festival a few years from now.

It's possible. No, it's inevitable. "I promise," she whispers one more time.

With a satisfied nod, she rubs her hands together to shake off the dirt, only her fingers and nails are as clean as if she had finished washing her hands, and her palms emit a soft glow similar to the bond between her and Ëólas. The light fades away, and Nan's words during their dream walk float into Adaline's mind. *With patience and an open heart, we can befriend the elements while guiding them, nurturing them, healing them.*

"Well, that's cool," Adaline mumbles.

As she walks over to Ëólas and the others, tents fill the background, along with the sounds of soldiers building fires and cooking dinner. The closer she approaches Ëólas, the more she feels at peace leaving behind the village, but her friends' expressions give her pause, their mouths hanging open and their eyes bright with wonder despite twilight casting shadows on their faces.

Adaline glances behind her but sees nothing of significance. "I didn't take too long, did I?"

Ëólas jumps down and approaches her slowly as if he were in a dream, his voice full of awe. "What happened?" He rubs the back of her hands with his thumbs, and the light resurfaces once more, a single pulse but warm and bright. "We saw a faint glow surrounding you."

"You did?" She flips her hands over, but no matter how she turns them, they look ordinary now. "I thought it was just my palms."

Sliding his hand over her cheek, Ëólas chuckles. "You are extraord—"

The thump of something hitting the ground makes Ëólas step aside and turn around. Between the horses, Elashor, on his knees, crumples into a ball. "I can feel it," he cries, his tears resting like dewdrops on the grass. "I can finally feel her spell."

He no longer looks like a proud king clinging to days long gone. Instead, he looks like a broken old man who forgot how to hope.

Kneeling in front of him, Adaline rests her hand on his back. "You know the truth now; wear it like armor as you fight with us to rebuild this world. I need your help, Grandfather."

When Elashor sits up, he catches her hand falling away from him. For the first time, he truly looks at her and holds her gaze as he searches her face, taking in the features she inherited from both sides of her family, and his expression contains slightly less pain. "You are so much like your grandmother."

Chapter Twenty-Six

THE DRUMS OF ALDERTON

Adaline pats the soft, short fur along Conleth's back as he tears out tufts of grass and chews his dinner. Leaving him to eat with his friends, she walks around the first groups of soldiers cooking over small fires and ignores their whispers along with the far-off look of awe in their eyes.

Ugh. I guess they saw me glowing like a giant fairy. Maybe that's a fae trait? So much for trying to keep that a secret.

Joining Sora and Merith in front of their own fire, Adaline sits next to Ëólas and holds her hands up to the flames, letting the warmth wash over her. With the sun retired for the night and the temperature dropping, the smallest breeze feels several degrees colder. She shivers once, and Tumin passes her a hot metal bowl filled to the brim.

Accepting her meal with both hands, she blows away the steam on top and savors the spicy broth, the shredded beef no longer dried out, and the large chunks of root vegetables. "Did you make this, Tumin?"

With a shy smile, he nods but says nothing.

"It's perfect, thank you. I'll cook tomorrow night."

His eyebrows jump upward. "No, my lady. That's unnecessary. Breton has cooking duty tomorrow night."

Concealing his amusement behind his bowl, Ëólas slurps his soup. "You'll offend the queen by not letting her help."

As Tumin gulps, Adaline elbows Ëólas. "Don't scare him."

When they're done eating, Ëólas cuts Sora off from dragging Adaline into the fields for training and holds open the flap to their tent, which the royal guard erected while she stood back and grumbled that she knows how to hammer stakes into the ground. But when Tumin and Moren proudly announced that they set up the queen's accommodations, she thanked them profusely. They didn't skimp either.

Inside the tent, the hexagonal shape and domed roof give her and Ëólas plenty of room to move about. The metal braziers shaped like upside-down mushroom caps warm the entire space, and carpets cover the ground, creating a cozy retreat. Someone also brought in the trunks containing their belongings, along with a wooden folding table and two chairs with fur pelts draped over them, all of which seems extreme given everything else the horses have pulled in the wagons. On the table, two pitchers and basins allow them to wash up, and someone rolled out thick sleeping mats that call Adaline's weary limbs.

Who the hell said I needed all of this? Does Magnus travel this way?

The glamping accommodations don't seem fair, given the communal long tents the human soldiers share in groups of ten. Many of the elves, however, lie down under the stars. To them, sleeping on the ground is like a mother cradling her children in her arms. If only that were true for the humans, which must be why the royal guard has pampered Adaline with more comfortable sleeping arrangements—that, or the royal guard encircling her tent, located in the middle of Lameiría's camp, doesn't like the idea of their queen visible to a thousand men at night.

Well, that's not something I want to think more about.

When Ëólas drops the flap, the canvas walls shield her from the murmur of conversation. She meanders to the table, eager to wash the grime off her skin, and toils away at unfastening her armor and the twenty-plus tiny buttons on her tailcoat. Ëólas, however, lingers in the center of the tent, drumming his thigh and bobbing his head as he waits for something.

Not sex. Definitely not sex. He probably has commander general stuff to do. "Are you going back outside?"

"After you've fallen asleep, yes. It makes sense for the elves to take watch."

Giving your limited need for sleep, of course.

She undoes the last button and slips the tailcoat off her shoulder, only to pull it back on. "Why don't I go outside too?"

With a chuckle, Ëólas removes his cloak, armor, belt, and leather overcoat, which he folds and tucks inside his trunk. On top, he rests his swords. Sitting in the fur-lined chair, he unlaces his boots. "Stop worrying about the special accommodations. They care about you. Consider it a kindness."

"I just—"

"Hate being a burden. I know. Now, if you're not going to lie down and stretch your back, then I will." Yanking off his boots, he lies down, closes his eyes, and folds his hands over his abdomen.

With a huff, Adaline strips down to her trousers and tunic that falls to her knees, washes off, and lays down next to him. Their shoulders rubbing against each other is the longest contact they've had all day. He smells like lavender and pine again, which makes Adaline's lips curl upward, until she hears Merith's voice outside their tent. "How badly is Merith disappointed in me?"

"He's not."

"Liar."

"Never."

"I saw you arguing."

Ëólas shuffles beside her, turning onto his side and propping his head up on his hand. "He's angry at me for teaching you mostly defense. He kept waiting for you to take the initiative and attack him."

"But—"

"I know. Going on the offense is not your style." When she grumbles, Ëólas strokes her cheek with the back of his hand, and his eyes travel to her lips. Swallowing hard, he drags his eyes back to meet hers. "My love, don't worry so much—"

She smushes her finger against his mouth. *It's my party, and I'll worry if I want to.*

He kisses her finger. Then, like a snapping turtle, he tries to bite the tip, making her yank her hand away in a panic.

"Jerk," she laughs, tucking her arm under her head like a pillow. Above her, the canvas ceiling comprises boiled leather dyed in shades of blue and purple and stitched together in patches. "Yesterday, we were at happy hour in Dupont Circle, drinking mojitos while I explained how Dirty Santa works and you pouted."

"That's because something called Dirty Santa should involve lingerie."

He always knows how to lighten the mood. She grazes his jawline with her knuckles, tracing the chiseled outline. Her legs don't feel as tired now. "We don't have audio privacy, huh?"

His eyes reflect the fire crackling in the brazier. "You could travel us home for a bit."

"Oh really."

"Just a thought." He rests his hand on her lower abdomen and gathers the tunic, collecting the fabric bunch by bunch, until he dips his thumb under her waistband and she slaps his hand.

"You don't think I already considered that?" She rolls onto her opposite side, giving him her back.

"So...that's not an option then?"

"Nope."

"Because that would be unfair to our troops. And we can't waste pointless time in Maryland."

She shifts around to face him, resting the side of her head on her bent arm. "I mean, *pointless* is rather harsh. But yeah."

"I understand. I'll be good."

Pinching her chin, he dances his lips over hers. She grabs his nape to stop him from escaping. Dragging his hand along her thigh, he grips her knee and pulls her leg around him. He crushes his mouth against hers and slips his tongue inside, and she feels like she's home again. When they're this close, fear has no room to breathe, to spread, to invade.

But she moans. Their eyes fly open, and they roll away from each other, neither comfortable with providing the elven soldiers the soundtrack to a porno.

We're not here for fun, Adaline. Get a hold of yourself.

"Hmm." Ëólas sits up and stares at the tent entrance. "Daven's outside."

Before Ëólas can say another word or finish relacing his boots, Adaline jumps up, throws on her boots, and ducks outside, wearing only her trousers and tunic. She rubs her arms as she approaches Daven. "Hey, is everything okay?" *The cold air is a godsend right now.*

"Yes, my lady." Angling himself away from her, his eyes dart to various people and objects, from the nearest royal guard standing at attention beside her tent to a pile of stakes left on the ground. "My men are accustomed to music before retiring for the night. My apologies. The distraction keeps up morale and—"

"Music?" Adaline perks up. "What kind of music?"

"Oh, um, drums, my lady."

"Drums! You brought the drums of Alderton here?" Adaline imagines the heft of the bass drumsticks in her hands. Granted, if she can muster energy to swing the drumsticks, maybe she shouldn't have ditched Sora's extra training session. *Yeah, no thank you.*

Daven coughs into his clasped hands. "Yes, my lady. It's tradition to—"

"Why would you bring drums when marching into enemy territory?" Elashor asks, appearing from the other side of the tent, his golden eyes fixated on Daven. "Those drums are the fastest way to draw Morgán's attention."

"Exactly." Pushing the canvas flaps aside, Ëólas emerges, wearing his swords again, and stands next to Adaline. "The sooner we can draw Morgán out, the faster we'll win. Drums are a brilliant idea."

"Woot!" Adaline bounces on her heels, despite her feet aching for a break. "Can I have a go at the drums?"

"Er, we brought the smaller ones." Daven scans his men far beyond the rows of elves separating her from the humans. "We, uh, could bring the drums up here."

"Don't bother." Adaline pats Daven's arm and marches toward the men, stopping only when Ëólas holds her coat out for her to slip her arms into the warmer layer.

Merith steps in front of her, blocking her path. "My queen, this perimeter is for your—"

"Lighten up, Merith. I'm going on the offence."

She claps him on the shoulder and leaves him stunned while she treks toward Alderton's various campfires and the soldiers circling them. Lost in their own thoughts, few of them speak as they stare into the flames, even as the queen and king weave through their camp, but Adaline studies as many faces as she can, hoping she'll recognize someone or, rather, an undeniable family resemblance. But face after face, she sees only strangers with somber expressions.

She slows down to walk beside Daven. "For how many of these men is this their first time leaving Alderton?"

"All of them."

And here they are on the fields of Aerytol, where five-hundred years ago, their ancestors died fighting Lameiría, fighting Elashor. Adaline glances at Sora and the royal guard that has spread out in a semicircle to protect their queen and king, none of whom protested entering Daven's camp.

Aerytol needs a united army. We'll have to build one as our population grows. Thank goodness Ëólas knows how to do that.

She reaches for his hand but then stops, not giving too much thought about why.

A soldier up ahead runs over to their group and, at Daven's nod, sprints off again to join the drummers. A few minutes later, the first bass vibrations roll over the camp. The soldiers, shedding the darker thoughts that had been weighing them down, look up from the fire and appear more youthful. Adaline quickens her pace, despite her legs wishing she had remained in bed. When she stops in front of the six musicians, Sora and Merith position themselves directly behind their lady and lord.

Even though Daven couldn't bring the massive taiko-like drums Alderton played at the ball, three of the soldiers hold the thinner hand-held drums with the backside open. Two other men stand in front of the waist-high barrel drums with animal skin stretched over the top and tacked to the sides. Another soldier carries a three-foot-long metal horn.

As the drummers wail on their instruments, the roar of rolling thunder carries Adaline back to her uncle's house, to him entertaining the kids while his wife made dinner. The cousins gathered at Uncle Jamie's feet, hitting the floorboards with their palms while he whacked the barrel drum. When Adaline was four, she rolled up the sleeves of her wool dress, pushed her unkempt curls out of her face, and asked him to let her try.

A proud son of Alderton, Uncle Jamie took one look at her scrawny arms, shook his grizzly dark-brown beard, and said, "Little girls are too weak."

After Aurellia slammed a plate on the dinner table, she tore the bass drumsticks out of her brother's hands, shoved one pointedly in his face, and reminded him who bought him that drum for his tenth birthday.

Given that his big sister knew how to whop his ass, Uncle Jamie raised his hands close to his shoulders and leaned away from her. "I said *little* girls, not girls."

Flashing her dark green eyes at him, Aurellia handed her daughter the sticks. Fearless like her mother, she banged the drum, and the vibration traveled through her body, making every inch of her feel more alive than ever before. From then on, Uncle Jamie let her practice at his home, even when Allex and Victor, her oldest cousins, sneered at the *little* girl in their way.

I kept playing, Mom.

Adaline nods her head in time with the beat as the soldiers hit the drums with their fists, their palms, and the bass drumsticks capped with large balls of fleece. Every soldier in their camp, no matter how far away, can relax this night as the drums take them home.

Song after song, different soldiers take turns showing off their skills and style. As one soldier steps down, he passes Adaline the drumsticks and disappears into the crowd. She cranes her neck, trying to see around Sora and the other royal guards, but she can't find the soldier with sandy-blond hair and matching stubble again.

He was too young. He wouldn't have known me.

With Ëólas elbowing her to get up there, she runs to the biggest barrel drum. Daven glances at Ëólas, as if waiting for the king to protest his wife standing among a group of towering, sweaty men, most of them shirtless and their abs glistening from pounding the drums for so long. Instead, Ëólas crosses his arms over his chest and waits for Adaline to do her thing.

When the soldier next to the queen recognizes her, he stumbles backward and drops his sticks. The other players, stopping mid-note, look to Daven for guidance. Stooping down, Adaline picks up the sticks rolling into her foot and offers them to the soldier.

"Beg your pardon," he mumbles and bows, "but the drums are not built for ladies."

Rolling her eyes, Adaline rests his fluffy sticks on top of his drum, raises her arms high above her head, and swings down the first drumstick. The entire barrel thunders. As the roar dies away, she counts beats in her head, letting the silence take hold, grow stronger, and make everyone anticipate the next strike. When she hits ten, she pounds the drum with the second stick. Again, the roar shatters the silence into oblivion.

The next time, she counts to eight, then six, letting each rumble build into a crescendo until she's wailing on the drums as fast as the men had been while also changing up her pattern, including strikes on the barrel's sides and outer edges. Dropping the sticks altogether, she also uses her hands as she blends the different pitches, the different tones, the different volumes—merging the sounds of Alderton with a changeup that's more reminiscent of modern rock and roll.

If only she had a drum kit here.

The sweat drips off her brow, and her hands move so fast that her motions turn into a blur. And in those strikes, she remembers practicing with Uncle Jamie, remembers her parents dancing in the background, remembers the town festivals that started and stopped with the drums, and remembers the school band concerts with her father and Nan in the front row.

The drums have been a part of her since birth, a part that no spell could make her forget, not really.

Halfway into her second song, the other musicians join in, and they continue their jam session for three more songs. When Adaline finally rumbles her hands to a stop, her palms are beet red. Her hair clings to her nape, and she's out of breath. But the soldiers throw their fists into the air, cheer her performance, and bow deeply as she returns to Ëólas's side.

When he slips his hand around her waist, she leans against him, her limbs deliciously numb and her eyelids droopy as if they just made love. Knowing he can hear her over the music, she whispers, "Okay, I can sleep now."

They turn to leave, and as Daven bids them goodnight, the familial glint in his eye resembles the discreet yet profound pride Uncle Jamie displayed when he invited Adaline to join him on stage at the harvest festival—in front of the entire village. That celebration was one of the last times they played together before she and her family disappeared.

Following Sora and Merith, she heads toward her tent, her spirits rejuvenated even as she leaves behind the drums. The men, peeking up from their groups, look at her more closely, as though they can see beyond her title, as though they might recognize one of their own—until she subconsciously reaches for Ëólas's hand. As he clasps his fingers around hers, the men's stares harden, and they turn away, their lips curled in disgust.

For the rest of the walk through Alderton's camp, she stares at Sora's boots and sighs with relief when they cross into Lameiría's side with its lack of tents and numerous mats rolled out under the stars. Only, the elves no longer gaze at her with awe; instead, setting down their flutes or abruptly ending their conversations, they glance at her as if she's on the wrong side of camp.

Holding on to Ëólas more tightly, she walks faster to her tent, to her respite, anticipating its warm interior and the chance to be alone, unseen, maybe even forgotten for the time being. The braziers illuminate the canvas walls, making them pulse with a soft golden glow that beckons her. Once inside, Ëólas reclines on their bed, crossing his ankles as he drifts to sleep. Adaline sheds her coat, strips down to her tunic, and scrubs the sweat off her skin, grinding the washcloth harder than necessary until patches of red mark her arms and legs.

Chapter Twenty-Seven

A Respite

Ëólas kneads Adaline's upper back, drawing her away from the dream realm. "My love, breakfast is ready."

She turns her head to face him, one cheek buried in the fur bedding, and peeks an eye open. "I said I'd make breakfast today."

Not once in the last five days has the royal guard let her cook or help set up the tent or do anything other than walk her horse or train with Sora. Worst yet, Adaline's been too tired to fight them on the matter. *They make it too damn easy for me to want to be pampered.*

"If you want to cook, you'll need to wake up earlier." Already dressed, Ëólas backs away from her and sits in the chair near the entrance, his hands hooked behind his head as he tilts backward as if he's been on holiday this entire time, not walking hundreds of miles and sleeping on the ground.

"Hmm. Okay. Wake me earlier tomorrow." *Yeah, right.*

Pushing herself to sit up on her knees, the furs fall down her back, exposing her to the icy morning air. Goosebumps form on her arms and legs, and her nipples scrape her nightgown. She stretches her arms overhead and stands up, stumbling toward the trunk with her clothes, while Ëólas flips through the papers and maps on the table, studying scribbled words and landmarks rather than his wife. She's not surprised though; everyone thought they'd run into Morgán or his demonic elves by now. Instead, the pressure keeps building with no release in sight. Even Ëólas has reduced his bantering to a minimum.

The honeymoon phase really is over. Hopefully, they can be themselves again when this is all over.

With a frown, Adaline rubs the sleep away from her eyes, digs through her trunk for fresh clothing, and dresses as quickly as possible. When she finishes buttoning her trousers, she sneaks a peek at Ëólas, but he's already gone, probably instructing his people to tear down camp and load the wagons.

Within an hour, the army sets off again, and a light yet chilly rain makes their march annoying as all hell. Her elven waterproof cloak keeps her dry, but the softer ground latches onto her boots, making her glutes burn ten times worse and making her pray for an early lunch break. Unfortunately, Ëólas and Daven agree that the lack of dark clouds means they should continue hiking through tall, wet grass that clings to everyone's boots and trousers.

When lunch saves them, Adaline nibbles her food to delay sword practice. Yet the moment she swallows her last bite, Sora jumps up, bows to Adaline, and leads her away from the group that gets to rest their legs longer. Given that the royal guard has tended to her every need so she has this time with Sora, Adaline ought to be grateful. Brushing her tears aside, she unsheathes her sword and assumes first position, her feet fighting the grass so she can spread her legs further apart and hunker down. She shakes her head so her hood falls off, letting the mist coat her face in a cool, light sheen, and grunts as she lifts her blade, which on day one weighed not much heavier than a baseball bat but on day six feels like a twenty-pound sledgehammer.

Maybe I should confess that I'm tired. I mean, what if Morgán shows up tomorrow? The thought of those red eyes and gnarled arms makes Adaline lift her sword higher. *Never mind. Let's go.*

But Sora takes one look at Adaline and drops her hand away from her hilt. With her fingers tapping her chin, she studies her queen while debating with herself. "I told Merith we should break today. He disagrees. What do you think, my lady?"

Adaline lowers her sword an inch, her arms screaming at her to stop holding that thing in the air and her mind yelling at her that this is some sort of mindset test. *Merith's being a hard ass.* "I trust you to know what's best."

For the first time since they left New Leira, Sora smiles. "Thank you, Your Majesty." Leaving her sword in its scabbard, she walks over to Adaline and sits down on her cape, gesturing for Adaline to do the same. "I think I need to know you more."

Careful not to sever her fingers as she shoves her blade into its sheath, Adaline pulls her hood over her brow and plops down next to Sora, away from the guys, away from the occasional glares whenever she gets too close to Ëólas, and away from the pampering. For the next half hour, the two ladies do nothing but talk.

When Sora's done playing a hundred questions, Adaline asks, "Do you practice enchantments or work well with a specific element?"

"Ha! No, I'm a soldier through and through. I did enchant my sword though, so I'm fairly good with metal."

"Really?" Adaline leans around Sora but sees only her black leather hilt. The silver pommel doesn't look particularly magical, and nothing glows. "Enchanted it how?"

Sora pulls out her long blade and lays it across her lap. "I added layers of protection so the metal along the edge doesn't easily chip away. The hilt is drawn to my palm, so my sword will find me within close proximity, and the stronger my opponent, the harder my strike."

"Seriously? That's amazing. Did Ëólas enchant his swords?"

"Nah. He's better with wood. I enchanted a number of his weapons though."

Adaline flips her scabbard around, pulling it off the grass so it rests on her lap. The occasional large drop of rain pings the diamond in the center of the hand guard wrapped in vines. "Is my sword enchanted?"

"Uh, no. You can't rely on the enchantments. You need to earn the skills first."

Well that's poop. "Why are you a soldier through and through?"

Sora drums her fingers on the sage and navy fabric strips wrapped around her leather hilt. "My parents were from Aerytol. They lived in the capital city, what was then called Lénorem. They used to tell me stories about the different cities they visited, the people they met from all over the world, spices and fruits I've never tasted, and their admiration for Queen Arraya. They'd often see her roaming the city, conversing with her citizens, building friendships among her people."

The nostalgia falls away from Sora's voice as she squeezes her scabbard. "And they told me about the day they lost everything, how they abandoned their family home and escaped the mob that tried to kill all elves, how neighbors turned against neighbors, save a few. I never wanted to see that happen to Lameiría, so I joined border patrol and eventually the royal guard," she looks at Adaline, "with the hope that maybe, someday, I could bring my parents home. They were there that day, when you shared your memories. You've given them hope again."

When Adaline summoned the sacred circle and dropped that stone in the water, she thought only about bringing Ëólas's family together. She never dreamed the truth would reach so many others. "I'd like to meet them someday, your parents."

"They'd love that, truly."

Because I'm Adaline, or because I'm the Queen of Aerytol? You know what, I'm not going to think about that. Let's see. What can we talk about that won't lead back to me sounding like some sort of elven savior? Oh!

Adaline waggles her eyebrows. "So, do you have someone special back home?"

"Ha! No." Sora twirls her fingers around the grass. "I had a lover about a decade ago, but I tired of him quickly."

"Why?"

"He was a newer recruit for the queen's guard and couldn't keep up with me." She curves her hand around her mouth and whispers, "I have zero resistance to solid, muscular arms."

Adaline laughs, and the sound and feeling remind her that the discomfort of this journey is temporary. "Ëólas's arms and abs make me want to lick him from top to—" She clamps her mouth shut and buries her face in her lap. "I'm so sorry." *Please don't gag at that.* She hears nothing but snorting from Sora. Her face burning like a hotplate, Adaline peeks up. "I didn't gross you out?"

"What? Why would—ugh." She sticks her tongue out at the group packing up behind them. "Forget those morons. How else are we supposed to get an heir? Besides, I'm happy my friend found his destined partner. Oh, you're going to—yep, you're a hugger alright."

"Sorry."

"Don't be."

As they walk back toward the others, Sora loops her arm around Adaline's. "Tomorrow, I'll be strict with your training again."

"Yeah, I figured."

"But you should know you're an excellent student."

Adaline takes those last four words and mentally tucks them away in a storage box inside her chest so she can retrieve that affirmation the next time she berates herself for failing at sword practice, for not living up to Merith's expectations, for embarrassing Ëólas in front of his people. Words like those are as strong as any magic spell.

With Adaline not trudging after Sora this evening, she wanders among Ëólas's troops setting up camp. Everyone moves together so much like a well-oiled machine that Adaline fears jumping in and breaking all the cogs.

I must be able to help in some way.

Beyond the sea of Ëólas's soldiers, Daven's men toil away at erecting tents to shield themselves from the rain and wind with the hope of warming up, drying off, and getting a decent night's sleep. The elves do the same, not keen to sleep outside tonight. While Elashor directs his own Secret Service, Daven and Ëólas tend to their shared priorities with rechecking maps and issuing orders about army stuff.

Maybe I should go listen and learn from them?

Of the fifty members of the royal guard, ten of them set up her accommodations by hauling items off the wagon, hammering stakes so her tent won't blow away, enchanting the surrounding grass to prevent a wildfire, and lighting the braziers. She walks toward one group responsible for making dinner, yanks off her gloves, and tucks them into her pockets, only to stop short when several elves sitting in a circle place dead rabbits in front of them. After bowing their heads to the pudgy creatures whose noses will never twitch again and whispering some Elvish about sacrifice and nature's path, the chefs tear the fur and flesh off the animals.

Adaline does an about-face and heads for the wagon. *I can carry stuff.*

Despite the constant light rain, the royal guard works in unison too. When a couple of elven ladies carry Ëólas's folding table off the wagon, Adaline climbs the ramp, lifts a tarp, and grabs a pile of fur blankets that make her arms sag and back hunch forward. The pelts fall around her feet until she throws half the length over her shoulder.

"My lady," a human royal guard rushes to Adaline, "let me carry that for you."

"I'm good, thanks." Adaline runs down the ramp, propelled by gravity, and gathers more fur around her arms to stop the pelt from dragging in the grass.

"But my lady, you needn't—"

"Here." Sora grabs a portion of the blankets, lifting them off the ground and away from Adaline's feet. "It's easier with two." She nods toward the tent and follows Adaline inside, where they drop the pelts on Ëólas's trunk. "We should bring in the second half of carpets next. Best to lay them first."

"Right."

After finishing with that massive tent, Adaline helps Sora hammer the stakes for her small, two-person tent made of the same canvas material. *Man, these guys should see how awesome retractable tent poles are.* Despite having zero modern conveniences, the preparation and teamwork remind her of scouting during middle school, and the unspoken yet understood camaraderie feels like being with family.

While Adaline observes the other guards working together, the soldier with the sandy-blond hair approaches Ëólas and Daven speaking with their generals. Pausing outside his commander's circle, the boy, with his baby face and new stubble, must be younger than most of the other soldiers. After Lord Bodlin barks his orders and brandishes his finger for emphasis, the boy bows and backs away from his commanding officer. As he turns to leave, the kid stares directly at Adaline, his cheeks blushing. She opens her mouth to ask him if he's from Meadowbrook, but the boy hurries away to rejoin his rank and buddies.

Ëólas walks up to her. "Hey."

She instinctively sidesteps closer to him, her gaze still following the boy long after he disappears, and extends her arm to fold it around Ëólas's waist, but he moves away from her, toward their camp, and waits for her to snap out of her trance and join him.

"Why don't you ask if that soldier hails from Meadowbrook?" Ëólas asks.

"Because I don't think he wants me to." Leaving the boy alone, Adaline stomps through a thick tuft of grass. "Hey, you have better vision than me. Did you notice any family resemblance?"

"I'm afraid not much, beyond his green eyes."

Huh.

During dinner, the rain stops and permits their group to observe the sunset while Sora and Adaline eat in silence near the fire, and Ëólas and Merith continue a heated discussion on the other side of the flames, painting their faces red and orange. The entire time Adaline gobbles her rabbit stew, Elashor steals glances at her from two rows away. She slows down her bites to a more lady-like pace and uses the back of her hand to wipe her chin clean. Without a word of warning, Elashor rises from his troops, cuts across camp, and sits next to Adaline. He remains silent as he takes an occasional bite of stew and studies the saturated dark-green fields with an intensity that would rival Cindy peering into a microscope.

Um, okay.

When Adaline stretches her neck back and forth and arches her spine, Elashor nods at Conleth grazing with his buddies between Lameiría and Alderton's camps. "Why don't you mount your horse? You shouldn't push yourself so much."

"Meh. This walk is nothing compared to what Ëólas and I dealt with when escaping the Wastelands." *Which is exactly where we'll be tomorrow. Oh goodie.*

Elashor tears off a piece of bread and nibbles the end. "Escaping?"

Gesturing at Ëólas, Adaline asks him to tell the story, and he uses this opportunity to warn everyone about the creature who steals souls. During this retelling, Adaline rubs her thumb along the underside of her wedding ring, which she almost left in the castle but then took with her as insurance. The ring means nothing compared to Ëólas's safety. Then again, Mr. Toad enjoys taking objects from the dead. He already has her father's knife. Maybe he'll want Nan's necklace next.

Please, let's avoid Mr. Toad altogether this time.

Elashor stitches his brows together. "You saved my grandson."

"He saved me first. Many times."

After Elashor stares dramatically at the fire for a long while, his distress morphs into a fond smile. "Erol saved my life. Before the borders shut down, I convinced him to explore the world with me."

That had to be, what, seven, eight hundred years ago? Shit, is he okay traveling so far from home with us? "What happened?" Adaline sets down her empty bowl, which Moren snatches and refills for her. "Thank you." She takes another large spoonful of salty, tender meat. *Sorry, bunnies.*

"The earth shook. I fell between the rocks and slipped into the heart of a deep cave. He tied a rope around his waist and dove in after me. Took us four days to climb out. We wouldn't have found the exit without that rope."

Dang, Grandad. That must have terrified them, being cut off from nature and dying. "Sounds like you two were close."

"We were. That's why when I became king, I made him my right hand."

"Whoa!" She slops broth onto her thighs but saves the rest of the ingredients. "My grandfather was like Merith?"

Elashor chuckles, but the melody uses only sad notes. "Not quite. He was my right hand in terms of politics. I didn't need a soldier always guarding me back then."

Adaline falls silent too, not wishing to hear how humans ruined Elashor's life. Dunking the last of her stale baguette into her soup, she savors the broth soaked into the bread. "How did Erol meet Nan?"

"The first time Arraya's mother summoned me to Aerytol as king, I took Erol with me. I lost my right hand that day." Despite his sarcasm, nostalgia softens his face.

He knew my great-grandmother too? Nan never mentioned her. "What was her name, Nan's mom?"

"Léna, but her family called her Lé-Lé."

Adaline chokes on a chunk of potato. *No way. That's the name of the fairy I used to draw at Nan's house—Lee-Lee.*

Setting aside her bowl, she locks eyes with Ëólas. He nods that he recognizes the connection too.

It can't be. But why would I know that? Maybe Nan did mention Lé-Lé's name before? I feel like I'm forgetting something.

Stirring her soup, Adaline watches the ingredients bump into each other and fall apart. "Thank you so much for sharing that."

With a silent nod, Elashor passes her the rest of his baguette, leans back on his hands, and counts the stars visible within the small patches of the cloudy sky, seemingly satisfied that he has fulfilled his promise to tell her about Erol. Maybe over time he'll tell her more.

When Ëólas finishes his meal, Elashor attempts small talk with this grandson, an awkward conversation that revolves a lot around bird migration, but Ëólas limits his replies to four-word sentences. Elashor has his work cut out for him in more ways than one.

As everyone cleans up their plates and says their goodnights, Elashor asks Adaline, "Why do you call your grandmother Nan?"

"Oh, um, it's a nickname for Grandma. She told me to call her that after I moved in with her."

Clasping his hands behind his back, he stares at his boots. "What was she like when you knew her?"

Adaline lets the memories wash over her, taking heed not to let them drown her. "Equally fierce and kind. No one dared to cross her, except me—sometimes. She loved to help people and volunteered a lot, both at my schools and in the community. She made the best tarts and would bake a hundred at a time and freeze them for me. And she spent most afternoons digging in the soil, planting flower beds, herbs, vegetables—anything really. She seemed happier there, like the sorrow that hovered behind her couldn't enter the garden."

Elashor's dark-gold eyes glow brighter, glossier. "Erol was the gardener, not Arraya."

Wait, what? Oh... Crossing her arms over her chest, Adaline hugs herself. The clouds release their mist again, coating her cheeks and braid. Raindrops hang from her lashes and fall onto her purple cloak. *So, Nan used the garden to stay connected to Grandad.*

Turning his back to Merith, Ëólas walks around Elashor and takes Adaline's hand. When their palms touch, a soft glow pulses between them, and she can sense the ache tearing into his chest too. He leads her into the tent and closes the flap, shutting out the rest of the world.

That won't be us, my love. Not us.

CHAPTER TWENTY-EIGHT

THE SAGE

After draping her damp cloak over her trunk, Adaline falls onto the bedding and buries her face in the furs, sighing as the braziers restore the color in her cheeks. Her exhaustion now rivals what she felt in the Wastelands, of the endless hours of walking. Her feet appreciate the carpets lining her tent and the soft soil on this side of the journey, even though the soggy ground made her legs and torso work harder today.

And tomorrow's when the real hardship begins.

As she rolls over, Ëólas yanks her boots and socks off and grinds his thumbs into her heel. His dirty-blond hair frames his high cheekbones and diamond-shaped jawline as if he visited the salon today. "You remember the first time I tended to your sore feet?"

"Uh-huh."

The stench mortified her. Then his ministrations made her moan, and she could have died right then and there. She still hates the idea of him inhaling her stinky feet, but at least she can't scare him off permanently. They're bound together, now and forever, in sickness and in health, which includes less favorable body odors that nullify his libido.

These last few days must have reminded Ëólas of the downsides to having a half-human wife. While he's remained pristine, she's used up most of the washing basin each night to make herself somewhat presentable. But her hair feels greasy, and a washcloth can remove only so much grime. Not that it matters. After going at it like rabbits—*aww, poor cooked bunnies*—every day in Maryland, this week of depravation has been the worst part of this trip thus far.

I really should be grateful we've had an easy start.

She lies back as Ëólas bends her foot forward, stretching her arch. Like every night prior, he won't touch her beyond this. After the massage, he'll sit at the table and read a book, and when she drifts off to sleep, he'll rejoin his soldiers and laugh quietly with his friends to keep up morale. Well, he'll laugh with everyone but Elashor and Merith.

"Are you going to cut your grandfather and best friend some slack?" she asks.

Ëólas pinches her toes and tugs on them, stretching the bones. "Eventually."

"I didn't know you hold on to grudges for so long."

"Ha. My grandfather's grudge lasted five centuries."

"Point taken. But he's trying."

"Yes, well, he needs to keep trying."

"And Merith?"

Ëólas sets down one foot and picks up the other, flexing her ankle back and forth. "Merith and I are fine."

"You don't look it."

"He doesn't grasp that you're..."

"Human?"

"Kind-hearted."

"You mean soft."

"Well, you are soft." He tickles the underside of her foot. When she yelps and yanks her leg away, he snatches her ankle and rubs circles up and down her calf muscle, his hair falling beside his eyes, making his gold irises glow in the dim light.

Adaline attempts to think about anything other than crossing the river into the Wastelands tomorrow, but Ëólas's rhythmic rubbing conjures images of his clothes on the floor and them making lewd sounds as his flesh smacks against hers for the entire army to hear.

Damn, I have a dirty mind.

"What are you thinking about?" Ëólas asks.

Shit. Don't tell me he sensed that. "Nothing important."

With a nod, he works his thumbs around her ankle bone, circling the nub slowly yet forcefully until her body temperature rises and a tingling sensation overtakes her inner thighs.

Fucking tease. She kicks his hand away.

Not easily dissuaded, he captures her again and digs his thumb into her heel, grinding back and forth to force that muscle to relax too. "When you were training with Sora during lunch, I received one of Magnus's birds. Lameiría's and Alderton's forces are a bit tense from both sides surrounding the city. I'm sure Magnus and Jorrel can handle that, but I thought you should know. No updates about Cindy or Dax though, sorry."

Adaline wriggles on the bedding and tilts her torso upward, resting on her elbows. "I hate leaving Magnus to watch over our people." *We should be there handling this, not him.* An idea pops into her head, and Adaline sits up straight. "We should go check in with him."

Kneading the ball of her foot, Ëólas peeks up. "You think? What about leaving our army behind?"

"Not the same thing. New Leira needs us too, and I'd like to check in on Cindy and Dax, see how they're coming along."

"Alright." Ëólas angles his head toward the tent entrance and keeps his voice at the same volume. "You caught that, Merith?" After a brief pause, Ëólas turns back to her. "He insists we announce our arrival the moment we return to camp."

"Will do, Merith."

Standing up, Adaline grabs Ëólas's hand and pulls him into their personal chambers. Along with the tent, the smell of damp horses, sweaty soldiers, and campfires disappears. Instead, silence, drawn curtains, a king-size bed, and plush carpets take their place. Adaline heads for the doors, but Ëólas grabs her wrist and yanks her back, pulling her against him. His hands latch onto her bottom, and he crushes his mouth against hers. He groans as he grinds his hips back and forth, his member hardening and pressing into her lower abdomen.

All the emotions and desire she's been suppressing erupt inside her, making her need one thing only. Grabbing his hard, muscular arms, she squeezes his biceps and slides her hands up to his neck, only to sniff the body odor emanating from her armpits. She pushes herself away from him. "I'm foul."

"Trust me."

He yanks off her tunic, tossing it across the room, far away from them both, and strips off the rest of her clothing, not taking his time to be gentle or giving her a chance to argue. His hands skate up her bare back and around to the front, and her body quivers as he palms her breasts. She envisions pushing him onto the bed and climbing on top, until his hands grind the grime into her skin.

Recoiling, she opens her mouth to protest, but Ëólas kisses her again, and the taste of him, the freedom to kiss him as deeply and as long as she wants without worrying about the soldiers overhearing her moans, makes her yank his belt off and throw it aside. He grins at his victory and tears his own clothes off, dumping them on the floor near hers. His abs flexing as he sheds his trousers makes Adaline lick her lips.

Standing in front of her unclothed, he pulls her into his arms again, his member slipping between her folds.

She suckles and nibbles his earlobe. "How can you want me right now?"

His tongue dives into her mouth, his groan his only response. He claps his hands onto her round bottom, making her cheeks jiggle, and picks her up so she's forced to wrap her legs around him. Pulling her braid loose, he twists his fingers in her greasy hair and carries her across the room, but instead of taking her to their bed, he pushes the door open to their bathroom.

"What are you—"

The extra-large wooden tub, filled with steaming water and infused with scents of lavender and chamomile, waits for them in the center of the room.

He lets her go, only to drop her legs into the hot water. "For the record, this is for your comfort. I'm so starved I'd rather take you first."

"But how did they—You! You planned this. When you heard from Magnus, you knew I'd want to check on everyone."

"If you hadn't, I would have insisted."

"What am I going to do with you?" As she lowers herself into the tub, the water wraps around her sore muscles. She pulls her legs to her chest, giving Ëólas room to climb in and sit down opposite her.

When he leans against the curved back of the tub and props his elbows on the rim, his golden eyes lock with hers. "I've had to control myself for days," he growls. "Do not keep your distance now."

She bites her lip, and his eyes flick to her mouth. With a coy smile, she swims to him, her breasts bobbing in the water and lapping against his chest. His smoldering gaze and taut jaw tell her she won't be able to tease him for long.

Still, she pushes him. "You know we can't stay here long. We do have people to greet and—"

He smacks her bottom bobbing out of the water and flips her around, settling her against him. Reaching over the side of the tub, he grabs the pitcher sitting on the nearby stool and pours it over her hair. With his fingertips, he massages her scalp and wrings her hair clean, twisting it off to the side and out of his way. As she lies backward, resting her head on his shoulder, he washes her body, his hands taking their time as he explores every inch, helping her to shed her physical ailments from the last several days.

"Ëólas, can we just stay here tonight? Is that selfish of me?"

"Mmm. I love that idea." He kisses the hollow of her neck, making her back arch. "We'll visit Cindy and Dax soon. Right now, I need you to hold on to the rim of the tub and bend over for me."

"What about Magnus?"

Ëólas tweaks her nipple. "What do you mean? I have no intention of sharing."

"That's not what I meant!" She tilts her head sideways and looks at him incredulously. "I was referring to making sure he's okay. You said—"

"Oh, that." He trails his lips along her shoulder, then pushes her forward onto her knees, and the water pouring off her splashes onto the stone floor. "I lied. He's fine."

"Ëólas!"

"Chastise me later. Bend over now."

"Are you mad at me?" Ëólas snaps his belt around his waist and adjusts the collar of his black coat, the gold tunic beneath highlighting his eyes.

"Ha!" Sitting on the disheveled bed, Adaline clips her curls back in a half bun, bends down, and pulls on a long pair of thick socks. "We should have spent our nights here. I would have better endured you keeping your distance during the day." Slipping on her boots, she drags her belt off the bed and tugs the leather strap through the buckle decorated with filagree and purple gemstones.

"You really think I distanced myself so much?"

"You know you did. But I get it. Sort of."

He leans against the door to the sitting room, blocking her path. "I catch the men staring at you. I don't blame them, but I don't want to encourage it either."

Yeah, they look at me, and then they remember I married an elf, and their stares turn to sneers.

She drums her palms on his chest a few times and peers up at him, her lips curled with mischief. "Everyone will need time to adjust to the idea of a couple like us, but I'm proud I'm yours and you're mine. Part of me doesn't care that might offend them. Maybe we should set an example."

"Mmm." He kisses her nose. "Maybe."

Leaving that thought to permeate in his head, Adaline opens the doors to their chambers and seeks Cindy while Ëólas checks in with Magnus—just in case he's been dealing with more than he's shared. As much as Adaline would love to visit with everyone, her bones ache for her to crawl into bed and stay there for the rest of the night. At AU, she taught later classes for a reason. She's never been an early riser. Thankfully, Cindy's her late-night-owl sister.

Adaline wraps her knuckles three times on a wide door with a wrought-iron circular handle hanging from a diamond plate decorated with vines and large grapes. When she hears Cindy say, "Come in," Adaline pushes open the door. Inside the makeshift lab located around the corner from the study, Cindy peeks up from her microscope, which rests on a long table with a butcher-block top. She's lined up two generators in the corner, next to her gray-blue analyzer, stacked boxes of latex gloves, hand sanitizer, and trays with empty test tubes. The science equipment combined with the lit torches on the walls and the antique velvet furniture opposite the lab create an impressive steampunk setting.

"Hey you!" Cindy takes off her work-only glasses, sets them on the table, and walks around to hug Adaline. In addition to a teal floor-length gown with a slim silhouette, most likely thanks to Seira's choosing, Cindy wears her white lab coat. "What are you doing back? Oh no. Did shit hit the fan?"

"No. I just wanted to check in on you before we cross into the Wastelands. How's it going? Love the scientific take on your dress, by the way."

"Oh, man. After you left, some lady yelled at me, insisting that I would embarrass you if I didn't wear something more appropriate."

"Yeah... Lady Marzella can be intense, but she means well. You know you'd never embarrass me, right? And you don't have to wear that snood."

"I figured, but I wanted to shut her up. Plus, teal's my favorite color. Seira's good at keeping the peace."

"That she is." Adaline walks over to the long counter and plucks an empty vial from a rack. "How's it going with the samples?"

"Good. Good. Really good."

Sliding the tube back in place, Adaline faces Cindy and props her elbows on the countertop behind her. "Three *goods* are scary."

"Like your three *fines*?"

"Thanks. I love when you call me out." She flips Cindy the bird. "What's going on?"

Cindy puckers her lips to the side. "I have twelve samples, including one from Seira that I can't use because of the whole heritage thing."

Ah, yes. The fae thing. "So eleven, huh?"

Cindy skirts around the table and sits on a metal stool, hiking up her skirts so she can tap her flats on the bottom rung. "I got more yesterday, thanks to Fólas helping me set up shop at an empty stall on Market Street. It used to belong to some stone carver guy."

"Oh." Adaline clicks her thumbnails together and waits a beat before replying. "That's, that's great. It's a good spot to make friends and connect with the people."

"Yeah. Me going to them has made things easier."

"That's awesome. Thank you, Cindy."

"Ah." She waves Adaline off. "How's your campaign going?"

"Long." That's the only answer she can give Cindy right now. Her brain doesn't want to think about the fact that both sides limit their interactions as much as possible. Then again, that's better than them turning on each other and fighting to the death. "Everything's okay here? Dax? Seira? Mercia?"

"Yeah, all's good. Mercia runs a tight ship. She reminds me of my boss."

"She's something alright." *Maybe I can catch her in the morning, since she's up with the sun.*

Adaline meanders toward the velvet sofa surrounded with fifteen plants of various heights and widths, her body slowing down with each step. She rubs a waxy leaf between her fingers. "Dax claimed this side of the room, huh?"

"What gave it away?" Cindy laughs. "He spends most of his time at the training grounds or in the elven garden."

I hope Cindy's having fun too.

Behind a small, potted Ficus-like tree, the white stone wall sparkles with a dull, rainbow-like shimmer. Adaline ducks around the glossy almond-shaped leaves, picks up a crate containing colorful glass bottles and crystals, and sets it on the sofa. "What's all this?"

"Oh." Turning her back to Adaline, Cindy returns to her lab station and grabs a pipette and a vial filled with dark-red liquid. "Lady Loríen dropped those off."

"Why?"

"Because she wants to help me with *magic*." She says that last word as if she's a cheap magician who's dazzling the audience with spirit fingers.

Adaline approaches Cindy slowly. "But magic is real, especially in this world. I mean, look at what I can do."

"I wouldn't call that magic." Holding her pipette at an angle, Cindy squeezes blood into a circular, enclosed disc with various clear chambers. "Traveling is a talent you were naturally born with."

Um, sure. I guess one could look at it that way. "And the elements, the way I connect with them?" *Correction—sometimes connect with them.*

Cindy pushes a button on the LED screen of her analyzer, and the rectangular box in the middle pops open a tray drawer. "So the elements are more alive here. I'm okay with that; I have faith, Adaline. I just don't buy the whole magic idea. That word makes it sound like we can make something from nothing, which isn't possible. Now, if Lady Loríen's vials and rocks have ingredients I can work with, I'm all for that."

She sets the disc on the tray, closes the drawer, and enters a few basic details about the sample. When she enters the patient's age, she punches in the numbers three and five. She glances at Adaline and grins. "I had to divide each patient's age by ten." Reading the test results, Cindy jots down a few notes on her clipboard.

"So this patient's actually three hundred and fifty. Sounds about right. Ew, wait a minute. You entered Ëólas's age as eighteen? That's so wrong."

"Ha, yeah. I thought the same thing."

They both laugh, and within the safety of that humorous moment, Adaline hooks her arm around Cindy's shoulders and bumps their heads together. "Hey, can you just keep an open mind, please?"

Cindy waves at the castle walls in a sweeping arch. "Chica, look where I am. I think I'm pretty damn open minded. But yeah, fine."

"Thank you, mi hermana. I really—"

"Adaline!" Dax bursts into the lab.

Having traded in his T-shirts, Dax wears a silky blue tunic that complements the blue undertones of his dark skin, a navy leather vest, and brown trousers. Leather straps crisscross over his chest, the pouches filled with who knows what, but the overall outfit makes him look like a proper ranger in a fantasy film. Adaline wouldn't be surprised if he's asked everyone here to call him Bosque.

"I heard you were back." He kisses Adaline's cheek and Cindy's lips. "Can you come outside, both of you? I have to show you something."

After Cindy pulls off her latex gloves and tosses them into a steel trashcan, they follow Dax outside to the private gardens. The moon's position indicates they're approaching midnight.

Damn, I have to go to bed ASAP.

They walk a few steps down the dirt path, and when Dax pauses, he spins around, kneels down, and touches his hand to the earth. Closing his eyes, he mutters a few words under his breath, and thin vines inch their way out of the ground and hook around Cindy and Adaline's ankles.

"Holy shit, Dax!" Adaline wriggles her foot. The vines hug her once and retreat into the soil, at least for her.

Cindy, literally rooted to the ground, doesn't fight to escape. Instead, she gawks at the vines with her mouth hanging open. "How? I don't understand." Dipping her hand into her lab coat pocket, she pulls out a pair of tweezers and tears off a piece of vine.

"I know, right?" When Dax whispers again, the vines around Cindy retreat. "I met this cool elf who's been teaching me about plants."

"But how did you do that?" *How the hell did you learn that in a few days when I've been struggling for months? And why the hell did no one tell me that elves can do shit like that?*

Resting his hands on his hips, Dax puffs out his chest. "Man, this is who I've always been. This world just knows it too."

Who you've always been—never were words so true. "Dax, that's one of the most brilliant things anyone's ever said to me."

Crawling into bed, Adaline flops down on her stomach, hugs her pillow, and sighs into its softness. Her eyelids drift shut, and her weight sinks into the mattress as Ëólas rolls half his body onto her, slides his leg between hers, and rubs her back, his warm hand soothing her muscles like hot stones during a massage.

Who I've always been. Who's that?

When Ëólas's breathing slows and his hand stops on her bottom, she too fades into nonexistence, into the void between realities. Her bedding turns into grass, the blades crunching under her palms and legs as she pushes herself up to standing. Her legs are much shorter and her hands smaller.

Without a tree or building obscuring the horizon, the entire sky reflects a kaleidoscope of pastel colors, and the birds threading themselves through the clouds beat their wings and roar a stream of liquid fire.

Dragons. They're dragons.

"Hello, Little One," calls a woman's voice. "You've wandered too far from home again."

As Adaline turns around, a lady with long legs, raven-black hair, and lavender eyes descends from the sky, her wings as delicate as a dragonfly's and their translucent silver sheen speckled with starlight. Her feet touch the ground without a sound, and when she folds her wings downward, they disappear altogether, as if Adaline imagined them.

"Lé-Lé!" Adaline sprints to the lady, who squats down and scoops Adaline into her arms. When she speaks, her voice has reverted to her native accent from Alderton. "I'm sorry. I didn't mean to wander."

"I know. That's just who you are."

Adaline tilts her head to the side. "Huh?"

With her eyes twinkling, Lé-Lé nuzzles her forehead against Adaline's. "You'll understand someday."

Understand who I am? Who am I?

But those thoughts are too mature. They don't belong in this familiar dream.

Laying her head on Lé-Lé's shoulder, Adaline sighs, and her vision blurs as if someone were pulling her eyelids down like heavy drapes blocking out the world. Whenever she wanders into Lé-Lé's home, Adaline feels like she could sleep for days. "Momma's calling me. I can hear her."

"Then you should go home, Little One."

"Soon. It's only the first time Momma's called." Adaline lifts her head and pushes a tired yet mischievous smile onto her face. "Lé-Lé, since I'm here, might we..." She points her finger up to the sky.

With a laugh that makes Adaline feel weightless, Lé-Lé lifts her wings. They flutter as quietly as a bird as she rises into the air, and Adaline squeals with glee, turning her face into the wind and spreading her arms wide.

She didn't mean to wander; she just needed to escape for a little while, to be wild and free. And at peace.

Chapter Twenty-Nine

THE RAVINE

The horses neigh and stomp their feet as Adaline, Ëólas, and a handful of their companions approach the edge of the ravine that separates Aerytol from the Wastelands. Across from them, the peak of the ravine towers above them, a foreboding rocky summit that conveys *turn around*. The highest portion resembles a giant's bulbous belly with both fists positioned beside his stomach. He must have devoured thousands of people to fill a stomach that large. From between his knuckles, two waterfalls cascade into the ravine, spraying an icy mist onto Aerytol's border.

At the base of the ravine, each waterfall fills a pool that spills in opposite directions, isolating the Wastelands from the rest of the continent and flowing into the ocean. Moss, grass, and wildflowers cover the steep cliffs and narrow ledges that could trick people into believing they might survive climbing down, but one slip, and the ravine would skin that person alive before tossing them into the rushing rivers.

Merith pulls on his steed's reins, guiding him to back up a few paces. "That must be a sizable lake on the other side."

Daven nods. "How many miles do we need to clear the waterfalls?"

"How do we make that decision?" Adaline asks Ëólas.

"That's partly why I sent spies to explore the Wastelands. Two said the terrain levels out about fifteen miles to the right of us."

"That puts us in Lameiría." Daven studies his men waiting less than a mile away. "The queen will permit our entrance?"

"She will," Sora says. "The queen has given us her blessing to do what's necessary to protect Aerytol."

"I'll ride ahead and speak with border patrol." Ëólas directs his horse to face Lameiría. "You won't have any issues. I give you my word."

Adaline pats Conleth's neck, helping him relax in front of the steep drop-off. "And we're going to get two thousand soldiers across those rope bridges you brought?"

"Of course. Our knots don't come undone." With a wink, Ëólas kicks his heels and rides off toward the trees designating Lameiría's border.

With Merith following Ëólas, Adaline lingers behind and studies the behemoth belly. She could travel to the other side and investigate—if she could clearly see where to land. *Damn it.* What's the point of having such gifts if she can't use them in times like these? She'll have to be patient and trust Ëólas. "Lord Daven, please tell everyone to head toward Lameiría."

He arches an eyebrow. "Everyone?"

Adaline sighs. "Tell Elashor the orders are mine."

He grunts but sets off, galloping back to the army.

"Perhaps we should go with him?" Sora says. "Lord Elashor won't be happy about this plan."

"I know." *Poor Elashor.* In a matter of minutes, hundreds of humans will filter into his woods. That must be his worst nightmare. But that's the plan. Besides, the fact that Élara's letting them do this speaks volumes about the progress Lameiría's already made—despite Elashor's thoughts on the matter. "But he came to help. If he meant that, then he won't put up a fuss, at least not verbally. Let's go support our commander general." Adaline nudges her horse and gallops after Ëólas.

A group of soldiers remains outside Lameiría to tend to the horses and watch the wagons. Now begins the portion of the journey that will be far more challenging, without the tents and extra accommodations that made their trek thus far relatively easy. They must also carry their own bedding and food.

With trees looming behind them, two of Ëólas's soldiers carrying bows and arrows walk to the edge of the ravine while the commanders stand back and watch. To their right, Lameiría's clifftop slopes downward until the land eventually levels with the river. The Wastelands, however, remains high and mighty as it looks down on the continent it left behind. Thankfully, Ëólas's spies identified a forty-foot-wide area where the clifftops measure at almost the same height.

The elven archers notch their arrows, the tips glowing bright white. At Ëólas's command, they release their bow strings with a twang. The arrows shoot across the ravine at a breathtaking speed and lodge themselves into the rock, close to the clifftop. The ropes themselves are maybe twenty feet apart but level with each other. Another set of elves tug the ends of the ropes around tree trunks as wide as Hummers, pulling as tightly as possible, before tying knots. The archers repeat the process two more times so two hand ropes hang parallel to each other with a third in the middle but four feet lower. Both sets look like a wobbly V that wants to toss people overboard.

That's a bridge? MoFo, who's going to cross those first?

Ëólas takes off his backpack and sets it on the ground next to his feet. "Alright, we'll send four over first, including Merith and myself, and—"

"What?" Adaline screeches. With everyone's eyes on her, she forces her eyebrows downward, into a more confident position. "Why are you going first?"

"Because I'm the commander general, my love."

Because Ëólas believes leaders should lead. "Well, considering we're leading this campaign together, I'm going with you." Adaline slips the straps off her shoulders, sets her backpack on the ground, and walks closer to the ravine.

"What? No, no." Shaking his head and looking at her as if she's the crazy one here, Ëólas blocks her path. "Absolutely not."

"So, the king can go first but not the queen?" *I will not be left behind, damn it.*

"That's not what I said." Ëólas angles himself so that he leans toward Adaline and blocks everyone's view of the disapproving expression on his face. Lowering his voice, he hisses in her ear, "There's no need for you to—"

"Set an example? Work together as a team? You and I have been over there already, and we found out the hard way that it's best we have both a human and an elf in case we run into either side. Besides, I'm lighter and more nimble than Daven."

"Nimbler."

"Whatever. Not the point."

Ëólas rubs his hands up and down his face while grinding his teeth and turning his back to whatever Merith's mouthing in Ëólas's direction. "And if Ãranol or the Morgai or vampire elves await us on the other side?"

Adaline envisions Ëólas crossing the bridge, only for Morgán to ambush, wound, or kill Ëólas before he steps foot on the clifftop. Curling her fingers around his vambrace, between the leather straps that fasten his armor to his forearm, she stares at him until he realizes she won't back down. "We do this together. Always."

He tightens his jaw and grunts. "Must you always be so insistent?"

Rising onto her toes, she kisses his cheek, not caring who's watching. "Yes. But you love that about me."

"Not at this moment."

"That's not true." She smiles coquettishly.

His eyes move to her mouth, prompting her to pucker the corner of her lips to tease him further. He pinches her chin and lifts her face, not allowing her to hide beneath her lashes. "If this goes sideways, I'm going to be extremely cross with you."

"Same. I'm glad we understand each other."

A low growl rumbles in the back of his throat. Then he drops his arms, giving up this fight, and turns to Daven and the generals. "Right, while we finish the first two bridges and secure the other side, Daven and Elashor will oversee making more bridges." Ëólas eyes them both, making certain they'll cooperate with each other.

Thank God the bridges aren't done. Whew.

While Ëólas speaks with Elashor privately, Sora approaches Adaline and bows. "My lady."

"Sora, you don't have to bow when you approach me. Or at all, really."

She straightens her back and shows Adaline a small leather strap like the one she uses to keep her hair in that high ponytail. "If I may?"

"Oh, yes. Thank you."

Adaline turns around and stares at the gap in the ridge. Too far back, she can't see the water below, but she can hear the river rushing toward the ocean, the same river she'd been in six months ago.

Wait a minute. Adaline counts on her fingers the number of days that have passed in this world since she landed on Lameiría's shore, recalling the horse ride to Gladríen, meeting Élara, revealing her memories to all of Lameiría, taking on her role as queen in New Leira, and their journey west. *I escaped that raft only ten days ago. Dang.*

Sora runs her fingers through Adaline's hair, starting at her temples and pulling the curls away from her face. As she weaves the first three sections together, Sora remains unusually quiet.

The sun overhead filters through the boughs far above them, creating shadows that dance around their feet. But she can't admire the setting with Sora's silence pressing down on Adaline's shoulders. "Do you want to say something, Sora?"

Her steady hands pause mid-air for half a second. Then Sora resumes weaving Adaline's hair into a braid one section at a time. "Are you always so competitive?"

"It's not competition." *It's me, still trying to prove I'm worthy.* "Ëólas and I have already dealt with a lot in the Wastelands, and I can't send anyone else ahead first. It'd feel like a sacrifice."

"One that your people would eagerly make to keep our queen safe."

With her braid tied off at the end, Adaline turns around and faces her friend. "Thank you. But I don't want to be that type of leader."

With a reluctant nod but a glint of admiration, Sora steps back and gestures toward the incomplete bridges. "After you, my lady."

When they join Ëólas and Merith, the four of them drape around their necks several strips of rope so thin that Adaline mistakes them for string until she pinches one close to her face and studies its miniature, fine weave. *Nice work.*

Taking the lead, Merith and Sora walk to the edge of the ravine. Gripping the two hand ropes, they take a couple of steps forward on the middle foot rope and squat down as if they're on a balance beam, not a tight wire. After tying the center of a string to the foot rope, they back up and tie the ends of the string to the hand ropes at an angle. They repeat this process, taking four steps forward and two steps back, effortlessly creating a monkey bridge in mid-air. With the first sixteen feet complete, Adaline and Ëólas follow their captains.

The elves stroll along the bridge with no visible concern of leaving behind solid ground, their footfalls sure and their grips casual. Adaline, not wanting to slow Sora down or give herself time to chicken out, charges ahead too, her palms grinding the hand ropes each time she must let go to move forward.

Within a few steps, Adaline stands over the river, the waves elbowing each other out of the way as they take turns reaching for anyone stupid enough to cross the river's path. If only she didn't have to look down. Carefully, she steps over Sora's knots and aligns her foot with the bottom rope until a series of violent gusts belts her face. Despite her prayers, holding her breath doesn't stop the bridge from swaying. She clutches the hand ropes and can't pry her fingers off.

Ëólas casts her a concerned look, as if he might leap across the fifteen feet that separate them. But that idea makes her heart beat faster and knuckles turn white.

Easy, he mouths. *You've got this. It's like dancing.*

She scrunches her nose and mouth into an incredulous expression. "What about any of this resembles dancing?" she hisses. Staring at her boots, she tries to ground herself, only to remember how far away the ground is. *Yep, this is getting old. Let's speed this up now, thank you.*

Reaching the mid-way point, Sora ties off her last string and turns to Adaline for the next. They continue along while Daven, Elashor, and everyone close enough to witness Adaline freak out keeps their eyes locked on the bridges. While the trees conceal most of Daven's men, who are most likely still guarding against sneak attacks from border patrol, Lameiría's army has the best view of the Queen of Aerytol.

Focus on what I'm doing, not who's watching me.

A burst of wind whips a few loose strands of hair into her face, and she squeezes her eyes shut. With the world turned off and the breeze swirling around her, Adaline feels as though she were flying in Lé-Lé's arms again. She had forgotten that dream and the pictures she used to draw afterward. The wind hadn't been scary then. The entire experience felt like playing tag with a friend.

When Adaline opens her eyes, her laughter permeates the air, bouncing off the cliffside and encouraging Ëólas to share in her mirth as he admires his wife. The currents leap around her, mimicking her joy, and rush off to ruffle Ëólas's hair and rattle his bridge, making his eyes double in size as both he and Merith freeze, their hands gripping the ropes tightly.

Adaline turns her face into the wind. "Okay, okay. Leave them be, please. I love that elf. And the other is a good friend, when he's not so grumpy." *Merith needs to find his soul mate.*

The wind kisses her cheek and relaxes into a delicate breeze, allowing the wisps framing her face to settle and no longer sting her eyes.

"Thank you," Adaline whispers. A moment later, the wind dashes up and over the cliffside, disappearing into the Wastelands. "Playful as ever."

With more than half the bridge complete, Adaline passes Sora another piece of string as the wind rushes back to Adaline, brushing against her ear and sharing two unfamiliar male voices.

"...elves..."

"Lameiría..."

"...invading..."

"Ëólas!" Adaline shouts.

His gaze fixated on the clifftop tells Adaline he heard them too. "Merith, Sora, we need to move faster."

Walking ahead to where he has yet to attach string, Merith drops onto his stomach, gripping the rope ahead of him with both hands. One leg hangs down like dead weight while he uses the top of his other foot, resting on the rope, to push his body forward. The speed with which he can crawl across the rope leaves Adaline speechless. At the same time, Ëólas ties the strings around his waist, preparing himself to follow Merith. Several of his soldiers don't wait either. With Elashor waving them on, they race across the completed portion of Ëólas's bridge.

Sora takes Adaline's strings and ties them around her waist. "We're heading back, now."

Adaline doesn't argue, but she doesn't move either. "We don't know who they are. If they're human, Ëólas needs me."

"I'm not taking that risk."

Adaline looks to Ëólas, who yells, "Listen to her. Go!"

Fuck!

Before Adaline turns around, two figures emerge at the top of the ravine. From thirty feet away, Adaline can't make out the shape of their ears, but their ragged clothing suggests humans. A large man unsheathes his sword and drops onto a ledge near the lodged arrows. He raises his blade overhead, and Merith swings his body downward, using that momentum to throw himself the last ten feet onto the cliffside. He slides several inches but latches onto the rocks.

Leaning around Sora, Adaline shouts, "We've come to help. I'm hum—"

The man swings his blade downward, and the bottom of Ëólas's bridge snaps.

"No!" Adaline screams as Ëólas jumps onto a hand rope and shimmies across like Merith.

The man lifts his sword again, and arrows from Lameiría's side soar overhead, two of them piercing the man's chest. Slipping off the ledge, he slides, tumbles, and free falls into the river.

"Adaline, move!" Sora barks.

With Ëólas nearing the cliffside and his soldiers catching up to him, Adaline hurries across the bridge toward Lameiría, where Elashor orders the archers to reload. She looks over her shoulder, and six more humans rush to the edge of the ravine. More arrows fly overhead while soldiers scale the second bridge, the foot rope swaying wildly but not enough to hinder the elves' speed.

Okay, fine. I was stupid.

Not yet halfway across the bridge, that female voice whispers in Adaline's ear, calling her name.

"Oh, fuck! Sora, hold on." Using both hands, Adaline latches onto the rope to her right and locks her eyes on Ëólas reaching the cliffside. The left side of her bridge spasms and falls away, leaving Adaline and Sora to sidle along the bridge like crabs.

Stupid, stupid, stupid, stupid.

Ëólas, hanging from the cliffside, pulls himself upward while the humans drop rocks on his head.

I'll fucking kill them! Her palms itch and burn like coal, and Adaline's blood drains away from her face. *Oh, no. Not now. Fire's a bad, bad, bad idea.*

The bridge quakes, making Adaline's arms and body vibrate. As her guardian angel calls out again, the second hand rope drops away—and not just on her bridge. Ëólas's people hang from their one remaining rope, many of them clinging to each other like monkeys from a barrel. But before she can worry about them, to pray for their safety, her head falls forward. Her body continues in the same direction, picking up momentum as her braid and her legs flip upside down.

Sora, with the ease of an Olympic gymnast, twists and flips around so she's holding on with one hand. She extends her other arm outward and swings toward her queen, stretching as far as possible. If Adaline held onto her own rope, Sora would have caught her easily.

But Adaline fails.

The shock of her weight yanking on her arms tears her fingers away from the rope, and the bridge swaying in the wind escapes her grasp.

CHAPTER THIRTY

THE CLIMB

The weightlessness of falling seizes Adaline's voice. But as distance shrinks Sora's face, she screams loud enough for them both until her captain lets go and follows her queen. As Ëólas bellows Adaline's name, his voice shredded like shrapnel, the wind whips around her, almost as if to tug her upward, but the gusts blow through her fingers.

Sometimes, flying with Lé-Lé felt like this, when she'd pause the fluttering of her wings and they'd plummet to the earth, only for her to spread her wings wide and sweep them skyward again. Adaline giggled the entire time.

They weren't dreams.

She wishes she were dreaming now. Wishes she had thought to travel somewhere else. Wishes she had flipped herself into more of an upright position so that the river colliding with her body doesn't feel like slamming into an iceberg.

The chilly water encompasses her, consumes her, claims her, pulling her downstream and tossing her about like a rag doll. Water invades her nostrils, her throat, and her lungs burn. Like her mother and father, she's lost within the currents. In her dreams, she begged her mother to ask the ocean for help. How stupid. Adaline can't open her mouth, can't speak. She can't even cry.

Not that the river cares.

No matter how much she flails her arms or kicks her legs, the river pulls her back under. Rocks along the bottom of the riverbed scrape her back, tearing at her coat that weighs her down like a boulder, and her leather trousers strangle her legs and knees. When her feet drag along the bottom, she pushes off, her hands clawing at the surface for air, for sound, for life.

Her head bobs above the water, the waves stinging her eyes and blinding her. For a moment, she can taste hope. Then she gasps for breath, and water floods her mouth. Choking and gasping, she spits the river out, and the waves toss her around. She can't focus. Can't think straight. Can't breathe.

But she sees a boulder ahead and thrashes her legs to propel herself in that direction, her arms and legs throbbing as she screams at them to do what's needed, her leather armor fighting her every movement. She slips underwater but fights the currents that seem to think she's playing a game, the water tugging her downward while she kicks fervently. The pounding in her skull makes keeping her eyes open painful, and all directions look the same, even down.

In between her feeble arm strokes and spitting out more water, she steals a few breaths and cries, "I don't want to die. Please."

Don't take me too.

But the river doesn't feel helpful today. She senses the currents' disappointment, then anger, that she's not enjoying the game, that she's not playing correctly, even though she doesn't know what the river wants of her. When the icy water saturates her bones, making her limbs heavier, slower, immobile, the river yanks her downward again. The burning in her lungs intensifies so much that her chest might self-combust.

Her palm pulses once, then twice, then grows warmer, begging her to open her eyes. Despite the soot churning in the water and stinging her eyes, she looks at her palm. Unlike the red embers of a dying fire, this golden glow reminds her of something vital.

Ëólas.

She presses her warm hand against her freezing chest and sees Ëólas's face, the tenderness in his eyes when she wakes up in the morning. Beyond the image, she can sense his terror, his desperation to find her, his urge to go berserk and slaughter everyone in his way.

Her boot catches on a large rock. Using her other foot, she launches herself upward. Only her fingers breach the surface, but she can't give up. She can't let the river take her too. She made a promise. A vow.

I'll never stop fighting to get back to...

Sinking lower, she scratches at her neck as if she can claw open her throat and get oxygen that way. Her thoughts shut down, and her lips tremble, ready to open, to breathe in the river water, to fill her lungs with whatever's available, to make the pain stop.

But I told him... I have to...

She wiggles her toes, trying to find solid ground so she can push off again, but something tugs at her waist and wrenches her toward the surface. The air hits her face, and she gasps several times as her chest heaves. With her armor too tight to let her take big enough breaths, her tears feed the river, and her limbs won't respond, her sodden clothing suffocating her movements.

"I have you," Sora says, one arm battling the river, the other hauling Adaline along.

Thank you.

When Adaline's teeth start rattling, Sora swims closer to the cliffside. "I see an alcove, my lady. We should," she takes a deep breath between arm strokes, "find shallow water there."

Adaline flips around, holding onto Sora's back and kicks her feet to help Sora reach the alcove where the water pools before streaming back into the river. A surge of currents knocks into their sides, pushing them diagonally toward the pool. Their feet find ground, and they stumble onto shallow rocks. Sora hooks an arm around Adaline's waist and drags her out of the river, the metal tips of their scabbards clanging against the stone.

In the alcove, the water swirls around their thighs. Adaline stands up on her own, bracing her hands on her knees, and heaves in and out. Her braid spills over her shoulder, the tip disappearing into the pool.

Panting, Sora points behind Adaline. "My lady, look."

Someone or something carved a cave entrance into the portion of the alcove that curves away from Lameiría's view.

"Oh my god." *We landed on the Wastelands' side of the ravine? How lucky is that! Or was the river pushing me here all along?*

Craning her neck upward, Sora assesses the height of the ravine. Lameiría's side is a few stories shorter, but they'd have to jump in the river again to reach the other side.

No thank you.

God knows how far they've drifted downstream or how long she's been away from Ëólas. She doesn't sense his fear anymore. She senses nothing. *I should have stayed back and stayed out of his way.* But what about the people he's fighting? How can she reach them?

Sora glares into the darkness deep within the cave. "My lady, are you well enough to travel us elsewhere?"

"Back to Lord Elashor? I, I can try." *I should have practiced traveling while walking or running—or drowning.*

With her head throbbing, her body shivering, and her legs wobbling, she conjures a doorway cloaked with a silver sheen beneath Lameiría's trees, where she stood before the archers launched their arrows, but she doesn't step through.

"I see Daven and Elashor, but they haven't built more bridges. Why would they stop trying to cross the ravine?" Adaline turns away from the portal and studies Sora's severe expression. "Because doing so would endanger Ëólas. The humans have him, don't they?"

Sora lowers her eyes. "I would assume as much, yes."

And I'm not there to help with negotiations. Humans will not listen to him, not if they're like Calvden. "Damn it." *What fucking good am I?*

If only she could see the other side of the ravine. Maybe then she could force herself to travel somewhere she's not been before. But that's not an option, and she will not trap herself with Elashor.

Sora glances at the cave entrance. "Go back to Elashor. I'll head through here. If I can—"

"No way." Shivering from head to toe, Adaline tucks her hands under her armpits and wades toward the entrance. "If you get caught too, that's it. We'll be out of options." She pushes down on the cave floor, which aligns with her chest, to haul herself up, but her arms wobble and buckle, and her chin hits the bottom. "Ouch."

Sora climbs up first, then locks onto Adaline's forearm, and pulls her up. With a lot of grunting and cussing and her feet searching for a ledge, Adaline scrambles onto the cave floor too. She sits with her back against the wall and closes her eyes, her body urging her to fall asleep. Except her heart aches at the thought of Ëólas in danger.

Don't go down that rabbit hole. She can't imagine all the horrific what-ifs. She'll fail him again.

I have to get up. Sora might be able to dry my hair, like Ëólas did. But her bones have turned to ice. Dry hair isn't enough. She's no good to him, not like this. "Sora, I need to warm up. I, I have to go home. To Maryland. So we won't lose time here. Do you need to—"

"Go. I'll wait here."

"Don't you need dry clothes?"

"I'll be fine. Temperature changes don't much affect us. Do what you need to, my lady."

"Sora, thank you."

After a moment of silence passes between them, Sora crosses her hand over her chest and bows low. "I won't let you down again."

"What? Sora, you saved me. I owe you everything." *You're too hard on yourself.*

When Adaline travels home, she's sitting on the floor of the guest bedroom that she and Ëólas claimed as theirs. Clamoring to her feet, she peels her armor, coat, and tunic away from her body, her limbs stiff, her teeth rattling. She tosses her sword onto the floor and sits down to yank off her trousers, but they refuse to roll down her red, raw thighs. Eventually, she wins and leaves the sodden pile on the area rug as she stumbles to the shower. Like pellets, the hot water beats her skin, but soon her muscles release their frozen tension.

She sinks to the shower floor, taking her shampoo and conditioner with her. But she doesn't lift her arms. Staying perfectly still, she breathes in the steam, letting it soothe her lungs. After her shower, she changes into her favorite pair of jeans, her Timberland boots, and a warm periwinkle shirt. She rolls the sleeves up to her elbows, pulls her hair back in a half bun, and wedges her dagger into her boot. Taking a few hesitant steps, she snatches her sword and ties it to her belt while she stares at their bed. Her fingers fall to the soft comforter, brushing away a wrinkle on Ėólas's side.

Sleeping isn't an option right now. She doesn't care how much her muscles ache. She needs to get her husband back. Because without him here, the house is dead again.

I'm coming for you. Do you feel that?

She gathers the heap of soaked clothing and drops them off in her castle chambers, placing the armor near the hearth, while making a mental note to thank Kayla the next time they meet. Then Adaline returns to the cave.

Sora shakes her ponytail back and forth, which dries in front of Adaline's eyes. "That was fast. Where's your armor?"

"Drying. I'll pick it up in about an hour. Are you sure you're okay?" *Please don't let the caves make her sick too.*

Sora glances at her damp trousers and tunic. Her breastplate with the tree of life pressed into the leather looks as strong as ever. "I am, my lady. But we can't advance without your armor."

"We don't have time to argue. Let's see what we're dealing with first."

With shared determination and Sora's frustration, they trudge forward. The cave floor slopes upward, and after ten minutes, Adaline's quads and glutes burn as if she's fallen into a new circle of hell. She also keeps one hand on her hilt in case the humans find them first. For maybe one mile, they have only the single tunnel to follow. The darker the tunnel becomes, the more Sora's sky-blue irises glow, and she leads the way, making certain Adaline doesn't stumble. When they reach a fork, they pause.

Which way?

If only the wind could bring Adaline voices down here, but stagnant, damp air fills the caves. While Sora listens and waits, Adaline holds her palm to her heart and thinks about Ėólas, about how she can't wait to fall asleep in his arms tonight. She senses him again, this time feeling his despair, his anguish. Are the humans torturing them? Killing his friends?

I'm keeping my promise, mé ellador. I'm coming back to you.

As her palm glows, a fine gold thread about five inches long rises from her hand and wafts without a single breeze toward the right tunnel in search of its other half. Adaline cups her palm close to her chest, her heart fluttering like the thread.

Ha! Our honeymoon did strengthen our bond.

Sora stares at the thread in disbelief and mouths, *How?*

"I don't know," Adaline whispers. With a burst of adrenaline, she follows the tether that also casts a dim glow on the cave walls, enabling her to walk faster.

After another twenty minutes or so, voices up ahead make them halt. Adaline curls her open palm into a fist, cutting off the thread. Pressing themselves against opposite sides of the cave wall, they creep forward. In a circular chamber, three people stand in a circle. Behind them, Adaline counts five tunnel entrances and mentally groans because the chamber might have more.

A giant man with broad shoulders, scruffy dark hair, and thick stubble that's on the verge of being a beard crosses his arms over his chest. "They won't talk no more."

"Make 'em talk! That's what you're here for." A gray hood covers the second man's face, but a torch held by the third illuminates Hoodie's beady black eyes and long face covered with smudges of dirt.

Giant and Hoodie look to Torch for answers, his back to Adaline and Sora and his frizzy dark hair pulled back in a haphazard bun at the base of his neck. He's the smallest in stature, but Giant and Hoodie lower their eyes while Torch thinks aloud.

When he speaks, Torch keeps his voice low and breathy, as if he fears elves might be listening. "They said she's from Aerytol. I want her found and brought to me."

Sora's blue irises snap to Adaline.

"You think they might be telling the truth?" Giant massages his fingers into his cheek.

"Of course not. Elves can't be trusted." Hoodie turns and spits a loogie on the cave floor, his eyes sweeping over the shadows hiding Adaline and Sora, who closes her blue eyes to not give them away.

Torch shakes his head. "I'll decide if they're lying. Just find her."

Sora quietly slides a few inches of her sword out of its sheath, but Adaline waves her hand to get Sora's attention and shakes her head fervently.

Killing them won't help us find Ëólas, Adaline mouths.

"Start with tunnels two and six," Torch says. Then he tosses his thumb over his shoulder, pointing in Adaline and Sora's direction. "I'll check this one."

Moving her hand to her hilt, Adaline steps out of the shadows, blocking Sora from leaping forward. "You don't have to find me. I'm right here. Where is—"

Turning around, Torch lifts his hand to stop the other two from advancing. Only, when Torch faces Adaline, he's not a he. He's a she. And despite the grime smeared across Torch's cheeks and brow, Adaline would know those green eyes anywhere, because they have been staring back at her for the last twenty years.

Chapter Thirty-One

Negotiations

Too many emotions, memories, and words flood Adaline at once. Images of her mother tucking her in at night resurface, along with a few verses of a forgotten lullaby, a tune about moonlight and a lost love that made Adaline cling to her mother's hand as she fell asleep. That image quickly disappears, replaced with Adaline returning to that broken cottage, their furniture smashed and her mother's paints strewn on the floor.

What can she possibly say? How does she explain choosing to forget her mother? How does she justify growing up happy and well cared for while her mother suffered God knows what? She should fall on her knees and beg for forgiveness—if only she could move her legs and arms.

"They follow you?" Aurellia asks, her chin lifting in Sora's direction. "The elves." Her voice may no longer be a whisper, but the texture has changed over the years. She sounds hoarse, bruised, aged even, though not a single wrinkle has touched her oval-shaped face.

I guess. "Yes."

With a nod, Aurellia turns to Giant and Hoodie. "Tell the others I'll be there soon. And to leave the elves be. For now." When her two goons don't budge, their eyes darting from Aurellia to Adaline to the elf behind her, Aurellia snaps, "You heard me! I need a moment."

As Aurellia's men scurry through the fourth tunnel, Sora steps closer, her hand on her hilt and her presence looming over Adaline's shoulder. "My queen," she whispers.

Sora must be worried about Ëólas and the others. What did Aurellia say? Leave the elves be. *Has my mother imprisoned my husband? Oh no.*

Aurellia's eyes fall on Sora. "I'd like a moment with your queen."

Sora doesn't budge. Maybe she doesn't recognize Aurellia. In the visions that the water sprites resurrected, Aurellia had silky light-brown hair that Adaline used to wind around her little fingers. At home, her mother never wore a snood. She didn't wear one when visiting Uncle Jamie either, much to his agitation. But here, in the dim cave light, her frizzy hair looks like dingy, matted-down fur.

How long have you been down here?

Adaline never takes her eyes off her mother, terrified she might vanish, that she's only a hallucination from a concussion. "I need a moment, Sora. Please."

"This way." Aurellia takes a different tunnel, the torch light leading the way.

With her brain switched off, Adaline mechanically follows her mother several feet into the tunnel and then a small hollowed-out room—as much as one can call a more private area of the cave a room. Sora remains outside but close enough to hear Adaline's shallow breaths.

A table with four different styles of wooden legs, all cut to the same height, fills the center of the room. A strip of bedding lies on the ground behind the table, its coverings made from ratty blankets with holes larger than quarters. The room has no other pieces of furniture, aside from a covered bucket in the corner. Not a fireplace to light and warm the space. Not a wash basin to clean her hands and body. Not a wardrobe for clothing gifted to her. Not a mattress to ease her sore muscles.

Aurellia sets the torch in a metal sconce pinned to the wall with a nail the size of a railroad spike and walks over to Adaline. She wipes her hands on her stained, musty gray tunic and cups Adaline's face, her thumbs brushing over her cheeks, her touch as gentle as a spirit's. "My goodness. Look at you."

Adaline places her hands over her mother's, and her bottom lip quivers. A well of tears fills her eyes, blurring her view of the one person she wants to see clearly, who's no longer a memory she's trying to preserve but flesh and blood and right here. When she tries to speak, her voice cracks, and tears spill down her cheeks. "Mom."

Releasing that one word is like pulling the plug, and now she can't stop. "Mom, mom. I'm so sorry. I, I wasn't. I didn't mean to. I tried to find you, but I, I wasn't strong enough, and I'm—"

"But you did find me."

Adaline falls into her mother's arms, pressing her cheek above Aurellia's heart that beats steadily. She doesn't smell like currants and warm bread anymore. Instead, she smells like flint and ash mixed with dried sweat, all scents that prove she's real. Her arms are as warm and strong as ever, and in them, Adaline knows everything will be okay. Because that's what moms do. They hold their children through the dark times.

I won't leave you behind again, I promise. I—

Aurellia lets go, allowing a cold void to take her place as she steps back. She nestles her hand under her daughter's chin, pushing up until their eyes are level. Although she keeps her voice soft, the firmness of her words stuns Adaline. "You're a queen now. Don't lower your head to anyone, not even to me."

Mom... But...

Backing up several more paces, Aurellia takes in her daughter's jeans and shirt and furrows her brow in skepticism. "I thought I'd find you soaked to the bone. Élara's boy said you fell in the river."

"I, I did. I changed quickly."

"I see."

Does she know I can travel?

"I'm sorry for that." Aurellia turns away from the torch, and her mossy-green eyes grow cooler. "My men saw the elves coming and panicked. You're okay though?"

"I, um, yeah." One by one, Adaline shuts down her emotions, leaving her as numb as if she never climbed out of that icy river. She doesn't have time to untangle her feelings right now or examine the odd yet pervasive disconnect between them. "What do you mean by *your men*?"

Aurellia's cheek jerks upward. "There's a lot of us down here, almost two hundred last time I counted. Most are malnourished, but I have seventy capable of fighting. I've been rallying them together, planning a rebellion."

My mom is Princess Leia? "We came to help."

"Help?" she asks, raising her voice. That one word reverberates off the cave walls, adding layers of sarcasm to her disbelief. "I lost six of my people today. That's the help Élara's boy brought me?"

He was defending his people. And he's not a boy. Adaline fiddles with the underside of her wedding band with her thumb. "Where are they? Are they okay?"

Aurellia clenches her jaw before answering. When she speaks again, she severs all emotions and sounds like a businesswoman addressing members of the board. "Zero dead on their side. Seems unfair to me."

"There's nothing fair about this entire situation." She surprises herself with the agitation in her voice. Once upon a time, she never would have spoken to her mother that way. Pressing her hands against her abdomen, Adaline resets her tone. "We came here to help, to stop Ãranol and Morgán, and to take Feídra né Morna. Ëólas—"

"Raged when he set foot on the Wastelands. He killed two of my men and maimed five within seconds. They'll be lucky to walk again, if they survive infection."

"They cut our bridges. What were we supposed to do?" *Aside from not falling.*

"My people didn't attack the elves directly. They sent a message to stay in Lameiría, but the elves shot arrows at us and slaughtered innocent people who have fought every day to keep their freedom. We have enough oppressors over here. We don't need more."

"How were we to know that when *your* people were scaring the crap out of us and dropping rocks on our heads? I tried to tell your men that I'm human, but they wouldn't hear me out." To rein in her hands that she had been waiving about, Adaline massages her temples and stares at the alternating shades of red and orange that the torch casts on the cave floor. The sound of the billowing flames eating away at the torch gives her a temporary reprieve from her mother's obstinacy. *I don't want to argue with you. Please, stop.*

For whatever reason, Aurellia backs down and lowers her voice. "Seeing more elves coming here makes us uneasy. It doesn't help that Lameiría still blames us for all that happened."

Us. She keeps saying us. These are her people now. "Lameiría knows the truth about Morgán's lies and betrayal."

Aurellia huffs a sad half laugh. "And you think it's that easy for them to let go of the animosity they've clung to for centuries?"

"I've seen it myself. Aerytol is all about bringing people together." Adaline sweeps her hand behind her, pointing toward the tunnel that must somehow lead her to Ëólas and their army. "Even Elashor came with us."

"Elashor! Oh, no. He can stay put. We don't need or want his help. I don't trust his grandson either."

Well, shit. "Why are we debating this? You married an elf, for crying out loud."

"Don't bring your father into this!" The pain that flashes across Aurellia's face cracks and shatters her anger. Leaning against the cave wall, she stares at the ceiling until her hands stop shaking. "He's the best of them," she murmurs, her expression mirroring the same unspoken ache Edwin displayed, until his daughter entered the room and he pretended he was fine.

But Aurellia allows the truth to surface for only a few seconds. Quickly, she flings off her grief and stands tall. "You trust Lameiría?"

Walking toward her mother until only an arm's length separates them, Adaline infuses her voice with a calm certainty. "Remember that conversation I overheard on the wind, that Magnus and Ëólas wanted to create a city where elves and humans could live side by side? They did it. The city is thriving. And when Lameiría learned the truth about Morgán, the queen and her citizens supported me claiming my birthright. So, yes, I trust them. Now, please, tell me Ëólas is safe."

"Of course he's safe. I wouldn't pass up ransoming him for weapons and supplies."

"Mom!"

"Okay, okay. I hear you." Aurellia squints at Adaline's insistence, at the panic in her daughter's voice, but doesn't press for details. "My men have him in custody. After he finally surrendered."

Adaline drops her hands. "He did?"

"Yes, so the fighting would stop and we would search for you. My men don't trust him though. I have to warn you; they said his intentions are impossible to read. Someone that ruthless and cold makes me nervous."

That damn neutral face of his. "I trust him implicitly. Is he down here?"

"Above. I'm not *that* cruel." Aurellia scrubs her face, wiping away her need for sleep, but the bags under her eyes remain. "You came to free Feídra né Morna. What about the others?"

"What others?"

"In the camps."

"What camps?"

Aurellia hangs her head, then gestures at the bedding. "Sit down. We have a lot to discuss."

"Yes, we really do. But not until after I see my people." Squaring her shoulders, Adaline turns her back on her mother but pauses at the room's exit. *Please, come with me. Please, help me fix this.*

After a drawn-out groan, Aurellia lifts the torch free from its holder and steps into the tunnel. The moment Adaline emerges, Sora jumps next to her and studies her queen to make sure she's alright, whereas Adaline hopes her face conveys her apologies for what Sora overheard. Sora pats Adaline's back and jerks her head toward the main chamber, wordlessly telling Adaline to focus on getting them the hell out of these caves.

They both follow Aurellia, and Adaline speed walks until she falls in step side by side with her mother. They continue in silence for a time with Adaline stealing glances at the woman who was, is, her mother. The torchlight, casting an orange glow on Aurellia's face, reminds Adaline of the countless nights they spent cuddled on the sofa in front of the fireplace, leaning into each other's warmth and sharing a blanket while Edwin read them a story. Most nights, when Aurellia stroked Adaline's forehead and the movement matched the rhythm of her father's deep voice and the fire's crackle, Adaline's eyelids would flutter shut until she passed out in her mother's arms.

And yet this woman, a leader of the rebel alliance, feels like a stranger. Their lives have diverged so much. Where do they go from here? How will Aurellia react when she learns Adaline married Ëólas, that she gets to reunite with her husband while Aurellia's still searching for hers? *Is she searching? Did she sense the accident?* "Mom, um, did Dad find you?"

Aurellia halts and places her hand on her heart. "No, he didn't. I can feel him, but...I don't know." Shaking her head, she resumes hiking upward.

What's that mean? "Do—"

"Your accent changed."

"Oh." Adaline's brain glitches as she pushes aside her questions about her father. "Yeah. Dad and I hid with Nan, um—"

"Arraya?"

"Um-hmm. I tried coming back and—"

Aurellia holds up her hand, and her face hardens. "We can't change the past, Adaline. Our only option is to keep moving forward."

I guess. But...

A few twists and turns later, their upward climb continues until Aurellia's head brushes the cave ceiling. Passing the torch to Sora, Aurellia pushes on the ceiling that gives way, revealing a large, flat rock that acts as a trap door. She climbs a few more steps, and a hairy arm descends into the cave, grabs onto her forearm, and pulls her out. Adaline follows, accepting the stranger's help, while Sora climbs out on her own, not taking the man's hand even if he had offered it to her.

Above ground, they blink several times until their eyes adjust to the blazing sun hovering over the horizon. At this rate, they have maybe six hours until nightfall. In front of Adaline, a massive lake reflects a gleaming blend of red, orange, and blue. In the center, a small island void of life interrupts the vivid colors with dark shades of slate gray. Spiky rocks, their tips dusted with frost, outline Alderton's side of the lake, its water flowing to the left where it falls over the ravine. The bank near Adaline slopes upward toward Lameiría and curves out of sight thanks to a series of boulders that would dwarf Stonehenge.

Cupping her hand above her eyes, Adaline scans their surroundings. "Where are my people?"

Aurellia points uphill, and they begin their hike along the lake, including Hoodie, who had helped them exit the caves. The wild grass makes the ascent slippery, but they use their hands when needed to balance and pull themselves along.

As Adaline's head emerges at the top, bodies litter the ground, their legs and arms twisted at odd angles because of the rocks and crevices. A group of men, including the Giant, surround five or six elves on their knees, their weapons discarded several feet away and their hands on the back of their heads while their captors point daggers and swords in their faces. In a gap between two men's legs, she spies Merith's silver hair.

Reaching the clifftop, Adaline snaps at the men who spin around to face her. "They've dropped their weapons. Let them up right now, or—"

"Adaline!" Ëólas shouts from somewhere beyond the Giant.

Her mother waves her hand, telling her men to step aside, but Ëólas doesn't wait. Jumping to his feet, he sprints between the Giant and another guard before anyone can redirect their sword or shout, and he pulls Adaline into a fierce hug, his body flat against hers, as he wraps one arm around her waist and cradles the back of her head with his hand. Looping her arms around his neck, she squeezes him tightly, inhaling his scent and channeling his warmth. His hard body against hers is all the tangible proof she needs to release the worries that had been silently clawing her from the inside out. If she could stop time so they could stay together, she would.

When someone clears their throat, Ëólas hesitantly loosens his grip and slides his hand out of her hair. Cupping her cheek, he searches her face as if to verify she's real. "I'm sorry. I—"

"No, it was me. I was stupid to think—"

"We needed you. I needed you."

You what? Rising onto her toes, she rests her chin on his shoulder and hugs him more tightly. Behind him, she counts the bodies of the fallen and the men treating the wounded, blood seeping through ragged bandages. Burying her face in the crook of Ëólas's neck, she allows herself one more moment of gratitude, then peels herself away from him. "We need to tend to the dead and injured."

As Adaline angles herself toward her mother and flashes an apologetic smile, Ëólas takes her hand and turns back to Merith and the other elves still on their knees. "We have medical supplies we can share."

The Giant stomps forward and slams his hands on his hips, his grizzly chiseled jaw grinding back and forth. "We'd rather die than allow you to build your bridges and help Morgán eliminate the rest of us."

"Let the elves come," Aurellia says, her voice loud, clear, and brokering no argument. "I always said we might need their help one day."

With the guys refusing to end their staring contest, Ëólas holds firmly onto Adaline and instructs his soldiers to rise. "Collect your weapons and keep them sheathed."

"How can we trust them?" the Giant asks.

"Because I said so." Flicking her chin at Ëólas, Aurellia adds in a matter-of-fact tone, "And because I wager this one here's my son-in-law."

Ëólas whips his head to Aurellia, his focus landing on her green eyes, and a kaleidoscope of emotions sweeps across his face. His frozen, indifferent features give way to a broad smile, until he glances at the people he fought and killed, and the corners of his mouth drop sharply. Squeezing Adaline's hand once, he lets go and walks up to Aurellia. Hoodie shifts sideways to shield her, but her glare tells him not to move.

Halting in front of Aurellia, Ëólas crosses his arm over his chest and bows his head. "I owe you my everything."

While the Giant gawks at them, his dark eyes not believing what he's heard, Aurellia rakes her eyes over Ëólas as if assessing whether he's housebroken or feral.

So much for finding a better moment to break the news. Adaline joins her husband and hugs his arm as he stands up straight. "Mom?"

Rather than acknowledging Ëólas's gesture, Aurellia looks past him and tells the Giant, "Daylight isn't on our side. Let the elves build their bridges." Turning to Adaline, she adds, "Descending this mountain can take a solid day, so we best get started. It isn't horribly steep, but watch your step."

Without waiting for a reply, Aurellia turns her back on them, passes Sora without concern, and leads them down the mountain toward the gray landscape that feels like purgatory.

Chapter Thirty-Two

THE CAMPS

With the bridges built, the dead and wounded tended to, and the army crossing into the Wastelands, Adaline and Ëólas weave around rocks and boulders, tufts of grass that conceal larger drops, and the swollen lake that feeds the rivers. The steep descent requires concentration and eventually squinting when the rocks and shadows merge. They move quickly, leaving their questions, doubts, and resentments to fester like blisters on their toes.

As the sun sets, the twinge in Adaline's spine hums louder. If only her leather backpack had chest and hip buckles to offset the load. At least her dry armor doesn't add much weight. When they pause for the night, Adaline drops her pack and dusts off her jeans that garner the occasional odd stare. Placing her hands above her bottom, she arches backward, stretching her spine and listening to her vertebrae click and crack.

After she straightens up, Ëólas grinds his fist into her lower back and, angling away from Daven, whispers in Elvish. Warmth radiates from his hand, heating her muscles until she can feel her cheeks bloom. Twisting her face closer to his, she murmurs, "Thank you." His lips brush her cheek as he steps away and drops his own pack.

Not once does he look her in the eyes.

With the rocks as their cushions tonight, they don't have flat surfaces wide or long enough to roll out blankets, so everyone plans to use their bedding as shields to block the wind. While the soldiers begin their evening routine, skipping the tents and proceeding with preparing meals, Merith and Sora instruct the royal guard to set up a perimeter around their queen and king. Likewise, Aurellia forms a group with ten of her own people, including the Giant and Hoodie. They don't invite Adaline to join them, and most stare at Ëólas as if imagining how to even the odds.

Squatting down, Adaline flips open her backpack, loosens the drawstring, and rummages for the cheese and dried fruit she packed this morning while holding the flap up like a blinder to block her view of her mother. *You have time to figure this out, Adaline. It's going to be okay.*

Ëólas's boots appear in front of her bag. When he doesn't speak, she pushes herself up to standing. Instead of talking, they study the soldiers huddling in protective groups. Not even Daven's men know what to say to Aurellia and her people.

"Hey," Ëólas says.

Her eyes fall to his swords flanking his hips. "Hey."

"Are you okay?"

"Yeah. Best day ever." Even though fae can't lie, Adaline's apparently not banned from deadpan sarcasm.

Adaline peeks at her mother, how her people lean closer to hear her every word, how this distance between them feels greater than the years they spent apart. After Adaline recovered her memories, she didn't allow herself to imagine finding her mother, but if she had, she never would have envisioned a scenario in which they would be on opposite sides.

Shoving his hands in his pockets, Ëólas's chest curls inward. "I'm sorry for making things worse."

"I get it." She yearns to reach for him, to ease his guilt, but doesn't. "Everyone's reactions were understandable. They just all sucked."

Both sides defaulted to their gut instincts. Including her husband. Her partner. Who shares her soul. Who promised that together they would set a better example. But they weren't together. Despite all her efforts to not be a liability, to keep up with him, she never considered the consequences of her absence, that she needs to temper his actions. They came here to help, damn it, not further traumatize these people.

He shouldn't have been on that bridge. Oh god, I hope he'll forgive me for this. "I think Daven and I need to take the lead from here on out."

Éólas's chest stops moving.

I'm sorry. "You, you know how it looks, right?"

Taking a deep inhale, he nods repeatedly. "I do. Of course." But he won't look her in the eyes.

She grabs his nape and presses her forehead against his. "You know I'd lose my mind if I lost you, that I wouldn't be able to think straight either."

He pecks her brow and walks away. "No. You wouldn't."

Not sure how to interpret that, Adaline watches his back until he disappears among his people to issue orders, to check in with his generals, to avoid the person who just stabbed him in the heart. The bruise in her chest grows large with every broken beat, knowing that she's sensing his pain. That she's the cause.

Is this what it means to be a leader? Are these the sacrifices she must make to do what's best for her people, while hurting those she loves most?

Sora approaches Adaline slowly. "Forgive me, my lady. Merith and I have stationed elves along the length of the mountain. They'll watch for movement throughout the night. Please," she touches Adaline's arm, "rest easy, so we can all start afresh tomorrow."

"Thank you, for everything."

With a bow, Sora takes her leave, giving Adaline space to sit within her circle of protection that cuts her off from everyone else.

When the clouds steal the night sky, the elves' glowing eyes become the only source of light. No one starts a fire that would serve as a beacon to Āranol's army, if they are nearby. Elashor steps onto a boulder beyond the royal guard and stares into the distance, having already begun his watch for the night. Every so often, Aurellia eyes him while her teeth tear into the dried meats Sora shared. Everyone's cold dinner comprises similar food, including nuts, dried fruit, and buttered bread, though Adaline suspects few others had the butter.

When Aurellia's done hissing at the Giant, she tells the royal guard to step aside and sits in front of Adaline. "Let's talk."

"Okay." With a gulp, Adaline folds a square of cheese cloth around her bread, sets down her dinner, and rests her hands on her lap. She can do this. She'll listen to whatever her mother has to say, to share, to get off her chest. No judgement. No making this about herself. This is about being there for her mother.

"You don't have a clear picture of what's been going on over here."

"Oh." Curling her fingers into fists, Adaline sits up and glances around her. "Sora, would you please gather all the generals and bring them here? Thank you."

Ten minutes later, the three groups form a jagged circle, some higher than others. To Adaline's right, Daven sits in front of his four generals. Elashor remains on his rock off to the side while his peers and the captains of the royal guard gather behind Adaline. Ëólas sits beside his wife with his mouth clamped shut, not a stitch of his clothing touching hers. Like everyone else, he gives Aurellia his full attention, but the guilt pressing down on his shoulders makes him hunch over, resting his forearms on his thighs.

Aurellia's council includes the Giant, who introduces himself as Torsden; Hoodie, who hides under his cloak and doesn't speak much; and Mags, a woman who appears to be in her late fifties with short silver hair, dark wrinkles etched beside deep-set brown eyes, and a sharp mouth that could cut anyone to the quick.

As the clouds part, granting the humans use of the waning moonlight, Aurellia uses a rock to draw a rectangle in a patch of dirt at her feet. "You know about Feídra né Morna, but you don't know about the camps."

While Adaline shakes her head, Daven scratches his gray beard and groans. "Shit. How many army encampments does Ãranol have?"

"No," Aurellia says. "These aren't elven camps. They're human farms Morgán established outside Feídra né Morna."

"What?" Adaline hugs her stomach. "Why?"

"To test his theories, four of them to be specific." Above the rectangle, Aurellia draws four circles that form a trapezoid, her hand firmly pressing down on the rock as it scrapes her dry skin.

Torsden worries his giant hands together. "The camps are all human, but the elves are in control. They decide who gets out, if ever."

Adaline sucks in a sharp breath and sits back. *Camps. Interment camps. Oh god, it's happening here too.* "What are they using these prisons for?"

"Camp One," Aurellia points to the corner of the trapezoid closest to Hell City, "is where elves select their hopefuls. The most obedient, who prove their devotion and purity, can earn the luxury of Feídra né Morna. Camp Two is where they test how best to subdue human emotions."

"Subdue?" Sora asks, her voice barely above a whisper.

"Drugs," Mags says. "Everyone's kept on drugs from the moment they're old enough to have a tantrum. The elves found that more effective than drilling into our heads."

Grounding herself, Adaline stares at the earth beneath her feet until the world stops spinning and her stomach stops churning. Ëólas slides his arm around her back, and she leans into his side.

Torsden points at the circle furthest from Hell City. "They test diseases in Camp Three, studying what will torture us and what will kill us faster. And Camp Four..." He drops his gaze to his hands, which he's rubbed raw.

"In Camp Four," Aurellia says, "only the most ruthless survive another day. They want continuous proof of the evils we're capable of."

With his sheathed sword between his knees, Merith grinds his hands on the hilt, and Sora looks as though she might throw up, if elves did such a thing. Daven's face reveals only a quiet rage that's waiting for the right time to erupt, a sentiment Adaline feels just as strongly, if not more. She clasps her hands together to snuff out the heat building beneath her skin.

Ëólas, placing his hand over hers, helping her to simmer down, hangs his head. "How could we ever believe someone as depraved as him?"

"Because it's easy to believe a lie when it's about people you already hate," Aurellia says.

"But how can anyone do this?" Adaline asks.

Torsden spits on the map. "He did it in memory of his late wife. That's what I heard."

After a long silence, Elashor, his eyes fixated on the clouds drawing nearer, whispers, "Her name was Orena. She kept to herself most of the time and loved nothing more than to listen to the birds sing. She used to grow day lilies around the palace all year long. Even in the winter, their color showed through the snow. Until her son died. Until she died." The clouds snuff out the moonlight, and Elashor turns sideways to face Aurellia, his golden eyes barely piercing the darkness. "Nothing justifies what Morgán has done, what anyone who believed him has done. I just thought you should know her name."

Orena. What happened when she died? Morgán should still feel the half of her soul within him. That should have given him peace and comfort. How could he think his actions were acceptable? That she'd condone this?

A blocked heart—that's what Loríen said. A blocked heart cannot see or judge clearly, so people make more mistakes that further weigh them down, that further dim their hearts, until escape feels impossible.

Morgán lost himself in the darkest labyrinth of all. Who's to say I wouldn't too, if I lost Ëólas?

Sensing her thoughts, Ëólas clasps her hands more tightly, and his words from earlier this night pierce her thoughts: *No. You wouldn't.*

Adaline kisses the back of his hand, stands up, and hides her red-hot palms inside her jean pockets. "Camp Three is the closest." She glances at Ëólas, who nods at her. "That's where we're going first. Daven, what say you?"

Rising to his feet, Daven hooks his thumbs over his wide belt. "Agreed. What do we need to know about the camps?"

When Aurellia doesn't speak, Mags cuts to the chase. "A fifteen-foot wall surrounds each camp with guards stationed up top every twenty feet, keeping an eye out for us. There's only one way in and out, and ten guards block that entrance at all times."

The clouds allow a portion of the night sky to illume Daven's weathered face, which looks ten years older but more determined than ever. "Will they barricade themselves inside when they see us coming?"

"Breaching the wall is easy," Sora says. "We have plenty of rope. But we'd need to be quick about it so no one inside gets hurt."

Aurellia lays the rock at her feet, its sharp point aimed at her scuffed black boots that are far too large for her small feet. "None of that matters because this whole thing is a trap."

"How do you know?" Adaline asks.

"When I learned Ãranol and Morgán were traveling this way, I tracked them. By the time I arrived here, Ãranol had already abandoned his mission and changed course toward Camp Three. We have yet to find Morgán again."

She's been hunting them. Wait, wait. Does that mean Morgán is in Aerytol? And what about Ãranol? If he was leading us into a trap, wouldn't he have told me about Camp Three? "What makes you think it's a trap?"

Merith cranes his neck, pointing at Daven and the thousand human soldiers behind them. "Disease. He means to wipe out half our forces."

"And if we don't go?" Daven asks, even though his hard tone states that's not a possibility.

"Who the hell knows?" Mags says, her voice as raspy as sandpaper scratching wood. "But it won't bode well for the people trapped in Camp Three."

We can't let more people die. I have to be there this time. "We must go."

Ëólas stands up and laces his fingers through hers. "What about you? You're human too."

"I've never had anything more than a cold."

His nostrils flaring tell her he wants to argue, to put his foot down this time. Maybe he's right. Maybe she should stay back, accept that the elves have the upper hand here. After all, they're immune to disease, except for whatever Morgán did to his five test subjects. But that's what she thought last time, that the elves knew better.

What if it's a trap for both of us?

Staying back isn't an option, and not going at all might lead to more deaths. She'd never forgive herself for that. She started this campaign to save as many lives as possible. To end these horrific practices. They can't back down now.

Sensing her decision, Ëólas says, "Alright."

Adaline looks her mother squarely in the eye. "Can you draw us a map?"

Upon first hearing that question, Aurellia looks like a panic-stricken mother watching her child run toward a cliff, but when she sees the determined woman standing before her, she rises and shakes Adaline's forearm. "I'll take you there myself."

CHAPTER THIRTY-THREE

THE WILLOW

Within a few days of trekking across the Wastelands, the green moors and sporadic trees give way to the gray landscape Adaline hoped to never see again, the endless expanse of nothingness that devours hope and leaves everyone hollow inside. In another world, the Childlike Empress would have already sent Atreyu on his quest to save Fantastica.

Meh, I still like the sound of Fantasia better. Oh man, am I Atreyu in this scenario? Then who's my Bastian?

Dreaming of riding her own Falkor across the Wastelands, Adaline hooks her thumbs under the straps of her knapsack and, like everyone else, trudges forward while she imagines what she'll say to the people in Camp Three when she and Daven knock down the gate and tell everyone they're free to go—and spread diseases across the world that might eradicate all of humanity.

I'll need to bring Cindy here. We'll have to start testing everyone and, I don't know, create Ellium's first pharmacy? Studying the inhabitants of Camp Three could trap Cindy and Dax here for decades. They'll have to develop another means.

Throughout this part of their journey, the division among the groups of leaders has grown more pronounced. Elashor's awkward, long bouts of silence rival Daven's and Aurellia's. Éólas, while tending to Adaline's feet and back pain, hasn't spoken much, and no one's been in the mood for stories—or Adaline hasn't been in the mood to share them, thanks to The Nothing feasting on her mind.

So much for bringing people together.

The troops, at least, huddle with their friends around the fire, and the murmurs of their conversations, of their quiet chuckles, rejuvenates Adaline's hope, until she questions why—despite the size of their army advertising their campaign—neither Morgán nor Āranol has attacked them yet. With each uneventful passing day, uncertainty and suspicion creep deeper into her gut.

During the night, Adaline shares her bedding with her mother, and they lie in silence while Adaline breathes through her nose—not that Adaline's spring fresh either. Despite several opportunities, Aurellia doesn't ask about Maryland, about who Adaline became. Maybe Aurellia doesn't want to know what she has missed, or maybe she fears Adaline asking similar questions that her mother doesn't want to answer. Then again, maybe Aurellia's still processing the fact that she now must warn her people about demonic elves.

Whatever the reason, Adaline doesn't feel like she got her mother back, and she's no closer to discovering the truth about her father, about whether he's lost or dead or worse.

When they stop for lunch, Adaline and Sora bring food to share with Aurellia's council. Torsden does most of the talking, acknowledging Adaline only when she asks why the Wastelands has no birds.

"You noticed that, huh?" He swallows a handful of roasted nuts. "I heard Morgán cast an enchantment about twenty years ago that banished all birds from this land, that they follow the orders of an evil fae who sent them to claw out the elves' eyes."

Torsden throws his head back and laughs loudly while slapping his hand on his thigh, his elbow out to the side, his muscular arm bulging so much that he looks as if he could break someone's neck with a snap of his fingers.

Adaline flashes back to the day the Morgai found her family, to the birds pecking out their eyes to save her. She excuses herself and hurries away, for once eager to train with Sora. *That's not fair to the birds. And I'm not evil.*

She heads toward the center of camp. Within the Wastelands, they can't slink off to the side for privacy, and Adaline's too on edge to feel embarrassed. Reaching for her hilt, she faces Sora, who seems to have turned into a confused statue.

"Hey, you okay?" Adaline asks.

"Hmm? Oh, yes. Sorry, I just—" She glances back at Torsden, still laughing, and whispers into Adaline's ear, "Do many men have arms that large? Is that normal?"

Adaline uses the last of her energy to lock her lips in a neutral position and not tease her friend. "Um, some."

"Huh."

After dinner and training, Adaline sits on her bedding and loosens the laces to her vambrace so she can better rotate and stretch her wrist that won't stop throbbing. Meanwhile, Aurellia chats with her friends, all of whom make her chuckle in a way Adaline's not achieved since their reunion.

To snuff out her burning palms, Adaline flattens them together, sealing away the red glow, but that only pushes the fire inward and generates considerable heartburn that flares throughout her chest, singeing her torso.

Behind her and thirty feet away, Ëólas and Merith speak quietly beside their campfire, their expressions nostalgic as they reminisce about something. She could ask what they're talking about or ask Ëólas to sit with her. Maybe then she could ease the discomfort between her and Ëólas, the guilt that's dimmed his golden eyes, but Adaline's not sure how to achieve that yet.

She could join Sora, Moren, and other members of the royal guard, but they deserve a break from tending to Adaline's needs, especially given that no one knows what will happen when they arrive at Camp Three tomorrow.

With Adaline trapped in her own thoughts, Aurellia bids her friends goodnight and lays down next to Adaline. They don't look at each other. Aurellia admires the stars while Adaline stares at her boots and wiggles her toes. Only the body heat between them feels alive.

Be brave. Again. This could be our last chance.

Adaline rests her chin on her knees. "When this war is over, will you come to Aerytol with me?" Under her legs, she clasps her hands together to stop them from shaking.

Her mother takes four slow breaths before replying. "My people need me here. But I'd like that, for a little."

A little. I can work with that. After testing several variations of the same question in her head, Adaline asks, "Can we go somewhere to talk privately?"

Sitting up, Aurellia scans the camp. "Where?"

Where, indeed? Adaline doubts Aurellia's ready to see their cottage again. Adaline's not either. Nan's house has too many ghosts, too many shadows of what Aurellia missed, and the castle seems too far removed from whom they used to be. "Do you remember the lake we passed when walking to Uncle Jamie's, the one with the old willow tree?"

Aurellia sticks her finger through a hole in her trousers. "Yes. Why?"

Touching her mother's arm, Adaline takes them there. The weeping willow looks almost the same, its tendrils dipping into the small lake that reflects the waning moonlight. The long, low croaks of bull frogs sound like cows mooing, and the serenade of bush crickets surrounds them, offsetting a barn owl's shrill shriek miles away.

"What?" Aurellia jumps up and spins in circles until she stops and stares down the dirt road, toward home. "How?"

"Sorry for not warning you. I'm a traveler. It's my—"

"Gift," Aurellia says, her expression a blank slate.

Without explaining her indifferent attitude, her mother hikes through the tall grass, takes off her boots, and climbs onto a low bough, the same one they used to sit on when taking a break on their way home from Uncle Jamie's. Back then, Adaline's toes couldn't touch the water. Now, side by side, they dip their sore feet into the cool water. So close to home. So close to family.

If only I could have brought Mom home sooner. "I'm sorry," she whispers.

Shaking her head, Aurellia rolls her threadbare trousers up to her knees. "Why do you keep saying that? I'm the one who's sorry."

"What for?"

"You and your father are so much stronger than me." She lifts her leg. The water runs down her calf and falls like rain back into the lake. "I got caught because I was weak. It was my fault."

Pulling her braid over her shoulder, Adaline flicks the tip up and down with her finger. "That's how I feel. All the time."

"How's that possible? Look at where we are right now, at what you can do. How can you think yourself weak?"

"Ëólas has been training his whole life to be a leader, a skilled fighter, a master strategist. You should see how thoroughly he thinks things through, planning for every scenario. I'm nowhere near his level. Fate gave me the most amazing partner, but I hate wielding a sword. I mean, I downright loathe it. And my magic, well, I'm still at the beginning of understanding how it works."

"First, he's the one whom fate has rewarded, meaning he must prove himself worthy of you." Aurellia's sharp tone insinuates that he's not up for the task. Placing her hands beside her, she leans forward and stares at her reflection, at her tattered clothes, frizzy hair, and the dirt smeared across her face. "It's a bit intimidating, being married to an Aerytolían."

"To be fair, the poor guy had no idea what he was getting into when he married me."

"Huh? What do you mean?"

"Neither of us knew about my lineage when, um," all the heat in Adaline's body rushes to her cheeks, "we said our vows."

Aurellia opens her mouth, closes it, then tries again. "You mean, he married you, thinking you were only—"

"Human. Yeah."

"Well, shit. I can't dislike him as much now."

"He also saved my life. Several times. And he—"

"Okay, okay." Aurellia sits up and pats Adaline's knee. "You don't have to keep talking him up."

Adaline drags her feet back and forth, creating ripples in the lake that remind her of the water sprites who re-enacted her memories. Despite all the ups and downs since then, he's been her rock. Even now, when he's hurting. Her mother doesn't know him. Not yet, anyway. "Ëólas isn't intimidated."

"You said he overthinks things—that's not a sign of confidence. Take another look at your husband."

Wait, what? All that meticulous planning... Holy shit. "Whoa."

Aurellia taps the surface, her splashing adding to the late summer chorus. "As for your magic, fear and regret—"

"And anger weaken our magic. I know. I know."

"Not for you!" Aurellia chuckles.

"What?"

"Must be the human in you, but anger makes you stronger. Haven't you noticed that yet?"

So, I am a source of chaos, like Āranol said. "I'm dangerous then."

"What? No." Aurellia brushes that idea aside. "You are the most passionate person I've ever met. That's why you have a natural affinity for fire. Oh, every time you conjured a flame and I asked you to put it back in the fireplace, your whole body turned four shades of red." She laughs at the memory as she moves her foot in circles, creating larger rings in the lake. The longer they sit on this bough and her mother plays with the water, the more lively her face appears, as if the lake were the fountain of youth.

"What do you mean a natural affinity? Don't fae have access to all four elements? I've been able to communicate with each of them, one time or another."

"Yes, but no one can be a master of everything. You're naturally connected to fire. Your father has an affinity for water. Arraya is also fire, although she developed a deep connection to earth thanks to—"

"Grandad."

"Yes. And as your father's partner, I too have a deep love for the water." Aurellia taps her foot on the surface of the lake again, and the face of a female water sprite emerges, her hair undulating within the water, her eyes bluer than the ocean. She waves once to Aurellia and then dives deep again.

That's how Mom survived jumping into the ocean. She didn't have to ask for help; the water just knew. Maybe the river was trying to push me to that cave entrance.

Adaline swings her legs back and forth. "I have so much to learn. But, Mom," she shifts sideways, the bark pressing into her hands, "you're not weak."

The stories Aurellia used to share proved that. After she lost her mother at a young age, Aurellia took care of her entire family, raising her siblings, burying the ones who didn't survive to adulthood, falling in love with a lost elf in hiding, and raising a daughter to lead with compassion and kindness regardless of her immense abilities. And look at Aurellia now, taking in refugees, organizing a rebellion, and guiding these people toward their best chance for freedom. What a role model.

"You're a leader, Mom. My determination comes from you."

Aurellia traces the curve of Adaline's cheek and smiles softly the way only a mother can, when she's looking at her legacy, at the person she poured her hopes and dreams into, believing beyond a shadow of a doubt that someday her child will come into her own and make a difference.

How could I betray her like that? How could I give up my memories of her?

Taking her mother's hand away from her face, Adaline looks down at her lap. Their hands are the same size now. "Mom, when I couldn't find you, I, I chose to, to—"

"Forget me?"

Adaline's gaze snaps to her mother's. "How did you know?"

"Before you were born, your father and I planned many contingencies, should the Morgai find us. We discussed that possibility too, if it meant keeping you safe."

Keeping me *safe. What about them?* "Why?"

"Because we'd do anything to give you your best chance, and we'd rather love you as a human daughter than mourn you as a dead Aerytolían."

They've endured so much. Because of me.

As those words sink into Adaline's heart, the tree, the crickets and frogs, the whole world vanishes. She can feel the pattern of the bark pressing into her legs, but she's so deep inside herself, swimming against the tide, trying to reach the shore, that she can't focus on anything else.

Studying her daughter's face, Aurellia grabs Adaline's shoulders and calls her back, her voice strict and unforgiving, demanding nothing less than her child's full attention. "Adaline, you listen to me right now. I knew what I was getting myself into. Edwin begged me to walk away, to break him, to reject what had grown between us. But I wouldn't. I knew our story would be difficult. That was my choice."

Aurellia leans closer until Adaline's eyes refocus. Knowing her daughter can see her, Aurellia continues, her voice still steadfast. "But the day I held you in my arms, felt you lay your head on my chest, watched you wrap those tiny fingers around mine, I knew *you* were meant for greatness, in this world or any other. So don't you dare let me be the thing that haunts you, that holds you back, that weakens you. What happened wasn't your fault. None of it was, my sweet girl."

As steady as a bass drum, Adaline's heart thumps so loudly that it cracks and breaks the guilt that has been building up like a residue for decades, suffocating her from the inside out. Her heart pushes against the walls of her chest, her gratitude and her mother's love too large to fit inside her anymore.

Leaning forward, Aurellia hugs her daughter, holding Adaline's head to her chest and rocking back and forth while Adaline convulses, her sobs drowning out the bull frogs. Even as a light rain pings the lake's surface and raindrops roll down the willow's leaves, falling onto their hair, soaking into their clothes, Adaline and Aurellia don't let go, not until they both forgive not each other but themselves.

When they return to the campsite, Sora stands at the edge of Adaline's bedding, staring down at her queen. "I can't keep you safe if you travel without me." She strides away, dropping onto her own blanket, her stare burning a hole into Adaline's backside.

Oops. I should have at least warned her.

"I think you should go to your husband." Aurellia jerks her chin at Ëólas sitting next to Merith.

"Yeah." After hugging her mother one more time, Adaline gets up and walks toward Ëólas, his eyes following her even though the rest of him remains as still as a statue.

Merith rises, giving her his seat, but before he dashes off, he bows at the waist. "Forgive me, my queen."

"For what?" *Being too harsh? Chastising my husband?*

"Underestimating you. You're tougher than you look."

Adaline's lips and eyebrows dip downward. "Why don't I look tough?"

"Ah. Um." He rakes his hand through his silver hair, and the amusement on his face reminds her of the night he caved to her pleas and allowed her to enjoy the festivities in the elven tavern. "You have too kind a persona. I mistook that for—"

"Weakness?" When Merith nods bashfully, Adaline punches him in the arm. "I'm going to consider that a compliment and one of my secret weapons."

"You have other secret weapons?"

Adaline winks and walks around him to sit next to Ëólas. The flames curl and ripple, their snaps and crackles music to her ears, their warmth a balm for her healing heart. "I take back what I said—about Daven and I taking the lead."

Propping his elbow on his bent knee, Ëólas rests the side of his face in his hand, his dirty-blond locks falling away from his wide, diamond jawline. He tosses a twig into the fire. "It was a wise choice."

"But it wasn't the right one."

Ëólas sits up, and his golden eyes find hers. "That doesn't make sense."

Hmm. Storytime.

Pulling Ëólas's arm onto her lap, she plays with his long fingers, lacing hers through his, then turning his hand over and tracing the lines on his palm. They've not had much time together these last few days, not since she began sharing her bedding with her mother. Sitting with him, just the two of them for now, is all she needs.

When her fingers dance over his skin, he snaps his hand shut, trapping her in his grasp. "You're going to tell me a story, aren't you?"

"How'd you know?"

"Because I know you. How's this one go?"

She wriggles her fingers until he lets go and resumes tracing his heart line across his palm. "Once upon a time, in days of old, when the world was still new, the birds and mammals wanted to play a game of soccer. Because Bat had wings, he chose to play with the birds, until their team started losing. Bat snuck off and told the mammals that he belonged on their side, and they let him play. But the moment the mammals started losing, Bat abandoned them to rejoin the birds. By the end, no one wanted Bat on their team because he was only a fair-weathered friend."

"You're not Bat."

"I know. But you and I are a team. Always. And whenever either of us makes a mistake, we'll work that out too. So, when we reach Camp Three tomorrow, no matter what's waiting for us, we'll face it together. Okay?"

Ëólas slides his hand under her ear and pulls her head closer, his fingers threading through her hair. Not caring who's watching, he brushes his lips over hers. "Agreed."

CHAPTER THIRTY-FOUR

THE DISEASED

When the camp comes into view, Adaline and Ëólas halt the army two miles away. A massive wall, as if risen from the Wastelands' rocky terrain, encircles the city and merges with the back of a mountain. Spires from a church peek above the wall, along with a few other buildings set on top of hills, but the rest of the city remains hidden, submerged, contained. The gates aren't yet visible, hidden to the right and most likely facing north.

Adaline gawks at her mother standing next to Daven. "You call this a camp?"

She oscillates her head from side to side. "It was a camp—five centuries ago."

Taking the forty-five elven members of the royal guard, Ëólas and Adaline advance closer to the city, leaving the rest of the army a safe distance away. As much as she wants the prisoners to see humans freeing them, she can't risk Daven and his men. She also doesn't want to terrify the humans with hundreds of elves descending upon them, so she and Ëólas agreed to begin with the royal guard.

Despite Adaline's pleas, her mother refuses to stay with Daven. "I've fought too hard and too long not to be here for this."

Elashor also begs to come with them, to face head on the extent of Morgán's depravity, but the worried yet admiring glances he casts toward his grandson tell an additional story that makes Adaline like him a little more.

I guess we're doing this with family. And I once thought I had none left. She chuckles to herself. *Okay, serious face.*

As their small group strides across the barren land—Adaline and Ëólas in the center, Sora and Aurellia to the queen's right, and Merith and Elashor to the king's left—Adaline marches swiftly and confidently, but half her brain does not yet believe they're on the cusp of a monumental moment that will alter this world's history, that she's in the lead instead of recreating this scene for her students.

The closer they get, the more Adaline's churning stomach warns her that something's not right. No guards line the wall. No one launches an arrow. No envoy comes out to inquire why they're here. What if they were wrong about Ãranol trying to infect Daven's men? What if Ãranol's army waits beyond the horizon, counting the miles that separate Adaline from the rest of the army?

She touches a star on her chest plate. *Please keep our troops safe.*

They continue toward the north side of the wall where they find two solid-steel gates about a mile away. Like the wall, the gates rise at least fifteen feet high. And someone has left them cracked open, enough for two people to enter side by side.

Yeah, because that doesn't give me the heebie-jeebies.

Unlike Feídra né Morna, not a single guard stands sentry, and Adaline's confidence plummets to the bottom of her stomach. Without thinking, she takes Ëólas's hand. His warmth combats the cold crawling up her spine, especially as she listens for clues beyond the wall, for the din of city life, for people crying or protesting or arguing, for the sounds of swords drawn and bowstrings notched. But she hears nothing. A chill rakes through her body, making her limbs stiff and breath catch.

Less than half a mile away, Ëólas squeezes Adaline's hand, and she halts, as does everyone else. Lifting his free arm high in the air, Ëólas waits half a second, then waves five of their guards ahead. With their blades drawn, the scouts sprint to the entrance, hiding behind the first gate. In the lead, Moren peeks around the steel door and disappears inside. The rest follow swiftly thereafter. As the seconds tick by, each feeling like minutes, Adaline's anxiety twists itself around her muscles.

It's going to be okay. We're going to free these people. We're going to get through this.

"What?" Ëólas takes one step forward, his brows dipping low.

"I don't understand," Elashor says as he, Merith, and Sora look to Ëólas for guidance.

The forty elves behind Adaline inhale sharply, but they quickly erase the surprise from their faces.

Adaline tugs Ëólas's hand. "What did you hear?"

When he faces her, his resolve wilts under the weight of having to be the barer of something so horrific that she can feel through their bond how desperately he wants to take her away from whatever lies on the other side of those doors.

"Ëólas, what's going on?" Aurellia asks.

Keeping his eyes anchored to Adaline's, he whispers, "They're dead."

"No." Adaline drops his hand. "No."

No, no, no, no, no.

She stares down the steel gates. Before she can sprint into the city, her mother bolts ahead. Adaline charges after her, with Ëólas, Sora, and everyone else close at her heels.

Why would he do this? How could this possibly help his cause?

On the other side of the gates, a wide street stretches through the center of the city. Squat buildings twist and bend away from the street, revealing narrow alleyways, sharp bends, and deep shadows. A heavy floral perfume, the kind the sick wear to mask their decay, pervades the air. The buildings of homes, shops, and trade stalls match the muted gray tones of the Wastelands, but the occasional flower box and green patch between homes offer hope. At least, they did.

Adaline and her mother run down the street, calling out that they're here to help and praying that someone responds. The rest of the royal guard spreads out to search for life too, but everywhere Adaline turns, death surrounds her.

A torso slumped over his workstation.

A pair of legs sticking out of an open door.

An arm draped over the side of a cart.

A shoe, smaller than Adaline's hand, peeking out from behind a barrel.

Where did they go wrong? What could she have done differently to avoid all this, to spare these people? *Oh god. Ëólas panicked and killed two people. I let a monster go, and he killed an entire city.*

Too many petrified bodies face her, most of them with their eyes shut as if they fell asleep in the middle of their day. A few eyes forever frozen open follow her as she stumbles around limbs, broken crates and baskets, their contents strewn across the street. When her mother aimlessly wanders closer, Adaline can't look at her. "I saw Ãranol days ago, when I learned about the demonic elves. I could have...I should have..."

Standing behind her, Ëólas places his hands on Adaline's shoulders, letting her lean against him. "We should have."

"No." Aurellia sweeps her hand across the street, her fury imprinted on her face. "This level of depravity—this has Morgán written all over it. He orchestrated this. He's to blame. And we will not let him get away with this."

As Aurellia disappears into nearby houses only to emerge empty-handed, Adaline turns around and forces herself to believe every word she utters so Ëólas feels that too. "This isn't our fault. We can't let him break us, weaken us, like this."

He hesitates a moment, not speaking until his determination mirrors Adaline's. "Agreed."

With Ëólas close behind, Adaline wanders down the street and looks at each face she passes, the pus-filled boils marring their skin, their blue lips, their peaceful expressions. She could close her eyes, but that wouldn't shut out the images. She can't turn off her phone and lose herself in the busyness of her day, pretending as if nothing happened, as if she can't do anything about this. Because she does have power. Power to hunt Morgán down. But more than that, power to make sure these people aren't forgotten, that he doesn't erase their story. Ellíum may not have mass media, but Adaline can make sure the world knows about this.

Closing her eyes, she listens to the wind that has helped her so many times, that has brought her those ethereal warnings, and finds the currents drifting past. "Come to me, please," she whispers. "I need your help, my friends."

The currents gather near, creating a docile funnel of gusts encircling her, brushing her loose curls across her face.

"Thank you." Adaline opens her eyes and clasps her hands over her heart. "In every corner of the world, tell them what happened here this day, that Morgán has betrayed his people. He's broken the laws of nature and defiled the sanctity of life. He orchestrated the slaughtering of a thousand human families in the

Wastelands because his hatred has consumed him, and Aerytol will not let this go unpunished."

When she extends her hand to the sky, the wind swirls around her, playing back echoes of her words. One by one, the currents peel away and fly off in various directions.

I'll make it so he can't hide ever again.

Turning around, she faces Ëólas and bites her lip to stop herself from crying. His golden eyes draw her nearer, giving her a safe refuge, a light when the world feels unbearably dark.

A few feet away, Elashor parts his lips, but he can't find any words. Adaline follows his line of sight down a side street that leads to a large, circular fountain with a single stream of water spraying upward. Around the fountain, bodies lie on the ground, their buckets over-turned.

But one living person sits on the fountain's ledge, his head dropped into his hands, his long brown hair falling forward and concealing the front of his turquoise overcoat.

Ëólas's breath hitches when he sees the lone figure too, but he doesn't advance. He looks to Adaline, who glances at the gates several blocks away. Should she scream for reinforcements or run toward the fountain, draw her sword, and ram the blade through Āranol's heart?

He decided his path.

Adaline staggers toward the fountain. In her periphery, her mother halts and watches her while more guards search the buildings nearby to no avail. Despite the silent commotion, Āranol doesn't move from the ledge. Adaline stops a few feet away with Ëólas beside her, their hands on their hilts, but the longer Adaline stares at Āranol, the lone soldier at the center of so much destruction, the more he looks like the last survivor, the remaining warrior who's lost everything.

She drops her hand from her hilt. "This is the world you wanted to make?"

Āranol lifts his head, his chartreuse eyes bloodshot, and meets her gaze, her judgment. "Not this. Never this."

Ëólas lunges forward, grabs a fistful of Āranol's silk garments, and hauls him onto his feet. "How did you do this?"

"I didn't." Āranol doesn't try to pry himself free, his arms hanging loosely at his sides. "I sent my army ahead while I followed my father. My soldiers were to wait for me here. But when I arrived, I found this."

As Aurellia stalks closer, Adaline expects her mother to pull a dagger from her boot and grip it like an ice pick, to scream at the person who stole her and locked her away. Instead, she glares at him like a bereft mother, her eyes barren, incapable of comprehending his choices. He evades her disappointed gaze.

Grabbing Ëólas's arm, Adaline pulls him away from Āranol, the person who's haunted her dreams for years. When Ëólas releases his hold, Āranol's shoulders slump forward. Not once does he fight to flee, even as Elashor, Merith, and Sora close in around him.

He's tricky. Don't fall for it again. Adaline visited her family's cottage at least a hundred times before he suckered her into taking his hand, until he promised to reunite her with her mother.

"Where's your army?" Sora asks.

Āranol glances toward the gates as if he could conjure his soldiers to return. "I don't know."

Keeping her sword drawn, Sora positions herself next to Adaline's left. "If they're not following your orders, then who's in charge?"

"Who do you think?" Āranol tosses an arm about, his voice brittle. "Who's been in charge since the beginning?"

Merith moves to Āranol's left, blocking any opportunity for escape, knowing he's good at playing the long game. "Where are Morgán's demonic soldiers? We've not seen them yet. They must be lurking somewhere."

"I'm no longer privy to my father's plans. Clearly." Āranol's eyes sweep from one dead body to another until his gaze falls on Adaline. "I imagine they're not far from you."

But I haven't sensed them. I haven't sensed much since that night with Morgán.

As the clouds drag across the sky, a rogue beam of sunlight reflects off a piece of glass near Āranol's heel. Adaline steps forward, and Āranol leaps to the side as if she's a viper about to strike. Arching a brow at him, she stoops down and picks up the long cylinder of glass, its cork lost elsewhere. She rolls the vial between her

thumb and pointer finger and lifts the bottom close to her eye. A crusty drop of
blood taints the bottom.

"Shit." Adaline drops the vial.

Taking a seat on the edge of the fountain, she touches the water's surface with
the tip of one finger. Much like when Morgán murdered the earth, nausea crawls
up her arm. She rips her hand away, but the discomfort travels into her chest and
settles in the pit of her belly, forcing her to hunch over, and she rocks back and
forth as if to expel a possession. "More blood magic."

While Sora and Merith keep Āranol cornered, Ëólas kneels in front of her and
brushes her hair away from her cheeks. "We need to go."

"No." Clutching her stomach, Adaline asks, "What's the custom here for
tending to the dead?"

"Funeral pyres," Āranol says.

"That's for elves." Aurellia's eyes fall to the body next to Adaline's feet. "We
bury our dead."

Adaline can't look away from the woman lying on her side, her brown eyes
staring at Adaline's shins. Crow's feet branch from the corners of her eyes, and
streaks of silver highlight her greasy blonde hair, her long locks lying on the dirt
road. Was she someone's wife? Someone's mother? And one person decided she
didn't deserve to keep living.

Adaline reaches for Ëólas, but something thumps and falls on top of her foot,
its weight as light as a sheet of paper. She cranes her head downward, and the dead
woman's thin, wiry hand rests on Adaline's boot.

But her arm had been at her side.

Like a lingering ember, Adaline's hope awakens, her eyes focused on that hand.
Time stretches into an eternity, and the city fades from view. She holds her breath
while Ëólas stands up and argues with Āranol, their words becoming increasingly
muffled.

Move. Please, move.

But blue and yellow blotches cover the woman's skin. Her stiff fingers, frozen
like a claw, don't move. Adaline's eyes skim over the arm, over the tattered sleeve

of a bland linen dress, over the woman's still chest and sunken eyes. A fly crawls on her immobile gray lips.

"...been dead for maybe two days," says a royal guard, maybe Moren.

That ember of hope crumples into a pile of ash.

With her stomach twisting inside out, Adaline pushes off the fountain and stands up, her hands trembling. She takes one step, but the dead woman's arm vibrates like a coin struggling to lift and attach itself to a magnet hovering overhead.

"Ëólas," Adaline whispers. The sudden silence tells her everyone's watching that arm.

For a few seconds, the fingers twitch, as if she's trying to open her hand. Then they lie still again, unmoving as they ought to be, until the hand snatches Adaline's ankle. As she shrieks, Ëólas hooks his arm around her waist and yanks her away from the body.

Everyone else leaps backward, including Ãranol, his calves hitting the fountain's edge and his teetering torso nearly falling into the water. Crouching down, Merith pokes the woman's side and flips her onto her back. Dirt cakes the cheek that had been on the ground.

Merith presses his fingers to the woman's neck. "No pulse."

"What the fuck?" Adaline shouts, her heart beating rapidly.

Ëólas tucks her against his side, angling her away from the body, from that hand. "A residual effect of whatever happened to them?"

"I'm not keen to see that again." Sora points her sword toward the exit. "Time to go."

"No," Adaline says. "We're not leaving until they're buried. All of them."

"How do you propose burying more than a thousand people?" Merith asks.

Adaline glances at the gates. "It'll take an army."

To verify she's not endangering Magnus's men, Adaline checks in with Cindy, who insists they travel to her lab in Maryland and retrieve two cases of latex gloves and trash bags to handle hazardous waste. Refusing to bring her best friend near Āranol, Adaline gives Cindy a long hug, pretending for a moment that they're parting ways after a lunch date, and leaves her at the castle.

At Adaline's instruction, Daven orders that anyone with an open wound stand watch at the main gate or guard the backpacks they left behind, where they'll set up camp; everyone would prefer another night of restless sleep on the hard, gray earth than spending a night inside the city on abandoned beds.

For the rest of the day, Adaline uses her army not to rescue people but to lay them to rest.

Everyone helps, including Āranol at his own insistence, his shaggy brown hair falling in front of his chartreuse eyes as he silently takes turns sharing a shovel and digging up the street. Adaline puzzles over Āranol's remorse, not sure what to make of his subtle display of grief.

No one speaks much. The sound of digging fills the city, and each shovelful chips away at Adaline's entire plan, at what she thought they'd accomplish here, at her hopes for the remaining camps Morgán could destroy.

Despite Ëólas never leaving her side, they fall into a pattern of digging, shifting, and filling in. They keep their thoughts to themselves, neither knowing how to comfort the other right now. Maybe they don't deserve such a reprieve from the task at hand, from the horror at hand.

Adaline thrusts her shovel into a dirt pile and tosses dry soil into a hole, her arms and back aching, sweat dripping down her spine. But she doesn't stop. The more she and Ëólas pile on, the less she has to see what they're doing, who they're burying. During her graduate years, she always hated images of mass graves. Now she's digging them.

If I take Seira with me and vow to never come back to Ellíum, would Morgán leave this world alone?

She knows the answer. Proof surrounds her. He may hate Aerytolíans, but Morgán won't rest until he's eliminated all of humanity.

How fucked up is that?

"Adaline?" Ëólas drives his shovel into the ground, leaving it standing upright. "We're almost done."

From the street below, Daven treks uphill, using the back of his hand to wipe his sweaty brow. He leads his four generals, three of whom appear as though they never touched a shovel, their uniforms as dirt-less as this morning.

When he reaches the top, Daven bows his head to Adaline. "My men are filling in the last graves now."

The soldiers finish their work with sullen faces, hunched backs, and hushed voices, their swords dangling uselessly at their sides. They look as though they've buried pieces of themselves too. Forget about demonic elves or disease. Morgán found another way to defeat this army.

We need to rally these soldiers. Constructing a memorial won't work this time; it's not feasible. How else can I encourage them to not give up hope?

"My lord!" A soldier sprints up the street, his face paler than those he passes, and halts in front of Daven. "From the north, about three miles away, an army approaches."

Son of a bitch. It is a trap—just not one Adaline would have ever imagined.

A PROMISE

With Daven taking the lead for the entire army, human and elven soldiers sprint from every corner of the city to the gate. Discarding blue latex gloves in their wake, they follow their commanders' orders, file outside, and set up their formations. They have maybe a half hour before Ãranol's army reaches the city. Carrying only their weapons, the enemy moves faster than seems fair. Then again, nothing about this day has been fair.

Tucked away on a side street off the main thoroughfare, Merith pushes down on Ãranol's shoulders, shoving him onto his knees, his empty hands resting on his thighs, his sword discarded on the ground several feet away. Without removing his hand, Merith moves aside, allowing Sora room to bend over and face Ãranol. A shabby two-story home with broken shutters looms behind them. Over Ãranol's shoulder, a window box houses a few green sprigs of basil, thyme, and drocken, their stems picked nearly clean. They resemble a wiry green claw beside his head.

She places the tip of her dagger beneath his chin. "What's your plan? What advantage have you given yourself by being in here with us?"

Several feet behind Sora, Adaline studies Ãranol's face, the way he stares past them all, his eyes vacant yet never leaving the fresh mounds of dirt in the center of the narrow street. Neither Ëólas nor Aurellia, standing beside Adaline, share their thoughts, but Adaline has little hope for this line of questioning. No matter what Sora or Merith ask him, Ãranol remains numb, not because he's calculating his options but because he thinks none are left.

Motioning for Sora to step aside, Adaline squats in front of Āranol, his vapid chartreuse eyes ignoring her. "Can you call off your army?"

His eyes roam past Adaline to Ëólas and Aurellia. When he speaks, he sounds like an irritable teenager. "Is she serious?"

"Yes." Ëólas keeps his tone curt, his patience ticking away quickly.

A herd of soldiers jogs down the street, lifting their feet high so they can jump over and dodge mounds. Their commander pauses and points for them to turn left at the cross street. "Unit fifteen, take up position in the southern flank. Let's go!"

Āranol rolls his eyes. "You have seasoned commanders at your disposal, and you're going to let a little girl take the lead here?"

"Watch it." Sora slaps her palm with the flat side of her dagger's blade. "You're alive because our queen hasn't given us permission to run you through yet. You think she's playing games when in fact she's giving you a chance, one no one else here would give you."

With Adaline in his face, Āranol can't escape her scrutiny while he considers Sora's words. "Not that you'll believe a word I say," his eyes flick to Aurellia, then back to Adaline, "but I doubt they'll listen to me. They're not following my orders."

Even if they're following Morgán's commands, Āranol must have friends among them. "Do you have enough who are loyal to you, who might listen to you?"

Agreeing with Merith's scoffs, Ëólas moves next to Adaline. "We can't trust him, my love."

"What do you propose?" She spins around, rises, and places her hands on her hips.

"We have leverage." Without looking at the prisoner, Ëólas gestures at Āranol. "We'll greet his army with a dagger to his throat. If he doesn't stop them, he dies."

"What? No!" *Do you know who you married? Have you forgotten who I am?* "I refuse to resort to that."

Walking around the corner, Elashor hurries over to join their group, having passed his orders onto his lieutenants so he can remain beside his family. "What have I missed?"

Ignoring his grandfather, Ëólas grips Adaline's shoulders. "We're at war, my love. Sacrifices—"

"Don't say it." Her fingers twitch, wanting to slap his hands away. Instead, she jabs his cheek, making him turn his head toward the end of the street where the royal guards block off access to their queen, each one standing at attention between mounds of dirt. "Look around you. We've been waist deep in sacrifices all day. I've had enough."

"I hear you. I truly do. But we're past negotiations. There's no reasoning with these people. What more evidence do we need? Please, take your mother back to the castle. Wait with Magnus. Come back in an hour, maybe three, and—"

"No." Adaline shoves his hands off her. "He said they're not following his orders."

"I'm sorry. I don't believe him, and I don't understand how you can."

"Because what if he is telling the truth? Then what? We follow through with our threat and kill someone who's essentially powerless? There's no honor in that."

Ëólas closes the distance between them and grabs her lower back, placing his hand over her scar. "We won't have to worry about him trying to kill you again."

Tilting her head to the side, Adaline smooths away the wrinkles creasing his brow and cups his cheeks. "I know you want to end the threat his family poses to me, to us, to this world. But I will not use fear to justify injustices. Call me naive. Call me a little girl. I don't care. I'm always going to try diplomacy first."

With his resolve weakening, Ëólas takes Adaline's hands and places them over his chest as he wars with himself. As his last chance, he looks to Aurellia for help. "Anything you'd like to add?"

Shit. No, that's not fair. She's completely biased in this matter—with good reason.

Aurellia yanks off her gloves, the latex's suction snapping away from her skin. She scrutinizes Āranol, his hunched shoulders and frozen expression, like a parent trying to sniff out a lie and debating whether to trust her child. As he shrinks under her gaze, she nods her head. "I think he's telling the truth."

Mom? "Really?"

Āranol drops his chin to his chest. He doesn't seem confused that Aurellia believes him, not even guilty. Hell, indifferent would also be understandable. Instead, he looks relieved, as if he might care what Aurellia thinks of him, and that reaction, no matter how impossible, niggles in the back of Adaline's mind, even as Ëólas stops arguing with her and tells Merith to let Āranol up.

Shoving his hand under Āranol's armpit, Merith hoists him onto his feet. "I advise against trusting him. The first chance he gets, he'll run to his soldiers, and we'll lose our leverage."

Yeah, I'm not so sure of this myself.

While Elashor asks Ëólas if he has a plan, the herbs in the window box behind Āranol wither, their greenery darkening until the stems turn black and crack, and the few remaining leaves fall like ash into the flower box. Adaline doubles over, her stomach retching with an onslaught of nausea that she hasn't felt since entering that dead circle and watching Morgán create his own abominations. Bile clogs her throat and burns her esophagus.

"My love, are you okay?" Ëólas asks.

That ethereal voice drifts close to Adaline's ear, a whisper on the wind that calls her name, its musical tone matching Lé-Lé's when she found Adaline wandering too far from home.

"Lé-Lé." *That's you, isn't it? And we're in danger.* "Ëólas, we need to go."

"Are you feeling alright? Do you—" Following her line of sight to the decayed herbs, Ëólas draws his sword and shouts at the royal guards. "Protect the queen!"

The guards abandon their stations and run toward Adaline. From the rooftop behind Āranol, a cloaked figure appears, its shadow stretching over their group and the few guards nearby. He leaps off the building, and his mangled hand draws a curved blade, his red eyes glowing beneath his hood. While Ëólas grabs Adaline and swings her behind him, Merith shoves Āranol out of the way, knocking him to the ground, before the figure lands where Āranol once stood. Charging forward, Sora locks blades with the demonic elf, the clang so forceful that her arms and knees buckle.

Two guards run to Sora's aid. Merith strikes at the enemy first, giving her a chance to escape and attack again, but the demonic elf pushes back both captains.

Impaling a guard behind him, the demonic elf hurls the body at Merith and Sora, who half catch, half drop their friend and stumble backward.

Two more enemies with red eyes jump off the rooftop to join the first. Both slash a guard with their gnarled hands, their razor-sharp nails tearing through the guards' vambraces. Clutching their forearms, the guards collapse on their knees and fall over. Sweat coats their brows, and their bodies convulse.

What the hell is happening?

Elashor places himself in front of Aurellia and fends off one of the demonic elves, giving her seconds to grab Āranol's sword, toss away the scabbard, and sprint to her daughter's side. Ëólas, keeping Adaline and her mother behind him, unsheathes his second sword.

Aurellia points down the street and shouts, "Over there!"

In between two dilapidated houses, another cloaked demonic elf, mostly concealed in shadow, pins his red eyes on Adaline. But he doesn't attack. He waits, counting the royal guards as they run to their queen, not yet aware of his presence.

"That's four. Look for one more." Ëólas scans the city, the dark corners, the closed windows, the blind bends.

Āranol scrambles to his feet beside them. "Um, about that..."

"What about what?" Ëólas asks.

"Remember when I said I followed my father for several days? Well, when I caught up to them, the original five were infecting more elves."

Half the royal guards rush to help Merith, Sora, and Elashor. The other half encircles their queen and king, Aurellia, and Āranol, creating several rows of protection. At the far end of the street, oblivious to the demonic elves, the last line of Daven's soldiers disappears around the bend to exit the city.

"What?" Adaline asks. "Infecting them how?"

"By drawing blood with their claws." Āranol points at the royal guards rolling on the ground and scratching at their arms as if trying to amputate the limb.

They are fucking vampire elves!

"How many did you see?" Ëólas asks.

Not one but at least twenty more vampires emerge from side streets and rooftops, all of them rushing at the royal guards to get to Adaline. As they snarl, fangs poke into their bottom lips.

Oh come on! What kind of magic changes teeth? That's just overkill.

Āranol eyes Ëólas's two blades. "Might I have a sword now? They don't like me either."

"I can't imagine why," Aurellia says with a smirk.

Āranol and her mother exchange a knowing glance that makes Adaline's arm hair bristle and palms sweat. *No, no, no. Don't freak out. I don't want to set my guards on fire.*

The vampires cut down and beat back the guards faster and harder than Adaline's brain can process, the two sides clashing together in a confusing blur of blades, punches, and screams that shrink the circle around her and Ëólas with each passing second.

Āranol twists around to look behind him. "Send guards to call back some of your soldiers."

"I'm not risking the battle between our forces and yours," Ëólas says.

"The battle won't matter if we're dead!"

As more guards fall, the vampires advance on Adaline's circle with Merith, Sora, and Elashor fighting from the outside. Even surrounded on both sides, the vampires never tire, never yield, and never scream when slashed as if Morgán removed their emotions. They move together with one goal, one purpose, and they won't allow anyone to get in their way.

A guard closer to Adaline shouts over his shoulder, "My lady, you must travel far away from here."

"Tumin!" *Where's Moren? They're always together.*

Adaline counts her guards, Ëólas's friends, their family; she can't carry this many people through a doorway. She could get Ëólas and Aurellia out of here. But carrying thirty, forty more people isn't possible, and the more people she saves, the faster the guards waiting for their turn will die. If only she and Ëólas vanish, will the vampires retreat or slaughter everyone in their fury? She can't sacrifice her people.

Lowering her weapon, Aurellia turns to her daughter, her mossy green eyes reflecting Adaline's fear. "You need to go."

She didn't say we. For a moment, Adaline's back in that meadow, a child listening to her mother's screams as the Morgai take her prisoner. *No, not again. I can't. I won't.*

Adaline pushes past her mother and steps in front of Ëólas, between his swords. Unfurling her fists, she cups his face, making him focus on her and cease his calculations. She peers into his golden eyes not in defeat but with fortitude. "They want me. They'll *follow* me."

Ëólas presses his forehead against hers, his eyes more vibrant than ever. Then he sheathes his second sword.

"Come on!" Ãranol cries, waving his empty hands about. "Give me one!"

Ignoring him, Ëólas points to a building far opposite the gates, its rooftop rising above most other buildings nearby, and takes her hand. "Can you get us there?"

Maybe two miles separate her from that rooftop, and with regular human eyesight, she can't see anything more than a smear of gray coloring. If she couldn't travel to the clifftop, how can she hope to get them so far away now?

Too much mind. Adaline imagines switching off her thoughts, but, like the guards' screams, other people's words invade her mind, words like abomination, half-breed, chaos, mule, little girl. Each one forms a fetter around her wrists and ankles, chaining her to the street.

Another guard two rows in front of her falls to his knees, a sword sticking through his backside. The vampire jerks his blade free, pushes the guard to the ground, and steps on the dead man's back to attack the next guard, his weapon inching closer to his primary target. Beyond the vampires, Merith, Sora, and Elashor don't give up, fighting desperately with every swing, every thrust, every block to save just one person.

It's not fair. It's my job to protect my people. That is who I've always been. And it's about damn time I know it too.

Ëólas laces his fingers with Adaline's. "You can do this."

"I know." Adaline cups her hand around her mouth and shouts over the swords clashing and the claws slashing, "Sora, I trust you to get my mother to safety. Merith, keep Āranol alive." With her free hand, she wraps her arm around Aurellia and buries her face in her mother's frizzy hair. "I love you, Mom. This time, I'll save you. I promise."

Turning off her logic brain, Adaline throws away the idea of limitations and sets her gaze on a closer rooftop, the one where the first vampire appeared.

"What do you mean?" Aurellia asks, her voice wavering. "No, Adaline. It's my job to pro—"

The city rotates around Adaline until the street turns into a flat gray rooftop, and she and Ëólas overlook their friends and family fighting off the vampires—a collision of black cloaks and dark-blue leather armor with more of her royal guards wounded, fighting off infection, or dead. Aurellia and Āranol blink at the sudden empty space between them, and the vampires scream like banshees as they double their efforts to skewer guards and search for their target.

Lifting their clasped hands, Ëólas kisses Adaline's knuckles. "A brilliant start, my love."

"Yeah, now we have to draw them away." Adaline waves an arm overhead and shouts, "Hey you former-elf-people-vampire-things, up here!"

While Sora screams for them to get out of the city, Adaline asks Ëólas, "Do you think they heard—"

"Yep." He yanks her away from the edge as every vampire halts, turns, and sprints toward Adaline. "Definitely heard. Next roof, next roof, next roof!"

Turning around, they run across the tiles. Adaline fixes her gaze on a rooftop two buildings ahead, comes to a complete stop, jerking Ëólas backward, and travels them forward. Pots, wooden beams, and an overgrown tomato plant picked clean litter the second rooftop. They resume running, and Adaline and Ëólas jump over a stack of boards. When Adaline tugs Ëólas's hand, they both freeze, and she pops them three buildings ahead.

Mid-run, Ëólas glances over his shoulder. "Go left. Take us uphill."

Behind her, eight vampires sprint closer with only two rooftops between them. "How do they move so quickly?"

Okay, now. No stopping this time. I can do this. It's like jumping out of a moving car onto a stationary target. Easy peasy.

Setting her sight on a flat rooftop to their left, Adaline travels them there, but the instant change of direction makes her head spin and her feet wobble, her brain telling her to turn left even though they already did.

Ëólas pulls her along though, locking his arm under her armpit to keep her upright, and points ahead. "That one!"

The next travel jump makes her ears pop and head swim. Before she can choose another building, a vampire leaps from the adjacent rooftop and lands in front of them. Adaline shrieks and jumps back while Ëólas, letting go of her, unsheathes his second weapon in a wide arc.

What are you doing?

Adaline chooses the next building a block away and touches Ëólas's back. When their feet touch down on the new rooftop, a cloaked vampire jumps up from the street, swinging his sword down between them. Adaline and Ëólas fly apart. She rolls over a broken pot, the shards digging into her arms, whereas Ëólas, landing on his feet, lifts both blades and charges the vampire.

Don't let him touch you!

A second vampire stalks Adaline from behind, his sword dragging along the tiles, the screeching worse than nails on a chalkboard. Further in the background, more vampires change direction and leap over rooftops, their gazes set on her. Scrambling to her feet, Adaline grabs her hilt, but the moment the vampire pounces at her, she lifts her palms and blasts a stream of fire into his face. His cloak catches fire, and the vampire falls to the ground, wailing and howling as he rolls around to smother the flames.

Oh god. I'm sorry.

As Adaline twists around to find Ëólas, he slides his blades between the first vampire's ribs and kicks his abdomen, sending him flying backward. The vampire catches his balance at the edge of the roof, but his hood falls away, revealing a youthful face with a slender nose, square jaw, and wide mouth that stretches into an exaggerated clown's snarl. Layers of scratches cover his cheeks, as if he clawed his flesh until it bled and scarred over, only for him to do so again and again, marring what must have once been a handsome face, and the whites of his eyes have turned solid black, making those dark-red irises glow brighter.

"Gandor?" Ëólas lowers his blades, his face pale and contorted in self-disgust.

"You knew him?" Adaline asks.

"He's one of the spies I sent ahead."

That's messed up on so many levels. Did he betray Ëólas, or can Morgán's disease make anyone do his bidding?

Falling on his knees, the vampire collapses sideways and coughs up blood, his gaze still fixated on Adaline, even as he takes his last gasps.

When Gandor's chest stops moving, Ëólas turns his back to his friend and points at vampire elves to their left and right. "They're fanning out. They mean to surround us."

Not if I can help it. Setting her sights on the tall building Ëólas initially pointed out, she grabs Ëólas's wrist and travels them half-way across the city.

Leaning over, she rests her hands on her knees, taking a few seconds for the fuzzy haze clouding her vision to clear. Down the main thoroughfare, Aurellia, Elashor, and their friends funnel toward the gates with several carrying a wounded guard around their shoulders. Beyond the city's wall, the soldiers hustle into formation and wait for Āranol's approaching army, those dots growing larger by the second. As their friends vacate the city and Merith pulls the gates shut, the vampires close in around Adaline and Ëólas.

They'll never stop coming for us. For me. For Seira. This can't go on.

CHAPTER THIRTY-SIX

THE HUNT

Adaline returned to the Wastelands to free the oppressed, to protect her family, to make a difference. She can't do any of that with these demonic elves hunting her. Was Ëólas right? Not about necessary sacrifices—she can't entertain that idea. But maybe she needs to accept that she's human, that she can't save everyone, and right now she needs to protect her husband and herself so they have a chance to find a cure, to end this war, to help those waiting for freedom.

The vampires spread out to create a wide net. Instead of rushing at her from all directions, each cloaked figure chooses a rooftop where they stand as still as gothic statues, their red eyes trained on her, limiting her escape options and her time to regroup between traveling. They don't need to swarm her; they just need one to claw her throat, to tear through her leather armor, or worse—to scratch Ëólas and kill her soul.

Ëólas widens his stance and lifts both blades, the steel catching glints of red sky as the sun begins its descent. "What's the chance they can't handle starlight?"

"Not one I'm willing to bet on."

"Now would be a good time for you to draw that sword, my love, or get us out of here."

The vampires watch her scan the horizon to choose their next destination. Before she selects another rooftop, the five nearest race toward her, either to kill her now or force her hand.

Oh, no you don't.

Adaline's skin itches and prickles. Unfurling her fists, she turns her hands over, and a spark ignites in the center of her palms. The warmth radiates up her arms and relaxes her shoulders. Losing herself in the flames, she inhales deeply, filling her lungs and expanding her chest. The world beyond the flames blurs out of focus. All other sounds become muffled, until she hears only the steady thumping of her heart like a bass drum, the hum of energy vibrating her limbs, the lush flickering of the flames, and the ethereal rhythm of her breath.

It's like playing music.

The flames glow brighter, hotter, their base turning blue where they dance over her skin.

As the vampires leap onto their rooftop, Ëólas studies their movements to predict the first assault, his feet planted to deny them access to Adaline. "My love," he calls over his shoulder, "I don't suppose you have a plan?"

We don't have time to form one.

Two vampires dive at Ëólas. Adaline whips her hands overhead, and the flames flare in a wide arc, erecting a wall of fire around her and Ëólas. The two vampires fly into the fire, only to stop short, yelp, and fling themselves backward.

Suddenly, all that research and practice, all the pieces she's picked up from friends and family, click into place like notes finding the right keys, and those notes create an internal harmony that Adaline recognizes, that she no longer has to doubt or analyze—because this is who she's always been. Tuning into the elements is like learning to play the guitar or practicing a new dance routine. First, she needs to find the right song that speaks to her. Then, she needs to find the right chords, the right steps, and let the music guide her, become her, as she funnels everything, all her passion, through the heart.

Adaline pushes her hands outward, and the wall of fire moves forward, giving her and Ëólas more room to breathe, to move. As if playing a harp, she swipes her hands sideways, making the flames spin faster, and twists her hands upward so the fire forms a dome around her and Ëólas while remaining an inch off the rooftop tiles.

With the dome complete, Ëólas relaxes his wrists and turns around, his blades dipping downward. A red and orange glow shimmers over his face like waves.

"Huh." He tilts his head to the side, his bottom lip arched upward. "I confess this scenario never occurred to me."

"I love surprising you?" With her arms stretched outward, she focuses on the dome, on maintaining the same tempo, her arms twitching and aching from all that shoveling. "Seriously though, I don't know how long this will last. We can't keep traveling away from them."

Moving behind her, Ëólas whispers in her ear, "Can you sneak me behind them, one at a time?"

"I, I can..." The fire sputters and wavers, sparks rolling toward her boots.

Ëólas hangs his head, his chin tapping her shoulder. "You want to try diplomacy first, don't you?"

"Please. I need to know if any part of who they were remains."

He moves beside her but a few feet in front, his blades at the ready. "On your mark."

Pressing the back of her hands together, she slowly spreads them a part until a gap the size of a head opens in the fire wall. A cloaked vampire peers through the window, his red and black eyes glowing brighter beneath his hood.

"Do you remember your name?" she asks.

He doesn't move or utter a sound, either because he doesn't understand her, doesn't care, or just wants to size up his next kill.

Adaline shudders but pulls her shoulders back. "We want to heal you, to help you return to who—"

The vampire jumps back and hurls a dagger at Adaline's face, but Ëólas swings his blade down on the dagger, sending it flying off to the side where it clangs on the roof tiles.

After sealing the window shut, Adaline smiles awkwardly at Ëólas. "At least I tried?"

He kisses her cheek. "Are you ready?"

"I don't think I'll ever be ready." Her elbows buckle, and the overlapping waves sizzle apart for an instant. Through the gaps, she counts at least eight vampires on this rooftop, leaving them about fifteen to deal with, fifteen more lives to take.

Ëólas rotates his wrist, turning one blade sideways to show her its length. The thin steel glows red, reflecting the dome. "Do you remember what I said these are for?"

She envisions the training room, the dummies lining the brick wall, the window facing the arena where the guards sparred with each other, and Ëólas gifting her a sword, holding the blade out to her with both hands. "Yes. They're for protecting what's important."

Lowering his weapons, Ëólas presses his temple against hers. "There's nothing more important to me than you. I'm going to end this threat one way or another. But," he lifts his head and peers into her eyes, "it'd be a lot easier with your help. I need you."

The fire surges faster around them, its crackling and sizzling building into a crescendo as the wall grows thicker. "Because we're a team," she says.

"Always."

Bending sideways, Adaline presses her lips against his. They linger in this safe space, neither wanting to end the moment, to take a life, or risk each other. But they can't escape this fight, not if they want to see tomorrow. And Adaline wants as many tomorrows as possible with Ëólas.

I can do this. "Get ready, my love."

Ëólas walks closer to the flaming wall and turns sideways, lifting both blades high, one overhead, the other at an angle. Parting her hands, Adaline cracks the dome open a few inches at a time until a vampire races through the gap, only for Ëólas to slice the vampire's throat. Adaline locks her gaze on the buildings ahead, not the person clutching his neck as he falls to his knees.

Turning his blades downward, Ëólas shifts into a sprint, but another vampire runs into the dome. With the enemy on his heels, Ëólas pumps his arms and legs and races to Adaline. The vampire lifts his gnarled hand, his red eyes targeting Ëólas's back. Adaline drops her arms. The fire dome collapses onto the tiled roof and peters out. She runs to Ëólas, throwing her arms around his neck as the vampire swipes downward, and travels them ten buildings away. While the vampires screech and hiss at the space she left behind and search the city's skyline, another cloaked figure jumps in front of Adaline still hugging Ëólas.

Here we go.

In the blink of an eye, Adaline and Ëólas reappear across the city and behind the vampire furthest away. As Adaline ducks down, Ëólas impales the vampire between his shoulder blades with one swift thrust. When the body hits the rooftop, Adaline twists behind Ëólas and checks the back of his coat for tears. Finding none, she hugs his back and chooses their next target standing on the edge of a roof that slants downward. The moment Adaline travels behind him, she and Ëólas slide down the slick tiles. As the vampire turns around, Ëólas slashes his abdomen and kicks him off the building, sparing Adaline from seeing the vampire's insides.

Again and again, Adaline travels Ëólas to different corners of the city, holding onto his shoulders and pausing every so often to choose a lone vampire for Ëólas to kill as quickly as possible.

In between the jump to their fifth target, when the next rooftop superimposes itself on the previous one, the vampire twists around, catching Ëólas's first blade mid-strike and thrusting his hips backward to avoid the second. The sudden closeness of his red eyes to theirs makes Adaline shriek, throw her arm next to Ëólas's cheek, and blast a stream of fire into the vampire's face. His hood catches fire, and the flames consume the entirety of his cloak as the vampire stumbles backward, throws the wool fabric away from his body, and releases a blood-curdling scream.

"Oh my god! I'm so sorry," Adaline cries, unable to tear her eyes away from the flames latching onto his trousers and eating away at the hem of his coat beneath his leather armor.

To end the vampire's agony, Ëólas swings one sword fast and furious like a baseball bat, severing the vampire's head from his body and blocking Adaline's view.

I don't want to do that again. Stepping into Ëólas's embrace, Adaline travels them far away from that rooftop, but not to another vampire. Instead, she travels around their enemies in three consecutive jumps, watching the vampires as they turn around the instant she vanishes, anticipating her arrival behind them.

"Did you see that?" She pushes the heels of her hands against her brow and drags them sideways, stretching her forehead to massage away the tension building behind her skull.

"I did. We need a distraction. How much longer can you keep this up?"

"It's not so bad. It's like I keep changing altitudes or something. The pressure clears quickly enough."

She jogs to the edge of the rooftop, the vampire elves following her every move. A few of them leap across buildings, but they take their time, like chess pieces choosing their next moves. Beyond the city wall, the first wave of each army runs toward each other, closing the half mile that now separates them.

We need to be there.

Adaline peers over the roof, at the rotten shutters falling away from their hinges, the debris littering the alleyway, the tattered bedsheets through the window. "I have a plan, but I need you to hold on to me. I might get dizzy."

Sheathing one sword, Ëólas clutches a leather strap across Adaline's back. "Alright."

She extends both arms, and fire cascades down the side of the building, engulfing everything flammable within seconds. The dried-out shutters flash like a bomb as they incinerate. As the flames take on a life of their own and spread from doorways to furniture, she travels along the perimeter of the city and sets buildings on fire, trapping everyone inside.

The vampire elves chase after her at full speed, their patterns erratic, their desperation mounting. Asking the wind for help, Adaline implores the gusts to fan the fire further, higher, hotter. The thick black smoke billowing into the sky conceals her momentarily, slowing the vampires down as they search around the plumes for her next appearance.

Each time she travels to a different rooftop, the pressure in her head compounds, and the charred air corrodes her lungs. Her legs wobble, and Ëólas holds her up, his arm hooked around her waist. Not even clamping down on the meaty flesh between her thumb and finger helps, but with the ring of fire encircling the city, she gives herself a few seconds of reprieve, allowing the pressure to dissipate naturally.

She can sleep later. Much later. She still has work to do.

Ëólas whispers in her ear, "Third from the left."

Adaline tracks the vampire racing toward a plume of smoke three-buildings wide. "Okay."

"On my count. Five, four, three, two—"

She travels behind the vampire the second he disappears behind the plume. He never sees Ëólas's blade coming, not until it pierces his torso. As the fire engulfs the city, she and Ëólas pick off the last of Morgán's assassins.

When Ëólas yanks his sword free from the last vampire, Adaline falls onto her knees, her jeans singed, her periwinkle blouse stained with soot, her leather armor too heavy. If she could take three migraine pills and a twenty-minute power nap, then she could last the rest of this night without issue.

Ëólas cleans off his swords, sheathes them, and shows Adaline the bloody rag. "Is this good enough for Cindy?"

She shakes her head, crawls over to the vampire elf, and gently closes his eyes. Digging into her denim pockets, she pulls out a small leather pouch with six test tubes, a dark-purple elastic tourniquet, and small needles. "I need to fill these."

With the fire roaring louder, Adaline lays the vampire elf's arm across her lap, unbuckles his vambrace, tossing the leather aside, and pushes up his linen sleeves. With the absence of silks and velvets, he must have been a commoner. A farmer or a carpenter maybe. Regardless, he was someone's son, maybe someone's father. Who's waiting for him to come home?

She ties off the tourniquet, places her thumb over the vein along the inside of his elbow, and angles the needle at thirty degrees the way she practiced with the fake arm Cindy bought online. As she slides the needle in, Ëólas turns away.

Seriously? He can slice and dice people, but a blood draw makes him squeamish? Thank God we have each other.

The first vial fills slowly but steadily. When she changes the tubes, the vampire's fingers twitch in her lap. Her heart thumps against her chest, and her hands spring away from his arm.

"Ëólas, what the hell is going on?"

He squats down and presses his fingers to the vampire's neck. "Nothing. He's gone."

Adaline fills the rest of the vials, her spine tingling and hands shaking the entire time. After returning the pouch to her pocket, she walks with Ëólas to the edge of the rooftop. In every direction, people's homes collapse, groaning their relief as they burn to the ground, as they leave behind the prison Morgán constructed. The inferno also provides the vampire elves with their funeral rites, their deaths adding to the lives she could not save today.

Ëólas takes her hand and points to the battle beyond the city wall, where Ãranol's army collides with Daven's, where their allies buckle and fall backward like the spray of an exhausted wave. "We need to get down there. Can you take us to the other side of the gates?"

Her insides feel squishy, like two moving walls have been pressing her into a pancake, but she conjures a doorway in front of the gates so she can preview what awaits them on the other side.

Sora, Merith, and Elashor guard Aurellia and the gates while arguing about whether to venture back inside the city or chase after Ãranol, whom Adaline doesn't see anywhere. In the distance, about half a mile away, mobs of elves and men attack each other, both sides focused on nothing but survival and destroying their enemies.

Will this day ever end? "Get ready, my love."

Chapter Thirty-Seven

THE CHOSEN PATH

Adaline and Ëólas appear outside the gates, inhaling deeply the cleaner air with less smoke and soot. After initially jolting sideways, Aurellia pulls her daughter into a fierce hug while Merith and Sora look on with palpable relief.

Elashor shakes Ëólas's forearm and looks at his grandson with new appreciation. "We were terrified when the fire started."

"Ah, that," Ëólas rejoins his wife, his hand finding her lower back, "was Adaline's idea."

When everyone looks at her with a mix of confusion and admiration, she holds out her palm and wills a small flame to flicker awake, making everyone except her mother gawk at such a visible display of magic. "I'll explain later."

In front of them, the fanned-out royal guards shield the gates, the captains, and their infected friends who cannot stand, their tunics drenched in sweat and their eyes rolling back in their heads. Behind the battle, two tents house cots and medical aid a few miles away where their army planned to set up camp tonight.

Why are the medical tents empty of patients? "Sora, we have to get these people help."

"Yes, but we need to reassign soldiers to reinforce your guard before depleting your protection."

"That's unnecessary." Ëólas calls Moren away from the first row of guards. "Take whomever you need and bring the injured to the tents now."

While Moren redirects his peers and the guards thin out, Adaline better sees the battle ahead. The generals must have some sort of order planned, but to Adaline the battlefield looks like overwhelming chaos. In every direction, soldiers slash and jab limbs. Wave after wave, sea-green armor rages against navy and burgundy.

"Where's Āranol?" Ëólas says over the shouts and screams.

"Where do you think?" Merith gestures with his thumb toward the center of the conflict. "He ran off the moment we exited the city."

But he helped us bury the dead. Was he really playing the long game again? Adaline touches her pocket where she tucked away Nan's necklace. *No. He looked genuinely devastated.*

"I'm going after him," Ëólas says.

"What?" Adaline asks.

"This is what we came here to do, my love."

Aurellia, not adding her thoughts to the conversation, holds on to the sword Āranol didn't reclaim when he ran into the fray. Why? So he wouldn't risk giving Merith and Sora a chance to stop him? But how can a soldier not take back his sword in the middle of a battle?

Please Āranol, don't prove yourself our enemy again. "I'm going with you."

Ëólas rakes his gaze over her body, his eyes darting to her shoulders, her eyes, her legs. Then he grabs her wrist and lifts her hand, watching her fingers and waiting for them to shake again. They don't. "I need you to be absolutely honest with me—no dodging the answer. Are you tired? You used a lot of magic back there."

She twists her hand free and bumps his chest armor with her own. "I am tired, but I'm not about to collapse, and I know once we run out there, I'll get another boost of adrenaline. I can do this."

Sliding his hand around her neck, Ëólas crushes his lips against hers, his fingers massaging her nape. He doesn't blush, doesn't pull away, doesn't cut their kiss short. Instead, he sinks into her, his tongue sweeping the inside of her mouth, his tenderness and need painting a tapestry of memories of everything they've overcome thus far. Absolutely nothing, not even a war, can come between them.

When she sighs, Merith clears his throat. "We have urgent matters at hand."

Ëólas steals one more kiss, then uses his no-nonsense commander general voice. "Alright. Merith, you'll follow up on our rear. Sora, Elashor, flank our sides. Aurellia, stay close to Adaline. My love—" Ëólas eyes her sheathed sword.

"I'll fight my way," she says.

"Of course you will. Let's go."

Ëólas draws his weapons and stays in the lead with Adaline behind his left shoulder. Together, they run into the cacophony of battle cries, groans, and clanging steel. Some soldiers lock swords with one specific opponent, their blades reflecting the dying daylight, while others chase a new target or retreat to catch their breath. Regardless of whether they're winning or losing, the soldiers all wear the same expression, their faces knotted with hatred and desperation, their blood mixing with the scents of smoke and sweat.

When a pack of soldiers besieges her group, Adaline releases a concentrated stream of fire that whips at their feet, forcing several soldiers to screech and scramble away from their worst nightmare. Sora, Merith, and Elashor hack at the elves who breech their circle until they fall back, bleeding in too many places. Another soldier charges Aurellia, but she sidesteps at the last second, slashes Āranol's sword diagonally down the soldier's backside, and swipes at his shins, knocking him to the ground.

Dang, Mom! Did Dad teach you too?

"Up ahead," Ëólas shouts, aiming one of his long, slender blades to a location at least sixty feet ahead.

Behind a wall of his own soldiers, Āranol yells at an elf with long, wavy black hair tied back in a half bun. The elf listens to his commander's every word with an apathetic, unblinking stare. Mid-discussion, he turns and stalks away, but Āranol yanks the soldier's arm and grabs the top of his chest plate, pulling his subordinate closer. At Adaline's request, the wind, ever her friend, brings her pieces of their conversation.

Āranol's voice teeters a fine line between demanding and pleading. "...no longer trust...lost his way..."

"Hypocrite! How could you..."

"...to end this war..."

"...abandoned your lord and..."

Releasing the elf's armor, Āranol shoves the soldier backward. "...you let this happen, Espestus. Don't you realize..."

Ãranol's army needs to see this. "Ëólas, wait a moment."

At Ëólas's orders, their group stops advancing, and her friends form a tighter circle around Adaline. Within seconds, Ãranol's soldiers swarm them, not giving her protectors time to breathe between their strikes and blocks that have become purely defensive. The perimeter around her shrinks as her friends scream their frustration, their pain, their fear.

I can do this.

Focusing on the ground beneath Ãranol's feet, Adaline forms a circle with her hands, as if trapping him and Espestus in a ring. Between her fingers, she feels the dirt, the soil, the rocky terrain as if they are a part of her, an extension of herself.

A sword jabs through her defenses, slicing her shoulder. She stumbles forward into Ëólas but doesn't cry out, doesn't panic. As she rises taller, Daven and his men attack the soldiers surrounding her group, and within that moment of relief, she sinks her feet into the ground and taps into the energy that binds all life to the earth that bore them.

Once again, she uses her hands to create a ring around Ãranol, who yells at Espestus to stand down. Through her fingers, Ãranol turns his back on his friend, but Espestus rams his shoulder into Ãranol's back. Instead of letting his commander fall forward, Espestus grabs Ãranol's shoulders, spins him around, and knees him in the gut, knocking the wind out of him. Ãranol falls onto his hands and knees, gasping for breath and clutching his belt where his scabbard and sword ought to be, while Espestus lifts his blade above Ãranol's head.

She could let him die. If she does nothing, Ãranol will never be a concern again, just like Ëólas wants. And maybe, just maybe, his death will weaken Morgán too.

As Espestus swings downward, Adaline wrenches her hands upward. The earth around the two elves shakes and shudders and rises like a platform, pulling the ground out from under nearby soldiers who tumble and roll away from the sloping stage. Espestus loses his balance and falls on his bottom while Ãranol catches his breath, his eyes seeking Adaline to understand what she's doing.

The fighting around Adaline slows as the soldiers on both sides back away and stare in awe at the spectacle before them, at the stage lifting Ãranol and Espestus eight feet high so everyone can see them.

As they clamber to their feet, Espestus gripping his sword tightly, Adaline travels next to Ãranol. They lock eyes for a moment, Ãranol slightly alarmed, but Adaline unties her sword from her belt and holds the scabbard out to him. "Protect what's important."

Ãranol stares at the blue and green hilt as if waiting for her to unsheathe the blade and run him through. But she doesn't move. When he takes the weapon, his movements unsure, cautious, Adaline travels to Ëólas's side. With his golden eyes burning brighter than the sun and his mouth flattened into a thin line, he hooks his arm around her waist and keeps her close.

"Trust me," she says.

"I do. It's him I don't trust."

With Espestus staring at the raised ground in horror, Ãranol scans his army, his friends, and lifts his sword in the air to command their attention. "Cease this battle immediately!"

He repeats himself, projecting his voice across the battlefield as loudly as possible, his reach aided by the wind. Gradually, the clanging of metal and screams dies down.

Having his army's attention, Ãranol lowers the sword and moves closer to the edge of the stage. "My father is no longer the leader you knew. He's using dark magic for his own personal vendetta. And you," he clenches his hand into a fist, "and *I* have been nothing more than his puppets. I have seen with my own eyes the blasphemy he's committed, the torment he's inflicted on his own people and those he claimed to take responsibility for. No more will we follow his orders blindly. No more will we—"

"Behind you!" a female voice shouts as Espestus lifts his blade and runs at Ãranol.

Unsheathing Adaline's sword, Ãranol spins around and blocks the strike, his heel sliding off the edge of the stage, the scabbard rolling downhill.

"I will never follow your orders again," Espestus yells. "You betrayed your own father, and you've aligned yourself with the mule. How can you trust such evil? She set the city on fire and murdered her own kind!"

What, wait?

Grinding his teeth, Āranol pushes with his entire weight, inching Adaline's blade toward Espestus's throat, forcing his arms to buckle. When Espestus takes two quick steps back to regain his balance, Āranol shoves hard. Their blades unlock, and Āranol slashes Espestus's thigh, making him clutch his leg and retreat halfway across the stage while holding his sword aloft with one hand.

Āranol lifts his palms to show he won't attack again, that he needs Espestus to listen. "The inhabitants of Camp Three were already dead. I helped bury them this—"

"They weren't dead. We watched them fall asleep after break time. We left them snoring two days ago, which you would have known if you'd stayed with us."

"Every single person in that city had been dead for a least a day."

Espestus shakes his head wildly. "Lies. You're the one we can't trust. That's why Lord Morgán gave me his orders; he knew you'd betray him, betray us."

"Enough!" Āranol snaps. "I'm taking command of my army and the Wastelands." He lowers his weapon and turns to his people. "I know many of you have struggled with Morgán's ideals. I value your loyalty, but we cannot keep going down this path. Stay with me. Help me re-envision our home. I will serve in my people's best interests, including the humans who wish to stay."

Well, would you look at that? Did you see this, Seira? He's chosen his path.

Āranol scans the crowd. "Those of you who disagree, who—"

Spittle flies from Espestus's mouth as he rages at Āranol. "I will never allow humans to—"

Finished with this argument, Āranol's hilt catches Espestus's strike. In one motion, Āranol spins his blade around the flat side of Espestus's and pierces him through the abdomen. The tip of Adaline's sword peeks out the backside.

Espestus falls to his knees and looks at his friend. "He, he's done with you too."

"I know." Āranol quickly pulls his sword free. Dropping his weapon, he catches Espestus's shoulders, helps him to lie down, and holds his hand until his chest stops moving.

Taking one last look at his friend, Āranol rises, picks up Adaline's sword beside him, and faces her. A few drops of blood roll off the blade pointed at the ground.

"Will you give me a chance to do what's right? Or will you continue your invasion and take our homes?"

Adaline studies his face, his struggle to stay on his own path. "Do you know what's right? What's fair?"

When Āranol looks away, looks to his people, no one seems to have an answer.

Aurellia rests her hand on Adaline's shoulder and brushes her curls away from her soot-stained cheek. Looking fondly at her, Aurellia lets go and walks past her daughter, her head held high like the queen she should have been.

Mom, what are you...

Āranol watches Aurellia, his expression riddled with guilt, like the obdurate child who can no longer ignore his errors and is searching for his way home in desperate need of support.

Aurellia stops in front of the stage. Using Āranol's sword as an anchor, she shoves the blade into the sloped side, pulls on the hilt, and climbs upward. Āranol offers her a hand, which she accepts—without fear that he'll slice her throat or run her through or feed her to his soldiers.

But, but... What the hell have I missed?

When she reaches the top, Aurellia dusts off her tattered rag of a tunic and extends her arm that he immediately shakes. "I will help guide you."

CHAPTER THIRTY-EIGHT

A NEW VIEW

Standing at the edge of camp, Adaline crosses her arms over her blouse that reeks of smoke. Behind her, the royal guard and her army lay out their sleeping mats and cook dinner, another stew of some sort. She spied a bag of potatoes earlier. Aside from the moans of the wounded, the only sound of clanging steel comes from spoons stirring against pots. Otherwise, the army remains quiet tonight, the drums silent.

The waning moon hangs low in the wide expanse of sky. Thick clouds dim its soft silver light. So too does the smoke rising from the smoldering remains of Camp Three. The stars also struggle to see through this darkness. That's only from this perspective though. If Adaline could fly, the clouds and smoke would have no bearing. But she's stuck on the ground, like everyone else, trying to find her way.

Her body wants to collapse, to end this day, to stop moving the bandages wrapped around her shoulder. She's tired of needing stitches too, but she has the least injuries of everyone. Watching Merith pierce Ëólas's skin with a needle along his thigh and the back of his hand was worse.

She strolls away from Camp Three with Sora following closely behind. Despite her black eye, Sora won't allow anyone else to watch her queen. About twenty feet away, a tall silhouette blocks the multitude of campfires marking Ãranol's army a mile away.

A second silhouette approaches the first, the voice feminine, almost sultry. "Are you certain about this? She's Aerytolían."

"I'm not certain about anything, Ameira, except that we need to stop my father." Āranol takes a sip of water and passes his bladder to the lady.

She takes a long drink and wipes her mouth with her hand. "Are you done with negotiations here?"

"Not yet. We all need time to cool down. You should head back to our camp, get some rest."

"I'm not leaving you."

Āranol leans forward, and their silhouettes merge for a moment.

Um, maybe I should walk in the other direction.

"When this is over," Ameira's voice dips low, her hands on his chest, "I think you'll need some help to unwind."

Ew, ew, ew. Cringing, Adaline takes one step backward as silently as possible.

"Thank you. I don't expect to sleep this night." He removes her hands, kissing one, and lets go. "But that's why I carry paints and parchment with me."

Adaline freezes mid-step. *He paints.*

She remembers her mother's paints strewn on the cottage floor, Āranol stepping in them.

No, it can't be. She wouldn't have taught him—couldn't have taught him. It's just a coincidence. Millions of people paint.

In her mind, she replays that lost look in his eyes when they found him alone in Camp Three, how her mother believed him.

"You paint?" Adaline screeches.

When Āranol's silhouette turns around, she marches up to him and jabs her finger into his chest, shoving his shoulder backward. "Tell me you didn't learn from my mother. Tell me that. Now."

Sora approaches behind her, but Adaline holds up a hand, instructing Sora not to interfere. At the same time, Ameira attempts to step in front of Āranol, but he blocks her with his arm and faces Adaline.

"Why would that matter?" he asks.

Fire burns up and down the inside of Adaline's arms, which she locks at her sides. "Seriously? What were you doing—standing outside her cell and taking painting classes? Why would you even bother to visit her?"

"His lordship showed her empathy when no one else did," Ameira says. "You ought to be grateful he—"

"Grateful?" Adaline yells. *Oh, let me at her. I'll punch her in the fucking—*

"Ameira, stay out of this." Āranol gestures for her to take several steps back. Under the moonlight, he turns his chartreuse eyes on Adaline. "Yes, I visited her. Alright? What's the harm in that?"

"You stole my mother, you fucking asshole!" Adaline punches his chest plate, which hurts her knuckles more than his stomach. She doesn't care. She hits him again.

He grinds his jaw back and forth. "I didn't steal her. I wasn't there that day. I came afterward, at my father's orders."

Adaline punches his abdomen, his bored expression fueling her anger. She keeps hitting his chest with the sides of her fists, not entirely to beat him up but to get rid of this hatred that's been eating away at her. When he rolls his eyes, she gives him an upper cut to his jaw, which snaps his head back.

"Ouch!" he shouts, backing away from her.

When she charges him again, he grabs her shoulders to keep her at arm's length. "What do you want from me? To say I'm sorry? Fine! I am. I'm sorry I loved my father and wanted to ease his pain. I'm sorry I believed his stupid lies. I'm sorry I took advantage of your desire to see your mother again and stabbed you in the back. Okay? Is that enough?"

Adaline pushes his arms off her, the flesh around her stitches stinging. "It's a start." Not daring to look behind her and see Ëólas and God knows who else watching her, she scowls at Āranol. "Why did you visit my mother?"

He closes his eyes and exhales slowly, his jowls pushing outward as he tenses his jaw. The memories he's recalling haunt his face. "Because when I told her you returned to the Immortal Realms," he opens his eyes and swallows hard, "her grief reminded me of my mother. She died when I was seven."

We lost our mothers at the same age. What did Elashor say her name was? Orena.

Behind Āranol, the flickering campfires remind Adaline of the fireflies she used to chase around her family's cottage. She'd spend at least an hour traipsing through the tall grass, following the tiny beacons that played hide and seek with her, all while her home grew smaller and darker as night pervaded the meadow. She never feared straying too far; her mother's call would eventually guide her home.

Adaline chews the inside of her cheek to fight back her tears. "I don't want to like you."

"Well, I don't want to like you either. Are you always so childish?"

"It was either that or burning you alive."

"Because that's normal."

"Do I need to separate you two?" Aurellia asks, stalking over to both of them. *Shit.*

"No," Ãranol says. "I think we're good here." He stares at Adaline, waiting for her response.

"We're on the right path."

Adaline closes the door to her armoire and pauses in front of the ornate floor-length mirror. She appears physically unscathed, her curls spilling down her back, her purple velvet tunic impeccable with hand-stitched flowers decorating her collar and cuffs. Her green eyes look exhausted.

Holding a bundle of clothing close to her chest, she walks over to her bathroom, cracks the door open, and places the clothes on the floor inside the room, next to a new pair of boots. "Here, Mom. Let me know if these don't fit right."

"Thank you!" Water splashes onto the floor as Aurellia steps out of the tub. When she finishes dressing, she enters Adaline's bedroom chambers, pulling the belt tight around her waist. She rubs her arms, smiling at the soft touch of velvet. "That was paradise."

Adaline gestures to the vanity where her mother takes a seat. She picks up the silver brush she'd never use on her curls and brushes her mother's light-brown hair that smells like roses. With her straight hair framing her oval face and gently rounded jawline, Aurellia looks more like the mother Adaline remembers.

Aurellia rests her hands on the vanity, the left on top of the right. Edwin never gave her a wedding band; he spent his earnings buying her paints and canvases.

A passion she now shares with Āranol, of all people.

"You okay?" Aurellia asks.

"That's a rather complicated question."

Cindy asked Adaline the same thing after she delivered the blood samples and traveled the infected guards into Loríen's care. Adaline didn't have the energy to recap everything that had happened since the ravine, since finding her mother, since entering the city of the dead. The lengthy negotiations and several arguments that occurred after Adaline punched Āranol used up the last of her strength.

Now, she wants to help her mother rest and enjoy this brief time alone, before they travel back to camp and set off for Feídra né Morna in the morning with those who survived the battlefield. This time, they'll march alongside three-quarters of Āranol's army. The rest left during negotiations in search of Morgán, none of them believing Āranol's warnings about the demonic elves.

Adaline gathers a fistful of Aurellia's long hair and brushes the ends. "Are you certain about staying there? With Āranol?"

"He has a chance to prove himself."

"And you trust that?"

In the mirror, memories invade Aurellia's mind until her expression grows so heavy that her gaze drops to her hands. "He left my cell unlocked and distracted the guards so I could escape."

Adaline quietly sets down the brush, her movements stilted while her mind struggles to process her mother's words. She slides her thumbs along her mother's temples, pulling her hair back in a half ponytail that she secures with a leather tie.

"Why did he do that?" Adaline asks.

"Because," Aurellia clasps Adaline's hand resting on her shoulder. "I thought I lost my child, and he was a lost child. I needed someone to talk to, and he listened."

"Did you know he was the one who almost killed me?"

"No." She turns around on the stool to face her daughter directly. "I'm not saying I trust him completely. Or that I've forgotten…" She lifts her head to the ceiling and rubs her arms until color returns to her cheeks.

Whatever's haunting her, Aurellia shakes the thought away. "Ãranol can't do this on his own, and neither can I. Freeing the other camps won't be easy. Even if we march into Camp One and fling those gates wide open, no one will leave. They're groomed to prove their worth, their loyalty. Camp Two, honestly, with how much they've been drugged, I'm afraid they'll walk off a cliff or forget to feed themselves."

Adaline pulls her hair at the roots. "That's so fucked up."

"Edwin has a foul mouth too." Her mother chuckles sadly.

Has.

An awkward silence takes up residence between them. The long-lost husband. The lying father.

"What about Camp Four?" Adaline asks. "You said they're—"

"Deplorable."

"But Ãranol and his father made them that way. They don't know better."

"Exactly. We also can't turn loose several hundred people whose only life skills for obtaining shelter and food are thievery and murder. We'll need time to teach them otherwise. And we need Feídra né Morna to initiate these changes."

Damn it. "You're right. They need you."

Aurellia's lips lift into a soft smile as she rises. "I'm proud of you. Even though in the face of so much loss, you showed everyone that compassion still exists, even in the Wastelands. I am in awe that I get to be your mother."

Adaline folds herself into Aurellia's open arms. She still has the ability to make everything feel a little less awful.

When they part, Adaline wipes her eyes. "Let me know if you need anything."

"Thank you. Right now, our main priority is reaching Feídra né Morna before Morgán can. But there is one thing I need you to do for me." Aurellia slides her palms beneath Adaline's ears and stares into her daughter's green eyes that emulate her own. "You don't have to hold on to me so tightly. You'll always know where to find me, and I'll be here when you need me. I promise."

She always gave Adaline space to be herself, to find her way, to trust her instincts—instincts that helped today. Adaline ought to return the favor.

Placing her hands over her mother's, Adaline travels them back to the Wastelands, back to her mother's people, and lets her go. "I'm proud of you too, Mom."

Aurellia kisses her daughter's brow. Then she backs away, turns around, and sits down next to Mags and Torsden.

I'm proud to be your daughter. I hope you know that.

"Hey," Ëólas says from behind.

"Hey." She spins around, eager to lie down beside him and put this day behind them. "Thank you for giving me and my mom time to—What's wrong?"

Ëólas inhales sharply. Taking one step forward, he cradles her head and peers into her eyes as if studying a work of art. "They're not green anymore."

"What?"

"Your eyes." Quiet wonder warms his face, similar to when he swings on the porch bench and gazes at the night sky. "They're the most beautiful shade of light purple. They're like the stars."

"Seriously?" Adaline pulls out her dagger and angles the flat side of the blade like a mirror. A violet outer band encircles her glowing eyes, the irises filled with flecks of lavender and silver.

Well, what do you know? "I'm me again."

In the morning, everyone moves slowly as they pack their gear, hoist their knapsacks onto their backs, and load the injured onto the wagons Ãranol's lent them. From a mile away, he and his soldiers move slowly too, and Adaline squints to read his lips as he talks to his people.

"You going to keep staring at him like that?" Ëólas passes her a cup of tea.

"No. I just forgot how much further I can see with my own eyes."

Ëólas laughs and hugs her waist. "You can't pass as entirely human now."

"I'm okay with that." She clasps the hot cup with both hands, its heat not bothering her.

He kisses her temple. "We're about to get going. We have a ten-day walk ahead of us."

"Can the army make the trek? They haven't had decent rest since we crossed the ravine, and now they're wounded."

"The elves are already healing. They'll be fine."

"And Daven's men? My mother's people?"

"Daven assures me his men are up to the task. They're more eager than ever to reach the city and prevent what happened yesterday from occurring again, and we'll be better able to tend to the wounded there too."

I wish I could spare them. I don't even know if that sandy-haired boy survived. Maybe she should ask to meet the soldiers from Meadowbrook. Her mother might like to see family again too. "It's not fair I can pop over there within seconds and they have to struggle."

"If only you didn't have to pull us through the doorways you've described."

"Yeah." Adaline lifts the metal mug to her lips but doesn't take a sip. *Huh. Wait a minute. I've always pulled people through when I travel instantly, but who ever said I have to guide them through the doorways?*

She lowers her mug and hugs it against her chest. "You know, I asked Cindy if she had any theories about why I didn't travel or display magic throughout my life in Maryland."

"Hmm. What did she say?"

"Mind over matter."

"I'm not sure I follow."

Adaline looks at her husband, the love of her life, the person who showed her time and again that he had fallen in love with her, but she couldn't believe that, couldn't believe he felt just as strongly about her, not until he said the words out loud. "I didn't display magic because I grew up in a world that doesn't believe in it. The idea never occurred to me. I thought it impossible."

"What are you saying?"

With a grin, Adaline faces Āranol's camp and shouts, "Hey, Āranol! Get your butt over here. I have an idea."

He rolls his head back and probably groans, but within ten minutes he and his girlfriend—or whatever Ameira is—line up beside Aurellia, Torsden, Sora, Merith, Elashor, Ëólas, and Daven.

Adaline paces in front of them, her mind buzzing at the possibility and from the butterflies in her stomach. "So far, I've always had to hold on to people when I travel with them. But," she halts and looks at everyone as if she's about to astound them. "What if I don't *have* to?"

Ëólas rubs his finger along the divot above his chin. "Explain."

"Okay, traveling has been getting easier, especially when I trust my gut. It's like when I'm writing a new lesson plan. When I overthink it, nothing gets done. But when I just start doing it, I finish in no time. Oh, wait. Wrong audience for that analogy."

"We get the sentiment, but what are you implying?" Sora asks, her arm lightly brushing against Torsden's giant biceps, without him cringing at her touch.

Um, okay. "One way I travel is through doorways. What if you can travel through one—without me having to hold your hand?"

Ëólas snaps and points his finger at her. "Yes, I like that, but we can't see those doorways."

"What if I hold the doorway open and tell you where to go? What if I can hold the door open for the whole army!"

"Oh my," Aurellia says. "You mean we could reach Feídra né Morna today?"

"Exactly!" Adaline bounces on her toes. "And we don't have to deal with Mr. Toad again."

Aurellia shudders. "He makes my skin crawl."

As if having stepped in something putrid, Āranol scrunches his face together. "How wide do you think you can make that doorway?"

"I don't know. Let's see." Facing Āranol's camp, Adaline opens a doorway, a shimmer of buckling light, in front of Hell City.

Without questioning *if* she can, she pulls her hands apart and imagines the doorway stretching. Sure enough, the billowing background widens, easily at first, but then she feels resistance, as if she's trying to push open antique pocket doors that have fallen off their tracks.

She walks up to the doorway, steps between it, and physically pushes the frame wider one side at a time, leaning her shoulder into the frame that balances the two different locations. After a few grunts and grumbles and curses, she stands up, massages her shoulders, and walks back to her friends to better assess the size, only she finds them with green faces and clutching their stomachs and Āranol gagging.

"What's wrong?" Adaline asks.

"You looked like you cut your body in half." Ëólas rubs his hand over his face. "It was like a horror movie."

"Oh." Adaline glances at the portal. "Oh! That's why I heard a muffled scream on the other side. Oops. Anyway," she claps her hands together, "I'd say we can fit four people closely together at the same time. Do I have any volunteers?"

Ëólas raises his hand. "Question. What's stopping someone from walking through now? From the city to us?"

Adaline shrugs. "Because I made the portal a mile away from the main gates?"

"Uh-huh. Sure, okay." Ëólas walks forward. "Like you said, best not to overthink it."

When Aurellia, Āranol, and Daven step up next to Ëólas, Adaline moves Torsden and Merith into position on both sides of the doorway, their arms marking the frame. Like a restaurant hostess, she ushers her volunteers forward with a wave of her hand. They glance at each other, then walk forward in a line until they disappear altogether.

"Woo-hoo!" Adaline jumps with her hands in the air.

Sora, Ameira, Elashor, and Adaline walk through next, followed by Torsden and Merith. The moment they cross over the threshold, Āranol's camp vanishes, replaced with Feídra né Morna's outer stone wall.

Āranol rests his fists on his waist. "Ameira, go back and get my soldiers into formation."

"Damn." Daven scratches his beard along his jawline. "Elashor and I will do the same."

But no one moves. The morning sunlight casts a golden glow over the stone wall and the squat buildings behind it, their shutters painted turquoise, sea green, and coral. The salty ocean air ruffles their hair, and the few guards standing sentry by the gates open the doors wide to welcome Ãranol home.

Adaline and Ëólas reach for each other, their hands coming together.

The people inside have no idea what's about to happen, how their lives will change, the new laws Ãranol and Aurellia will put into effect. Some will support their efforts. Others won't—that's a guarantee—like the lieutenant who praised Morgán's breeding methods and wanted Adaline to mate with his wards.

Part of her can't wait to stare into that lieutenant's smug face as her mother tells him that his wards are free to do as they please, that all citizens have equal rights from here on out. And when that creep and people like him fight to maintain their positions of power, Adaline, Ëólas, and the friends they've brought with them will prove that those in charge are united in this goal.

Sure, hard work awaits them. But that's okay. Because today marks a new beginning.

Squeezing Ëólas's hand, Adaline heaves a sigh of relief. "We made it."

EPILOGUE

A daline walks through the corridors of Ãranol's mansion, her periwinkle satin gown rustling over the stone floor, its cool surface chilling her bare feet. She moves with purpose, though she's not sure where she's going or why. Moonlight streams through the arched windows, and the open glass panes usher in the fresh salty air that tousles her curls draped over her chest. Beyond the balcony, the sounds of the ocean waves breaking against the cliffs rise and fall, along with the murmurs of Daven's and Lameiría's troops camping throughout Feídra né Morna. She fell asleep to those same sounds only moments ago.

A beam of gold light from a room up ahead cuts across the floor. Inside, her mother argues with Ãranol about permits and food distribution and something about surgeries that makes her mother more furious than Adaline's ever seen before. Although Ãranol wears a bored expression, he doesn't argue with Aurellia, just waits for her to finish her tirade and occasionally nods.

A few doors down, another light flashes across the floor and flickers against the light-blue walls. When Adaline peers into that room, she finds the study back in New Leira. Magnus slams his fist onto his desk and throws his hands about as he yells at Thoren, whose face has turned redder than his beard. For once, the goliath keeps his mouth shut. Underneath the anger consuming his face are deeper layers of guilt and regret.

Slowly backing away from the study, Adaline peeks into more rooms. One shows the ballroom in New Leira as Adaline watches herself teaching Ëólas how to waltz. Another opens onto a balcony where Seira overlooks the castle's courtyard. Leaning over the balustrade, Seira watches Magnus gallop toward the castle with Adaline sitting behind him and hiding under Ëólas's cloak. The room opposite the balcony reveals the den in Nan's house, and Adaline, lying on the floor with her feet in the air, clicks her heels together as she watches *The Wizard of Oz*.

The memories appear out of order. And some aren't Adaline's, like Seira, no older than twelve, drifting into Lameiría all alone, her eyes vacant as she knocks on the door to Gladríen's palace and meets a teenage Ëólas for the first time.

Even though Adaline wants to watch this moment, the soft whimpers of someone crying further ahead lure her away from the palace steps. She follows the sound. The small voice's quivers echo down the hall.

When Adaline turns the corner, she steps outside into a lush green forest, the colors so bright she has to shield her eyes. A small white cottage with a thatched roof hides between the trees, its wooden door barred shut. The terror crawling up Adaline's spine screams at her not to go in there under any circumstances.

Turning around, she reappears inside Āranol's mansion, and the whimpering has changed direction. She hurries after the sound, past the row of mirrors framed in sand dollars. As the lady's cries grow deeper, more mature, the sobs seep into Adaline's chest until her own heart aches so much that she'd rather gouge out the organ than continue onward.

Adaline rests her back against the wall and slides onto her bottom. She shouldn't be here. This isn't her dream.

The lady's sobs turn into the panic-stricken screams of someone fleeing for her life. A door down the hall swings open. Seira runs into the hallway, her chest heaving as she pulls the circular handle and slams the door shut. On the other side, several people hiss and scream like banshees while they pry the door open. Leaning backward, Seira pulls the door shut again, and the mansion shakes, knocking a mirror off the wall. The glass shatters at her feet.

Hurrying to stand up, Adaline rushes to her cousin, ignoring the glass cutting the bottom of her feet, her skirts collecting the shards, and grabs the handle, using her weight to help keep the door shut.

"Adaline!" Seira's periwinkle eyes widen as her pinky overlaps her cousin's. "I wasn't sure I'd find you in time."

"Did you pull me into your dream?" *Is this what it's always like inside your mind?*

Seira shrieks as the door opens a crack. "You must come home now. They're almost here!"

ALSO BY ERIN P.T. CANNING

Adaline and Ëólas's adventure continues!

Join them as they unite their allies to stop Morgán in book four, **Siege and Sacrifice**, coming soon.

If you enjoyed reading this, please consider leaving a review. Nothing more helps authors to keep going and encourages other readers to take a chance on a book than your reviews. Thank you again.

All of my books blend fantasy, adventure, and romance as my characters explore other cultures, make unexpected friends, and discover their hidden strengths as they fight for what they desire most.

For regular updates, bonus chapters, free book recommendations, and more, you can subscribe to my newsletter by visiting my author website.

Promises and Possibilities

Available through Amazon, or get a free copy by signing up for my newsletter at www.erinptcanningauthor.com.

A promise becomes a shackle when Emelie discovers her true desires.
When Emelie meets Henrick, neither can deny the connection between them, but when Henrick learns Emelie's father has promised her to someone else, she'll need more than passion to chase the future she wants.

This novelette includes a strong female lead, mystical elves, first love, and hidden evil. As a standalone story, this spicy fantasy romance delivers an HEA and exists within The Elves of Aerytol *universe.*

ELVISH LANGUAGE GUIDE

As a lifelong lover of fantasy stories, I had to create pronunciation rules for my book. Here's how these Elvish words and names should sound.

Ameira (uh-mear-uh)

Āranol (ah-ruh-nol)

Ëólas (ee-oh-lus)

Élara (ee-lara)

Elashor (el-uh-shore)

Ellíum (el-lee-um)

Espestus (eh-spess-tuss)

Feídra né Morna (fay-druh knee more-nuh)

Fólas (foe-lus)

Gladríen (glad-ree-en)

inlūmras né leira (in-loom-russ knee lear-uh)

Jósep (joe-sep)

Lameiría (la-mear-ee-uh)

Loríen (lore-ee-en)

mé ellador (mee el-luh-door)

Morgán (more-gain)

neir nía (near knee-ah)

Seira (sear-uh)

tíer nía (tea-er knee-ah)

Acknowledgments

To my readers, thank you for your constant support and enthusiasm as we dive deeper into Adaline and Ëólas's story. The hundreds of hours I spend at my laptop mean nothing without you because you are the key to an author's success. If this story entertained you, please consider leaving a review. You don't even have to include words. Those stars matter too. I also hope you'll stay in touch by connecting with me online so I can send you free stories and bonus scenes. Just visit www.erinptcanningauthor.com.

Michelle S., Nadia, and Rita—my beta reader team—you ladies rock! Thank you for your time, for your patience while you bite your nails waiting for the next round of chapters, and for your honest feedback. You're the best.

Elisabeth, my real-life Adaline, you are the coolest with your dance and sword fighting background. Thank you for giving me the inside scoop on what it's like to be a part of both those worlds. Your insight and suggestions are priceless, as is your friendship.

Michelle L., our lunch dates and your support helped me stay sane with this tight deadline. You are one of the best human beings I've ever met. I think Ëólas would agree.

To my David, mé ellador, thank you for always believing in me. You are my destined partner, and every day with you is a blessing. I also promise to start doing the laundry again now that this book is complete.

ABOUT THE AUTHOR

Erin P.T. Canning has worked for twenty years as an editor, encouraging other writers' individual voices and teaching them how to hone their writing skills. She always planned to write a book. While she focused on her family, she stopped writing for six years. But something deep inside was missing. Depression, anxiety, and anger forced her to search for herself, both for her sake and her family's.

Despite fearing her skills had atrophied, Erin started writing again. For as long as she can remember, her imagination has been her safe place—a never-ending adventure where she can travel to far-off lands, find people who believe in her potential, and be the hero. By giving herself permission to be imperfect, she finished writing her own shitty first draft in 2022. *Ruins and Redemption* celebrates Erin making her own dreams come true.

Now, she spends her days helping writers become the authors they're meant to be and her evenings writing a blend of fantasy, adventure, and romance as her characters explore other cultures, forge unlikely friendships, and discover their hidden strengths as they fight for what's right and what they desire most.

She earned her BA in Literature from The American University and MA in Writing from Johns Hopkins University, and she lives with her husband and their two boys in Maryland.

You can find Erin on Facebook and Instagram (@erinptcanningauthor). You can also catch up with her regularly by going to her website, www.erinptcanningauthor.com.